D0617168

2-0

# SPEAKING OF
# GREED
### Stories of Envious Desire

# SPEAKING OF

# GREED

### Stories of Envious Desire

## Edited by Lawrence Block

The seven DEAdly Sins series

### Cumberland House
### Nashville, Tennessee

Copyright © 2001 by Lawrence Block and Tekno Books

Published by
    CUMBERLAND HOUSE PUBLISHING, INC.
    431 Harding Industrial Drive
    Nashville, TN  37211
    www.CumberlandHouse.com

Cover design by Gore Studio

Library of Congress Cataloging-in-Publication Data

Speaking of greed : stories of envious desire / edited by Lawrence Block.
    p. cm. — (The seven deadly sins series)
  ISBN 1-58182-221-9 (alk. paper)
    1. Greed—Fiction. I. Block, Lawrence. II. Series.

PS648.G74 S63 2001
813'.0108353–dc21

                                                                    2001042458

Printed in the United States of America
1 2 3 4 5 6 7—06 05 04 03 02 01

# CONTENTS

BEFORE WE BEGIN . . . *Lawrence Block* . . . . . . . . . . . . 7

*REED* *F. Paul Wilson* . . . . . . . . . . . . . . . . . . . 13

HITLER, ELVIS, AND ME *Doug Allyn* . . . . . . . . . . . 35

ONE HIT WONDER *Gabrielle Kraft* . . . . . . . . . . . 51

THE $5,000 GETAWAY *Jack Ritchie* . . . . . . . . . . . 67

ROTTEN TO THE CORE *Jeremiah Healy* . . . . . . . . . 81

FRONT MAN *David Morrell* . . . . . . . . . . . . . . 91

WATER'S EDGE *Robert Bloch* . . . . . . . . . . . . . 123

A TASTE OF PARADISE *Bill Pronzini* . . . . . . . . . . 139

BITS *Matt Coward* . . . . . . . . . . . . . . . . . . . 147

COME DOWN FROM THE HILLS *John F. Suter* . . . . . . 159

THE WRONG HANDS *Peter Robinson* . . . . . . . . . . 173

THE HIGH COST OF LIVING *Dorothy Cannell* . . . . . 191

MY HEART CRIES FOR YOU *Bill Crider* . . . . . . . . . 203

INSIDE JOB *Ed Gorman* . . . . . . . . . . . . . . . . 225

DEADLY FANTASIES *Marcia Muller* . . . . . . . . . . . 235

DEATH SCENE *Helen Nielsen* . . . . . . . . . . . . . . 249

GOODBYE, SUE ELLEN *Gillian Roberts* . . . . . . . . . 259

DEATH AND DIAMONDS *Sue Dunlap* . . . . . . . . . . 275

A TICKET OUT *Brendan DuBois* . . . . . . . . . . . . 291

SPEAKING OF GREED *Lawrence Block* . . . . . . . . . 305

AUTHORS' BIOGRAPHIES . . . . . . . . . . . . . . . . 353

COPYRIGHTS & PERMISSIONS . . . . . . . . . . . . . . 359

# BEFORE WE BEGIN . . .

*Lawrence Block*

This is the second installment of the Seven Deadly Sins series, a collection of anthologies with each volume centered upon a particular sin. In introducing the previous volume, *Speaking of Lust*, I prefaced my remarks by pointing out their utter superfluity. The stories, I said, needed no introduction.

That said, I went on to find some seven hundred words to serve as the very introduction I'd already decried as unnecessary. Because, in another sense, the introduction was essential, in that it was part of my job. My task as anthologist in this particular series is three-fold: first, I have to pick the stories; then I have to write a novella with my four series characters, whom we know only as the priest, the doctor, the soldier, and the policeman; finally, I have to hammer out an introduction for the volume. That's my job, and it's two-thirds done, but how can I best complete it? What will serve to introduce this book?

What I won't do is comment on the individual stories that appear herein. What on earth is the point of that? Shall I assure you that I think highly of them? That would appear to go without saying. If I hadn't liked them, do you suppose I would have chosen them? And what can I say about them that will in any way enhance your appreciation of them? You'll like them or not, making your own judgments, and that's as it should be.

Of course denying the need for an introduction is a time-honored way of supplying one, and I'm doing that very thing right now, aren't I? (I almost wrote "amn't I," and thought that I could then explain the usage and that Joyce liked the construction; I could go on to comment on the inconsistency of *aren't* as a contraction for *am I not*. That would fill some space and hurry this job toward completion, but I decided not to cheat that way.) Done skillfully, begging the reader to skip one's own words and proceed directly to the wonderful stories that follow, one can even manage to appear humble.

There is, though, another use for an introduction. It can be a bully pulpit, providing its author with an opportunity to Say Something which he feels Needs Saying.

I've never much felt that my fiction's the place for a message. "If you've got something to say," Nolan Miller told a class of us at Antioch, "hire a hall. Don't screw up a story with a message." I've taken his advice to heart, writing stories with no higher purpose than to get them well and truly told. Just now, however, I find myself with a little something to say, so I'll skip a space and get to it.

❦　❦　❦

There are stories I would have liked to use in this series of anthologies, and I couldn't do so.

For *Speaking of Lust*, I had hoped to include stories by John O'Hara and Erskine Caldwell. O'Hara, as I've mentioned before, is my favorite writer, and I'd happily shoehorn a story of his into every anthology I edit. Several of his stories would be at home in a collection of crime fiction—I did use one in the first volume of Master's Choice—and I found one with lust as a central element and wanted to include it. I hadn't picked a particular Erskine Caldwell story, but it would be hard to point to one that did not have lust as a key component, and I'd always thought highly of Caldwell and would have liked to include him.

My partner in this enterprise, Marty Greenberg, told me we couldn't afford the stories. Our editorial budget is limited, and the persons in charge of the two writers' estates would insist on more money than we could justify paying, far more than any of our other writers would receive.

I'm not whining about this. The stories we wound up including have nothing to apologize for, and I don't know that the book would have been any better for the inclusion of the O'Hara and Caldwell stories. I didn't get to do what I wanted, which always tends to piss me off, but that's my problem, and in and of itself wouldn't be worth mentioning here.

What bothers me more, and may well be worth mentioning, is that I do not believe the interests of the writers, O'Hara and Caldwell, were well served.

Writers write for money, certainly. But I know almost no one who writes solely for money. We write, most of us, to be read. And, while we all know nothing lasts forever, we tend to hope that some of what we write might endure beyond our own lifespan, that readers might continue to take some pleasure from our work after we're no longer around to cash the royalty checks.

Nowadays, sad to say, most of us will see most of our works go out of print during our lifetime. The stuff may still be read—libraries and used bookstores will still carry us, even if our publishers have given up—but, once we shuffle off this mortal coil and cease to prime the pump with new material, how are readers to know enough about us to go looking for our out–of–print works?

Often, short fiction can keep a writer's memory alive. New readers encounter it in anthologies, and, liking what they find, go looking for more of the writer's work—other short stories, naturally, and novels as well.

But when some grasping dolt of an heir—or, far more often, some illiterate jerk in the trust department of a bank—decides to price an author out of the anthology market, what's the net effect? The ultimate beneficiaries don't get the money the anthologist would have been able to pay, and the stories don't get reprinted, and the author slides inevitably toward oblivion.

The people in charge don't care. It's easier for them to say no; the heirs won't complain because they'll never even know there was an offer on the table. But it's all in the worst interests of all concerned. It's a different story with movie rights, or anything you can't sell more than once. There you have a duty to get the best possible price, and turn down less attractive offers in the hope that a better one comes along. With anthology use of short fiction, however, you're selling something you can go on selling forever. Anthologists buy one-time non-exclusive rights—and our contributors have a proportionate share in the book's earnings, in addition to the up-front fee. If anything, a writer enhances the value of his story by placing it in an anthology; another anthologist may see it there, and select it for something else. The more you sell these things, the more people want to buy them.

Enough. I'll cut this rant short before someone hires me away to be the color commentator on Monday Night Football. I don't expect to change the system, and that's not the point. What I would suggest is that those of you reading this who are in fact writers might want to make some provision to prevent this sort of thing from happening to you. A lawyer can certainly tell you how to stipulate, in your will or in a letter of intent to a literary executor, that you want your stories to be read after you're no longer around to write any more of them.

—Lawrence Block

# SPEAKING OF
# GREED
### Stories of Envious Desire

# RAMPID

*F. Paul Wilson*

True to his word, the first installment of Dennis Nickleby's *Three Months to Financial Independence* arrives exactly two weeks after I called the toll-free number provided by his infomercial. I toss out the accompanying catalogs and "Occupant" bulk mail, then tear at the edges of the cardboard mailer.

This is it. My new start. Today is the first day of the rest of my life, and starting today my life will be very different. I'll be organized, I'll have specific goals and a plan to achieve them—I'll have an *agenda*.

Never had an agenda before. And as long as this agenda doesn't involve a job, that's cool. Never been a nine-to-fiver. Tend to ad lib as I go along. Prefer to think of myself as an *investor*. Now I'll be an investor with an agenda. And Dennis Nickleby's tapes are going to guide me.

Maybe they can help me with my personal life too. I'm sort of between girlfriends now. Seem to have trouble keeping them. Denice was the last. She walked out two weeks ago. Called me a couch potato—said I was a fat slob who doesn't do anything but read and watch TV.

Not fair. And not true. All right, so I am a little overweight, but not as overweight as I look. Lots of guys in their mid-thirties weigh more than I do. It's just that at five-eight it shows more. At least I still have all my hair. And I'm not ugly or anything.

As for spending a lot of time on the couch—guilty. But I'm doing research. My folks left me some money and I'm always looking for a better place to put it to work. I've got a decent net worth, live in a nice high-rise in North Jersey where I can see the Manhattan skyline at night. I make a good income from my investments without ever leaving the house. But that doesn't mean I'm not working at it.

Good as things are, I know I can do better. And the Nickleby course is going to take me to that next level. I can feel it. And I'm more than ready.

My hands shake as I pull the glossy vinyl video box from the wrapper.

Grinning back at me is a young, darkly handsome man with piercing blue eyes and dazzling teeth. Dennis Nickleby. Thirty years old and already a multimillionaire. Everything this guy touches turns to gold. But does he want to hoard his investing secrets? No way. He's willing to share them with the little guy—guys like me with limited capital and unlimited dreams. What a *mensch*.

Hey, I'm no sucker. I've seen Tony Robbins and those become-a-real-estate-millionaire-with-no-money-down infomercials. I'm home a lot so I see *lots* of infomercials. Trust me, they roll off me like water off a duck. But Dennis Nickleby . . . he's different. He looked out from that TV screen and I knew he was talking to me. To *me*. I knew what he was offering would change my life. The price was stiff—five hundred bucks—but well worth it if he delivered a mere tenth of what he was offering. Certainly a better investment than some of those do-nothing stocks in my account.

I whipped out my credit card, grabbed the phone, punched in his 800 number, and placed my order.

And now it's here. I lift the lid of the box and—

"Shit!"

There's supposed to be a videotape inside—lesson one. What do I find? An audio cassette. And it's not even a new one. It's some beat-up piece of junk.

I'm fuming. I'm so pissed I'm ready to dump this piece of garbage on the floor and grind it into the carpet. But I do not do this. I take three deep breaths, calm myself, then I march to the phone. Very gently I punch in Mr. Nickleby's 800 number—it's on the back of the tape box—and get some perky little babe on the phone. I start yelling about consumer fraud, about calling the attorney general, about speaking to Dennis Nickleby himself. She asks why I'm so upset and I'm hardly into my explanation when she lets loose this high-pitched squeal.

"*You're* the one! Ooh, goody! We've been hoping you'd call!"

"Hoping?"

"Yes! Mr. Nickleby was here *himself*. He was *so* upset. He learned that *somehow* the *wrong* kind of tape got into one of his *Three Months to Financial Independence* boxes. He instructed us that should we hear from *anyone* who got an *audio* cassette instead of a *video* cassette, we should tell them not to worry. A brand new *video* cassette of *Three Months to Financial Independence* would be *hand* delivered to them *immediately*! Now, what do you think of *that*?"

"I . . . I . . ." I'm flabbergasted. This man is on top of everything. Truly he knows how to run a business. "I think that's incredible."

"Just give us your name and address and we'll get that replacement to you *immediately!*"

"It's Michael Moulton." I give her the address.

"Ooh! Hackensack. That's not far from here!"

"Just over the G. W. Bridge."

"*Well*, then! You should have your replacement *very* soon!"

"Good," I say.

Her terminal perkiness is beginning to get to me. I'm hurrying to hang up when she says, "Oh, and one more thing. Mr. Nickleby said to tell you *not* to do *anything* with the audio cassette. Just *close* it up in the box it came in and *wait* for the replacement tape. The messenger will take it in *exchange* for the videotape."

"Fine. Good—"

"Remember that now—close the audiotape in the holder and wait. Okay?"

"Right. Cool. Good-*bye*."

I hang up thinking, Whatever she's taking, I want some.

Being a good boy, I snap the video box cover closed and am about to place it on the end table by the door when curiosity tickles me and I start to wonder what's on this tape. Is it maybe from Dennis Nickleby's private collection? A bootleg jazz or rock tape? Or better yet, some dictation that might give away one or two investment secrets not on the videotape?

I know right then there's no way I'm not going to listen to this tape, so why delay? I pop it into my cassette deck and hit PLAY.

Nothing. I crank up the volume—some static, some hiss, and nothing else. I fast-forward and still nothing. I'm about to hit STOP when I hear some high-pitched gibberish. I rewind a little and replay at regular speed.

Finally this voice comes on. Even with the volume way up I can barely hear it. I press my ear to the speaker. Whoever it is is whispering.

"*The only word you need to know:* RROAD."

And that's it. I fast-forward all the way to the end and nothing. I go back and listen to that one sentence again. "*The only word you need to know:* RROAD."

Got to be a garble. Somebody erased the tape and the heads missed a spot. Oh well.

Disappointed, I rewind it, pop it out, and close it up in the video box.

☙  ☙  ☙

So here I am, not an hour later, fixing a sandwich and watching the stock quotes on FNN when there's a knock on my apartment door. I check through the peephole and almost choke.

Dennis Nickleby himself!

I fumble the door open and he steps inside.

"Mr. Nickleby!"

"Do you have it?" he says. He's sweating and puffing like he sprinted the ten flights to my floor instead of taking the elevator. His eyes are darting everywhere so fast they seem to be moving in opposite directions—like a chameleon's. Finally they come to rest on the end table. "There! That's it!"

He lunges for the video box, pops it open, snatches the cassette from inside.

"You didn't listen to it, did you?"

Something in his eyes and voice tell me to play this one close to the vest. But I don't want to lie to Dennis Nickleby.

"Should I have? I will if you want me to."

"No-no," he says quickly. "That won't be necessary." He hands me an identical videobox. "Here's the replacement. Terribly sorry for the mix-up."

I laugh. "Yeah. Some mix-up. How'd that ever happen?"

"Someone playing games," he says, his eyes growing cold for an instant. "But no harm done."

"You want to sit down? I was just making lunch—"

"Thank you, no. I'd love to but my schedule won't permit it. Maybe some other time." He extends his hand. "Once again, sorry for the inconvenience. Enjoy the tape."

And then he's out the door and gone. I stand there staring at the spot where he stood. Dennis Nickleby himself came by to replace the tape. Personally. Wow. And then it occurs to me: check the new box.

I pop it open. Yes sir. There's the *Three Months to Financial Independence* videotape. At last.

But what's the story with that audio cassette? He seemed awful anxious to get it back. And what for? It was totally blank except for that one sentence—*The only word you need to know:* Rɪɢ. What's that all about?

I'd like to look it up in the dictionary, but who knows how to spell something so weird sounding. And besides, I don't have a dictionary. Maybe I'll try later at the local library—once I find out where the local library is.

Right now I've got to transfer some money to my checking account so I can pay my Visa bill when the five-hundred–buck charge to Nickleby, Inc. shows up on this month's statement.

I call Gary, my discount broker, to sell some stock. I've been in Castle Petrol for a while and it's doing squat. Now's as good a time as any to get out. I tell Gary to dump all 200 shares. Then it occurs to me that Gary's a pretty smart guy. Even finished college.

"Hey, Gary. You ever hear of Reprisal?"

"Can't say as I have. But if it exists, I can find it for you. You interested?"

"Yeah," I say. "I'm very interested."

"You got it."

Yeah, well, I *don't* get it. All right, maybe I do get it, but it's not what I'm expecting, and not till two days later.

Meantime I stay busy with Dennis Nickleby's videotape. Got to say, it's kind of disappointing. Nothing I haven't heard elsewhere. Strange . . . after seeing his infomercial, I was sure this was going to be just the thing for me.

Then I open an envelope from the brokerage. Inside I find the expected sell confirm for the two hundred shares of Castle Petrol at 10.25, but with it is a buy confirm for *two thousand* shares of something called Thai Cord, Inc.

What the hell is Thai Cord? Gary took the money from Castle Petrol and put it in a stock I've never heard of! I'm baffled. He's never done anything like that. Must be a mistake. I call him.

"Hey, dude," he says as soon as he comes on the line. "Who's your source?"

"What are you talking about?"

"Thai Cord. It's up to five this morning. Boy, you timed that one perfectly."

"Five?" I swallow. I was ready to take his head off, now I learn I've made nine thousand big ones in two days. "Gary . . . why did you put me into Thai Cord?"

"Why? Because you asked me to. You said you were very interested in it. I'd never heard of it, but I looked it up and bought it for you." He sounds genuinely puzzled. "Wasn't that why you called the other day? To sell Castle and buy Thai? Hey, whatever, man—you made a killing."

"I know I made a killing, Gary, and no one's gladder than me, but—"

"You want to stay with it?"

"I just want to get something straight: Yesterday I asked you if you'd ever heard of RELOAD."

"No way, pal. I know ParkerGen. NASDAQ—good high-tech, speculative stock. You said Thai Cord."

I'm getting annoyed now. "RELOAD, Gary. RELOAD!"

"I can hear you, Mike. ParkerGen, ParkerGen. Are you all right?"

At this moment I'm not so sure. Suddenly I'm chilled, and there's this crawly feeling on the nape of my neck. I say one thing—*The only word you need to know*—and Gary hears another.

"Mike? You still there?"

"Yeah. Still here."

My mind's racing. What the hell's going on?

"What do you want me to do? Sell the Thai and buy ParkerGen? Is that it?"

I make a snap decision. There's something weird going down and I want to check it out. And what the hell, it's all found money.

"Yeah. Put it all into ParkerGen."

"Okay. It's running three-and-an-eighth today. I'll grab you three thousand."

"Great."

I get off the phone and start to pace my apartment. I've got this crazy idea cooking in my brain . . .

. . . the only word you need to know: RELOAD.

What if . . . ?

Nah. It's too crazy. But if it's true, there's got to be a way to check it out.

And then I have it. The ponies. They're running at the Meadowlands today. I'll invest a few hours and check this out. If I hurry I can make the first race.

I know it's completely nuts, but I've got to know . . .


I just make it. I rush to the ten-dollar window and say, "RELOAD in the first."

The teller doesn't even glance up; he takes my ten, punches a few buttons, and out pops my ticket. I grab it and look at it: I've bet on some nag named Yesterday's Gone.

I don't bother going to the grandstand. I stand under one of the monitors. I see the odds on Yesterday's Gone are three to one. The trotters are lined up, ready to go.

"*And they're off!*"

I watch with a couple of other guys in polo shirts and polyester pants who're standing around. I'm not too terribly surprised when Yesterday's Gone crosses the finish line first. I've now got thirty bucks where I had ten a few minutes ago, but I've also got that crawly feeling at the back of my neck again.

This has gone from crazy to creepy.

With the help of the Daily Double and the Trifecta, by the time I leave the track I've parlayed my original ten bucks into sixty-two hundred. I could have made more but I'm getting nervous. I don't want to attract too much attention.

As I'm driving away I can barely keep from flooring the gas pedal. I'm wired—positively giddy. It's like some sort of drug. I feel like king of the world. I've got to keep going. But how? Where?

I pass a billboard telling me about "5 TIMES MORE DICE ACTION!" at Caesar's in Atlantic City.

My question has been answered.

I pick Caesar's because of the billboard. I've never been much for omens but I'm into them now. Big time.

I'm also trying to figure out what else I'm into with this weird word. *The only word you need to know . . .*

All you need to know to *win*. That has to be it: the word makes you a winner. If I say it whenever I'm about to take a chance—on a horse or a stock, at least—I'm a guaranteed winner.

This has got to be why Dennis Nickleby's such a success. He knows the word. That's why he was so anxious to get it back—he doesn't want anybody else to know it. Wants to keep it all to himself.

Bastard.

And then I think, no, not a bastard. I've got to ask myself if I'm about to share the word with anybody else. The answer is a very definite en-oh. I get the feeling I've just joined a very exclusive club. Only thing is, the other members don't know I've joined.

I also get the feeling there's no such thing as a game of chance for me any more.

Cool.

The escalator deposits me on the casino floor at Caesar's. All the way down the Parkway I've been trying to decide what to try first—blackjack, poker, roulette, craps—what? But soon as I come within sight of the casino, I know. Flashing lights dead ahead:

PROGRESSIVE SLOTS! $802,672!!!

The prize total keeps rising as players keep plunking their coins into the gangs of one-armed bandits.

I wind through the crowds and the smoke and the noise toward the progressive slots section. Along the way I stop at a change cart and hand the mini-togaed blonde a five.

"Dollars," I say, "even though I'm going to need just one to win."

"Right on," she says, but I can tell she doesn't believe me.

She will. I take my dollar tokens and say, "You'll see."

I reach the progressive section and hunt up a machine. It isn't easy. Everybody here is at least a hundred years old and they'd probably give up one of their grandkids before they let somebody use their damn machine. Finally I see a hunched old blue-hair run out of money and leave her machine. I dart in, drop a coin in the slot, then I notice the machine takes up to three. I gather if I'm going to win the full amount I'd better drop two more. I do. I grab the handle . . . and hesitate. This is going to get me a lot of attention. Do I want that? I mean, I'm a private kind of guy. Then I look up at the $800,000-and-growing jackpot and know I want *that*.

Screw the publicity.

I whisper, "RETROD," and yank the handle.

I close my eyes as the wheels spin; I hear them begin to stop: First window—*choonk!* Second window—*choonk!* Third window—*choonk!* A bell starts ringing! Coins start dropping into the tray! I did it!

Abruptly the bell and the coins stop. I open my eyes. There's no envious crowd around me, no flashing cameras. Nobody's even looking my way. I glance down at the tray. Six dollars. I check out the windows. Two cherries and an orange. The red LED reads, "Pays 6."

I'm baffled. Where's my $800,000 jackpot? The crawling feeling that used to be on my neck is now in the pit of my stomach. What happened? Did I blow it? Is the word wearing out?

I grab three coins from the tray and shove them in. I say, "RETROD," again, louder this time, and pull that handle.

*Choonk! Choonk! Choonk!*

Nothing this time. Nothing!

I'm getting scared now. The power is fading fast. Three more coins, I damn near shout, "RELOAD" as I pull the goddamn handle. *Choonk! Choonk! Choonk!*

Nothing! Zip! Bupkis!

I slam my hand against the machine. "Damn you! What's wrong?"

"Easy, fella," says the old dude next to me. "That won't help. Maybe you should take a break."

I walk away without looking at him. I'm devastated. What if I only had a few days with this word and now my time is up? I wasted it at the track when I could have been buying and shorting stocks on margin. The smoke, the crowds, the incessant chatter and mechanical noise of the casino is driving me to panic. I have to get out of here. I'm just about to break into a run when it hits me.

The word . . . what if it only works on people? Slot machines can't hear . . .

I calm myself. Okay. Let's be logical here. What's the best way to test the word in a casino?

Cards? Nah. Too many possible outcomes, too many other players to muddy the waters.

Craps? Again, too many ways to win or lose.

What's a game with high odds and a very definite winner?

I scan the floor, searching . . . and then I see it.

Roulette.

But how can I use the word at a roulette table?

I hunt around for a table with an empty seat. I spot one between this middle-aged nerd who's got to be an optometrist, and a mousy, thirtyish redhead who looks like one of his patients. Suddenly I know what I'm going to do.

I pull a hundred-dollar bill from my Meadowlands roll and grip it between my thumb and index finger. Then I twist up both my hands into deformed knots.

As I sit down I say to the redhead, "Could I trouble you to place my bets for me?"

She glances at my face through her Coke-bottle lenses, then at my twisted hands. Her eyes dart back to my face. She gives me a half-hearted smile. "Sure. No problem."

"I'll split my winnings with you." *If I win.*

"That's okay. Really."

I make a show of difficulty dropping the hundred-dollar bill from my fingers, then I push it across the table.

"Tens, please."

A stack of ten chips is shoved in front of me.

"All bets down," the croupier says.

"Put one on RED, please," I tell the redhead, and hold my breath.

I glance around but no one seems to hear anything strange. Red takes a chip off the top of my pile and drops it on 33.

I'm sweating bullets now. My bladder wants to find a men's room. This has got to work. I've got to know if the word still has power. I want to close my eyes but I don't dare. I've got to see this.

The ball circles counter to the wheel, loses speed, slips toward the middle, hits rough terrain, bounces chaotically about, then clatters into a numbered slot.

"Thirty-three," drones the croupier.

The redhead squeals and claps her hands. "You won! Your first bet and you won!"

I'm drenched. I'm weak. My voice is hoarse when I say, "You must be my good luck charm. Don't go anywhere."

Truth is, it *could* be luck. A cruel twist of fate. I tell Red to move it all over to "RED."

She looks shocked. "All of it? You sure?"

"Absolutely."

She pushes the stack over to the 17 box.

Another spin. "Seventeen," the croupier says.

*Now* I close my eyes. I've got it. The word's got the power and I've got the word. *The only word you need to know.* I want to pump a fist into the air and scream "YES!" but I restrain myself. I am disabled, after all.

"Ohmigod!" Red is whispering. "That's . . . that's . . . !"

"A lot of money," I say. "And half of it's yours."

Her blue eyes fairly bulge against the near sides of her lenses. "What? Oh, no! I couldn't!"

"And I couldn't play without your help. I said I'd split with you and I meant it."

She has her hand over her mouth. Her words are muffled through her fingers. "Oh, thank you. You don't know—"

"All bets down," says the croupier.

No more letting it ride. My winnings far exceed the table limit. I notice that the pit boss has materialized and is standing next to the croupier. He's watching me and eyeing the megalopolis skyline of chips stacked in front of me. Hitting the winning number two times in a row—it happens in roulette, but not too damn often.

"Put five hundred on sixteen," I tell Red.

She does, and 22 comes up. Next I tell her five hundred on nine. Twelve comes up.

The pit boss drifts away.

"Don't worry," Red says with a reassuring pat on my arm. "You're still way ahead."

"Do I took worried?" I say.

I tell her to put another five hundred on "RED." She puts the chips on 19.

A minute later the croupier calls, "Nineteen." Red squeals again. I lean back as the croupier starts stacking my winnings.

No need to go any further. I know how this works. I realize I am now the Ultimate Winner. If I want to I can break the bank at Caesar's. I can play the table limit on one number after another, and collect a thirty-five-to-one payout every couple of minutes. A crowd will gather. The house will have to keep playing—corporate pride will force them to keep paying. I can *own* the place, damn it!

But the Ultimate Winner chooses not to.

Noblesse oblige.

What does the Ultimate Winner want with a casino? Bigger winnings await.

Winning . . . there's nothing like it. It's ecstasy, racing through my veins, tingling like bolts of electricity along my nerve endings. Sex is nothing next to this. I feet buoyant, like I could float off this chair and buzz around the room.

I stand up.

"Where are you going?" Red says, looking up at me with those magnified blue eyes.

"Home. Thanks for your help."

I turn and start looking for an exit sign.

"But your chips . . ."

I figure there's close to thirty G's on the table, but there's lots more where that came from. I tell her, "Keep them."

What does the Ultimate Winner want with casino chips?

❧   ❧   ❧

Next day, I'm home in my apartment, reading the morning paper. I see that ParkerGen has jumped two-and-one-eighth points to five and a half. Sixty-one percent profit overnight.

After a sleepless night, I've decided the stock market is the best way to use the word. I can make millions upon millions there and no one will so much as raise an eyebrow. No one will care except the IRS, and I will pay my taxes, every penny of them, and gladly.

Who cares about taxes when you're looking at more money than you'll ever spend in ten lifetimes? They're going to take half, leaving me to eke by with a mere five lifetimes' worth of cash. I can hack that.

A hard knock on the door. Who the hell—? I look through the peep-hole.

Dennis Nickleby! I'm so surprised, I pull open the door without thinking. "Mr. Nickle—!"

He sucker punches me in the gut. As I double over, groaning, he shoves me to the floor and slams the door shut behind him.

"What the *fuck* do you think you're doing?" he shouts. "You lied to me! You told me you didn't listen to that tape! You bastard! If you'd been straight with me, I could have warned you. Now the shit's about to hit the fan and we're both standing downwind!"

I'm still on the floor, gasping. He really caught me. I manage a weak, "What are you talking about?"

His face reddens and he pulls back his foot. "Play dumb with me and I'll kick your teeth down your throat!"

I hold up a hand. "Okay. Okay." I swallow back some bile. "I heard the word. I used it a few times. How'd you find out?"

"I've got friends inside the Order."

"Order?"

"Never mind. The point is, you're not authorized to use it. And you're going to get us both killed if you don't stop."

He already grabbed my attention with the punch. Now he's got it big time.

"Killed?"

"Yeah. Killed. And I wouldn't give a rat's ass if it was just you. But they'll come after me for letting you have it."

I struggle to a crouch and slide into a chair.

"This is all bullshit, right?"

"Don't I wish. Look, let me give you a quick history lesson so you'll

appreciate what you've gotten yourself into. The Order goes way back—
*way* back. They've got powers, and they've got an agenda. Throughout history they've loaned certain powers to certain carefully chosen individuals."

"Like who?"

"Like I don't know who. I'm not a member so they don't let me in on
their secrets. Just think of the most powerful people in history, the movers
and shakers—Alexander the Great, Constantine, some of the Popes, the
Renaissance guys—they all probably had some help from the Order. I've
got a feeling Hitler was another. It would explain how he could sway a
whole nation the way he did."

"Oh," I said. I knew I had to be feeling a little better because I was also
feeling sarcastic. "An order of evil monks, ruling the world. I'm shaking."

He stared at me a long moment, then gave his head a slow shake. "You
really are an ass, Moulton. First off, I never said they were monks. Just
because they're an order doesn't mean they skulk around in hooded robes.
And they don't rule the world; they merely support forces or movements or
people they feel will further their agenda. And as for evil . . . I don't know
if good or evil applies to these folks because I don't know their goals. Look
at it this way: I'll bet the Order helped out the robber barons. Not to make
a bunch of greedy bastards rich, but because it was on the Order's agenda to
speed up the industrialization of America. Are you catching the drift?"

"And so they came to you and gave you this magic word. What's that
make you? The next Rockefeller?"

He seems to withdraw into himself. His eyes become troubled. "I don't
know. I don't have the foggiest idea why I was chosen or what they think
I'll accomplish with the Answer. They gave me the tape, told me to memo-
rize the Answer, and then destroy the tape. They told me to use the
Answer however I saw fit, and that was it. No strings. No goals. No instructions whatsoever other than destroying the tape."

"Which you didn't do."

He sighs. "Which I didn't do."

"And you call *me* an ass?" I say.

His eyes harden. "Everything would have been fine if my soon-to-be-ex-
wife hadn't raided my safe deposit box and decided to play some games
with its contents."

"You think she's listened to the tape?"

He shrugs. "Maybe. The tape is ashes now, so she won't get a second
chance. And if she did hear the Answer, she hasn't used it, or figured out its

power. You have to be pretty smart or pretty lucky to catch on."

Preferring to place myself in the former category, I say, "It wasn't all that hard. But why do you call it the Answer?"

"What do you call it?"

"I've been calling it 'the word.' I guess I could be more specific and call it 'the Win Word.'"

He sneers. "You think this is just about winning? You idiot. That word is the *Answer*—the *best* answer to any question asked. The listener hears the most appropriate, most profitable, all-around *best* response. And that's power, Michael Moulton. Power that's too big for the likes of you."

"Just a minute now. I can see how that worked with my broker, but I wasn't answering questions when I was betting the ponies or playing roulette. I was telling people."

The sneer deepens. "Horses . . . roulette . . ." He shakes his head in disgust. "Like driving a Maserati to the local 7–Eleven for a quart of milk. All right, I'll say this slowly so you'll get it: The Answer works with all sorts of questions, including implied questions. And what is the implied question when you walk up to a betting window or sit down at a gaming table? It's 'How much do you want to bet on what?' When you say ten bucks on Phony Baloney, you're answering that question."

"Oh, right," I say.

He steps closer and stands over me. "I hope you enjoyed your little fling with the Answer. You can keep whatever money you made, but that's it for you."

"Hey," I tell him. "If you think I'm giving up a gold mine like that, you're nuts."

"I had a feeling you'd say something like that."

He reaches into his suit coat pocket and pulls out a pistol. I don't know what kind it is and don't care. All I know is that its silenced muzzle is pointing in my face.

"Hey! Wait!"

"Good-bye, Michael Moulton. I was hoping to be able to reason with you, but you're too big an asshole for that. You don't leave me any choice."

I see the way the gun wavers in his hand, I hear the quaver in his voice as he keeps talking without shooting, and I flash that this sort of thing is all new to him and he's almost as scared as I am right now.

So I move. I leap up, grab the gun barrel, and push it upward, twisting it with everything I've got. Nickleby yelps as the gun goes off with a *phut!*

The backs of his legs catch the edge of the coffee table and we go down. I land on him hard, knocking the wind out of him, and suddenly I've got the gun all to myself.

I get to my feet and now I'm pointing it at him. And then he makes a noise that sounds like a sob.

"Damn it!" he wails. "Damn it to hell! Go ahead and shoot. I'm a dead man anyway if you go on using the Answer. And you will be too."

I consider this. He doesn't seem to be lying. But he doesn't seem to be thinking either.

"Look," I tell him. "Why should we be afraid of this Order? We have the word—the Answer. All we have to do is threaten to tell the world about it. Tell them we'll record it on a million tapes—we'll put it on every one of those videotapes you're peddling. Hell, we'll buy airtime and broadcast it by satellite. They make one wrong move and the whole damn world will have the Answer. What'll *that* do to their agenda?"

He looks up at me bleakly. "You can't record it. You can't tell anybody. You can't even write it down."

"Bullshit," I say.

This may be a trick so I keep the pistol trained on him while I grab the pen and pad from the phone. I write out the word. I can't believe my eyes. Instead of the Answer I've written gibberish: RFOAD.

"What the hell?"

I try again, this time block printing. No difference—RFOAD again.

Nickleby's on his feet now, but he doesn't try to get any closer.

"Believe me," he says, more composed now, "I've tried everything. You can speak the Answer into the finest recording equipment in the world till you're blue in the face and you'll hear gibberish."

"Then I'll simply tell it to everybody I know!"

"And what do you think they'll hear? If they've got a question on their mind, they'll hear the best possible answer. If not, they'll hear gibberish. What they won't hear is the Answer itself."

"Then how'd these Order guys get it on your tape?"

He shrugs. "I don't know. They have ways of doing all sorts of things—like finding out when somebody unauthorized uses the Answer. Maybe they know every time *anybody* uses the Answer. That's why you've got to stop."

I don't reply. I glance down at the meaningless jumble I've written without intending to. Something big at work here. Very Big.

He goes on. "I don't think it's too late. My source in the Order told me that if I can silence you—and that doesn't mean kill you, just stop you from using the Answer—then the Order will let it go. But if you go on using it . . . well, then, it's curtains for both of us."

I'm beginning to believe him.

A note of pleading creeps into his voice. "I'll set you up. You want money, I'll give you money. As much as you want. You want to play the market? Call me up and ask me the best stock to buy—I'll tell you. You want to play the ponies? I'll go to the track with you. You want to be rich? I'll give you a million—two, three, four million a year. Whatever you want. *Just don't use the Answer yourself!*"

I think about that. All the money I can spend . . .

What I don't like about it is I'll feel like a leech, like I'm being kept.

Then again: All the money I can spend . . .

"All right," I tell him. "I won't use the word and we'll work something out."

Nickleby stumbles over to the sofa like his knees are weak and slumps onto it. He sounds like he's gonna sob again.

"Thank you! Oh, thank you! You've just saved both our lives!"

"Yeah," I say.

Right. I'm going to live, I'm going to be rich. So how come I ain't exactly overcome with joy?


Things go pretty well for the next few weeks. I don't drag him to the track or to Atlantic City or anything like that. And when I phone him and ask for a stock tip, he gives me a winner every time. My net worth is skyrocketing. Gary the broker thinks I'm a genius. I'm on my way to financial independence, untold wealth . . . everything I've ever wanted.

But you know what? It's not the same. Doesn't come close to what it was like when I was using the Answer myself.

Truth is, I feel like Dennis Nickleby's goddamn mistress.

But I give myself a daily pep talk, telling myself I can hang in there.

And I do hang in there. I'm doing pretty well at playing the melancholy millionaire . . .

Until I hear on the radio that the next Pick 6 Lotto jackpot is thirty million dollars.

Thirty million dollars—with a payout of a million and a half a year for the next twenty years. That'll do it. If I win that, I won't need Nickleby any more. I'll be my own man again.

Only problem is, I'll need to use the Answer.

I know I can ask Nickleby for the winning numbers, but that won't cut it. I need to do this myself. I need to feel that surge of power when I speak the Answer. And then the jackpot will be *my* prize, not Nickleby's.

Just once . . . I'll use the Answer just this once, and then I'll erase it from my mind and never use it again.

I go driving into the sticks and find this hole-in-the-wall candy store on a secondary road in the woods. There's a pimply faced kid running the counter. How the hell is this Order going to know I've used the Answer one lousy time out here in Nowheresville?

I hand the kid a buck. "Pick 6 please."

"You wanna Quick Pick?"

No way I want random numbers. I want the *winning* numbers.

"No. I'll give them to you: RELOAD."

I can't tell you how good it feels to be able to say that word again . . . like snapping the reins on my own destiny.

The kid hits a button, then looks up at me. "And?"

"And what?"

"You got to choose six numbers. That's only one."

My stomach lurches. Damn. I thought one Answer would provide all six. Something tells me to cut and run, but I press on. I've already used the Answer once—might as well go all the way.

I say RELOAD five more times. He hands me the pink-and-white ticket. The winning numbers are 3, 4, 7, 17, 28, 30. When the little numbered Ping-Pong balls pop out of the hopper Monday night, I'll be free of Dennis Nickleby.

So how come I'm not tap-dancing back to my car? Why do I feel like I've just screwed up . . . big time?

I stop for dinner along the way. When I get home I check my answering machine and there's Nickleby's voice. He sounds hysterical.

*"You stupid bastard! You idiot! You couldn't be happy with more money than you could ever spend! You had to go and use the Answer again! Damn you to hell, Moulton! They're coming for me! And then they'll be coming for you! Kiss your ass good-bye, jerk!"*

I don't hesitate. I don't even grab any clothes. I run out the door, take the elevator to the garage, and get the hell out of there. I start driving in circles, unsure where to go, just sure that I've got to keep moving.

Truthfully, I feel like a fool for being so scared. This whole wild story about the Order and impending death is so ridiculous . . . yet so is that word, the word that gives the right answer to every question. And a genuinely terrified Dennis Nickleby *knew* I'd used the Answer.

I make a decision and head for the city. I want to be where there's lots of people. As I crawl through the Saturday night crush in the Lincoln Tunnel I get on my car phone. I need a place to stay. Don't want some fleabag hotel. Want something with brightly lit halls and good security. The Plaza's got a room. A suite. Great. I'll take it.

I leave my car with the doorman, register like a whirlwind, and a few minutes later I'm in a two-room suite with the drapes pulled and the door locked and chained.

And now I can breathe again. But that's about it. I order room service but I can't eat. I go to bed but I can't sleep. So I watch the tube. My eyes are finally glazing over as I listen to the same report from Bosnia-Herzewhatever for the umpteenth time when the reporter breaks in with a new story: Millionaire financial boy-wonder Dennis Nickleby is dead. An apparent suicide, he jumped from the ledge of his Fifth Avenue penthouse apartment earlier this evening. A full investigation has been launched. Details as soon as they are available.

I run to the bathroom and start to retch, but nothing comes up.

They got him! Just like he said they would! He's dead and oh God I'm next! What am I going to *do*?

First thing I've got to do is calm down. I've got to think. I do that. I make myself sit down. I control my breathing. I analyze my situation. What are my assets? I've got lots of money, a wallet full of credit cards, and I'm mobile. I can go on the run.

And I've got one more thing: the Answer.

Suddenly I'm up and pacing. The Answer! I can use the Answer itself as a defense. Yes! If I have to go to ground, it will guide me to the best place to hide.

Suddenly I'm excited. It's so obvious.

I throw on my clothes and hurry down to the street. They probably know my car, so I jump into one of the waiting cabs.

"Where to?" says the cabbie in a thickly accented voice. The back seat smells like someone blew lunch here not too long ago. I look at the driver

ID card and he's got some unpronounceable Middle East name.

I say, "Rford."

He nods, puts the car in gear, and we're off.

But where to? I feel like an idiot but I've got to ask. I wait till he's made a few turns, obviously heading for the East Side.

"Where are you taking me?"

"La Guardia." He glances over his shoulder through the plastic partition, his expression fierce. "That is what you said, is it not?"

"Yes, yes. just want to make sure you understood."

"I understand," he says. "I understand very good."

La Guardia . . . I'm flying out of here tonight. A new feeling begins to seep though me: hope, But despite the hope, let me tell you, it's très weird to be traveling at top speed with no idea where you're going.

As we take the La Guardia exit off Grand Central Parkway, the driver says, "Which airline?"

I say, "Rford."

He nods and we pull in opposite the Continental door. I pay him and hurry to the ticket counter. I tell the pretty black girl there I want first class on the next flight out.

"Out to where, sir?"

Good question. I say, "Rford."

She punches a lot of keys and finally her computer spits out a ticket. She tells me the price. I'm dying to know where I'm going but how can I ask her? I hand over my American Express. She runs it through, I sign, and then she hands me the ticket.

Cheyenne, Wyoming. Not my first choice. Not even on my top twenty list. But if the Answer tells me that's the best place to be, that's where I'm going. Trouble is, the flight doesn't leave for another three hours.


It's a comfortable trip, but the drinks I had at LaGuardia and the extra glasses of Merlot on the flight have left me a little groggy. I wander about the nearly deserted terminal wondering what I do now. I'm in the middle of nowhere—Wyoming, for Christ sake. Where do I go from here?

Easy: Trust the Answer.

I go outside to the taxi area. The fresh air feels good. A cab pulls into the curb. I grab it.

"Where to, sir?"

This guy's American. Great. I tell him, "RELOAD."

He says, "You got it."

I try to concentrate on our route as we leave the airport, but I'm not feeling so hot. That's okay. The Answer's taking me in the right direction. I trust it. I close my eyes and rest them until I feel the cab come to a halt.

I straighten up and look around. It's a warehouse district.

"Is this it?" I say.

"You told me 2316 Barrow Street," the cabbie says. He points to a gray door on the other side of the sidewalk. "Here we are."

I pay him and get out. 2316 Barrow Street. Never heard of it. The area's deserted, but what else would you expect in a warehouse district on a Sunday morning?

Still, I'm a little uneasy now. Hell, I'm shaking in my boxer shorts. But I can't stand out here all day. The Answer hasn't let me down yet. Got to trust it.

I take a deep breath, step up to the door, and knock. And wait. No response. I knock again, louder this time. Finally the door opens a few inches. An eye peers through the crack.

A deep male voice says, "Yes?"

I don't know how to respond. Figuring there's an implied question here, I say, "RELOAD."

The door opens a little wider. "What's your name?"

"Michael Moulton."

The door swings open and the guy who's been peeking through straightens up. He's wearing a gray, pin-striped suit, white shirt, and striped tie. And he's big—damn big.

"Mr. Moulton!" he booms. "We've been expecting you!"

A hand the size of a crown roast darts out, grabs me by the front of my jacket, and yanks me inside. Before I can shout or say a word, the door slams behind me and I'm being dragged down a dark hallway. I try to struggle but someone else comes up behind me and grabs one of my arms. I'm lifted off my feet like a Styrofoam mannequin. I start to scream.

"Don't bother, Mr. Moulton," says the first guy. "There's no one around to hear you."

They drag me onto a warehouse floor where my scuffling feet and their footsteps echo back from the far walls and vaulted ceiling. The other guy holding me is also in a gray suit. And he's just as big as the first.

Hey, look, I say. "What's this all about?"

They don't say anything. The warehouse floor is empty except for a single chair and a rickety table supporting a hard-sided Samsonite suitcase. They dump me into the chair. The second guy holds me there while the first opens the suitcase. He pulls out a roll of silver duct tape and proceeds to tape me into the chair.

My teeth are chattering now. I try to speak but the words won't come. I want to cry but I'm too scared.

Finally, when my body's taped up like a mummy, they walk off and leave me alone. But I'm alone only for a minute. This other guy walks in. He's in a suit, too, but he's smaller and older; gray at the temples, tanned, with bright blue eyes. He stops a couple of feet in front of the chair and stares down at me. He looks like a cabinet member, or maybe a TV preacher.

"Mr. Moulton," he says softly with a slow, sad shake of his head. "Foolish, greedy Mr. Moulton."

I find my voice. It sounds hoarse, like I've been shouting all night. "This is about the Answer, isn't it?"

"Of course it is."

"Look, I can explain—"

"No explanation is necessary."

"I forgot, that's all. I forgot and used it. It won't happen again."

He nods. "Yes, I know."

The note of finality in that statement makes my bladder want to let go. "Please. . ."

"We gave you a chance, Mr. Moulton. We don't usually do that. But because you came into possession of the Answer through no fault of your own, we thought it only fair to let you off the hook. A shame too." He almost smiles. "You showed some flair at the end . . . led us on a merry chase."

"You mean, using the Answer to get away? What did you do—make it work against me?"

"Oh, no. The Answer always works. You simply didn't use it enough."

"I don't get it." I don't care, either, but I want to keep him talking.

"The Answer brought you to an area of the country where we have no cells. But the Answer can't keep you from being followed. We followed you to La Guardia, noted the plane you boarded, and had one of our members rush up from Denver and wait in a cab."

"But when he asked me where to, I gave him the Answer."

"Yes, you did. But no matter what you told him, he was going to bring you to 2316 Barrow Street. You should have used the Answer before you got in the cab. If you'd asked someone which cab to take, you surely would have been directed to another, and you'd still be free. But that merely would have delayed the inevitable. Eventually you'd have wound up right where you are now."

"What are you going to do to me?"

He gazes down at me and his voice has all the emotion of a man ordering breakfast.

"I'm going to kill you."

That does it. My bladder lets go and I start to blubber.

"Mr. Moulton!" I hear him say. "A little dignity!"

"Oh, please! Please! I promise—"

"We already know what your promise is worth."

"But look—I'm not a bad guy . . . I've never hurt anybody!"

"Mr. Nickleby might differ with you about that. But don't be afraid, Mr. Moulton. We are not cruel. We have no wish to cause you pain. That is not our purpose here. We simply have to remove you."

"People will know! People will miss me!"

Another sad shake of his head. "No one will know. And only your broker will miss you. We have eliminated financiers, kings, even presidents who've had the Answer and stepped out of line."

"Presidents? You mean—?"

"Never mind, Mr. Moulton. How do you wish to die? The choice is yours."

*How do you wish to die?* How the hell do you answer a question like that? And then I know—with the best Answer.

I say, "REDACTED."

He nods. "An excellent choice."

For the first time since I started using the Answer, I don't want to know what the other guy heard. I bite back a sob. I close my eyes . . .

. . . and wait.

# HITLER, ELVIS, AND ME

*Doug Allyn*

'Twas a month before Christmas, and all through the Delmore not a creature—well, actually one creature was stirring. Philly Lacey, a blocky, dreadlocked musician from Grand Rapids was creeping down the lobby staircase, suitcase in one hand, guitar case in the other. Giving up on his neon dreams? Or had he packed them in the chipboard case with his battered Strat?

Either way the kid was late with his rent. I sympathized. Been there, done that.

Lacey was built like a blockhouse, and night clerks at the Delmore Arms don't get combat pay. I could have played dead, let him sneak past the counter. But later I'd wonder whether I'd let him skate by out of the goodness of my heart or weaseled out because he was built like a jailhouse iron pumper. I've been there, done that, too. Don't care to go there again.

"Hey, Philly, what's up? Kinda late, isn't it?"

His shoulders slumped, but at least he didn't pony for the door. Instead he trudged over to the desk, facing the music like a grownup. Which he might be someday.

"I'm movin' on, Ax. Can't find any gigs around here."

"Detroit's a tight market now," I nodded. "A few years back, the town was cookin', a hundred clubs pumpin' seven nights a week, Hitsville cuttin' platinum by kids fresh off a bus from Georgia. I was one of 'em."

"Yeah? When was that?"

"Blew in from Mississippi in '85, green as okra, playing bass in a blues band. The group broke up, but I stayed on, jammin' around town, tending bar, whatever. Hoping. Until I dumped a motorcycle, rearranged my face, and the mirror told me it was time for a career change."

"You ever come close to makin' it?"

I eyed him a moment. He meant no offense. He needed to know.

"I did in a way; worked with people I liked, had a helluva good time.

Most folks never have that much fun their whole lives."

"But you never really got anyplace, right? And now you're down to working nights in this dump."

"Temporarily. I've got a little detective agency, mostly making collections for clubs, agents, musicians, whoever. It's the only job where having a face like mine pays off. And I'm not the one trying to skate out the door at four in the morning."

"Look, I know I'm a little behind with the rent—"

I glanced at the monitor. "A little over six bills."

"All I got on me is busfare, Mr. Axton. You can beat the hell out of me and that's still all I'll have."

"Nobody's beatin' anybody over back rent, Philly. In my playing days the folks who own this place carried me a few times. Now Tooey's in the hospital, Greta has to run things alone, so I'm helping out nights until they can find somebody steady. Payback time, you know? So I'll be expecting a payback from you as soon as you get it together. Send installments if you want, but send it. Unless you want to see my ugly ass comin' after it."

"No, sir."

"Good. Have a nice trip, Philly. Stay in touch, hear?"

"I will, thanks, Mr. Axton, you're the bomb, man. I sure do—"

He was gone before he finished telling me what I nice guy I am. Pity. Because it was the only pay I'd get for this gig. But just because a job's a freebie doesn't mean I don't take it seriously.

As soon as the kid hit the snowy streets, I locked up, hung a BACK IN FIVE MINUTES placard on the door, and rode the rickety elevator to the ninth floor to check Lacey's ex-room.

Philly wasn't the trashing type, but in his rush to cut out he might have forgotten his stash, hash pipe, or God knows what. The Man shakes the Delmore down for fugitives on a regular basis. Finds a few, too. The last thing Greta needs is having some kid's dope turn up in a roust.

Using the master key I let myself in. Empty. And nothing's as empty as a vacant hotel room. Checked under the pillows and mattress first. Zip. Closets clear, no shoes under the bed, nothing hidden behind dresser drawers or taped under them. Medicine cabinet bare, toilet tank—damn.

A large plastic bag was nestled neatly at the bottom of the tank behind the inlet tube. Rolling up my sleeve, I reached into the tank and lifted it out.

Knew what it was as soon as I touched it. A gun. A long-barreled pistol of some sort. Double damn.

After carefully wiping my prints off the bag, I used a washcloth to carry it to the bed, popped the waterproof Baggie seal with a thumbnail, and dumped my find onto the faded chintz bedcover.

Whoa! I'd never actually seen one up close and personal, but I recognized it instantly. A German Luger, weapon of choice for every movie villain since the thirties, cold, black and deadly.

This one differed from the usual movie prop, though. Barrel was longer, for one thing, ten inches or so, and the frame was ornately engraved with filigree and an inscription. Kneeling, I tried to read it. German, naturally.

"Nussink," I muttered. "I know nuss-ink!"

Checked the magazine. Empty. Immaculate, in fact. I doubt it had ever been loaded. Or fired. The Luger looked showroom new, but it couldn't be. The checkered ivory grips had yellowed with age, taking on a wonderful patina. I'm no gun freak, but I know beauty when I see it. This was machinery elevated to another level, sleek and Teutonic as Marlene Dietrich in her prime.

So what was a kid from Grand Rapids doing with it? Sticking up 7-Elevens? Not likely. Philly'd been looking hard for gigs, auditioning, sitting in around town. I'd given him a few phone numbers, but nothing happened for him. No surprise. Music's corporate now. Studios want programmers, not players.

No stickup guy would use this thing anyway. The piece was too bulky to pack and too pretty to shoot. Strictly a decorator. And more than likely, slightly hot.

Which was a problem. I couldn't prove the kid had dumped it, the Delmore is already on the Detroit P.D.'s short list, and possessing an unregistered firearm is an automatic two-year felony in Michigan.

Solution? Lose it. Quick. Preferably at a profit.

Made a few calls and arranged to meet a bud at a Shoney's truck stop in Dearborn just off I-94. Tony Tallman's name suits him. Six-four with a black shoulder-length mane, he's an Odawa from Marquette and works at the look, flannel shirt, o.d. pants tucked into steel-toed jump boots. Bear claw necklace. A face like Tony's is probably the last thing Custer ever saw.

He was in a corner booth at the back of the restaurant, away from other customers. We rapped fists for hello, then I slid in across from him, parking the briefcase on the floor beside me.

"Hey, Axton, how you been?"

"Good, Tony, but I'm working nights. Let's get to the biz before I nod out. You still making the Motown to Miami run for Generous Motors?"

"Twice a week. Baltimore in between. Why?"

"I got some merch to move. South Florida sounds right."

"Why Florida?"

"It's gun country, loose laws, a lot of collectors." I slid the briefcase across to him. "Take a look."

He glanced casually around the dining room; nobody was paying attention to us. Shielding the case with his torso, he popped the lid, eyed it a moment, then nodded.

"Nice. Navy Luger, P'08 model, 9 millimeter." He hefted it, checking the balance. "Original or a reproduction?"

"I don't know. How can you tell?"

"The finish. Old bluing has a softer luster and . . ." He hesitated, staring at the gun, puzzled. Sliding it back into the case, he wiped his hands on his dungarees.

"What?" I asked.

"I don't know, something . . . Where'd you get this thing?"

"Some hump dumped it at the Delmore for back rent, swear to God."

"How much back rent?"

"A few hundred, why?"

"If it's a reproduction, it's worth a few yards. If it's original, and I think it is, we're talkin' five, six grand, maybe more."

"Sixty-forty to you?"

"Maybe. There's somethin' wrong about this piece."

"You mean it's fake?"

"No, I'm pretty sure it's the real deal. Bluing's right; the grips are definitely ivory, and you can't get the real thing any more."

"So what's the problem?"

"I don't know." Tony shook his head slowly, bemused at his own confusion. "Ever feel like somebody stepped on your grave? I got a jolt from that piece that felt like an eighteen-wheeler backed over mine."

"A truck? Terrific. What are you givin' me, man? Some Indian medicine thing?"

"What do I know from medicine? I'm Lutheran, for chrissake. I'm just saying I got a bad feeling about it."

"Get a grip. It's never even been fired."

"Hey, Ax, I know it's stupid, but I didn't live this long by dumpin' on my hunches. Somethin's up with this piece. You want me to deal it, fine, but I want to know more about it first. Provenance, collectors call it. If it's right-eous, we'll twitch the split, sixty-forty to you for your trouble. You're some kind of detective, right? So detect. Call me when you got somethin'. Or don't."


As I was driving back to the Delmore, it occurred to me that Tony was half right. There was definitely something wrong about the piece, but it wasn't a mystical eighteen-wheeler.

The problem was the provenance he'd mentioned. Bottom line, if the Luger were worth a couple of yards minimum, why would Philly Lacey leave it behind? He was sneaking out anyway, why not carry the gun, too?

Because it was hot? Then why leave it in the one place where it could be traced to him? Why not just pitch it in the nearest dumpster?

Answer: Philly didn't ditch the piece. Someone else had. Most likely a previous tenant.

I found Greta behind the registration counter, asleep on her feet after catnapping in a chair beside Tooey's bed all night. I sent her around the corner to Starbuck's for some caramel mocha and a breather. She was so grateful I felt like dog dump for using her exhaustion to backcheck the occupants of Room 914. Most recently, Philly Lacey and before him . . .

Janeen M. Husted, 419 Cherrymist Drive, Rochester Hills. Half an hour away by freeway? Ah, checked in at eleven A.M., no checkout time. A nooner. Lunch hour love or something like it. An unlikely candidate for stashing pistols in toilet tanks.

Before Husted? Rashaan Ali Salameh, a Lebanese from Beirut. Stayed at the Delmore two days before moving on. If I bought into profiling, Rashaan should be my guy, a transient Arab. Terrorist, right?

But I remembered Salameh, had checked him in myself. A Detroit Metro taxi brought him straight from the airport with the customs stickers still on his luggage. And since airport security types really are into profiling, there's no way a Lebanese national could smuggle a bulky pistol through security. Which let Rashaan off the hook, too.

That left . . . nobody. The room had been unoccupied for a month before Salameh, and the gun couldn't have been there more than a week or two.

When in doubt, scout. Using a borrowed code card, I logged onto the Law Enforcement Information Net and ran all three names. Philly Lacey, a pot bust a year earlier, paid a fine, drew no time. No arrests since, no wants or warrants. Rashaan Ali Salameh . . . with no credit I.D., three Rashaans came up, one doing double life in Milan, the other two out-of-staters. None of them could be my guy.

I ran his passport number. Got a hit. It listed Detroit Metro as his port of exit five days ago. Home to Beirut. Dead end. If Rashaan had dumped the gun, I doubted he'd talk to me about it over a long distance line.

Ran Janeen M. Husted . . . sweet Jesus Jenny on a bike! Multiple hits. Convictions for burglary, firearms possession, and robbery while armed, four years in Coldwater. Paroled seven months ago. No current wants or warrants but I'd just found my candidate—

"What are you doing?" Greta asked, peering over my shoulder.

"Abusing my computer privileges," I admitted, "but in a good cause. Do you remember this one?" I pulled up the notorious Janeen's pic and enlarged it.

"Yeah. A nooner but new at it. Used her real name, paid with a credit card."

"There's no checkout time."

"She didn't check out. Ran out of here like her hair was on fire. We got raided, bigtime, a swat team looking for Roland Dukes, the guy who knifed that cop over on Dequindre? I told 'em he wasn't here, but they had a hot tip, kicked in three or four doors on eight and nine. Probably scared that poor girl to death."

"Just her? What about her boyfriend?"

"Never saw him." Greta frowned. "I don't think he showed. Cops probably scared him off. Why? Who is she?"

"Just someone I'm looking up for a friend."

"She's somebody's wife, fooling around, right? I thought you didn't take divorce cases."

"If I did, I wouldn't be working nights for you. What makes you think she's married?"

"Because she was so green about it all. She even came back a few days later, asked for the same room but Lacey was in it by then. Besides, she looked very . . . elegant. That picture doesn't do her justice."

"It's a five-year-old booking picture, Greta. She did time for armed robbery."

"Get outa here! That girl? I thought she was some society type from Grosse Pointe with a rich hubby in Who's Who."

"Nope. But she's definitely got me wondering what's what."

❦   ❦   ❦

Hardtime ex-con or not, she was an amateur at office flings. Office couples looking to love their lunch hour away at the Delmore are an everyday affair, no pun intended. They pay cash, never show identification, and list phony license plate numbers. Janeen left a trail a beagle with a head cold could follow. Or a part-time night clerk.

Using her charge card number I called up her current credit status: nearly broke; no surprise, since she'd only been out of jail seven months. What was surprising was her current job.

Janeen Husted, presently on parole for burglary and robbery while armed, was listed as employed at the Bondurant Metropolitan Museum of Grosse Pointe. In what position? I couldn't imagine.

So I thought I'd ask.

The BMMGP is housed in the former Bondurant estate in Grosse Pointe, four multilevel flat-roofed buildings with glass walls bordered by Arkansas stack-stone fountains and swooping enclosed ramps that soar up from the parking lot below.

I'd actually worn a topcoat and a tie. Don't know why I bothered.

Most of the patrons were U. of Detroit students dressed like street people.

A quick scan of the video program at the entrance: "Manet et la Monde Nouvelle," . . . "Krieg Kunst—Masterworks of Browning, Borchardt and Their Contemporaries," "Auto-erotica: Sensuality in the Designs of Raymond Loewy." Whoopee.

Clueless, I began drifting through the exhibits, keeping a weather eye out for Janeen Husted.

The Manet display was French art depicting . . . colorful stuff. Baffling to me, but then they like Jerry Lewis. And snails.

I drifted along with a crowd of college kids up a glass tunnel to the next building, the auto-erotica exhibit. Starlets enjoying themselves in roadsters? Hardly. It was a collection of airy engineering drawings, most of which seemed to be cars.

Leaving the kids to ooh, aah, and take notes, I wandered up the next ramp alone, stepped through a doorway and found myself staring down a gun muzzle. A cannon, in fact. An honest-to-God automatic anti-aircraft gun. Designed by John Browning, the placard said. Glass-fronted display cases were filled floor to ceiling with firearms, most of them magnificently engraved with gold or silver filigree—rifles, shotguns, revolvers . . . and there it was.

I was drawn across the carpeted room by a magnet of a display. Five Luger automatics were arranged in a circle on green felt. In the center of the group was the handsomest weapon of all. Mine. Or its twin brother.

Leaning closer, I read the placard below. "Luger '08 Naval Model, presented by Admiral Erich Raeder to Chancellor Adolf Hitler, July 1936, in commemoration of the launching of the battle-cruiser *Scharnhorst*. Acquired from the Elvis Aron Presley Graceland Collection in 1971 by Robert Bondurant, curator 1959 to 1974."

Elvis? And Hitler? The gun—I sensed someone approaching and edged to my right, feigning interest in a rack of engraved bolt action rifles.

"Fascinating pieces, aren't they?" He was a compactly built man, five eight or so, wearing a gray vested suit that cost more than my car. Narrow face, heavy brows, wavy David Niven curls dyed chestnut with a sliver of silver at his temples.

"Uh, yeah. Pretty cool stuff."

"You seemed quite interested in the Luger display."

"Not really. I'm just surprised that Elvis owned 'em."

"Actually, Mr. Presley was quite an avid collector, both of firearms and edged weapons. His commissions helped foster interest in the work of more recent artisans such as Gilbert Hibben and others."

"No kidding? I thought he was just a singer—you know, 'Hound Dog,' 'Don't Be Cruel,' and all that?"

"Of course. Well, if you have any questions, feel free to consult our staff. Excuse me."

He bustled off, not bothering to hide his disdain. And annoyance. He'd probably have to disinfect his sleeve where it had brushed my coat.

No matter. The main reason for my visit to the Bondurant was sitting at a desk in an open office in a far corner of the room. After glancing around to be sure we were alone, I rapped lightly on her door. She glanced up.

Greta was right, she didn't look much like her booking picture any more. A small woman with blonde close-cropped hair worn in a pageboy, she looked every bit the suburban socialite, subdued navy dress with a sweater draped artfully over her shoulders, clunky Doe Martens shoes. And ice-gray eyes that could see a thousand yards.

"Janeen Husted?"

"That's right. Can I help you?"

"Maybe we can help each other. I believe I have something of yours. From the Delmore Arms."

She didn't even blink, continued reading me with those liquid eyes. "You're not the law," she said at last.

"No, ma'am, I'm private. My name's Axton, R. B." I showed her my investigator's license. She read every word of it. Carefully.

"What is it you want, Mr.—"

"Axton. My friends call me Ax. And what I don't want is trouble, for you or from you. We've got a situation, but it's nothing we can't work out. Where can we talk?"

"Not here. Do you know Papa Grappa's in Greektown?"

"Sure. What time?"

"Three?"

"Works for me. But don't be late."

She wasn't. I staked out the restaurant forty minutes early, watching it from a parking lot across the street on the off chance that my date might send a kneecapper in her place.

Instead she pulled into the lot five minutes after I did in a battered Volvo, parked behind a snowdrift two rows up, and settled in to wait and watch. Exactly as I was.

I gave it five minutes, then tapped my horn twice. Our eyes met in her rear view mirror. I trudged over to her car.

"Hi. You're not a very trusting lady."

"Would you trust somebody who looked like you?"

"No, ma'am. But now that we've established that neither of us is an amateur, can we talk?"

"Do you mind if I drive? I think better behind the wheel."

"Do you?" I said, climbing in. "Is that why you drove for your boyfriend when he held up the NBD branch in Inkster?"

"I was young, stoned, and in love," she said coolly, guiding the Volvo into early afternoon traffic. "What's your excuse?"

"For what?"

"Your face. Car wreck? Or did somebody remodel you?"

"Motorcycle accident. I've got your Luger."

"Good for you. Do you have a figure in mind?"

"It's not that simple. I need to know what's up."

"No you don't. Look, Mr. Axton—"

"Ax."

"Whatever. Trust me, you don't want to deal yourself into this. Take the money and run."

"I can't. I'm already involved in whatever's going on. If it breaks bad, do you think the law will believe I didn't know diddly? Or believe the first hump who offers to swap me for a reduced sentence?"

"You're not a very trusting sort either."

"Nobody loves me but my mama and she could be jivin', too."

"What?"

"It's a song. B. B. King. Look, Janeen, here's how it is. I've got the piece, which leaves you with exactly two options. Tell me what's up so we can work out a deal that protects me and mine. Or don't tell me, in which case the gun goes straight to the law."

"You won't make a dime that way."

"I won't be making license plates either. What's it gonna be?"

She didn't answer for a mile or two. I passed the time counting the new VeeDubs on Woodward. Bright as gumdrops. A green. Two reds and a yellow—

"I don't know what's going on," she said slowly. "In the slam I knew people who couldn't take it on the outside any more. Needed prison, the discipline, to stay sane."

"Institutionalized, you mean?"

"Yeah. I'm wondering if it's happened to me. Lately nothing seems to make much sense."

"Then you've got nothing to lose. Tell me."

"I did four years in Coldwater, the last two on work release, mopping floors at a Wal-Mart at night. I thought it would be better when I got out, but I couldn't find any kind of a job. Applications all over town but no takers; meanwhile I'm still mopping floors. Then I finally caught a break. I thought. Bumped into a guy I knew from the old days. He's the assistant curator at the museum, hired me on the spot. Eighteen bucks an hour."

"I'm missing something. How does a guy in the life wind up running a museum?"

"He marries it. His wife's a Bondurant. Besides, he wasn't into anything heavy, we'd just seen each other around in the dance clubs, you know? Knew some people in common."

"What people?"

"Dopers," she said, glancing the challenge at me. "He smoked a little weed. So did I. So did everybody else I knew."

"So he hired you. Are you qualified for this job?"

"I am now. I worked in the prison library, and I'm a quick study. It's been great, everything I ever hoped for. Dennis helped me get charge accounts at Hudsons and Winkelmans, showed me how to dress—"

"Dennis?"

"Mr. Garland. You were talking to him earlier."

"Actually I wasn't, but go on. And what did Dennis expect for all this help?"

"Not the wild thing, if that's what you're wondering. His wife Alise is older and a lot heavier. Dennis runs around on her, all right, but I'm not his type. You might be."

"Not yet. Okay, you've got a great job, life is Fat City, where does the gun come in?"

"After a few months he started asking me to do little favors for him, mostly deliver packages to people. Money. Ten grand here, fifteen there."

"How do you know it was money?"

"I looked. I also checked out the people I was dealing with. Two were bookies, one was Marko Rothstein."

"The loan shark from Ecorse?"

"He does sports betting, too. Poor Dennis has a jones for gambling. And he's unlucky. Two weeks ago, Rothstein and one of his goons came around. They were in his office a long time. He was scared spitless afterward."

"So what happened?"

"Nothing for a few days. Then Dennis asked me to make another delivery, but instead of dropping it off, I was supposed to meet a guy at the Delmore and give him the package."

"But this time it wasn't money?"

"No, it was the Hitler Luger. Scared the hell out of me when I realized it. If I get caught with a gun, I'm gone automatically, four more years. So I'm waiting for my contact, watching the street, when five squad cars roll up, no lights or sirens. Didn't know if they were there for me, didn't wait to find out. I stashed the gun and went out the window."

"From the ninth floor?"

"I've been in tougher spots back when I was doing burglaries. I just crawled along the ledge to a cornice, hid in the shadows until the prowl cars left, and split."

"But the Hitler Luger's back on display."

"When I came back without it, Dennis got pretty panicky, but somehow he fixed the exhibit."

"I see." And I was beginning to. "Did Garland tell you to check into the Delmore under your real name?"

"Yeah, so the contact could ask for me. Why?"

"Just wondered. So you told him about the raid, then what?"

"I thought he'd tell the contact where to pick up the package, end of problem, but he had a hairy, said I was the one who lost it, I had to recover it. I went back the next day, but the room was already rented."

"Yeah, to Philly Lacey." I shook my head slowly, smiling. "You were in the life, right? Ever hear of a Hendrix hustle?"

"What are you talking about?"

"A scam, Janeen. A Hendrix is what they call it in the music business, but this sounds like the same game. Here's how it works. Guitar collectors will pay huge bucks for some instruments, not because they are rare or special but just because some rock star played them once. A '63 Fender Stratocaster might be worth a few thousand, but if Jimi Hendrix played it on an album, the same guitar can bring three hundred grand."

"For the same guitar? That's crazy."

"No crazier than Beanie Babies or baseball cards, just more expensive. A few years ago, when the Japanese got into the collector guitar market, prices went to Mars. And before long somebody came up with a hustle. You buy a famous star's guitar, one that Hendrix, Clapton, or whoever played. Then you arrange to have it stolen, but you also make damn sure the police recover it."

"I don't get it."

"You will. The police and insurance people verify that it's the original and return it to you, the press is all over the story, rare guitar lost and found, blah blah. Then later on, some guy offers to sell your Hendrix guitar to a shady collector. The collector knows about the theft, so he calls you to find out if you got the original back. You say sure you did, but you're very, very interested in any copies he hears about."

"I don't—" But then she did, nodding slowly. "Ahh. And because the collector's a sleaze, he figures you're lying. That the original's still missing and you're looking to buy it back?"

"Exactly. Now, if he's honest, he gives you the seller's name, and he's your own guy anyway. But more likely he pays big bucks for the copy, stashes it away, and you move on to run the scam on the next fish."

"But wouldn't the copies have to be perfect?"

"Sort of, but that's the beauty of the hustle. We're not talking about the *Mona Lisa* here. Guitars and Lugers aren't works of art, they're *things*, mass-produced by machines. If you have a piece from the right era, any competent forger can alter its serial number. After that, it literally is the same as the original. Remember, it's not valuable because it's unique, it's valuable because it belonged to some famous hotshot once and you've got the news stories to prove it. Fame's a funny thing. Whether the person was good or not, people will pay monster bucks for a piece just because it belonged to somebody . . . famous."

"My God. And that Luger was owned by Hitler *and* Elvis."

"And me," I added.

"And you," she echoed, glancing warily at me. "So, back to question one. How much do you want?"

"Same answer, it's not that simple. You see, in the hustle, the burglar either doesn't get caught at all or the owner drops charges later on. Nobody gets hurt, everybody gets what they want, even the crooked collectors. But in this case . . ."

An angry flush rose above her collar as the implications sank in. "My God, Dennis set me up, didn't he? I was supposed to get caught with the gun in that raid. He didn't hire me in spite of my record, he hired me because of it. Even if I go to the cops it's his word against mine. Who'd believe me? That bastard!"

"I'd say that covers it."

"So what do we do?"

"That depends. He needs the original Luger to make the hustle work, but as soon as he gets it back, he'll either set you up again or get rid of you and run the scam with somebody else. Unless . . ."

"Unless what?"

"Roll with me a minute. Suppose a clerk at the Delmore calls to say the room you asked about is available? If you're not around, Dennis would have to go himself, yes?"

"Where would I be?"

"Out sick, at a funeral, whatever. Gone. Any problem with that?"

"No."

"Good. Now, since I still have the real piece, the gun in the exhibit must be a duplicate. When you came back without the original, how quick did Dennis get a replacement for the display?"

"Five minutes. Maybe less. I went in the john to clean myself up, and

and the showcase was fixed before I was."

"He must have the duplicates stashed nearby, probably someplace in the building. Any idea where?"

"There's a strongroom for valuable artifacts in the museum basement," Janeen mused, "but I'm familiar with the stock there. Whenever Dennis gave me packets to deliver, he always got them from the safe in his office. A walk-in safe. If the dupes are in the building, that's where they'd have to be."

"I see," I said carefully. "So, Miss Husted. In your . . . professional opinion, just how good a safe is it?"


Antiques Incroyable is a garishly painted three-story hock shop a few blocks east of Saginaw's old downtown district. Johnno Habash, proprietor. He's Syrian, I think. His store's in a high crime area, but nobody ever rips Johnno off. Ever.

I pressed the buzzer just after closing, and the door hummed open electronically. A man-mountain stood just inside, black, in a black suit, pristine white shirt, red skullcap, and a maroon bow tie. Street Sweeper shotgun cradled casually in the crook of his arm.

"Yo, Ax, how you been doin'?"

"Good, Mr. Bass. You?"

"Fine as frog hair. Are you packin,' Ax?"

"No, but I've got pieces in this briefcase. You can check it if you like."

"No need, just so you understand you'll be pickin' up the tab for anything that goes wrong."

"Understood. Is Johnno in his office?"

"Like Mohammed on the mountain. Go ahead on."

The shop is a huge, open warehouse with its steel superstructure exposed, walls and aisles stacked with floor-to-ceiling shelving, every inch filled with an array of antiques and collectibles from Rookwood china to crosscut saws. The center of the store is dominated by a two-and-a-half story office tower encircled with a winding, wrought-iron staircase. I took a deep breath and started up, keeping away from the railing. Pausing to pant halfway up, I scanned the room. A mistake.

I hate heights, and I was already above the second story light fixtures. A long way down. I moved on.

The top is a mesa, an elegant, open-air square girded by a tall oak railing, offering a spectacular overview of the aisles below. Johnno was sitting at an exquisitely carved Victorian desk, his feet resting on a footstool. A bloated toad of a man built like a suet block, his black suit makes him look like a toad in a tuxedo. Even his face is amphibian: bulbous eyes, petulant lips, frog-belly pallor.

"Ax," he nodded curtly. "Time's money. What you got for me?"

"Five pre-war naval Lugers, mint condition, strictly for the collector market." I placed one of the guns on the table. He glanced at it, then back at me.

"Warm, are they?"

"They're not on any hot sheets, and nobody's looking for them. But there is one small problem."

"Which is?"

"They all have the same serial number."

He digested that a moment, sucking on a tooth.

"Let me guess. Five navy Lugers with the same serial as the one from that museum heist last month?"

"It wasn't a heist exactly. The cops busted an assistant director in a cheap hotel with one of the museum's guns. He was in hock to a loan shark and was tying to peddle it. Or so they figure. The museum fired him but didn't press charges."

"I remember now. The gun belonged to Hitler once, right? But I thought the museum got that gun back."

"So they said," I acknowledged. "Of course, there's a slight possibility that they were mistaken. The gun was out of their possession for a time, and navy Lugers aren't all that uncommon. I have five of them right here, for instance, identical to the . . . mishandled gun. A reasonable person would have to admit there's a possibility that one of them could be the original."

"A possibility?"

"Right. Just a possibility."

He bobbed his squat head, mulling it over. "I might know a few people interested in buying a . . . possibility. How much?"

"Ten K apiece."

"Fifty grand? That's a lot of—"

"It isn't ten percent of what you'll get for 'em, Johnno, and I've got partners to take care of. The offer's open for the next thirty seconds, and then I'm outa here."

He glanced at his watch, a Patek Phillipe, drumming his sausage fingers on the desk for what seemed a very long time. Then shrugged. "Deal."

Picking up the Luger, he hefted it, eyeing it critically. "This belonged to Hitler?"

"That's what the papers said. And later on Elvis owned it."

"No kidding? Hitler and Elvis both?"

"And me."

"No offense, Ax, but you don't exactly rank up there with Hitler and Elvis."

"Never really wanted to."

"Bull. Deep down, everyone wants to be famous."

"Funny, a kid said something like that to me awhile back. But he was wrong. Hitler and Elvis were famous, Johnno. Bottom line, would you rather be them? Or us?"

"Point taken," he nodded. "So when I deal these, you won't mind if I don't mention your name as a previous owner?"

"No," I said. "I won't mind at all."

# ONE HIT WONDER

*Gabrielle Kraft*

You probably don't remember me, but ten years ago I was very big. Matter of fact, in the record business I was what we call a one hit wonder. You know, the kind of guy you see on talk shows doing a medley of his hit? That was me, Ricky Curtis.

Remember "Ooo Baby Oooo"? Remember? "Ooo baby oooo, it's you that I do, it's you I truly do?" That was me, Ricky Curtis, crooning the insistent vocal you couldn't get out of your head, me with the moronic whine you loved to hate. Big? Hell, I was huge. "Ooo Baby Oooo" was a monster hit, triple platinum with a million bullets. That was Ricky Curtis, remember me now?

My God, it was great. You can't imagine how it feels, being on top. And it was so easy! I wrote "Ooo Baby Oooo" in minutes, while I was waiting for my teenage bride to put on her makeup, and the next day I played it for my boss at the recording studio where I had a job sweeping up. He loved it. We recorded it with some girl backup singers the next week, and it was alakazam Ricky.

For one long, brilliantly dappled summer, America knew my name and sang the words to my tune. People hummed me and sang me and whistled me, and my voice drifted out of car radios through the airwaves and into the minds of the world. For three sun-drenched months, I was a king and in my twenty-two-year-old wisdom I thought I would live forever.

Then, unaccountably, it was over. Because I didn't have a follow-up record, I was a one hit wonder and my just-add-water career evaporated like steam from a cup of coffee. I was ripped apart by confusion and I didn't know what to do next. Should I try to write more songs like "Ooo Baby Oooo"? I couldn't. Not because I didn't want to, but because I didn't know how. You see, I'd had visions of myself as a troubadour, a road-show Bob Dylan, a man with a message. A guy with heart. I hadn't envisioned myself as a man with a teenage tune wafting out across the shopping malls of the land, and "Ooo Baby Oooo" was merely a fluke, a twisting mirage in the desert. I was battered by doubt, and so, I did nothing. I froze, paralyzed in the klieg lights of L.A. like a drunk in a cop's high beams.

The upshot of my paralysis was that I lost my slot. My ten-second window of opportunity passed, and like a million other one hit wonders, I fell off the edge of the earth. I was yesterday's news. I couldn't get arrested, couldn't get a job. Not even with the golden oldies shows that go out on the tired road every summer, cleaning up the rock-and-roll dregs in the small towns, playing the little county fairs, not the big ones with Willie and Waylon, but the little ones with the racing pigs. I was an instant dinosaur, a joke, a thing of the past.

It hit me hard, being a has-been who never really was, and I couldn't understand what I'd done wrong. I'd signed over my publishing rights to my manager and dribbled away my money. In my confusion I started to drink too much—luckily I was too broke to afford cocaine. I drifted around L.A., hanging out in the clubs nursing a drink, telling my then-agent that I was "getting my head together," telling my then-wife that prosperity would burst over us like fireworks on the glorious Fourth and I'd have another big hit record any day now. Telling myself that I was a deadbeat washout at twenty-two.

Fade out, fade in. Times change and ten years pass, and Ricky Curtis, the one hit wonder, is now a bartender at Eddie Style's Club Dingo above the Sunset Strip, shoving drinks across a huge marble bar stained a dark faux-malachite green, smiling and giving a *c'est la vie* shrug if a well-heeled customer realizes that he's a guy who had a hit record once upon a sad old time.

But inside, I seethed. I smoldered. I didn't know what to do and so I did nothing. You don't know how it feels, to be so close to winning, to have your hand on the lottery ticket as it dissolves into dust, to feel the wheel of the red Ferrari one second before it slams into the wall. To smell success, taste the elixir of fame on your tongue, and then stand foolishly as your future rushes down the gutter in a swirl of brown, greasy water because of your inability to make a decision.

So I worked for Eddie Style. I had no choice. I groveled for tips and tugged my spiky forelock like the rest of the serfs; I smiled and nodded, but in the abyss I called my heart there was only anger. My rage at the crappy hand I'd been dealt grew like a horrible cancer eating me alive, and at night I dreamed of the Spartan boy and the fox.

I'd wake up every morning and think about money. Who had it, how to get it, why I didn't have it. In this town, the deals, the plans, the schemes to make money mutate with each new dawn. But I said nothing. I had nothing to say. I smiled, slid drinks across the bar and watched the wealthy enjoying themselves, waiting for crumbs to fall off the table. In a joint like the Dingo where the rich kids come out to play at night and the record business execs plant their cloven hooves in the trough at will, a few crumbs always fall your way.

Like when Eddie Style offered me a hundred thou to kill his wife.

Edward Woffard Stanhope III, known as Eddie Style to his friends and foes alike, owned the Club Dingo, and he was also a very rich guy. Not from the Dingo, or movie money, not record business money, not drug money, not at all. Eddie Style had something you rarely see if you float around the tattered edges of L.A. nightlife the way I do. Eddie Style had inherited money.

Edward Stanhope III, aka Eddie Style, came from a long line of thieves, but since they were big thieves, nobody called them thieves; they called them Founding Fathers, or Society, or the Best People. Eddie's granddad, Edward Woffard Stanhope Numero Uno, known as "Steady," was one of the guys who helped loot the Owens Valley of its water, real *Chinatown* stuff. You know Stanhope Boulevard over in West Hollywood? Well, Eddie Style called it Me Street, that's the kind of money we're talking about here.

Trouble was, Eddie Style had bad taste in wives. He was a skinny little guy, and he wasn't very bright in spite of the fact that the accumulated wealth of the Stanhope family weighed heavy on his narrow shoulders. Plus, he liked tall women. They were always blond, willowy, fiscally insatiable and smarter than he was. Chrissie and Lynda, the first two, had siphoned off a hefty chunk of the Stanhope change, and Suzanne, the third blond beauty, had teeth like an alligator. At least, according to Eddie. I didn't know. They'd only been married two years and she didn't come around the Dingo. It was going to take another big slice of the pie to divest himself of Suzanne, and Eddie was getting cagey in his old age. After all, he wouldn't come into any more dough until his mother croaked, and she was only fifty-seven. He had a few siblings and half siblings and such scattered around, so a major outlay of capital on a greedy ex-wife didn't seem prudent.

So, one night after closing, he and I are mopping up the bar—I'm mopping up the bar, he's chasing down mimosas—and he starts complaining about his marital situation, just like he's done a thousand nights before.

"Suzanne's a nice girl," he sighed, "but she's expensive." His voice echoed through the empty room, bouncing off the upended chairs on the café tables, the ghostly stage and the rock-and-roll memorabilia encased in Plexiglas.

"You don't say?" In my present line of work, I've learned that noncommittal responses are the best choice, and I switch back and forth between "You don't say" and "No kidding" and "Takes all kinds." Oils the waters of drunken conversation.

"I *do* say. Ricky boy, I've been married three times," he said ruefully, "so I ought to know better by now. You see a girl, you think she's . . ." He narrowed his eyes, looked down the bar to the empty stage at the end of the room and gave an embarrassed shrug. "I dunno . . . the answer to a question you can't quite form in your mind. A hope you can't name."

"Takes all kinds." I nodded and kept on mopping the bar. Like I said, the Dingo was empty, Eddie Style was in a philosophical mood, and I had a rule about keeping my trap shut.

But he wouldn't quit. "You get married and you realize she's just another broad who cares more about getting her legs waxed than she does about you. I can't afford a divorce," he said, pinging the edge of his glass with his forefinger. It was middle C. "I don't have enough money to pay her off."

I felt my brain start to boil. He didn't have enough money! What a laugh! Isn't that the way the song always goes in this town? I love you baby, but not enough. I have money but not enough. To me, Eddie Style was loaded. He owned the Club Dingo, he drove a classic Mercedes with a license plate that read STYLEY, he lived in a house in the Hills, he wore Armani suits for business and Hawaiian shirts when he was in a casual mood. Oh yeah, Eddie Style had it all and Ricky Curtis had nothing.

"See, Ricky boy," he nattered as he took a slug of his fourth mimosa. "Guy like you, no responsibilities, you think life's a ball. Hey, you come to work, you go home, it's all yours. Me, I got the weight of my damn ancestors pushing on me like a rock. I feel crushed by my own history."

"Sisyphus," I said, wringing out the bar towel. After my divorce I'd gone to a few night classes at UCLA in hopes of meeting a girl with brains. Some fat chance. Even in *Myths and Legends: A Perspective for Today*, all the girls knew "Ooo Baby Oooo."

"Whatever," Eddie sighed. Ping on his glass again. "I can't take much more of this kinda life." He gestured absently at his darkened domain. "If only she'd die. . ." He looked up at me and shot a loud ping through the empty club. His lids peeled back from his eyes like skin from an onion, and he gave me a wise smile. "If only somebody'd give her a shove . . ."

"Hold on," I told him. "Wait a minute, Eddie. . . ."

He didn't say anything else, but it was too late. I could smell dark blood seeping over the layer of expensive crud that permeated the Dingo. He'd planted the idea in my brain, and it was putting out feelers like a science-fiction monster sprouting a thousand eyes.

For three nights I lay in my bed, drinking vodka, staring out the window of my one-bedroom apartment on Ivar, at the boarded-up crack house across the street, and thinking about money. If I had money, I could take a few months off, vacation in Mexico and jump-start my life. I had no future as a bartender at the Club Dingo. If I stayed where I was—as I was—I would never change, and I *had* to revitalize my life or I would shrivel and die. If I could get out of L.A., lie on the beach for a month or two, maybe I could start writing songs again, maybe I could have another hit. Maybe *something* would happen to me. Maybe I'd get lucky. The way I saw things, it was her or me.

Three days later Eddie made me the offer. A hundred thou, cash, no problems. He'd give me the keys to the house; I could pick the time and place and kill her any way I wanted.

"Look, Ricky boy, you've got a gun, right?" he said.

"A thirty-eight." I shrugged. "L.A.'s a crazy town."

"Great. Just shoot her, OK? Whack her over the head, I don't care. Do it fast so she won't feel anything. Make it look like a robbery, steal some jewelry. She's got it lying all over her dressing table; she won't use the damn safe. Christ, I gave her enough stuff the first year we were married to fill a vault; just take some of it, do what you want. Throw it down the drain, it doesn't matter. I just gotta get rid of her, OK?"

"OK, Eddie," I said. By the time he asked me to kill her, it was easy. I'd thought it all out; I knew he was going to ask me, and I knew I was going to do it. Ultimately, it came down to this. If murder was the only way to finance another chance, I would become a killer. I saw it as a career move.

I told him I'd do it. Eddie gave me a set of keys to his house and planned to be at the Dingo all night on Wednesday, my night off. He said it would be a good time to kill Suzanne, anxiously pointing out that he wasn't trying to tell me my job. It was all up to me.

I drove up to his house in the Hills; I'd been there for the Club Dingo

Christmas party, so I was vaguely familiar with the layout. It was a Neutra house from the thirties, a huge white block hanging over the edge of the brown canyon like an albino vulture, and as I parked my dirty Toyota next to the red Rolls that Suzanne drove, I felt strong, like I had a rod of iron inside my heart. Suzanne would die, and I would rise like the phoenix from her ashes. I saw it as an even trade—my new life for her old life.

I opened the front door with Eddie's key and went inside, padding silently on my British Knights. My plan was to look around, then go upstairs to the bedroom and shoot her. Eddie said she watched TV most nights, used it to put her to sleep like I used vodka.

The entry was long, and there was a low, flat stairway leading down to the sunken living room. The drapes were pulled back, and I could see all of Los Angeles spread out through the floor-to-ceiling windows that lined the far wall. The shifting shapes of moving blue water in the pool below were reflected on the glass, and in that suspended moment I knew what it meant to live in a world of smoke and mirrors.

"Who the hell are you?" a woman snapped.

It was Suzanne and she had a gun. Dumb little thing, a tiny silver .25 that looked like it came from Le Chic Shooter, but it was a gun all the same. Eddie never mentioned that she had a gun, and I was angry. I hadn't expected it. I hadn't expected her either.

I'd met her at the Christmas party, so I knew she was gorgeous, but I'd been pretty drunk at the time and I wasn't paying attention. Suzanne Stanhope, nobody called her Suzie Style, was a dream in white. She was as tall as I was, and she had legs that would give a lifer fits.

"Eddie sent me," I said brightly. "He forgot his datebook. Didn't he call you? He said he was gonna . . ." I let my voice trail off and hoped I looked slack-jawed and stupid. I thought it was a damn good improvisation, and my ingratiating grin must have helped, because she lowered the gun.

"You're the bartender, the one who used to be a singer, right?" she asked. "Now I recognize you." She loosened up, but she didn't put down the gun.

This was going to be easy. I'd bust her in the head, steal the jewelry and be a new man by morning. I smiled, amazed that one woman could be so beautiful.

She was wearing a white dress, loose, soft material that clung to her body when she moved, and the worst part was, she wasn't even trying to be beautiful. Here she was, probably lying around in bed watching TV, painting her toenails, and she looked like she was going to the Oscars. Once again I saw the futility of life in L.A. without money.

"Tell Eddie I could have shot you," she said, very mild. "He'll get a kick out of that." She still had the little silver gun in her hand, but she was holding it like a pencil, gesturing with it.

"Sure will, Mrs. Stanhope," I said, grinning like an intelligent ape.

"Oh, cut the crap, will you? Just call me Suzanne." She looked me over, and I got the feeling she'd seen better in the cold case.

"You want a drink, bartender? What's your name, anyway?"

"Ricky Curtis."

"Rick, huh?" She frowned and started humming my song. "How does that thing go?" she asked.

I hummed "Ooo Baby Oooo" for her. Her hair was shoulder length, blond, not brassy. Blue eyes with crinkles in the corners like she didn't give a damn what she laughed at. "Ooo baby oooo, it's you that I do . . . ," I hummed.

"So how come you don't sing anymore, Rick?" she asked as she led me down the steps into the sunken living room. I could see the lights of the city twinkling down below and idly wondered if, on a clear day, I'd be able to see my apartment on Ivar or the boarded-up crack house across the street.

"How come nobody asks me?" I said.

She went behind the bar, laughing as she poured herself a drink. Sounded like wind chimes. She put the little gun down on the marble bar, and it made a hollow clink.

"Vodka," I told her.

She poured me a shot in a heavy glass, and I drank it off. I had a strange feeling, and I didn't know why. I knew Eddie Style was rich, but this was unlike anything I'd ever seen before. The sheer weight of the Stanhope money was crushing me into the ground. Heavy gravity. I felt like I was on Mars.

She sipped her drink and looked thoughtfully out the huge windows, past the pale translucent lozenge of the pool toward the city lights below. "It's nice here," she said. "Too bad Eddie doesn't appreciate it. He'd have a better life if he appreciated what he has, instead of running around like a dog. The Dingo is aptly named, don't you think, Rick?"

I wanted another drink. I wanted to be drunk when I killed her, so I wouldn't feel it. I hadn't planned on killing a person, just a . . . a what? Just a blond body? Just a lump in the bed that could be anything? I hadn't counted on looking into her clear blue eyes as the light went out of them. I pushed my glass across the counter, motioning for another drink.

"So why are you here, Rick?" she asked softly. "It was a good story about the datebook but Eddie's too frazzled to keep one. I'm surprised you didn't know that about him. Maybe you two aren't as close as you think."

I didn't know what she meant. Was she kidding me? I couldn't tell. What was going on? I had that old familiar feeling of confusion, and once again, I was in over my head. Did she *know* I was there to kill her? I couldn't let her think that, so I did the next best thing. I confessed to a lesser crime.

"I'm broke," I said shortly, "and Eddie said the house was empty. I was here at the Christmas party and I figured I could bag some silver out of the back of the drawer. Maybe nobody would miss a few forks. It was a dumb idea but it's tap city and Eddie has more than he needs. Of everything," I said, looking directly at her. "You gonna call the cops?"

"Robbery? That's an exciting thought," she said, clinking the ice in her glass as she leaned her head back and popped an ice cube in her mouth. She took it out with her fingers and ran it over her lips. "You value Eddie's things, his lifestyle. Too bad he doesn't."

"In this town it's hard to appreciate what you have," I said slowly, wondering how her lips would feel, how cold they really were. "Everybody always wants what they can't get."

"Don't they," she said meaningfully as she dropped the ice cube back in her glass. "What do *you* want, Rick? Since you brought it up."

"Me? I want money," I said. As the phrase popped out of my mouth I realized how pathetic it sounded. Like a teenager wanting to be a rock star, I wanted money. That's the trouble with L.A. Being a bartender isn't a bad gig, but in L.A., it's just a rest stop on the freeway to fame, a cute career to spice up your résumé.

"That shouldn't be tough for a good-looking guy like you. Not in this town." She refilled our glasses and led me over to a white couch. There were four of them in an intimate square around a free-form marble table. I felt like I was somebody else. I'd only had a couple short ones and I was wondering what she wanted in a man. I wondered if she was lonely.

"Sit down," she said, her white dress splitting open to show me those blond legs. "Let's talk, Rick," she said.

❧     ❧     ❧

"Sure I married him because he's rich, just like he married me because I'm beautiful," she said, running a finger across my stomach. "But I thought there was more to it than that. He was sweet to me at first. He didn't treat me like some whore who spent her life on her knees. Christ, I'm tired of men who want me because I'm beautiful and then don't want me because I'm smart. Am I smart, Rick?" she asked, pulling the sheet around her body as she got out of bed. "Want anything?"

Mars. I was on Mars. You hang around L.A., you think you know the words to the big tune, but you don't. You think you've seen a lot, know it all, but you don't, and as I lay in his bed caressing his wife, I wondered how it would feel to be Eddie Style. Live in his house, sleep with his wife. If I had a room like this, why would I ever leave it? If I had a wife like that, why would I want to kill her? The sheets were smooth, some kind of expensive cotton the rich like; the carpet was soft—was it silk? The glinting perfume bottles on her dressing table were heavy, geometrically cut glass shapes twinkling with a deep interior light far brighter than the city below. If I unstoppered one of those bottles, what would I smell?

She let the sheet drop to the floor as she lowered herself into the bubbling blue marble tub at the far end of the room. I lay in Eddie's bed and watched her as she stretched her head back and exposed a long white highway of throat pointing to a dark and uncharted continent. I thought about killing her and realized it was too late.

"This is insane," I said.

She laughed. "It's so L.A., isn't it? The bartender and the boss's wife, the gardener and the . . ."

"Yeah, I read *Lady Chatterly*. I'm not a complete illiterate," I told her. "What do you want to do about it?"

"Oh, we could get together afternoons in cheesy motels," she said. "Think you'd like that?"

"Sounds great," I said ironically. "Don't you think you'd find cheesy motels boring after a while? Say, after a week or so?" I got up out of bed, went over to the tub and got in with her. The water warmed me to the bone. "You could come live with me in my one-bedroom. You'd fit in just fine. Course, you'd have to leave this house behind," I said as I slipped my hands underneath her body and lifted her on top of me. "And there wouldn't be much time for shopping since you'd have to get a job slinging fries. Think you'd miss the high life?"

"Probably," she gasped.

"Yeah, I think so too. But we can talk about it later, right?"

"Right," she said, clutching at my back with those beautifully sculpted nails. "Yessss."


Of course, I left without killing Suzanne. Then I went back to the Dingo and yelled at Eddie, which was a laugh since rolling around with his wife all evening. Funny thing, though. As I stared at Eddie Style, sitting on his usual stool at the long faux malachite bar, I felt contempt for him. He had everything, Eddie did. Money, cars, a beautiful wife. But he didn't know what he had, and that made him a bigger zero than I was. Even with all that money.

"Why the hell didn't you tell me she had a gun?" I snarled over the blast of the head-banging band onstage. I'd never snarled at him before, and it felt good.

"I forgot," he said, very apologetic as he tugged on his mimosa. "Really, Ricky boy, I didn't think about it. It's just a little gun. . . ."

"Easy for you to say," I grumbled. "Don't worry about it, man. I'll take care of it for you."

But I didn't.

I called Suzanne a few days later, she came over to my apartment and we spent the afternoon amusing ourselves.

"Why don't you fix this place up?" she said. "It doesn't have to look like a slum, Rick."

"Sure it does. It *is* a slum," I told her, stroking the long white expanse of her back. "You think it's *La Bohéme*? Some sort of arty dungeon? Look out the window, it's a slum."

"Don't complain, you've got me. And," she said as she got out of bed and went over to her purse, "now you've got a nice watch instead of that cheapo."

You think your life changes in grand, sweeping gestures—the day you have your first hit, the day you get married, the day you get divorced—but it doesn't. Your life changes when you stretch out your hand and take a flat velvet-covered jeweler's box with a gold watch inside that costs two or three thousand dollars. Your life changes when you don't care how you got it.

When you're a kid, you never think the situation will arise. You think you'll be a big star, a hero, a rock legend; you don't think you'll be lying in bed in a crummy Hollywood apartment with another guy's wife and she'll be handing you a little gift. Thanks, honey, you were great.

I took the watch. A week later, I took the five hundred bucks she gave me "for groceries." You see the situation I was in? Here I was, supposed to kill Eddie Style's wife for a hundred thousand dollars, and I was too busy boffing her to get the job done. Me, the guy who was so hungry for cash that his hands vibrated every time he felt the walnut dash on a Mercedes.

I was swept by the same confusion I'd felt after "Ooo Baby Oooo." Once again I was staring out over a precipice into an endless expanse of possibilities, and I didn't know what to do. I was looking at a row of choices lined up like prizes at a carnival, and the barker was offering me any prize I wanted. But which one should I take? The doll? The stuffed monkey? The little toy truck? Reach out and grab it, Ricky boy. How do you make a decision that will determine the course of your life? A thick, oozing paralysis sucked at me like an oil slick.

All I had to do was kill her and I couldn't do it. When she wasn't around I fantasized about taking her out for a drive and tossing her down a dry well out in Palm Desert or giving her a little shove over the cliff as we stared at the sunset over the Pacific. But when she was around, I knew it was impossible. I couldn't kill Suzanne. Her beauty held me like a vise.

Beautiful women don't understand their power; their hold on men is far greater than they comprehend. Women like Suzanne sneer at their beauty; they think it's a happy accident. Mostly they think it's a commodity, sometimes they think it's a gift, but they don't understand what the momentary possession of that beauty does to a man, how it feels to see perfection lying beside you in bed, to stare at flawless grace as it sleeps and you know you can touch it at will.

The flip side of my problem was that a rich guy like Eddie Style didn't understand that possessing a woman like Suzanne made me his equal. Within the four corners that comprise the enclosed world of a bed, a fool like me is equal to generations of Stanhope money.

"So, Ricky boy, when you gonna do that thing?" Eddie asked me late one night, giving me a soft punch on the arm. He's acting like it's a joke, some kind of a scene. Kill my wife, please.

"Don't pressure me, Eddie; you want it done fast, do it yourself." Now that I was a hired gun, I no longer felt the need to kiss the hem of his garment quite so fervently or quite so often. Weird, what power does to you. You start sleeping with a rich guy's wife, you feel like a superhero, an invincible Saturday morning kiddie cartoon. "If you'd told me about the gun, I would have killed her that first night. Now the timing's screwed up."

This was true, and it creased a further wrinkle into my murderous plans. The vacationing couple was back at work at Eddie's big white house in the daytime, so it was no longer possible to slip in and kill Suzanne even if I'd had the guts to do it. Too many people around.

Besides, I was no longer an anonymous cipher, a faceless killer. I was a piece of Suzanne's life, although Eddie didn't know it. Now that she was coming to my apartment for nooners, I knew we'd been seen together. The elderly lady with ten thousand cats who lived across the courtyard and peeked out between her venetian blinds at people coming in and going out, Suzanne's big red Rolls parked on Ivar—there were too many telltale traces of my secret life, traces that would give me away if I *did* kill her.

So there I was, stuck between skinny Eddie Style and his beautiful wife, and it was at this point that a brilliant idea occurred to me. What if I killed Eddie Style? What if I killed the husband and not the wife? Assuming Suzanne approved of the idea, it would have a double-edged effect; it would cement Suzanne to all that Stanhope money and it would cement me to Suzanne. For I had no intention of allowing her to remain untouched by Eddie's death, if I chose to kill him instead of her.

Turnabout.

But would Suzanne take to the idea of killing her husband? Would she see me as a lout, as a sociopathic lunatic, or merely as the opportunistic infection I truly was? Or would she, too, see murder as a career move?

At night I worked at the Dingo, and though I poured drinks, laughed and chatted with the customers, I was changed inside, tempered by my connection to death. Now that I was concentrating on murder, I was no longer a failure, a one hit wonder. I was invaded by the knowledge that I possessed a secret power setting me apart from the faceless ants who surrounded me in the bar. A few weeks ago, I was a shabby, sad wreck tossed up on the shores of Hollywood with the rest of the refuse, the flotsam and jetsam of the entertainment business. Now that I was dreaming about murder, I was on top again, and I had the potential of ultimate power.

A week later I decided to talk to Suzanne about killing Eddie. I had no intention of bringing up the question directly; I was too clever for that. I planned to approach her crabwise, manipulate our pillow talk in the direction of murder. If she picked up the cue, well and good. If not, I'd have to alter my plans where she was concerned.

It was Wednesday, my night off, and Eddie was at the Dingo. I called Suzanne and said I'd be at her house that night. She wasn't too happy that

I was coming over, but I let my voice go all silky and told her I felt like a hot bath.

The white Neutra house was lit up by soft floodlights, and as I knocked on the door, it reminded me of the glistening sails of tall ships flooding into a safe harbor bathed in sunshine.

The door opened. It was Eddie Style. "Do you think you should be here, Ricky boy?" he asked, very mildly.

Not a good sign. I had a moment of fear, but I covered it. I was feeling omnipotent, and besides, I had my .38 in my jacket pocket. "You mean we've got to stop meeting like this?" I mocked. Simultaneously, I knew I was in over my head and apprehension started nibbling at my shoes.

He held open the door for me, and I went inside, automatically stepping down into the sunken living room. Suzanne, wearing a white kimono with deep, square sleeves, was sitting on the couch, a drink in her hand. Her nails shone red as an exploding sun and her face was flat, expressionless. All the beauty had drained out of it, and there was only the molded mask of a mannequin staring back at me from behind a thick sheet of expensive plate glass. Who was she?

Confusion swept me, and I was carried off down the river like a dinghy in a flash flood.

"Here we all are," Eddie said. "Drink?"

I nodded yes. "Vodka."

"Ricky boy," he said as he went behind the bar, "I've had you followed and I know you're sleeping with my wife. I'm afraid I can't stand still for that," he said slowly. "When the help gets out of line it makes me look foolish and I simply can't allow it to go unpunished." He reached underneath the bar and pulled out the shiny silver .25 Suzanne pointed at me that first night.

Now the dinghy was caught in a whirlpool. "I'm sorry, Eddie," I said. "These things . . . just happen." I indicated Suzanne. "I'm sorry."

"Ricky boy, I know what you think. I've seen you operate."

His voice was cold and he was still holding the gun. "You think because I'm rich you can come along, skim a little cream off the top and I'm so stupid I won't notice. You think you're as good as I am, street-smart Ricky boy, the one hit wonder. Wrong, buddy. Dead wrong. You're not as good as I am and you never will be."

The absurd little gun was firmer in his hand, and I had the cold, cold feeling he was going to shoot me. He'd claim I was a robber, that his faith-

ful minion had betrayed his trust. Who'd dare to call Edward Woffard Stanhope III a liar? With his beautiful wife Suzanne by his side to back up his
story, why would anybody try?

I looked at Suzanne. Her face was unmoved. I felt empty and desperate
in a way I hadn't felt since I'd started sleeping with her. I'd had a taste of
invincibility in her bed, but she was giving me up without a backward
glance; I could read the news on the shroud that passed as her face. I felt
like a fool. What made me think she'd choose me instead of the unlimited
pool of Stanhope money? Once Eddie killed me, she'd have him forever.
He'd never be able to divorce her; they'd be locked in the harness until the
earth quit spinning and died.

"Eddie, that's not it," I said. I heard the helplessness in my own voice. I
sounded tinny, like a playback. "OK, man, it was a mistake to get involved
with your wife. I know that. I'm sorry." I was trying to sound contrite, once
again the serf tugging his forelock. I walked over to him and shifted my
right side, the side with the gun in the pocket, up against the bar so neither
of them could see what I was doing. Slowly, I dropped my hand and began
to inch my fingers toward the gun.

"Yeah?" he laughed, an eerie sound like wind whining down a tunnel.
"Tell me how sorry you are."

Confusion butted heads with omnipotence. This was the time, the
moment, my last chance for a comeback, and I gave omnipotence free rein
as I kept inching my hand toward the gun in my pocket. "Ever try, Eddie?
Ever try and fail? You've never had to work, rich boy. You have it all. The
house, the wife, the car. You want to own a nightclub? Buy one. You want
your wife killed? Hire it done."

Suzanne gasped out loud. "Killed?" she said slowly. "You wanted me
*killed?*" she asked Eddie, her voice thick with distaste.

"He promised me a hundred thou to get rid of you, princess. Ain't that a
kick in the head?"

"Rick, you were going to kill me?" she asked. "That first night, you were
here to kill me. . . ." Now she was thoughtful, pondering her own murder
like a stock portfolio.

Eddie Style said nothing.

My fingers closed on the gun and I turned toward him, slowly. "Think
about living without that mass of cash behind you, that blanket of money.
Ain't easy, Eddie. But you'll never know 'cause whatever happens, you've
always got a fallback position. The rich always do."

It wasn't until I said it that I realized how much I hated him, how much I hated his flaccid face, his thin shoulders that had never seen a goddamn day's work, his weak mind that never had to make a tough decision, his patrician arrogance. I pulled the gun out of my pocket, fired and caught him right between the eyes.

I heard Suzanne shriek as blood sprayed out of the back of Eddie's head, splattering the polished sheen of the mirror on the back bar with a fine mist. His body crashed to the floor, taking a row of heavy highball glasses with it, shattering a few bottles. The smell of blood and gin filled the air. I didn't give a damn.

It was all mine. At last I'd turned myself inside out, and the mildewed scent of failure that had clung to me was gone. I was no longer a grinning monkey at the Club Dingo, but Zeus. A king. I was on top, a winner at last.

"Your turn, love," I said softly. "What's it gonna be? The way I see things," I said, pocketing the gun as I went over and sat down on the couch beside her, "Eddie just struck out and I'm on deck. He's dead, I'm alive and you're rich. Time to choose up sides for the Series."

She shuddered like a stalled Ford. "You killed him. You killed Eddie." Her voice was quiet and she sounded vaguely surprised.

"Yeah. I did. Now, you got two choices. You can do what I tell you to do or you can die."

"I thought you said two choices, Rick. I only heard one," she said carefully. Her voice had changed, and her face was no longer an expressionless mask. "Can I go look?" she asked as she got up and went behind the bar. She stood there for a minute, looking down at her dead husband; then she bent down and touched his cheek. "What do you want me to do?" she asked me as she straightened up.

"First thing I want, I want you to come over here and wrap your prints around my gun," I told her. "That'll keep you in line just in case you get tired of me, some faraway night when we're under the stars on the Mexican Riviera. I'll keep the gun for insurance."

"Don't you trust me?"

"This is L.A. I don't trust anybody who's ever breathed smog. Then I give you a black eye and leave. I won't hurt you, much. You call the cops and say a bad, bad robber broke in and killed hubby. You'll have a rough few months, but I'll take care of the Dingo and we can meet there once in a while. Maybe next year, we'll get married. Think you'd like a June wedding?"

"You're a cold son of a bitch; how come I didn't notice it before?"

"You weren't interested in my mind, Suzanne. Look, baby, now that Eddie's out of the picture we can have it all. Don't you understand, I can't afford to blow this off. I had one hit, I blew it. Usually, one hit is all you get in this town but I got a second chance tonight and I'm taking it. I'm not gonna get another. Ever."

"Why did he want me killed?" she said, looking down at Eddie's bloody body.

"Do you have to know? Money, OK? Isn't it always money? He said you cost too much and he didn't have enough money to pay you off."

"Greedy hog," she said and made an ugly snorting noise. "But that's what they all say, right, Ricky boy?"

I walked over to her, very fast, and slapped her in the face, very hard. "Never call me Ricky boy again, Suzanne," I said, a tight hold on her arm. "Call me honey or sweetie or baby or call me you jerk, but don't ever call me Ricky boy."

She pulled away from me, rubbing the red spot on her cheek where I'd hit her. "Why'd you have to hit me? I wish the hell you hadn't hit me. . . ." Her voice trailed off like a little girl's as she stepped back, leaned against the bar and buried her hands in the deep sleeves of her white kimono. She looked up at me and I saw death in her eyes. My death.

I saw it all and there was nothing I could do. She smiled and seemed to move very, very slowly, though in the back of my mind I knew everything was happening normally, skipping along in real time. The little silver gun slipped into her hand like a fish eager for the baited hook, and I realized she'd picked it up when she'd knelt down next to Eddie's dead body. She aimed it at me and fired. I watched as the gun leapt back in her hand and the bullet jumped straight for my heart.

I felt the slug sink into my body, only a .25, I told myself, a girl's gun, nothing to worry about. But Suzanne's aim was true. I put my hand to my chest and it felt scorched and fiery, like I'd fallen asleep with the hot water bottle on my naked flesh. I took my hand away and looked at it foolishly. Red. I had a red hand. Where the hell did I get a red hand? I was hot and tired and all of a sudden I thought a nap would do me good. Somewhere far away I heard her voice. . . .

"You were right, Rick. In this town, one hit is all you get."

# THE $5,000 GETAWAY

*Jack Ritchie*

O'Hanlon and I were in the guard's dining room having a cup of coffee with Lieutenant Farley before going on duty.

"It's impossible," Farley said.

I lit a cigar. "You mean it hasn't been done."

He shook his head. "I mean it's impossible. Nobody ever got off this rock unless we let him."

"What about Hilliard?"

Farley snorted. "Maybe he got off, but what good did it do him? His little wooden flippers didn't do much to improve his swimming. The current and the cold finished him and he drowned."

I grinned slightly. "For two weeks, until we found his body, we thought he made it."

"Not me," Farley snapped. "I would have bet plenty against it."

O'Hanlon looked pained, the way he always does when I argue with the lieutenant.

I watched a fleck of cigar ash drop to the floor. "It's only a mile and a half across the bay to the city. Or about two and a half to the point. A good swimmer shouldn't have trouble."

"There's the fog and the cold, Regan," Farley said. "Don't forget about them. And the current is tricky and strong."

"That's what the newspapers say."

Farley pounded the table. "That's what I say, too. I been here since the place opened and I know what I'm talking about."

I rolled the cigar in my mouth. "I read about Henderson and Wallace in '37. Their bodies were never found. Some people like to think that they crawled out of the bay on the other side and went on to a happy life in South America."

Farley's voice rose. "Their bodies were carried out to sea."

I rubbed my jaw. "We'll never know."

Farley glared at me. "We never heard a thing about them."

O'Hanlon glanced at his watch. "It's nearly four, Regan. Time for us to go."

He sighed as we left the room. "You're just a rookie guard, Regan. He's the lieutenant. It isn't smart to make him sore."

I knocked the light off my cigar when we reached the cell house. The gatekeeper waited while the armory officer checked us through his vision panel.

O'Hanlon's eyes took in the tool-steel bars. "Farley's right. Nobody gets off this place and lives."

The armory officer pressed his buzzer and the shield pulled off the lock.

"People sure go through a lot of trouble to get out of some places," O'Hanlon said. "Like a break I read about in Kansas City. This guy was in a cell on the sixth floor of the police station waiting to go to trial. He'd been there a couple of months, and then one night he sawed through the window bars and climbed down the side of the building."

Inside the first gate we waited until the keeper opened the door.

"It seemed like something impossible," O'Hanlon said.

"But when the police got him back later, he told them how he'd done it. For six weeks he practiced in his cell for hours every day strengthening his fingers with exercises. Finally, he could actually support the full weight of his body for over half an hour with just his fingertips. He went down the side of that building just that way, with his fingertips and using every crack and joint for a hold."

We relieved Gomez and Morgan in Cell Block C.

The late afternoon sun made the place bright, and two orderlies were polishing Broadway between the three-tiered cells. One of them was Turpin.

The rest of the men were at the shops, and the cell doors were all open. I walked along the shelves, glancing inside each cell. Some were plain and bare, with no more than the bed, the toilet bowl, the sink and fountain, and others looked like miniature law offices, art studios, or chapels, depending on the nature of the men who occupied them.

I stopped at Turpin's cell on the second tier and went inside. It was one of the plain ones, not a thing that wasn't issued, except for Volume 18 of the library's encyclopedia. I rifled through the pages, and the book still opened to the same place, the same subject. The pages were a little grimy. Turpin really should have memorized that section by now. The article was short and clear.

When I came out of his cell, Turpin was looking up. He went back to polishing the floor.

During the break for the orderlies, I went down to talk to him. "Not smoking, Turpin?"

"No, sir. I gave it up."

"Now, I wish I could do that," I said. "Tobacco's bad for the wind."

There was the faintest flicker in his eyes. "Yes, sir."

I looked through the incurved bars at the window to where buoys marked the forbidden zone two hundred yards off shore. "This is a lot better than Dog Block, isn't it, Turpin?"

His tone was expressionless. "Yes, sir."

"At least you get more sun and air," I said. "The walls are a little farther apart and you get a chance for exercise." I studied him. "Just be a good boy and you might even get more sun and air. Maybe a job with the garbage crew or the wharf gang."

"I think I'd like that, sir."

I looked out at the bay again. "Look at all that water, Turpin. I'll bet you never saw anything like that in Arizona. That's where you were born and raised, isn't it?"

His eyes were on the bay. "Yes, sir."

"Nice place," I said. "But dry." I looked back at him. "I'm a little worried about you, Turpin."

He was startled. "Why, sir?"

"Your hour in the recreation yard," I said. "Real healthy. Keeps you in condition." I pursed my lips. "You ought to keep your mind occupied too, Turpin. Take correspondence courses and stuff like that."

"I'll think about it, sir."

"We got a guy here who made himself a world authority on canary birds," I said. "Just imagine that. From books. And some of the boys in here have been making out so many writs and petitions that they know more about law than most lawyers." I smiled slightly. "A man can do almost anything if he sets his mind to it."

I walked back down the hall and joined O'Hanlon.

He watched Turpin. "That man used to give us a lot of trouble, but it looks like he's tamed."

"He doesn't care much for the isolation cells or solitary," I said. "Not much opportunity there."

O'Hanlon grinned. "He didn't much want to come to this rock in the first place. He made a break for it before the launch even got here."

I looked back down the corridor at Turpin. "That right?"

"It was before you came here, Regan. About three years ago when Farley was bringing him here from the mainland, he tried to get away. Just as the boat pulled away, he slipped his cuffs and made a jump back for the dock."

O'Hanlon chuckled. "I guess he waited a second too long because he landed in the water instead of on the dock. Went down like a stone. If Farley hadn't fished him out, he would have drowned."

At five-thirty, the prisoners were marched from the dining hall into the cell block. After the count bell, we locked them up for the night.

At eight, Lieutenant Farley came around to see how things were. He looked down the lines of closed cell doors. "Quiet," he said. "Just like always."

I covered my smile. "Not like always. This place can get noisy. Like the time seven were killed."

He scowled. "But nobody got out of the cell blocks."

"That's right," I said. "This isn't the place to try anything."

"Maximum security," Farley said. "Minimum privilege. No radios or newspapers. Correspondence and visiting restricted. No commissary. And the silence system."

"Not much to live for."

He grunted. "But only one ever took the easy way out. Everybody likes to live, no matter how hard things can get."

I looked up toward the skylights in the cell block. "I keep wondering what happened to Henderson and Wallace."

Farley scowled. "Stop wondering. The sharks chewed them up twenty years ago."

"We just don't know. Maybe they do their thinking in Spanish now."

Farley glared at me.

I smiled a little. "Did you know that a year before this became a federal pen, two women swam out here from the city, bucking those awful currents, went all around the island, and back to the mainland. Did you ever hear about it?"

Farley's face was mottled. "Sure I heard about it. But I don't believe it. And if they did, I'll bet they were like those professionals. Like the ones who swim that channel over in Europe."

"It takes a lot of practice to do something like that."

He slapped the railing and grinned. "That's it, Regan. Hours and hours of practice. Years maybe. And where are these cons going to practice swimming? We ain't got a pool here, you know."

"That's right Lieutenant," I said. "No pool."

Farley was still pleased. "Nobody here could make it across."

I nodded. "Especially if he couldn't swim in the first place."

He patted my shoulder. "Let me know if you see anybody in the water."

I made my round of the tiers at eight-thirty instead of nine-fifteen that night. On the second shelf I walked softly and stopped in front of Turpin's cell.

He was doing push-ups.

They were easy for him now. He wasn't breathing hard at all.

I watched the number on his back, 1108-AZ, until I counted fifty push-ups, and then I made a noise with my heel.

Turpin stopped and got to his feet, slowly.

"Letting off steam?" I asked.

"Yes, sir. Letting off more steam."

"That's fine," I said. "Real intelligent."


On Tuesday, after the noon meal, O'Hanlon and I went down to the beach for our monthly target practice. I scored a 197 with the .45 automatic.

O'Hanlon shook his head. "How come you're so good with that thing?"

"I put in an hour a day at it."

He thought that over. "You don't get a bit more practice than the rest of us. Once a month we all come down here and fire twenty rounds."

"But I still put in an hour a day."

He regarded me skeptically. "The government don't give you that many free bullets."

I lifted my empty automatic in line with the target, expelled my breath, and squeezed the trigger. "That's the way I practice, Pete. I don't need bullets."

O'Hanlon was dubious. "It can't be as good as the real thing."

"Some people think it's better," I said. "And it works."

We walked over to the truck and waited for the others to finish on the range.

"Maybe you got something," O'Hanlon said after awhile. "I once saw a movie short where some diving coach was training a couple of girls for the Olympics. Instead of using a pool, he had them jump off a springboard, do their twists, and land feet-first in a pit of sand. They didn't need water at all."

Three weeks later, the deputy warden assigned Turpin to the wharf gang. That meant that every morning, Turpin and a half a dozen other prisoners unloaded the supply boat at the dock.

That evening when I made my nine-fifteen tour everything was the way it was supposed to be; the single fifty-watt bulb burning in every cell, and the prisoners in their bunks. Including Turpin.

A half an hour later I went up to the second tier again, this time on tiptoe.

Turpin was on the floor, face down. He was kicking his legs rhythmically, toes pointed.

When he knew I was there, he stopped and got to his feet.

I smiled. "Sick?"

He licked his lips. "No, sir."

"I thought you might be having convulsions."

"No, sir."

I kept smiling. "Maybe I ought to get the medical orderly?"

"No, sir. I feel all right."

"Then why aren't you in your bunk?"

He looked worried. "You're not going to put me on report?"

"I don't know," I said. "Not if you're sick. I don't like to be hard on any-body."

He nodded quickly. "Sort of sick, sir. Stiff muscles. I was just loosening them up so that I could get some sleep."

I nodded. "How do you like your new job?"

"Just fine, sir."

"I notice you got a little sunburn. A few more nice days like this and you ought to be able to get yourself a tan."

"Yes, sir."

"We get a lot of nice weather here," I said. "Bright, sunny, and clear. Most people seem to think we have nothing but fog."

Turpin said nothing.

"But when we get fog," I said, "we really get it. Can't see your hand in front of your face."

A week later at two in the afternoon, I was in my quarters when the siren began its two-minute wail. I went to the window and cursed softly. He can't be that much of a fool, I thought fiercely. This isn't the time. There isn't enough fog, and what there is will clear up soon.

Along with the other guards not on duty, I reported to the armory where I was issued a rifle. Lieutenant Farley got the launch keys from the board and we began making our way to our emergency stations down at the dock.

"It's Will Stacey," Farley said.

I could feel the tension leaving me. "How did he do it?"

"Sawed his way through one of the bars in the laundry and managed to squeeze through," Farley said. "The laundry officer figures he hasn't got more than a fifteen minute start, but that was enough for him to scale the wall and get through the cyclone fence and barbed wire on top. The tower man didn't see him because a patch of fog moved in. As far as we know, Stacey was the only one who made the break, but we'll be certain after we take a count."

On the way down to the dock, we passed the men being marched from the shop building back to the cell blocks. The wharf gang's truck came through the sally gate. Turpin was on one of the side seats in the bed, and he was watching the fog thoughtfully.

I grinned and almost waved to him.

At the dock, I cast off the lines and Farley eased the boat into the bay. The fog was wispy and drifting. Clear spots were beginning to appear.

"If he decided to swim," Farley said, "he can't be out too far."

We cruised out almost to the mainland and then turned and made our way slowly back to the island, sweeping far to the right and left as we went.

Farley grinned. "You look thoughtful, Regan."

"I was a little surprised," I said. "I didn't think anybody would try it at this time of the year."

"I'm never surprised," Farley said. "I know they can't make it, but I'm never surprised when they try. Most of them got nothing to lose but their lives."

We turned up our coat collars against the chill breeze and kept our eyes on the water.

Inside of half an hour we found Stacey floundering in the water, and Farley turned the wheel toward him.

I stood up with the rifle, but O'Hanlon chuckled. "There's no fight in him, Regan. Put that thing down and save the man."

Stacey was taking desperate gulps of air when we got to him, and his eyes were wide. He was just about dead exhausted.

I pulled him aboard and slipped the cuffs over his wrist.

Stacey's lips were blue, and he shivered uncontrollably.

Farley felt generous. "Give the fool a blanket and a cigarette."

After he radioed the island, Farley watched Stacey take deep puffs of the smoke. "You were a damn fool, boy."

Stacey kept his eyes on the floorboards. "I didn't count on the fog lifting."

Farley laughed. "You were glad to see us. You didn't get one-quarter of the way across and you were about to come to pieces."

Stacey was silent for a few seconds, then a tired grimace came to his lips. "Drowning is a terrible way to die," he said softly.

Farley winked at me. "The trouble with Stacey is that he's out of condition. He needs more practice in our swimming pool. A couple of hours a day. I'll see if I can arrange it."

A detail of guards met us at the dock and took Stacey back up the hill for a medical examination and dry clothes. After questioning, he would be put in one of the solitary cells in Dog Block.

Farley and I went to the mess hall for some coffee.

He chuckled. "Disappointed, Regan?"

I shrugged. "Why should I be disappointed?"

He grinned. "I just thought you might be."

I sipped my coffee. "If the fog hadn't lifted, a good swimmer would have made it."

Irritation came to his face. "I'd bet a thousand it can't be done."

"All right," I said quietly.

He glared at me. "All right, what?"

"I was just thinking," I said, "that if anybody gave me odds, say five to one, I'd be willing to put up a thousand that somebody will make it across within the next year."

Farley frowned. "You know what you're saying?"

I put a little more sugar in my coffee. "It would have to be kept quiet, a bet like that."

Farley watched me for a half a minute. Then his eyes went over the room. A couple of off-duty guards were drawing coffee from the urn at the far end of the hall. Otherwise the place was empty.

"I got the thousand," I said softly.

Farley watched the flame of his match as he lit a cigar. "Suppose somebody was stupid enough to make a crazy bet like that with you. How would anybody know whether a man made the swim or not? If he didn't make it, his body might be washed out to sea and never recovered. Like with Henderson and Wallace."

"I'd lose the bet," I said. "We'd have to know for certain that he made it."

Farley glanced at the guards again. "But suppose he did make it and then skipped off to South America? How would we know? He isn't likely to phone us."

"That's why I get the five-to-one odds," I said. "We'd have to know for sure. I'd be counting on the fact that he'd be seen on the mainland by responsible witnesses or that he'd be picked up by the police within a year." I put down the coffee cup. "But we'd be betting only on the fact that he did or didn't make a successful break from the rock. What happens after that doesn't matter."

Farley was thoughtful. "You're betting in the teeth of a lot of things."

"That's why I want the odds."

His eyes met mine. "Like you said, the whole thing would have to be kept quiet. The government wouldn't like to hear about it."

"There's one other thing I'd have to worry about," I said. "If I win, would I get paid?"

Farley's face got glowering red. "I never welshed on a bet in my life. Just be sure you got a thousand."


That evening I stopped in front of Turpin's cell.

He was sitting on the bunk, idly paging through a magazine.

"That's it," I said. "Improve your mind."

He looked up.

"Stacey should have done that," I said. "Spent his time improving his mind instead of trying to escape." I shook my head sadly. "He was plain stupid. Even if he had been able to go the distance, he should have made it his business to know about the fog."

Turpin waited.

"He should have figured it would clear up and we'd be waiting for him when it did. The fog's a tricky thing here. When it rolls in from the southwest you can bet it won't stay around long. It's different when it comes from the north."

    ❦    ❦    ❦

Several days later Turpin came back from the wharf wringing wet.

The guard bringing the detail back to the cell block grinned. "Turpin got too close to the edge of the dock and fell off."

I looked at one of the windows. The day was bright and clear. "How was the water, Turpin?"

There was no expression on his face, but there was a gleam of what might have been triumph in his eyes. "It was a little cold, sir."

I talked to the guard. "Going to put that on report?"

He looked surprised. "What for? It was just a little accident."

"Just wondering," I said. "Did you have any trouble fishing him out?"

He shook his head. "No. It was only a few feet from the dock. Turpin swam back himself, grinning like a monkey."

In September, Turpin was transferred to the garbage crew. It was still outside work. Every afternoon he was down at the incinerators at the beach.

And the fog weather began.

I was in my room in the guard's quarters when I saw the first heavy concentration coming from the northwest—from the sea. This would be the time he would try it. I could almost feel that.

The siren cut through the fog at two-thirty. I put my cigar in the ashtray and made my way to the armory.

Lieutenant Farley was assigning the search details. "This time it's Turpin. The fog came down on the garbage gang so fast that the guard was caught by surprise. He started herding the prisoners to the truck, but Turpin slipped away and disappeared into the fog."

Farley grinned at me. "Relax. You're not winning any bet today. I happen to know for a fact that Turpin can't swim a stroke."

I shrugged. "Then why would he run away?"

Farley chuckled. "He lost his head when he saw a chance. He wasn't thinking. Now the best he can do is to hide out in some cave or corner of this island for a couple of days and hope that we'll think he's gone out and drowned himself. He probably figures that when we stop looking for him, he can smuggle himself aboard the supply boat."

I pocketed two clips of ammunition. "Then it won't be much good to take out the launch?"

Farley showed his teeth again. "No good at all. But we take it out just the same. That's our job."

A half a dozen more guards reported, and Farley began giving them instructions.

I picked the launch keys off the board. "I'll wait for you down at the dock."

Outside, it was like walking through smoke. Every object was shrouded and strange, and the trip down to the dock took me almost fifteen minutes.

I checked the boat compass and headed the launch northeast, out into the bay. The fog misted my face, and nothing was visible more than a few feet from the bow.

I could imagine what Farley would say when I got back.

"Why the hell didn't you wait for me?"

"I'm sorry, Lieutenant. But I thought I heard something out in the water."

Farley would probably grin. "You got some imagination. Why didn't you come back when you found he wasn't out there?"

I would look embarrassed. "I couldn't find the dock, Lieutenant. The fog was too thick."

"And what about the radio?" Farley would demand. "Why didn't you get in touch with us?"

"But the radio doesn't work, Lieutenant."

Now I kept the launch going until I was about halfway across the bay and a few miles north. Then I cut the motor and let the boat drift.

I wouldn't have been able to do that if Farley were with me. We'd be cruising back and forth and there would be a chance that we might find Turpin.

I didn't want that.

I disconnected a lead-in wire on the radio and sat down to wait. The current would bring me back near the island in a few hours.

The sea was calm, with just enough swelling to let you know that it was still alive. I tried to figure how long it would take a man to swim a mile and a half. It was difficult to know how good all of Turpin's practice had made him.

The time passed slowly. It was silent except for the breathing of the ocean and the faint foghorn of the coast guard boat searching near the mainland.

The cold and damp began to get into my bones after an hour. I checked my watch and decided to wait at least another half an hour before I started the motor and went back to the island.

And then I heard the sound, muffled in the distance.

I held my breath as it came again.

It was the hoarse cry of a man calling for help.

I cursed softly. Turpin had gotten himself lost in the fog. Instead of going straight, he had veered to the left. He was swimming parallel to the coast.

His calls were closer now, desperate in the emptiness.

I shook my head savagely. If he drowned here, the current would carry his body back to the island. It would be found in a few days, a week or two.

I started the motor and kept the launch slow as possible while I searched. It was hard work, but I kept at it, shutting off the power now and then to listen.

When I found Turpin he was treading water and taking deep gasps for air.

His eyes met mine, and I saw the same thing that I'd seen in Stacey's when we picked him up. There was defeat because his try had failed and relief because he would soon be out of the water.

I pulled him aboard and put him in the stern.

His face was dead white and he shivered with cold. I tossed him a blanket and watched him huddle inside it.

Turpin's teeth chattered. "How close did I get?"

"Not close at all," I said. "You were headed straight for Seattle."

Turpin sighed. "I was in the water a long, long time."

"An hour and a half," I said.

"I could have made it," he said softly. "If only I'd kept going straight. You knew what I was going to do, didn't you?"

I grinned, but said nothing.

"You were waiting for me to make the break. You wanted a little fun to fight the dullness of life. You knew what I was going to do, and where, and when. Maybe you even wanted to use that rifle."

I ignored what he'd said. I studied him for a half a minute, thinking it out. Then I searched through my pockets until I found an old letter. I carefully tore off a blank section at the bottom of one page. It would have to do.

I handed it to Turpin and gave him my fountain pen. "I want you to write the warden a little note."

His mouth gaped slightly.

"Go ahead," I snapped. "Write what I tell you."

He hesitated and then shrugged.

"Dear Warden," I said. "It was a cold swim, but it was worth it."

Turpin looked up, trying to figure it out. Then he shook his head, and moved the pen across the paper.

"Now wish him a Merry Christmas and a Happy New Year."

Turpin's mouth dropped again.

I glared at him. "Write it and sign your name."

He did what he was told.

I took the paper from him and examined it. The handwriting made it good enough, but I wanted more. "Put your fingers in some of that grease on the floorboards and let's have ten little fingerprints under your signature."

When that was done, I folded the paper carefully and put it in my wallet. It was worth five thousand dollars to me.

"Stand up, Turpin," I said. "And turn around."

He got up wearily and turned.

I brought the rifle stock down hard on the back of his head and he dropped without a sound.

After I made sure that he was dead, I got the anchor from the bow locker and tied it to him.

I took the launch three miles west, out to sea, and dumped Turpin's body overboard.

Then I lit a cigar, checked with the compass, and headed back for my chat with Farley.

In a month or two, when I got to the city on one of my days off, I'd mail Turpin's note in a plain, typed envelope.

The postmark ought to make news, and it would start all the world looking for the first man to escape from the rock.

# ROTTEN TO THE CORE

*Jeremiah Healy*

Thirty-three years old, and I'm still working for my mother.
Life can really suck, you know it?

I mean, if we're still turning a profit growing apples, that'd be one thing. But ever since the old man bit the big one five years ago and the land came to be all hers, Ma's been getting fat around the middle and thin around the business.

Not that it's all her fault, mind. We ain't got but a hundred acres of trees, which used to be enough to compete, long as you had two strong backs to help out most of the year. Come picking season, we hire another twenty, plus enough grading ladies on the packing line to tell the good apples from the ones bound for cider.

Only now, it ain't enough to know how to *grow* good product. No, these days, the fruit's in oversupply. Washington State is killing us, and China is killing them.

Ma says to me, "Orrin, I don't know how they can do it. I mean, whoever heard of *Chinese* apples?"

And I says to her, "Ma, how they can do it is if everybody in that country plants just one miserable tree, they've got four billion of them."

And she says to me, "Oh, I don't think there are that many people in China, do you?"

You see what I'm up against, a woman who can't keep her facts straight?

And, even without the overseas competition, the regional wholesaler here can play one of us little growers against the rest, which means we got to give away another dollar a box to keep that wholesaler's business. Only way to make a go of it at all is to build a pissy little retail store on the country road next to our packing barn, with apple jelly, apple potpourri, apple everything for sale to the dumbos up from the city, driving past and making believe they're some kind of country gentry by buying our stuff for twice what it'd cost in any supermarket worth its name.

Except that Ma don't believe in having a retail store. No sir, not Mrs. Jeannette T. Weems.

She believes in baking apple pies. With her little "JTW" initials as a "mark of quality" in the center of the crust. But without preservatives or anything else "unnatural." And guess what that means.

Right the first time. It means I got to be on the road pretty near every day, driving this old panel truck with shelves in it that the Nissen Bread folks pitched away. One pie to a box, nine boxes to a bread rack, thirty racks to the truck. And drive that sucker I do, fifty, sixty hours a week, delivering Ma's fresh, unpreserved apple pies to gourmet shops and fancy restaurants. Even a few of the big estates, too, think it's cool to have a local peasant drive up to the servants' entrance with the "fruit of the land," as I heard one of the whales in a whale-patterned shirt and tweed skirt say once.

Goldarnit, but I do hate the smell of apples.

You'd think working in a fish market or a slaughterhouse'd be worse, the stench of death all around you, getting into your clothes, your hair, even your skin. But nothing's worse than apples when you can't get away from them, especially if one's rotten to the core. It's a stink that . . . penetrates, that's what it does. Goes *past* your skin, all the way to the bone. And it festers there, like some kind of infection, till it drives you near crazy.

As you drive over half the county in that goldarn panel truck with those goldarn racks of pies in the back.

I says to her, "Ma, you should just sell the farm for real estate development."

"Now, Orrin, your father wouldn't like that."

"Ma, the old man's got his own land. Measures about eight by three and six feet under."

Which naturally made Mrs. Jeannette T. Weems cry, to hear me bring up the truth.

Even so, though, I thought I had her leaning—I *know* I did—until that Earle Shay showed up two months ago.

We'd lost the other fella working the orchard with us to a selling job at the Wal-Mart, so Ma put an ad in the county weekly for "Hired Help, No Room or Board, Must Be Clean and Polite and Willing to Work Hard."

And, wouldn't you know it, Earle had to be all three?

He's also black as coal, with a chest like a pickle barrel and a shaved head so shiny you dast not look at him on a sunny day without a good pair of dark glasses on you. I think Earle's around Ma's age—I can't never tell how old black people are, at least until they hit seventy or so, when their skin just seems to go into raisin mode and they start shuffling instead of walking right. But Earle's a long way from shuffling. He can work all day and keep Ma laughing in her kitchen half the night. She's been laughing so hard, Ma's dropped about ten pounds or so of that weight around her middle, and she's even taken to going to Bessie's Hair-a-Dome again, first time since the old man went in the ground.

But that's not the worst part.

No, the worst part is, Earle's got Ma believing we—and "we" don't mean just me and her—can run the farm at a profit again.

In that deep, booming voice he has, Earle says to Ma, "Why, Jeannette, all we have to do is put in a retail store and devote a couple of acres to speciality veggies for the gourmet shops and restaurants."

"But Earle, who would tend this store and garden?"

"I've got relatives aplenty in the city who'd love to come up here, stay in the county for a time. Clean air, no crime. And Orrin's already visiting most of the places we'd sell the veggies to with his panel truck and your pies."

"Well," Ma says to him, "it might work."

Might work. And if it did, I'd be stuck in the goldarn panel truck for the rest of my natural life. Only then I'd have goldarn garden dirt under my fingernails to go with the goldarn apple stench in my bones.

In fact, I couldn't hardly see a light at the end of the tunnel.

Until I finally got The Idea.


It happened on a cold, rainy day in late October, maybe a month after Earle'd used the John Deere forklift to stack the bins of McIntoshes eight tiers high in our C.A. room. The "C.A." stands for "controlled atmosphere." Basically, if you've got a hundred acres of apples, a lot of them are gonna get ripe in the same two week stretch, so you bring in the pickers and box the fruit quick as you can. Unless you want the product breaking down and getting soft, though, you got to seal it up in C.A. storage. Where the air's maybe 90 percent nitrogen—like they must have on the planet Mars? Put in a refrigeration unit to cool and blow that Martian air around the apples, and they'll keep preserved for a good five months.

I'd already parked the panel truck outside the packing barn, between the John Deere tractor that tows our AgTec crop sprayer—a big white thing, looks a little like a ten-foot dog kennel with tubes and nozzles at the back—and the Agway rototiller—which, long as I'm describing things, looks a lot like a gasoline–powered wheelbarrow with little propellers that dig into the ground. I walked past the brush chopper—this heavy flail mower that rolls behind the tractor, too, only it can chop-and-chip pieces of junk timber two inches thick. In the barn, I was on my way to the little fridge where I keep some cold beers when I realized the packing line looked a little longer than the day before.

Jesus God, I remember thinking. They've gone and done it.

Earle'd been after Ma for weeks to spring for a waxing machine. Even she thought seventeen thousand dollars—seventeen *thousand!*—was kind of steep, but Earle kept pressing her and teasing her with that Darth Vader voice. His idea was that we—"we" as in "three" again—could sell to the wholesalers who supply the big supermarkets that want their apples to sparkle like fire trucks. Takes another six hundred dollars of wax to polish fifteen thousand bushels of apples, but they come out looking better than the one Eve must have flashed at Adam back in their garden.

I had to sit down hard, on an old slatted crate in the packing barn.

Ain't no grower in this whole county—or, hell, even over there in *China*—that's gonna burn the price of a new pickup truck for her one and only son if she's really leaning towards selling the land for development. As apple orchard, our land wasn't worth spit, and we didn't have the kind of houses around us that'd let us carve off a small building lot here and there at the edges. But I knew we could divide the whole shebang up into "mini-estates," and get a fortune for every five-acre chunk. Sure, we'd have to put in a road and run the electric and arrange for probably half a dozen other things, but I knew it'd all work from the numbers side.

Only right then, sitting on that packing crate, I couldn't see it working at all, not with Ma doing whatever Earle told her he thought it was made sense. Next thing'd be the designer veggies and a retail store, with even more "employees"—dark in color—on our land.

Or Ma's land, I guessed. At least until . . .

I jumped back up and ran outside. Our crop sprayer looked mean enough, but I didn't see how showering Mrs. Jeannette T. Weems with pesticide would solve my problem. The rototiller had those little prop blades, but at best they'd take off some toes or maybe a finger, you got careless clearing a jam. Then I stared—long and hard—at our brush chopper. It'd do the job all right, but despite what Ma was doing to me, I couldn't quite stomach her being spritzed like hamburger spread over a row of our trees.

Scuffing my boots in the dust, I went back inside the packing barn.

And saw . . . the packing line?

No. No, even with the new waxing machine, the equipment at most might mangle an arm. And, anyway, with the crop already in storage, there'd be no reason to run the line, nor for Ma to be fiddling with the different stages, not with Earle around.

But that's when I heard it. A simple little noise, though maybe more beautiful than any country tune Garth Brooks ever wailed.

The noise was coming from our C.A. room. That metal-on-metal shear of a bearing going bad in the refrigeration unit's blower.

I went over to the big steel door we have bolted on the storage. You got to keep the room sealed absolute tight, otherwise the nitrogen air inside would seep out, rotting the apples and maybe killing you, you breathed deep enough close enough. Of course, nobody could predict when something might go wrong with the refrigeration unit either, so we had a little kitty-cat trap-door on the bottom of the steel one. The little door was hinged on top and bolted at the corners, too. But it'd give you a way in and out of the C.A. room in case some kinda repair was necessary. And we even had an old airpac Ma bought off the Volunteer Fire—the kind that rides on your back, like the tanks in this scuba-diving flick I saw one time? Our tank's yellow, with a hose running to the nose-and-mouth cover that you strap on over your head, the way fighter pilots do in those old war movies.

Right then, though, I pushed all the Hollywood stuff out of my head. Sitting down on that packing crate again, I closed my eyes to recollect the inside of our C.A. storage. Solid cement floor, ceiling twenty feet high, walls made from white insulated foam. Over the years, we'd spackled food-grade tar here and there to patch leaks, so the whole room'd look to you like the hide of a pinto pony. And most of the space was filled with those eight tiers of weathered-wood bins with the McIntoshes in them.

But every other cubic foot was 90 percent nitrogen. That only a Martian could breathe without an airpac.

I took The Idea as an omen. Especially since that same night—after driving my old pickup over to Clete's Tap to celebrate—I met Honey.


Clete's ain't nothing more than a taproom, one of maybe ten in the county. It's about the only place where the races mix much, though, and so I wouldn't go there but for it's the closest by far to the farm, and I don't fancy getting stopped by a sheriff's deputy for Driving Under the Influence account of I'm already Driving Without a License from another such encounter.

Anyway, I go into Clete's that night, and the crowd—fortunately—is mostly white. Oh, there're a couple of big young bucks bellied up to the bar, but I move over to a table by itself and tell Amy the airhead waitress to bring me a bottle of champagne, they had one cold. She asks me if I was sure I wanted that and not a Miller High Life, "the champagne of bottled beers." I say I'm sure, and as Amy turns away, airhead shaking like one of those ballplayer dolls on the TV, the stunner standing at my end of the bar turns a little.

The girl was black, technically, but her skin really glowed the color of honey, her hair maybe two shades darker. About five-five or so in jeans and a pair of those spiky cowboy boots, she was all legs and had just the cutest little rump I ever did see. She seemed to know she'd caught my eye, too, because before I could even get up, the girl'd click-clacked over to my table, asking if she could sit.

I says to her, "Honey, you can sit on anything you'd like."

All of a sudden, she looks sorta funny, like maybe I offended her kinda.

But all she says to me is, "How'd you, like, know that's my name?"

And I says to her, "What is?"

"'Honey.'"

"Only on account of that's what you remind me of, girl. A gorgeous itty-bitty thing just spun out of honey."

Which made her smile, and as Amy finally arrived with my champagne—in this spittoon with ice—I knew the chair across from me in Clete's Tap wasn't the only thing Honey'd be sitting on that night.


Honey says to me, "So, you're gonna kill your mama?"

It was afterwards, and now she's towards the passenger's side of my pickup, still at the turnaround off the dirt road we'd parked at beforehand. To this moment, I can't remember how The Idea'd come up in our conversation. But it seemed natural enough, telling her about it. Especially since Honey'd already told me she was up from the city for just the weekend, visiting relatives until she had to get away from all the "My, child, how you have growed up" talk.

I says to Honey, "Well, yeah, I have to kill her. But like I said, I couldn't feature Ma scattered over half an acre by the brush chopper like so much ground chuck."

Honey looked a little funny again, but this time more like she might urp up. All she says to me, though, is "How you gonna use that storage room?"

I told her about the bearing in the refrigeration unit, how I could hear it was going, and why we'd have to replace it or risk losing the fruit to a system failure.

"And your mama's just gonna, like, walk in there through that little trapdoor you have?"

I says to her, "No, Honey. All's I have to do is tell her about it when Earle ain't around. Then she'll have to go out to the packing barn with me and stand a ways off, because the safety rule is, nobody goes into C.A. storage without somebody else being on the outside."

"Like Lassie."

"Huh?"

"Like Lassie," Honey says to me. "That dog who'd go get help when some person was in trouble."

I shake my head, but I says to her, "Yeah, like that. Only I'm not going in there myself."

"What are you gonna do?"

"I'm gonna wear that airpac, and use a wrench on the trapdoor, and then say to Ma, 'Come over closer, I need help with this last bolt.' And when she's close enough, I'm gonna rap her upside the head with that wrench. Once Mrs. Jeannette T. Weems is for sure out cold, I'm gonna open the kitty-cat door on its hinge, push her in through it, and close the door again."

"I don't, like, get it."

I close my eyes. She might have a body like spun honey, but the brain was more like spun cotton. "I wait maybe two minutes, just to be sure Ma's a goner. Then I bleed out all that's left in the airpac, and I slide it off me. I take a deep breath, open the trapdoor again, and push the airpac inside. After that, I toss the wrench in, too."

Honey looked kind of sick again, but she says to me, "Oh, so everybody will think your mama was, like, trying to fix the bearing thing and ran out of good air."

"Right the first time. And, once the lawyers get through with doing her estate, I'm rich as that Trump fella."

Honey puts on a smile, a cousin to the last one she gave me at Clete's Tap. "You know, Orrin, I probably don't have to be back to my relatives for, like, another hour or so."

Omens. I'm telling you, they were everywhere for me, that afternoon and night.


Next morning in the kitchen, I says to Ma, "Where's Earle?"

Mrs. Jeannette T. Weems looks up from a pie she's making her little "mark of quality" in the crust of. "He said he had to run into town for something."

"Well, maybe Earle oughta spend a little less time running to town and a little more time checking the barn."

"Why, what do you mean, Orrin?"

"I mean, I was in there yesterday after I broke my back delivering all your pies, and I could hear this bearing starting to go on the C.A. blower."

"Oh, my goodness, no."

"Oh, my goodness, yes," I says to her. "I think you and me ought to go over there, quick as we can."

"Of course, Orrin. Let me just get this last batch out of the oven."

Last batch. I especially liked the sound of that first part.


"Ma," I says to her, over my shoulder and casual as can be, considering how the nose-and-mouth cover of the airpac's muffling my voice. "I'm having a little trouble with this last bolt."

Her voice comes from a corner of the packing barn. "Is it safe for me to join you there?"

"Sure it's safe. The room's still sealed. I just need a little help with the wrench is all."

"Well, if you really can't do it without me . . ."

"No, Ma," I says to her, my face against the trapdoor so she won't see me grinning ear-to-ear. "Take my word on this. I can't make it work without you."

I hear footsteps, only they're sounding heavy, like Ma was before Earle answered her ad in the weekly. I get ready anyway, figuring to just stand up a little and—


—I wake up in the dark, lying on my right side.

My head hurts behind my left ear. When I reach back there, I can feel a lump the size of a small hen's first egg.

I also feel the strap of the nose-and-mouth cover of the airpac.

I try to sit up, but when I do, the yellow tank part makes a scraping noise on the cold cement floor.

Cold? Cement?

"Orrin?" Ma yells to me from outside somewheres. "Can you hear me, Orrin?"

"Yeah," I says to her, muffled by the cover, but . . . echoing, too.

Like I'm in a room with twenty-foot walls.

"Orrin, I never believed you would consider doing such a thing to your own mother."

"What such a thing?"

"Murder for profit," booms Earle's voice, and I have a pretty good idea whose footsteps I heard coming up behind me on the other side of the kitty-cat door.

I says to him, "I don't know what you're talking about."

He booms to me, "Lucky thing that when I was in town this morning, my niece up from the city told me what you laid out for her last night."

"Laid" was the only word I really focused on.

Ma yells to me, "Orrin, how could you even have *contemplated* that?"

I says to her, "Ma, she's the one picked *me* up in Clete's."

"That's not what I mean, young man. I'm talking about killing your own mother."

I didn't like the way my air from the yellow tank was tasting. "Let me out of here."

"No, Orrin," Ma yells. "Earle believes Honey, and I believe Earle. What I don't believe is that you haven't even the decency to own up to the things they've said."

"Ma—"

"What?"

"Let . . . me . . . out . . . of . . . here."

Her voice goes different. "I couldn't bear to have Earle kill you the way he wanted to, after you'd planned to kill his beloved."

His "beloved"? Things were just getting better and better.

"So we compromised," Ma yells to me now. "We slid you in there with the airpac on and rebolted the trap here. I don't know how much time you have left, but at least you'll go quickly after reflecting on the horrible deed you intended."

"Ma—"

She yells this time till her voice about cracks. "And then we'll take a page from your book, Orrin. Earle will unbolt the trap again and toss in the wrench, so everyone will think the same tragic accident that you so diabolically aimed at me simply befell you instead."

"Ma, listen—"

Earle booms to me, "Poetic justice for a boy that just went rotten, rotten to the core."

I started saying a whole string of words Ma never liked to hear. When I'm done, neither of them's yelling or booming to me anymore.


So here I sit, in the dark and the cold. I really don't like the taste of my air from the yellow tank at all now. It's sour, like everything's going stale, and I practically have to whistle in reverse to feel anything reach down towards my lungs.

Then I remember something else from that scuba-diving flick I saw. One of the jerks you know is going to die anyway runs out of air when he's maybe three hundred feet down. Even though he knows it's stupid, he pulls off the mouthpiece from under his mask and starts breathing in water.

I guess it's like a reflex or something. Which means that, pretty soon, I'll probably be doing the same thing.

Which oughta bother me a lot, but somehow it don't. No, what does bother me is something else.

I'm in a controlled atmosphere storage room. When I take off the nose-and-mouth cover and draw in that first—and last—breath of Martian air, I'm also gonna smell . . . *them*.

The last goldarn thing on God's green earth I'll ever experience is the goldarn stench of goldarn apples.

Didn't I tell you that life can really suck?

# FRONT MAN

### David Morrell

T ell me that again," I said. "He must have been joking."
   "Mort, you know what it's like at the networks these days." My agent
sighed. "Cost cutting. Layoffs. Executives so young they think *L.A. Law* is
nostalgia. He wasn't joking. He's willing to take a meeting with you, but
he's barely seen your work, and he wants a list of your credits."

"All *two hundred and ninety* of them? Steve, I like to think I'm not vain,
but how can this guy be in charge of series development and not know
what I've written?"

This conversation was on the phone. Midweek, midafternoon. I'd been
revising computer printouts of what I'd written in the morning, but frustration at what Steve had told me made me press my pencil down so hard I
broke its tip. Standing from my desk, I clutched the phone tighter.

Steve hesitated before he replied. "No argument. You and I know how
much you contributed to television. You and Rod Serling and Paddy
Chayefsky practically invented TV drama. But that was then. This executive just started his job three months ago. He's only twenty-eight, for
Christ's sake. He's been clawing his way to network power since he gradu-
ated from business school. He doesn't actually *watch* television. He's too
damned busy to watch it, except for current in-house projects. What he
does is program, check the ratings, and read the trades. If you'd won your
Emmys for something this season, he might be impressed. But *The Sidewalks
of New York*? That's something they show on Nickelodeon cable reruns, a
company he doesn't work for, so what does he care?"

I stared out my study window. From my home on top of the Hollywood
Hills, I had a view of rushing traffic on smoggy Sunset Boulevard, of Spago,
Tower Records, and Château Marmont. But at the moment, I saw none of
them, indignation blinding me.

"Steve, am I nuts, or are the scripts I sent you good?"

"Don't put yourself down. They're better than good. They don't only grab me. They're fucking smart. *I believe* them, and I can't say that for . . ." He named a current hit series about a female detective that made him a fortune in commissions but was two-thirds tits and ass and one-third car chases.

"So what's the real problem?" I asked, unable to suppress the stridency in my voice. "Why can't I get any work?"

"The truth?"

"Since when did I tolerate lies?"

"You won't get pissed off?"

"I *will* get pissed off if—"

"All right already. The truth is, it doesn't matter how well you write. The fact is, you're too old. The networks think you're out of touch with their demographics."

"*Out of*—"

"You promised you wouldn't get pissed off."

"But after I shifted from television, I won an Oscar for *The Dead of Noon.*"

"Twenty years ago. To the networks, that's like the Dark Ages. You know the axiom—What have you done for us lately? The fact is, Mort, for the past two years, you've been out of town, out of the country, out of the goddamn *industry.*"

My tear ducts ached. My hurried breathing made me dizzy. "I had a good reason. The most important reason."

"Absolutely," Steve said. "In your place, I'd have done the same. And your friends respect that reason. But the movers and shakers, the new regime that doesn't give a shit about tradition, *they* think you died or retired, if they give you a moment's thought at all. *Then* isn't *now.* To them, last week's ratings are ancient history. What's next? they want to know. What's new? they keep asking. What they really mean is, What's *young?*"

"That sucks."

"Of course. But young viewers are loose with their dough, my friend, and advertisers pay the bills. So the bottom line is, the networks feel unless you're under thirty-five or, better yet, under *thirty,* you can't communicate with their target audience. It's an uphill grind for writers like you, of a certain age, no matter your talent."

"Swell." My knuckles ached as I squeezed the phone. "So what do I do? Throw my word processor out the window, and collect on my Writers Guild pension?"

"It's not as bad as that. But bear in mind, your pension is the highest any Guild member ever accumulated."

"But if I retire, I'll die like—"

"No, what I'm saying is be patient with this network kid. He needs a little educating. Politely, you understand. Just pitch your idea, look confident and dependable, show him your credits. He'll come around. It's not as if you haven't been down this path before."

"When I was in my twenties."

"There you go. You identify with this kid already. You're in his mind."

My voice dropped. "When's the meeting?"

"Friday. His office. I pulled in some favors to get you in so soon. Four P.M. I'll be at my house in Malibu. Call me when you're through."

"Steve . . ."

"Yeah, Mort?"

"Thanks for sticking with me."

"Hey, it's an honor. To me, you're a legend."

"What I need to be is a *working* legend."

"I've done what I can. Now it's up to you."

"Sure." I set down the phone, discovered I still had my broken pencil in one hand, dropped it, and massaged the aching knuckles of my other hand.

The reason I'd left L.A. two years ago, at the age of sixty-eight, was that my dear wife—

—Doris—

—my best friend—

—my cleverest editor—

—my exclusive lover—

—had been diagnosed as having a rare form of leukemia.

As her strength had waned, as her body had gradually failed to obey her splendid mind, I'd disrupted my workaholic's habit of writing every day and acted as her constant attendant. We'd traveled to every major cancer research center in the United States. We'd gone to specialists in Europe. We'd stayed in Europe because their hospice system is humane about pain-relieving drugs. We'd gotten as far as Sweden.

Where Doris had died.

And now, struggling with grief, I'd returned to my career. What other meaning did I have? It was either kill myself or write. So I wrote. And wrote. Even faster than in my prime, when I'd contributed every episode in the four-year run of *The Sidewalks of New York*.

And now a network yuppie bastard with the cultural memory of a four-year-old had asked for my credits. Before I gulped a stiff shot of Scotch, I vowed I'd show this town that *this* old fuck still had more juice than when I'd first started.

Century City. Every week, you see those monoliths of power behind the credits on this season's hit lawyer show, but I remembered, bitterly nostalgic, when the land those skyscrapers stood upon had been the back lot for 20th Century–Fox.

I parked my leased Audi on the second level of an underground ramp and took an elevator to the seventeenth floor of one of the buildings. The network's reception room was wide and lofty, with lots of leather couches where actors, writers, and producers made hurried phone calls to agents and assistants while they waited to be admitted to the Holy of Holies.

I stopped before a young, attractive woman at a desk. Thin. No bra. Presumably she wanted to be an actress and was biding her time, waiting for the right connections. She finished talking to one of three phones and studied me, her boredom tempered by the fear that, if she wasn't respectful, she might lose a chance to make an important contact.

I'm not bad looking. Although seventy, I keep in shape. Sure, my hair's receding. I have wrinkles around my eyes. But my family's genes are spectacular. I look ten years younger than I am, especially when I'm tanned, as I was after recent daily half-hour laps in my swimming pool.

My voice has the resonance of Ed McMahon. "Mort Davidson to see Arthur Lewis. I've got a four o'clock appointment."

The would-be-actress receptionist scanned a list. "Of course. You're expected. Unfortunately, Mr. Lewis has been detained. If you'll please wait over there." She pointed toward a couch and picked up a Judith Krantz novel. Evidently she'd decided that I couldn't promote her career.

So I waited.

And waited.

An hour later, the receptionist gestured for me to come over. Miracle of miracles, Arthur Lewis was ready to see me.

✧   ✧   ✧

He wore an Armani linen suit, fashionably wrinkled. No tie. Gucci loafers. No socks. His skin was the color of bronze. His thick, curly black hair had a calculated, windblown look. Photographs of his blond wife and infant daughter stood on his glass-topped desk. His wife seemed even younger and thinner than he was. Posters of various current hit series hung on the wall. A tennis racket was propped in a corner.

"It's an honor to meet you. I'm a fan of everything you've done," he lied.

I made an appropriate humble comment.

His next remark contradicted what he'd just said. "Did you bring a list of your credits?"

I gave him a folder and sat on a leather chair across from him while he flipped through the pages. His expression communicated a mixture of boredom and stoic endurance.

Finally his eyebrows narrowed. "Impressive. I might add, astonishing. Really, it's hard to imagine anyone writing this much."

"Well, I've been in the business quite a while."

"Yes. You certainly have."

I couldn't tell if he referred to my age or my numerous credits. "There used to be a joke," I said.

"Oh?" His eyes were expressionless.

" 'How can Mort Davidson be so prolific?' This was back in the early sixties. The answer was 'He uses an electric typewriter.' "

"Very amusing," he said as if I'd farted.

"These days, of course, I use a word processor."

"Of course." He folded his hands on the desk and sat straighter. "So. Your agent said you had an idea that might appeal to us."

"That's right."

The phone rang.

"Excuse me a moment." He picked up the phone. Obviously, if he'd been genuinely interested in my pitch, he'd have instructed his secretary that he didn't want any calls.

An actor named Sid was important enough for Arthur Lewis to gush with compliments. And by all means, Sid shouldn't worry about the rewrites that would make his character more "with it" in today's generation. The writer in charge of the project was under orders to deliver the changes by Monday morning. If he didn't, that writer would never again work on something called *The Goodtime Guys*. Sid was a helluva talent, Arthur Lewis assured him. Next week's episode would get a 35 ratings share at least. Arthur chuckled at a joke, set down the phone, and narrowed his eyebrows again. "So your idea that you think we might like." He glanced at his Rolex.

"It's about an at-risk youth center, a place where troubled kids can go and get away from their screwed-up families, the gangs, and the drug dealers on the streets. There's a center in the Valley that I see as our model—an old Victorian house that has several additions. Each week, we'd deal with a special problem—teenage pregnancy, substance abuse, runaways—but mostly this would be a series about emotions, about people, the kids, but also the staff, a wide range of interesting, committed professionals, an elderly administrator, a female social worker, an Hispanic who used to be in the gangs, a priest, whatever mix works. I call it—"

The phone rang again.

"Just a second," Arthur Lewis said.

Another grin. A producer this time. A series about a college sorority next to a fraternity, *Crazy 4 U*, had just become this season's new hit. Arthur Lewis was giving its cast and executives a party at Le Dôme tomorrow evening. Yes, he guaranteed. Ten cases of Dom Pérignon would arrive at the producer's home before the party. And beluga caviar? Enough for an after-party power party? No problem. And yes, Arthur Lewis was having the same frustrations as the producer. It was mighty damned hard to find a preschool for gifted children.

He set down the phone. His face turned to stone. "So that's your idea?"

"Drama, significance, emotion, action, and realism."

"But what's the hook?"

I shook my head in astonishment.

"Why would anyone want to watch it?" Arthur Lewis asked.

"To feel what it's like to help kids in trouble, to *understand* those kids."

"Didn't you have a stroke a while ago?"

"*What?*"

"I believe in honesty, so I'll be direct. You put in your time. You paid your dues. So why don't you back away gracefully?"

"*I didn't* have a stroke."

"Then why did I hear—?"

"My wife had cancer. She died . . . I caught my breath. "Six months ago."

"I see. I'm sorry. I mean that sincerely. But television isn't the same as when you created—he checked my list of credits—*The Sidewalks of New York*. A definite classic. One of my absolute personal favorites. But times have changed. The industry's a lot more competitive. The pressure's unbelievable. A series creator has to act as one of the producers, to oversee the product, to guarantee consistency. I'm talking thirteen hours a day minimum, and ideally the creator ought to contribute something to every script."

"That's what I did on *The Sidewalks of New York.*"

"Oh?" Arthur Lewis looked blank. "I guess I didn't notice that in your credits." He straightened. "But my point's the same. Television's a pressure cooker. A game for people with energy."

"Did I need a wheelchair when I came in here?"

"You've lost me."

"Energy's not my problem. I'm full to bursting with the need to work. What matters is, what do you think of my idea?"

"It's—"

The phone rang.

Arthur Lewis looked relieved. "Let me get back to you."

"Of course. I know you're busy. Thanks for your time."

"Hey, *anytime.* I'm always here and ready for new ideas." Again he checked his Rolex.

The phone kept ringing.

"Take care," he said.

"You too."

I took my list of credits off his desk.

The last thing I heard when I left was "No, that old fuck's wrong for the part. He's losing his hair. A wig? Get real. The audience can tell the difference. For God's sake, a hairpiece is death in the ratings."


Steve had said to phone him when the meeting was over. But I felt so upset I decided to hell with phoning him and drove up the Pacific Coast Highway toward his place in Malibu. Traffic was terrible—rush hour, Friday evening. For once, though, it had an advantage. After an hour, my anger began to abate enough for me to realize that I wouldn't accomplish much by showing up unexpectedly in a fit at Steve's. He'd been loyal. He didn't need my aggravation. As he'd told me, "I've done what I can. Now it's up to you." But there wasn't much I *could* do if my age and not my talent was how I was judged. Certainly that wasn't Steve's fault.

So I stopped at something called the Pacific Coast Diner and took the advice of a bumper sticker on a car I'd been stuck behind—CHILL OUT. Maybe a few drinks and a meditative dinner would calm me down. The restaurant had umbrella-topped tables on a balcony that looked toward the ocean. I had to wait a half hour, but a Scotch and soda made the time go quickly, and the crimson reflection of the setting sun on the ocean was spectacular.

Or would have been if I'd been paying attention. The truth was, I couldn't stop being upset. I had another Scotch and soda, ordered poached salmon, tried to enjoy my meal, and suddenly couldn't swallow, suddenly felt about as lonely as I'd felt since Doris had died. *Maybe the network executives are right*, I thought. *Maybe I am too old. Maybe I don't know how to relate to a young audience. Maybe it's time I packed it in.*

"Mort Davidson," a voice said.

"Excuse me?" I blinked, distracted from my thoughts.

My waiter was holding the credit card I'd given him. "Mort Davidson." He looked at the name on the card, then at me. "The screenwriter?"

I spared him a bitter "Used to be" and nodded with what I hoped was a pleasant manner.

"Wow." He was tall and thin with sandy hair and a glowing tan. His blue eyes glinted. He had the sort of chiseled, handsome face that made me think he was yet another would-be actor. He looked to be about twenty-three. "When I saw your name, I thought, *No, it couldn't be. Who knows how many Mort Davidsons there are? the odds against this being . . .* But it *is* you. The screenwriter."

"Guilty," I managed to joke.

"I bet I've seen everything you ever wrote. I must have watched *The Dead of Noon* twenty-five times. I really learned a lot."

"Oh?" I was puzzled. What would my screenplay have taught him about acting?

"About structure. About pace. About not being afraid to let the characters talk. That's what's wrong with movies today. The characters don't have anything important to say."

At once it hit me. He wasn't a would-be actor.

"I'm a writer," he said. "Or trying to be. I mean, I've still got a lot to learn. That I'm working here proves what I mean." The glint went out of his eyes. "I still haven't sold anything." His enthusiasm was forced. "But, hey, nothing important is easy. I'll just keep writing until I crack the market. The boss is . . . I'd better not keep chattering at you. He doesn't like it. For sure, you've got better things to do than listen to me. I just wanted to say how much I like your work, Mr. Davidson. I'll bring your credit card right back. It's a pleasure to meet you."

As he left, it struck me that the speed with which he talked suggested not only energy but insecurity. For all his good looks, he felt like a loser.

Or maybe I was just transferring my own emotions onto him. This much was definite—getting a compliment was a hell of a lot better than a sharp stick in the eye or the meeting I'd endured.

When he came back with my credit card, I signed the bill and gave him a generous tip.

"Thanks, Mr. Davidson."

"Hang in there. You've got one important thing on your side."

"What's that?"

"You're young. You've got plenty of time to make it."

"Unless . . ."

I wondered what he meant.

"Unless I don't have what it takes."

"Well, the best advice I can give you is never doubt yourself."

As I left the restaurant and passed beneath hissing arc lamps toward my car, I couldn't ignore the irony. The waiter had youth but doubted his ability. I had confidence in my ability but was penalized because of my age. Despite the roar of traffic on the Pacific Coast Highway, I heard waves on the beach.

And that's when the notion came to me. A practical joke of sorts, like stories you hear about frustrated writers submitting Oscar-winning screenplays, *Casablanca*, for example, but the writers change the title and the characters' names. The notes they get back from producers as much as say that the screenplays are the lousiest junk the producers ever read. So then the writers tell the trade papers what they've done, the point being that they're trying to prove it doesn't matter bow good a writer you are if you don't have connections.

Why not? I thought. It would be worth seeing the look on those bastards' faces.


"What's your name?"

"Ric Potter."

"Short for Richard?"

"No. For Eric."

I nodded. Breaking-the-ice conversation. "The reason I came back is I have something I want to discuss with you, a way that might help your career."

His eyes brightened.

At once, they darkened, as if he thought I might be trying to pick him up.

"Strictly business," I said. "Here's my card. If you want to talk about writing and how to make some money, give me a call."

His suspicion persisted, but his curiosity was stronger. "What time?"

"Eleven tomorrow?"

"Fine."

"Come over. Bring some of your scripts."

That was important. I had to find out if he could write or if he was fooling himself. My scheme wouldn't work unless he had a basic feel for the business. So the next morning, when he arrived exactly on time at my home in the hills above West Hollywood, we swapped: I let him see a script I'd just finished while I sat by the pool and read one of his. I finished around one o'clock. "Hungry?"

"Starved. Your script is wonderful," Ric said. "I can't get over the pace. The sense of reality. It didn't feel like a story."

"Thanks." I took some tuna salad and Perrier from the refrigerator "Whole-wheat bread and kosher dills okay? Or maybe you'd rather go to a restaurant."

"After working in one every night?" Ric laughed.

But I could tell that he was marking time, that he was frustrated and anxious to know what I thought of his script. I remembered how I had felt at his age, the insecurity when someone important was reading my work. I got to the point.

"I like your story," I said.

He exhaled.

"But I don't think it's executed properly."

His check muscles tensed.

"Given what they're paying A-list actors these days, you have to get the main character on screen as quickly as possible. *Your* main character doesn't show up until page fifteen."

He sounded embarrassed. "I couldn't figure out a way to—"

"And the romantic element is so familiar it's tiresome. A shower scene comes from a washed-up imagination."

That was tough, I knew, but I waited to see how he'd take it. If he turned out to be the sensitive type, I wasn't going to get anywhere.

"Yeah. Okay. Maybe I did rely on a lot of other movies I'd seen."

His response encouraged me. "The humorous elements don't work. I don't think comedy is your thing."

He squinted.

"The ending has no focus," I continued. "Was your main character right or not? Simply leaving the dilemma up in the air is going to piss off your audience."

He studied me. "You said you liked the story."

"Right. I did."

"Then why do I feel like I'm on the *Titanic?*"

"Because you've got a lot of craft to learn, and it's going to take you quite a while to master it. If you ever do. There aren't any guarantees. The average Guild member earns less than six thousand dollars a year. Writing screenplays is one of the most competitive enterprises in the world. But I think I can help you."

". . . Why?"

"Excuse me?"

"We met just last night. I was your waiter, for God's sake. Now suddenly I'm in your house, having lunch with you, and you're saying you want to help me. It can't be because of the force of my personality. You want something."

"Yes, but not what you're thinking. I told you last night—this is strictly business. Sit down and eat while I tell you how we can both make some money."

"This is Ric Potter," I said. We were at a reception in one of those mansions in the hills near the Hollywood Bowl. Sunset. A string quartet. Champagne. Plenty of movers and shakers. "Fox is very hot on one of his scripts. I think it'll go for a million."

The man to whom I'd introduced Ric was an executive at Warners. He couldn't have been over thirty. "Oh?"

"Yeah, it's got a youth angle."

"Oh?" The executive looked Ric up and down, confused, never having heard of him, at the same time worried because he didn't want to be out of the loop, fearing he *ought* to have heard of him.

"If I sound a little proud," I said, "it's because I discovered him. I found him last May when I was giving a talk to a young screenwriters' workshop at the American Film Institute. Ric convinced me to look at some things and . . . I'm glad I did. My *agent's* glad I did." I chuckled.

The executive tried to look amused, although he hated like hell to pay writers significant money. For his part, Ric tried to look modest but unbelievably talented, young, young, young, and hot, hot, hot.

"Well, don't let Fox tie you up," the executive told Ric. "Have your agent send me something."

"I'll do that, Mr. Ballard. Thanks," Ric said.

"Do I look old enough to be a 'mister'? Call me Ed."

We made the rounds. While all the executives considered me too old to be relevant to their sixteen-to-twenty-five audience, they still had reverence for what they thought of as an institution. Sure, they wouldn't buy anything from me, but they were more than happy to talk to me. After all, it didn't cost them any money, and it made them feel like they were part of a community.

By the time I was through introducing Ric, my rumors about him had been accepted as fact. Various executives from various studios considered themselves in competition with executives from other studios for the services of this hot new young writer who was getting a million dollars a script.

Ric had driven with me to the reception. On the way back, he kept shaking his head in amazement. "And that's the secret? I just needed the right guy to give me introductions? To be anointed as a successor?"

"Not quite. Don't let their chumminess fool you. They only care if you can deliver."

"Well, tomorrow I'll send them one of my scripts."

"No," I said. "Remember our agreement. Not one of your scripts. One of *mine*. By Eric Potter."


So there it was. The deal Ric and I had made was that I'd give him ten percent of whatever my scripts earned in exchange for his being my front man. For his part, he'd have to take calls and go to meetings and behave as if he'd actually written the scripts. Along the way, we'd inevitably talk about the intent and technique of the scripts, thus providing Ric with writing lessons. All in all, not a bad deal for him.

Except that he had insisted on fifteen percent.

"Hey, I can't go to meetings if I'm working three to eleven at the restaurant," he'd said. "Fifteen percent. And I'll need an advance. You'll have to pay me what I'm earning at the restaurant so I can be free for the meetings."

I wrote him a check for a thousand dollars.


The phone rang, interrupting the climactic speech of the script I was writing. Instead of picking up the receiver, I let my answering machine take it, but I answered anyhow when I heard my agent talking about Ric.

"What about him, Steve?"

"Ballard over at Warners likes the script you had me send him. He wants a few changes, but basically he's happy enough to offer seven hundred and fifty thousand."

"Ask for a million."

"I'll ask for nothing."

"I don't understand. Is this a new negotiating tactic?"

"You told me not to bother reading the script, just to do the kid a favor and send it over to Warners because Ballard asked for it. As you pointed out, I'm too busy to do any reading anyhow. But I made a copy of the script, and for the hell of it, last night I looked it over. Mort, what are you trying to pull? Ric Potter didn't write that script. *You* did. Under a different title, you showed it to me a year ago."

I didn't respond.

"Mort?"

"I'm making a point. The only thing wrong with my scripts is an industry bias against age. Pretend somebody young wrote them, and all of a sudden they're wonderful."

"Mort, I won't be a part of this."

"Why not?"

"It's misrepresentation. I'd be jeopardizing my credibility as an agent. You know how the clause in the contract reads—the writer guarantees that the script is solely his or her own work. If somebody else was involved, the studio wants to know about it—to protect itself against a plagiarism suit."

"But if you tell Ballard I wrote that script, he won't buy it."

"You're being paranoid, Mort."

"Facing facts and being practical. Don't screw this up."

"I told you, I won't go along with it."

"Then if you won't make the deal, I'll get somebody else who will."

A long pause. "Do you know what you're saying?"

"Ric Potter and I need a new agent."



I'll say this for Steve—even though he was furious about my leaving him, he finally swore, for old times' sake, at my insistence, that he wouldn't tell anybody what I was doing. He was loyal to the end. It broke my heart to leave him. The new agent I selected knew squat about the arrangement I had with Ric. She believed what I told her—that Ric and I were friends and by coincidence we'd decided simultaneously to get new representation. I could have chosen one of those superhuge agencies like CAA, but I've always been uncomfortable when I'm part of a mob, and in this case especially, it seemed to me that small and intimate were essential. The fewer people who knew my business, the better.

The Linda Carpenter Agency was located in a stone cottage just past the gates to the old Hollywoodland subdivision. Years ago, the "land" part of that subdivision's sign collapsed. The "Hollywood" part remained, and you see that sign all the time in film clips about Los Angeles. It's a distance up past houses in the hills. Nonetheless, from outside Linda Carpenter's stone cottage, you feel that the sign's looming over you.

I parked my Audi and got out with Ric. He was wearing sneakers, jeans, and a blue cotton pullover. At my insistence. I wanted his outfit to be self-consciously informal and youthful in contrast with my own mature, conservative slacks and sport coat. When we entered the office, Linda—who's thirty, with short red hair, and loves to look at gorgeous young men—sat straighter when I introduced Ric. His biceps bulged at the sleeves of his pullover. I was reminded again of how much—with his sandy hair, blue eyes, and glowing tan—he looked like an actor.

Linda took a moment before she reluctantly shifted her attention away from him, as if suddenly realizing that I was in the room. "Good to see you again, Mort. But you didn't have to: come all this way. I could have met you for lunch at Le Dôme."

"A courtesy visit. I wanted to save you the long drive, not to mention the bill."

I said it as if I was joking. The rule is that agents always pick up the check when they're at a restaurant with clients.

Linda's smile was winning. Her red hair seemed brighter. "Anytime. I'm still surprised that you left Steve." She tactfully didn't ask what the problem had been. "I promise I'll work hard for you."

"I know you will," I said. "But I don't think you'll have to work hard for my friend here. Ric already has some interest in a script of his over at Warners."

"Oh?" Linda raised her elegant eyebrows. "Who's the executive?"

"Ballard."

"My, my." She frowned slightly. "And Steve isn't involved in this? Your ties are completely severed?"

"Completely. If you want, call him to make sure."

"That won't be necessary."

But I found out later that Linda did phone Steve, and he backed up what I'd said. Also he refused to discuss why we'd separated.

"I have a hunch the script can go for big dollars," I continued.

"How big is big?"

"A million."

Linda's eyes widened. "That certainly isn't small."

"Ballard heard there's a buzz about Ric. Ballard thinks that Ric might be a young Joe Eszterhas." The reference was to the screenwriter of *Basic Instinct*, who had become a phenomenon for writing sensation-based scripts on speculation and intriguing so many producers that he'd manipulated them into a bidding war and collected megabucks. "I have a suspicion that Ballard would like to make a preemptive bid and shut out the competition."

"Mort, you sound more like an agent than a writer."

"It's just a hunch."

"And Steve doesn't want a piece of this?"

I shook my head no.

Linda frowned harder.

But her frown dissolved the moment she turned again toward Ric and took another look at his perfect chin. "Did you bring a copy of the script?"

"Sure." Ric grinned with becoming modesty, the way I'd taught him. "Right here."

Linda took it and flipped to the end to make sure it wasn't longer than 110 pages—a shootable size. "What's it about?"

Ric gave the pitch that I'd taught him—the high concept first, then the target audience, the type of actor he had in mind, and ways the budget could be kept in check. The same as when we'd clocked it at my house, he took four minutes.

Linda listened with growing fascination. She turned to me. "Have you been coaching him?"

"Not much. Ric's a natural."

"He must be to act this polished."

"And he's young," I said.

"You don't need to remind me."

"And Ballard *certainly* doesn't need reminding," I said.

"Ric," Linda said, "from here on in, whatever you do, don't get writer's block. I'm going to make you the highest paid new kid in town."

Ric beamed.

"And, Mort," Linda said, "I think you're awfully generous to help your friend through the ropes like this."

"Well"—I shrugged—"isn't that what friends are for?"


I had joked with Linda that our trip to her office was a courtesy visit—to save her a long drive and the cost of buying us lunch at an expensive restaurant. That was partly true. But I also wanted to see how Ric made his pitch about the script. If he got nerves and screwed up, I didn't want it to be in Le Dôme, where producers at neighboring tables might see him get flustered. We were trying out the show on the road, so to speak, before we brought it to town. And I had to agree with Linda—Ric had done just fine.

I told him so, as we drove along Sunset Boulevard. "I won't always be there to back you up. In fact, it'll be rare that I am. We have to keep training you so you give the impression there's very little about writing or the business you don't understand. Most of getting along with studio executives is making them have confidence in you."

"You really think I impressed her?"

"It was obvious."

Ric thought about it, peering out the window, nodding. "Yeah."


So we went back to my home in the hills above West Hollywood, and I ran him through more variations of questions he might get asked—where he'd gotten the idea, what actors would be good in the roles, who he thought could direct the material, that sort of thing. At the start of a project, producers pay a lot of attention to a screenwriter, and they promise to keep consulting him the way they're consulting him now. It's all guff, of course. As soon as a director and a name actor are attached to a project, the producers suddenly get amnesia about the original screenwriter. But at the start, he's king, and I wanted Ric to be ready to answer any kind of question about the screenplay so he could be convincing that he'd actually written it.

Ric was a fast study. At eight, when I couldn't think of any more questions he might have to answer, we took a drive to dinner at a fish place near the Santa Monica pier. Afterward, we strolled to the end of the pier and watched the sunset.

"So this is what it's all about," Ric said.

"I'm not sure what you mean."

"The action. I can feel the action."

"Don't get fooled by Linda's optimism. Nothing might come of this."

Ric shook his head. "I'm close."

"I've got some pages I want to do tomorrow, but if you'll come around at four with your own new pages, I'll go over them for you. I'm curious to see how you're revising that script you showed me."

Ric kept staring out at the sunset and didn't answer for quite a while. "Yeah, my script."


As things turned out, I didn't get much work done the next day. I had just managed to solve a problem in a scene that was running too long when my phone rang. That was around ten o'clock, and rather than be interrupted, I let my answering machine take it. But when I heard Ric's excited voice, I picked up the phone.

"Slow down," I said. "Take it easy. What are you so worked up about?"

"They want the script!"

I wasn't prepared. "Warners?"

"Can you believe that this is happening so fast?"

"Ballard's actually taking it? How did you find this out?"

"Linda just phoned me!"

"Linda?" I frowned. "But why didn't Linda . . . ?" I was about to say, "Why didn't Linda phone *me?*" Then I realized my mistake. There wasn't any reason for Linda to phone me, except maybe to tell me the good news about my friend. But she definitely had to phone Ric. After all, he was supposedly the author of the screenplay.

Ric kept talking excitedly. "Linda says Ballard wants to have lunch with me."

"Great." The truth is, I was vaguely jealous. "When?"

"Today."

I was stunned. Any executive with power was always booked several weeks in advance. For Ballard to decide to have lunch with Ric this soon, he would have had to cancel lunch with someone else. It definitely wouldn't have been the other way around. No one cancels lunch with Ballard.

"Amazing," I said.

"Apparently he's got big plans for me. By the way, he likes the script as is. No changes. At least, for now. Linda says when they sign a director, the director always asks for changes."

"Linda's right," I said. "And then the director'll insist that the changes aren't good enough and ask to bring in a friend to do the rewrite."

"No fucking way," Ric said.

"A screenwriter doesn't have any clout against a director. You've still got a lot to learn about industry politics. School isn't finished yet."

"Sure." Ric hurried on. "Linda got Ballard up to a million and a quarter for the script!"

For a moment, I had trouble breathing.

"Great." And this time I meant it.


Ric phoned again in thirty minutes. He was nervous about the meeting and needed reassurance.

Ric phoned thirty minutes after that, saying that he didn't feel comfortable going to a power lunch in the sneakers, jeans, and pullover that I had told him were necessary for the role he was playing.

"You have to," I said. "You've got to look like you don't belong to the Establishment or whatever the hell it is they call it these days. If you look like every other writer trying to make an impression, Ballard will *treat* you like every other writer. We're selling nonconformity. We're selling youth."

"I still say I'd feel more comfortable in a jacket by . . ." Ric mentioned the name of the latest trendy designer.

"Even assuming that's a good idea, which it isn't, how on earth are you going to pay for it? A jacket by that designer costs fifteen hundred dollars."

"I'll use my credit card," Ric said.

"But a month from now, you'll still have to pay the bill. You know the whopping interest rates those credit card companies charge."

"Hey, I can afford it. I just made a million and a quarter bucks."

"No, Ric. You're getting confused."

"All right, I know Linda has to take her ten percent commission."

"You're still confused. *You* don't get the bulk of that money. *I* do. What *you* get is fifteen percent of it."

"That's still a lot of cash. Almost two hundred thousand dollars."

"But remember, you probably won't get it for at least six months."

"*What?*"

"On a spec script, they don't simply agree to buy it and hand you a check. The fine points on the negotiation have to be completed. Then the contracts have to be drawn up and reviewed and amended. Then their business office drags its feet, issuing the check. I once waited a year to get paid for a spec script."

"But I can't wait that long. I've got . . ."

"Yes?"

"Responsibilities. Look, Mort, I have to go. I need to get ready for this meeting."

"And I need to get back to my pages."

"With all this excitement, you mean you're actually writing today?"

"*Every* day."

"No shit."


But I was too preoccupied to get much work done.

Ric finally phoned around five. "Lunch was fabulous."

I hadn't expected to feel so relieved. "Ballard didn't ask you any tricky questions? He's still convinced you wrote the script?"

"Not only that. He says I'm just the talent he's been looking for. A fresh imagination. Someone in tune with today's generation. He asked me to do a last-minute rewrite on an action picture he's starting next week."

"*The Warlords?*"

"That's the one."

"I've been hearing bad things about it," I said.

"Well, you won't hear anything bad anymore."

"Wait a . . . Are you telling me you accepted the job?"

"Damned right."

"Without talking to me about it first?" I straightened in shock. "What in God's name did you think you were doing?"

"Why would I need to talk to you? You're not my agent. Ballard called Linda from our table at the restaurant. The two of them settled the deal while I was sitting there. Man, when things happen, they happen. All those years of trying, and now, wham, pow, all of a sudden I'm there. And the best part is, since I'm a writer for hire on this job, they have to pay some of the money the minute I sit down to work, even if the contracts aren't ready."

"That's correct," I said. "On work for hire, you have to get paid on a schedule. The Writers Guild insists on that. You're learning fast. But, Ric, before you accepted the job, don't you think it would have been smart to read the script first—to see if it *can* be fixed?"

"How bad can it be?" Ric chuckled.

"You'd be surprised."

"It doesn't matter *how* bad. The fee's a hundred thousand dollars. I need the money."

"For *what?* You don't live expensively. You can afford to be patient and take jobs that build a career."

"Hey, I'll tell you what I can afford. Are you using that portable phone in your office?"

"Yes. But I don't see why that matters."

"Take a look out your front window."

Frowning, I left my office, went through the TV room and the living room, and peered past the blossoming rhododendron outside my front window. I scanned the curving driveway, then focused on the gate.

Ric was wearing a designer linen jacket, sitting in a red Ferrari, using a car phone, waving to me when he saw me at the window. "Like it?" he asked over the phone.

"For God's sake." I broke the connection, set down the phone, and stalked out the front door.

"Like it?" Ric repeated when I reached the gate. He gestured toward his jacket and the car.

"You didn't have time to . . . Where'd you get . . . ?"

"This morning, after Linda phoned about the offer from Ballard, I ordered the car over the phone. Picked it up after my meeting with Ballard. Nifty, huh?"

"But you don't have any assets. You mean they just let you drive the car off the lot?"

"Bought it on credit. I made Linda sign as the guarantor."

"You made Linda . . ." I couldn't believe what I was hearing. "Damn it, Ric, why don't you let me finish coaching you before you run off and . . . After I taught you about screenplay technique and industry politics, I wanted to explain to you how to handle your money."

"Hey, what's to teach? Money's for spending."

"Not in *this* business. You've got to put something away for when you have bad years."

"Well, I'm certainly not having any trouble earning money so far."

"What happened today is a fluke! This is the first script I've sold in longer than I care to think about. There aren't any guarantees. "

"Then it's a good thing I came along, huh?" Ric grinned.

"Before you accepted the rewrite job, you should have asked me if I wanted to do it."

"But you're not involved in this. Why should I divide the money with you? *I'm* going to do it."

"In that case, you should have asked yourself another question."

"What?"

"Whether you've got the *ability* to do it."

Ric flushed with anger. "Of course I've got the ability. You've read my stuff. All I needed was a break."


I didn't hear from Ric for three days. That was fine by me. I'd accomplished what I'd intended. I'd proven that a script with my name on it had less chance of being bought than the same script with a youngster's name on it. And to tell the truth, Ric's lack of discipline was annoying me. But after the third day, I confess I got curious. What was he up to?

He called at nine in the evening. "How's it going?"

"Fine," I said. "I had a good day's work."

"Yeah, that's what I'm calling about. Work."

"Oh?"

"I haven't been in touch lately because of this rewrite on *The Warlords*."

I waited.

"I had a meeting with the director," Ric said. "Then I had a meeting with the star." He mentioned the name of the biggest action hero in the business. He hesitated. "I was wondering. Would you look at the material I've got?"

"You can't be serious. After the way you talked to me about it? You all but told me to get lost."

"I didn't mean to be rude. Honestly. This is all new to me, Mort. Come on, give me a break. As you keep reminding me, I don't have the experience you do. I'm young."

I had to hand it to him. He'd not only apologized. He'd used the right excuse.

"Mort?"

At first I didn't want to be bothered. I had my own work to think about, and *The Warlords* would probably be so bad that it would contaminate my mind.

But then my curiosity got the better of me. I couldn't help wondering what Ric would do to improve junk.

"Mort?"

"When do you want me to look at what you've done?"

"How about right now?"

"Now? It's after nine. It'll take you an hour to get here and—"

"I'm already here."

"What?"

"I'm on my car phone. Outside your gate again."

Ric sat across from me in my living room. I couldn't help noticing that his tan was darker, that he was wearing a different designer jacket, a more expensive one. Then I glanced at the title page on the script he'd handed me.

## THE WARLORDS
### revisions by Eric Potter

I flipped through the pages. All of them were typed on white paper. That bothered me. Ric's inexperience was showing again. On last-minute rewrites, it's always helpful to submit changed pages on different-colored paper. That way, the producer and director can save time and not have to read the entire script to find the changes.

"These are the notes the director gave me," Ric said. He handed me some crudely typed pages. "And these"—Ric handed me pages with scribbling on them—"are what the star gave me. It's a little hard to decipher them."

"More than a little. Jesus." I squinted at the scribbling and got a headache. "I'd better put on my glasses." They helped a little. I read what the director wanted. I switched to what the star wanted.

"These are the notes the producer gave me," Ric said.

I thanked God that they were neatly typed and studied them as well. Finally I leaned back and took off my glasses.

"Well?"

I sighed. "Typical. As near as I can tell, these three people are each talking about a different movie. The director wants more action and less characterization. The star has decided to be serious—he wants more characterization and less action. The producer wants it funny and less expensive. If they're not careful, this movie will have multiple personalities."

Ric looked at me anxiously.

"Okay," I said, feeling tired. "Get a beer from the refrigerator and watch television or something while I go through this. It would help if I knew where you'd made changes. Next time you're in a situation like this, identify your work with colored paper."

Ric frowned.

"What's the matter?" I asked.

"The changes."

"So? What about them?"

"Well, I haven't started to make them."

"You haven't . . . ? But on this title page, it says, 'Revisions by Eric Potter.'"

Ric looked sheepish. "The title page is as far as I got."

"Sweet Jesus. When are these revisions due?"

"Ballard gave me a week."

"And for the first three days of that week, you didn't work on the changes? What have you been doing?"

Ric glanced away.

Again I noticed that his tan was darker. "Don't tell me you've just been sitting in the sun?"

"Not exactly."

"Then *what* exactly?"

"I've been thinking about how to improve the script."

I was so agitated I had to stand. "You don't *think* about changes. You *make* changes. How much did you say you were being paid? A hundred thousand dollars?"

Ric nodded, uncomfortable.

"And the Writers Guild insists that on work for hire you get a portion of the money as soon as you start."

"Fifty thousand." Ric squirmed. "Linda got the check by messenger the day after I made the deal with Ballard."

"What a mess."

Ric lowered his head, more uncomfortable.

"If you don't hand in new pages four days from now, Ballard will want his money back."

"I know," Ric said, then added, "But I can't."

"What?"

"I already spent the money. A deposit on a condo near Malibu."

I was stunned.

"And the money isn't the worst of it," I said. "Your reputation. *That's* worse. Ballard gave you an incredible break. He decided to take a chance on the bright new kid in town. He allowed you to jump over all the shit. But if you don't deliver, he'll be furious. He'll spread the word all over town that you're not dependable. You won't be hot anymore. We won't be able to sell another script as easily as we did this one."

"Look, I'm sorry, Mort. I know I bragged to you that I could do the job on my own. I was wrong. I don't have the experience. I admit it. I'm out of my depth."

"Even on a piece of shit like this."

Ric glanced down, then up. "I was wondering . . . Could you give me a hand?"

My mouth hung open in astonishment.

Before I could tell him no damned way, Ric quickly added, "It would really help both of us."

"How do you figure that?"

"You just said it yourself. If I don't deliver, Ballard will spread the word. No producer will trust me. You won't be able to sell another script through me."

My forehead began to throb. He was right, of course. If I wanted to keep selling scripts, if I wanted to see them produced, I needed him. I finally had to admit that, secretly, I had never intended the deception with Ric to be a one-time-only arrangement.

I swallowed and finally said, "All right."

"Thank you."

"But I won't clean up your messes for nothing."

"Of course not. The same arrangement as before. All I get out of this is fifteen percent."

"By rights, you shouldn't get anything."

"Hey, without me, Ballard wouldn't have offered the job."

"Since you already spent the first half of the payment, how do I get that money?"

Ric made an effort to think of a solution. "We'll have to wait until the money comes through on the spec script we sold. I'll give you the money out of the two hundred thousand that's owed to me.

"But you owe the Ferrari dealer a bundle. Otherwise Linda's responsible for your debt."

"I'll take care of it." Ric gestured impatiently. "I'll take care of all of it. What's important now is that you make the changes on *The Warlords*. Ballard has to pay the remaining fifty thousand dollars when I hand in the pages. That money's yours."

"Fine."


The script for *The Warlords* was even worse than I had feared. How do you change bad junk into good junk? In the process, how do you please a director, a star, and a producer who ask for widely different things? One of the rules I've learned over the years is that what people say they want isn't always what they mean. Sometimes it's a matter of interpretation. And after I endured reading the script for *The Warlords*, I thought I had that interpretation.

The director said he wanted more action and less characterization. In my opinion, the script already had more than enough action. The trouble was that some of the action sequences were redundant, and others weren't paced effectively. The biggest stunts occurred two thirds of the way into the story. The last third had stunts that suffered by comparison. So the trick here was to do some pruning and restructuring—to take the good stunts from the end and put them in the middle, to build on them and put the great stunts at the end, all the while struggling to retain the already feeble logic of the story.

The star said he wanted less action and more characterization. As far as I could tell, what he really wanted was to be sympathetic, to make the audience like the character he was playing. So I softened him a little, threw in some jokes, had him wait for an old lady to cross a street before he blew away the bad guys, basic things like that. Since his character was more like a robot than a human being, any vaguely human thing he did would make him sympathetic.

The producer said he wanted more humor and a less expensive budget. Well, by making the hero sympathetic, I added the jokes the producer wanted. By restructuring the sequence of stunts, I managed to eliminate some of the weaker ones, thus giving the star his request for less action and the producer his request for holding down the budget, since the preponderance of action scenes had been what inflated the budget in the first place.

I explained this to Ric as I made notes. "They'll all be happy."

"Amazing," Ric said.

"Thanks."

"No, what I mean is, the ideas you came up with, *I* could have thought of them."

"Oh?" My voice hardened. "Then why didn't you?"

"Because, well, they seem so obvious."

"*After* I thought of them. Good ideas always seem obvious in retrospect. The real job is putting them on paper. I'm going to have to work like crazy to get this job done in four days. And then there's a further problem. I have to teach you how to pitch these changes to Ballard, so he'll be convinced you're the one who wrote them."

"You can count on me," Ric said.

"I want you to . . ." Suddenly I found myself yawning and looked at my watch. "Three A.M.? I'm not used to staying up this late. I'd better get some sleep if I'm going to get this rewrite done in four days."

"I'm a night person myself," Ric said.

"Well, come back tomorrow at four in the afternoon. I'll take a break and start teaching you what to say to Ballard."


Ric didn't show up, of course. When I phoned his apartment, I got his answering machine. I couldn't get in touch with him the next day, or the day after that.

But the day the changes were due, he certainly showed up. He phoned again from his car outside the gate, and when I let him in, he was so eager to see the pages that he barely said hello to me.

"Where the hell have you been?"

"Mexico."

"*What?*"

"With all this stress, I needed to get away."

"What have you done to put you under stress? *I'm* the one who's been doing all the work."

Instead of responding, Ric sat on my living-room sofa and quickly leafed through the pages. I noticed he was wearing yet another designer jacket. His tan was even darker.

"Yeah," he said. "This is good." He quickly came to his feet. "I'd better get to the studio."

"But I haven't coached you about what to say to Ballard."

Ric stopped at the door. "Mort, I've been thinking. If this partnership is going to work, we need to give each other more space. You take care of the writing. Let me worry about what to say in meetings. Ballard likes me. I know how to handle him. Trust me."

And Ric was gone.


I waited to hear about what happened at the meeting. No phone call. When I finally broke down and phoned *him*, an electronic-sounding voice told me that his number was no longer in service. It took me a moment to figure out that he must have moved to the condo in Malibu. So I phoned Linda to get the new number, and she awkwardly told me that Ric had ordered her to keep it a secret.

"Even from me?"

"Especially from you. Did you guys have an argument or something?"

"No."

"Well, he made it sound as if you had. He kept complaining about how you were always telling him what to do."

"Of all the . . ." I almost told Linda the truth—that Ric hadn't written the script she had sold but rather *I* had. Then I realized that she'd be conscience bound to tell the studio. The deception would make the studio feel chilly about the script. They would reread the script with a new perspective, prejudiced by knowing the true identity of the author. The deal would fall through. I'd lose the biggest fee I'd ever been promised.

So I mumbled something about intending to talk with him and straighten out the problem. Then I hung up and cursed.


After I didn't hear from Ric for a week, it became obvious that Linda would long ago have forwarded to him the check for the rewrite on *The Warlords*. He'd had ample time to send me my money. He didn't intend to pay me.

That made me furious, partly because he'd betrayed me, partly because I didn't like being made to feel naive, and partly because I'm a professional.

To me, it's a matter of honor that I get paid for what I write. Ric had violated one of my most basic rules.

My arrangement with him was finished. When I read about him in *Daily Variety* and *Hollywood Reporter*—about how Ballard was delighted with the rewrite and predicting that the script he had bought from Ric would be next year's smash hit, not to mention that Ric would win an Oscar for it—I was apoplectic. Ric was compared to Robert Towne and William Goldman, with the advantage that he was young and had a powerful understanding of today's generation. Ric had been hired for a half-million dollars to do another rewrite. Ric had promised that he would soon deliver another original script, for which he hinted that his agent would demand an enormous price. "Quality is always worth the cost," Ballard said.

I wanted to vomit.

As I knew he would have to, Ric eventually came to see me. Again the car phone at the gate. Three weeks later. After dark. A night person, after all.

I made a pretense of reluctance, feigned being moved by his whining, let him in and offered a beer. Even in the muted lights of my living room, he had the most perfect tan I had ever seen. His clothes were even more expensive and trendy. I hated him.

"You didn't send me my money for the rewrite on *The Warlords*."

"I'm sorry about that," Ric said. "That's part of the reason I'm here."

"To pay me?"

"To explain. My condo at Malibu. The owners demanded more money as a down payment. I couldn't give up the place. It's too fabulous. So I had to . . . Well, I knew you'd understand."

"But I don't."

"Mort, listen to me. I promise—as soon as the money comes through on the script we sold, I'll pay you everything I owe."

"You went to fifteen percent of the fee, to fifty percent, to one hundred percent. Do you think I work for nothing?"

"Mort, I can appreciate your feelings. But I was in a bind."

"You *still* are. I've been reading about you in the trade papers. You're getting a half million for a rewrite on another script, and you're also promising a new original script. How arc you going to manage all that?"

"Well, I tried to do it on my own. I handed Ballard the script I showed you when we first met."

"Jesus, no."

"He didn't like it."

"What a surprise."

"I had to cover my tracks and tell him it was something I'd been fooling with but that I realized it needed a lot of work. I told him I agreed with his opinion. From now on, I intended to stick to the tried and true—the sort of thing I'd sold him."

I shook my head.

"I guess you were right," Ric said. "Good ideas seem obvious after somebody's thought of them. But maybe I don't have what it takes to come up with them. I've been acting like a jerk."

"I couldn't agree more."

"So what do you say?" Ric offered his hand. "Let's let bygones be bygones. I screwed up, but I've learned from my mistake. I'm willing to give our partnership another try if you are."

I stared at his hand.

Suddenly beads of sweat burst out onto his brow. He lifted his hand and wiped the sweat.

"What's the matter?"

"Hot in here."

"Not really. Actually I thought it was getting chilly."

"Feels stuffy."

"The beer I gave you. Maybe you drank it too fast."

"Maybe."

"You know, *I've* been thinking," I said.


The beer was drugged, of course. After the nausea wore off, giddiness set in, as it was supposed to. The drug, which I'd learned about years ago when I was working on a TV crime series, left its victim open to suggestion. It took me only ten minutes to convince him it was a great idea to do what I wanted. As I instructed, Ric giddily phoned Linda and told her that he was feeling stressed out and intended to go back down to Mexico. He told her he suddenly felt trapped by materialism. He needed a spiritual retreat. He might be away for as long as six months.

Linda was shocked. Listening to the speaker phone, I heard her demand to know how Ric intended to fulfill the contracts he'd signed. She said his voice was slurred and accused him of being drunk or high on something.

I picked up the phone, switched off the speaker, and interrupted to tell Linda that Ric was calling from my house and that we'd made up our differences, that he'd been pouring out his soul to me. He was drunk, yes, but what he had told her was no different than what he had told *me* when he was sober. He was leaving for Mexico tonight and might not be back for quite a while. How was he going to fulfill his contracts? No problem. Just because he was going on a retreat in Mexico, that didn't mean he wouldn't be writing. Honest work was what he thrived on. It was food for his soul.

By then, Ric was almost asleep. After I hung up, I roused him, made him sign two documents that I'd prepared, then made him tell me where he was living in Malibu. I put him in his car, drove over to his place, packed a couple of his suitcases, crammed them into the car, and set out for Mexico.

We got there shortly after dawn. He was somewhat conscious when we crossed the border, enough to be able to answer a few questions and to keep the Mexican immigration officer from becoming suspicious. After that, I drugged him again.

I drove until midafternoon, took a back road into the desert, gave him a final lethal amount of the drug, and dumped his body into a sinkhole. I drove back to Tijuana, left Ric's suitcases minus identification in an alley, left his Ferrari minus identification in another alley, the key in the ignition, and caught a bus back to Los Angeles. I was confident that neither the suitcases nor the car would ever be reported. I was also confident that by the time Ric's body was discovered, if ever, it would be in such bad shape that the Mexican authorities, with limited resources, wouldn't be able to identify it. Ric had once told me that he hadn't spoken to his parents in five years, so I knew *they* wouldn't wonder why he wasn't in touch with them. As far as his friends went, well, he didn't have any. He'd ditched them when he came into money. They wouldn't miss him.

For an old guy, I'm resilient. I'd kept up my energy, driven all night and most of the day. I finally got some sleep on the bus. Not shabby, although toward the end I felt as if something had broken in me and I doubt I'll ever be able to put in that much effort again. But I had to, you see. Ric was going to keep hounding me, enticing me, using me. And I was going to be too desperate to tell him to get lost. Because I knew that no matter how well I wrote, I would never be able to sell a script under my own name again.

When I first started as a writer, the money and the ego didn't matter to me as much as the need to work, to tell stories, to teach and delight, as the Latin poet Horace said. But when the money started coming in, I began to depend on it. And I grew to love the action of being with powerful people, of having a reputation for being able to deliver quality work with amazing speed. Ego. That's why I hated Ric the most. Because producers stroked his ego over scripts that I had written.

But not anymore. Ric was gone, and his agent had heard him say that he was going, and I had a document, with his signature on it, saying that he was going to mail in his scripts through me, that I was his mentor and that he wanted me to go to script meetings on his behalf. The document also gave me his power of attorney, with permission to oversee his income while he was away.

And that should have been the end of it. Linda was puzzled but went along. After all, she'd heard Ric on the phone. Ballard was even more puzzled, but he was also enormously pleased with the spec script that I pulled out of a drawer and sent in with Ric's name on it. As far as Ballard was concerned, if Ric wanted to be eccentric, that was fine as long as Ric kept delivering. Really, his speed and the quality of his work were amazing.

So in a way I got what I wanted—the action and the pleasure of selling my work. But there's a problem. When I sit down to do rewrites, when I type "revisions by Eric Potter," I suddenly find myself gazing out the window, wanting to sit in the sun. At the same time, I find that I can't sleep. Like Ric, I've become a night person.

I've sold the spec scripts that I wrote over the years and kept in a drawer. All I had to do was change the titles. Nobody remembered reading the original stories. But I couldn't seem to do the rewrites, and now that I've run out of old scripts, now that I'm faced with writing something new . . .

For the first time in my life, I've got writer's block. All I have to do is think of the title page and the words *by Eric Potter* and my imagination freezes. It's agony. All my life, every day, I've been a writer. For thirty-five years of married life, except for the last two when Doris got sick, I wrote every day. I sacrificed everything to my craft. I didn't have children because I thought it would interfere with my schedule. Nothing was more important than putting words on a page. Now I sit at my desk, stare at my word processor, and . . .

Mary had a little . . .

I can't bear this anymore.

I need rest.
The quick brown fox jumped over . . .
I need to forget about Ric.
Now is the time for all good men to . . .

# WATER'S EDGE

## Robert Bloch

The fly-specked lettering on the window read *The Bright Spot Restaurant.* The sign overhead urged *Eat.*

He wasn't hungry, and the place didn't look especially attractive, but he went inside anyway.

It was a counter joint with a single row of hard-backed booths lining one wall. A half dozen customers squatted on stools at the end of the counter, near the door. He walked past them and slid onto a stool at the far end.

There he sat, staring at the three waitresses. None of them looked right to him, but he had to take a chance. He waited until one of the women approached him.

"Yours, mister?"

"Coke."

She brought it to him and set the glass down. He pretended to be studying the menu and talked without looking up at her.

"Say, does a Mrs. Helen Krauss work here?"

"I'm Helen Krauss."

He lifted his eyes. What kind of a switch was this, anyway? He remembered the way Mike used to talk about her, night after night. "She's a tall blonde, but stacked. Looks a lot like that dame who plays the dumb blonde on television—what's-her-name—you know the one I mean. But she's no dope, not Helen. And boy, when it comes to loving. . . ."

After that, his descriptions would become anatomically intricate, but all intricacies had been carefully filed in memory.

He examined those files now, but nothing in them corresponded to what he saw before him.

This woman was tall, but there all resemblance ended. She must have tipped the scales at one-sixty, at least, and her hair was a dull, mousy brown. She wore glasses, too. Behind the thick lenses, her faded blue eyes peered stolidly at him.

She must have realized he was staring, and he knew he had to talk fast. "I'm looking for a Helen Krauss who used to live over in Norton Center. She was married to a man named Mike."

The stolid eyes blinked. "That's me. So what's this all about?"

"I got a message for you from your husband."

"Mike? He's dead."

"I know. I was with him when he died. Just before, anyway. I'm Rusty Connors. We were cell-mates for two years."

Her expression didn't change, but her voice dropped to a whisper. "What's the message?"

He glanced around. "I can't talk here. What time do you get off?"

"Seven-thirty."

"Good. Meet you outside?"

She hesitated. "Make it down at the corner, across the street. There's a park, you know?"

He nodded, rose and left without looking back.

This wasn't what he had expected—not after the things Mike had told him about his wife. When he bought his ticket for Hainesville, he had had other ideas in mind. It would have been nice to find this hot, good-looking blonde widow of Mike's and, maybe, combine business with pleasure. He had even thought about the two of them blowing town together, if she was half as nice as Mike said. But that was out, now. He wanted no part of this big, fat, stupid-looking slob with the dull eyes.

Rusty wondered how Mike could have filled him with such a line of bull for two years straight—and then he knew. Two years straight—that was the answer—two years in a bare cell, without a woman. Maybe it had got so that, after a time, Mike believed his own story, that Helen Krauss became beautiful to him. Maybe Mike had gone a little stir-simple before he died, and made up a lot of stuff.

Rusty only hoped Mike had been telling the truth about one thing. He had better have been, because what Mike had told Connors, there in the cell, was what brought him to town. It was this that was making him cut into this rat-race, that had led him to Mike's wife. He hoped Mike had been telling the truth about hiding away the fifty-six thousand dollars.

She met him in the park, and it was dark. That was good, because nobody would notice them together. Besides, he couldn't see her face, and she couldn't see his, and that would make it easier to say what he had to say.

They sat down on a bench behind the bandstand, and he lit a cigarette.

Then he remembered that it was important to be pleasant, so he offered the pack to her. She shook her head.

"No thanks—I don't smoke."

"That's right. Mike told me." He paused. "He told me a lot of things about you, Helen."

"He wrote me about you, too. He said you were the best friend he ever had."

"I'd like to think so. Mike was a great guy in my book. None better. He didn't belong in a crummy hole like that."

"He said the same about you."

"Both of us got a bad break, I guess. Me, I was just a kid who didn't know the score. When I got out of Service, I lay around for a while until my dough was gone, and then I took this job in a bookie joint. I never pulled any strong-arm stuff in my life until the night the place was raided.

"The boss handed me this suitcase, full of dough, and told me to get out the back way. And there was this copper, coming at me with a gun. So I hit him over the head with the suitcase. It was just one of those things—I didn't mean to hurt him, even, just wanted to get out. So the copper ends up with a skull-fracture and dies."

"Mike wrote me about that. You had a tough deal."

"So did he, Helen." Rusty used her first name deliberately and let his voice go soft. It was part of the pitch. "Like I said, I just couldn't figure him out. An honest John like him, up and knocking off his best friend in a payroll stickup. And all alone, too. Then getting rid of the body, so they'd never find it. They never did find Pete Taylor, did they?"

"Please! I don't want to talk about it any more."

"I know how you feel." Rusty took her hand. It was plump and sweaty, and it rested in his like a big warm piece of meat. But she didn't withdraw it, and he went on talking. "It was just circumstantial evidence that pinned it on him, wasn't it?"

"Somebody saw Mike pick Pete up that afternoon," Helen said. "He'd lost his car keys somewhere, and I guess he thought it would be all right if Mike took him over to the factory with the payroll money. That was all the police needed. They got to him before he could get rid of the bloodstains. Of course, he didn't have an alibi. I swore he was home with me all afternoon. They wouldn't buy that. So he went up for ten years."

"And did two, and died," Rusty said. "But he never told how he got rid of the body. He never told where he put the dough."

He could see her nodding in the dimness. "That's right. I guess they beat him up something awful, but he wouldn't tell them a thing."

Rusty was silent for a moment. Then he took a drag on his cigarette and said, "Did he ever tell you?"

Helen Krauss made a noise in her throat. "What do *you* think? I got out of Norton Center because I couldn't stand the way people kept talking about it. I came all the way over here to Hainesville. For two years, I've been working in that lousy hash-house. Does that sound like he told me anything?"

Rusty dropped the cigarette stub on the sidewalk, and its little red eye winked up at him. He stared at the eye as he spoke.

"What would you do if you found that money, Helen? Would you turn it over to the cops?"

She made the noise in her throat again. "What for? To say, 'Thank you,' for putting Mike away and killing him? That's what they did, they killed him. Pneumonia, they told me—I know about their pneumonia! They let him rot in that cell, didn't they?"

"The croaker said it was just flu. I put up such a stink over it, they finally took him down to the Infirmary."

"Well, *I* say they killed him. And *I* say he paid for that money with his life. I'm his widow—it's mine."

"Ours," said Rusty.

Her fingers tightened, and her nails dug into his palms. "He told you where he hid it? Is that it?"

"Just a little. Before they took him away. He was dying, and couldn't talk much. But I heard enough to give me a pretty good hunch. I figured, if I came here when I got out and talked to you, we could put things together and find the dough. Fifty-six gees, he said—even if we split it, that's still a lot of money."

"Why are you cutting me in on it, if you know where it is?" There was an edge of sudden suspicion in her voice, and he sensed it, met it head-on.

"Because, like I told you, he didn't say enough. We'd have to figure out what it means, and then do some hunting. I'm a stranger around here, and people might get suspicious if they saw me snooping. But if you helped, maybe there wouldn't be any need to snoop. Maybe we could go right to it."

"Business deal, is that it?"

Rusty stared at the glowing cigarette butt again. Its red eye winked back at him.

"Not *all* business, Helen. You know how it was with Mike and me. He talked about you all the time. After a while, I got the funniest feeling, like I already knew you—knew you as well as Mike. I wanted to know you better."

He kept his voice down, and he felt her nails against his palm. Suddenly his hand returned the pressure, and his voice broke. "Helen, I don't know, maybe I'm screwy, but I was over two years in that hole. Two years without a woman, you got any idea what that means to a guy?"

"It's been over two years for me, too."

He put his arms around her, forced his lips to hers. It didn't take much forcing. "You got a room?" he whispered.

"Yes, Rusty—I've got a room."

They rose, clinging together. Before moving away, he took a last look at the little winking red eye and crushed it out under his foot.


Another winking red eye burned in the bedroom, and he held the cigarette to one side in his hand so as to keep the light away. He didn't want her to see the disgust in his face.

Maybe she was sleeping now. He hoped so, because it gave him time to think.

So far, everything was working out. Everything *had* to work out, this time. Because before, there had always been foul-ups, somewhere along the line.

Grabbing the satchel full of dough, when the cops raided the bookie joint, had seemed like a good idea at the time. He had thought he could lam out the back door before anyone noticed in the confusion. But he had fouled that one up himself, and landed in stir.

Getting buddy-buddy with that little jerk Mike had been another good idea. It hadn't been long before he knew everything about the payroll caper—everything except where Mike had stashed the loot. Mike never *would* talk about that. It wasn't until he took sick that Rusty could handle him without anybody getting wise. He had made sure Mike was real sick before he put real pressure on.

Even then, the lousy fink hadn't come across—Rusty must have half killed him, right there in the cell. Maybe he'd overdone it, because all he got out of him was the one sentence before the guards showed up.

For a while there, he had wondered if the little quiz show was going to kick back on him. If Mike had pulled out of it, he'd have talked. But Mike hadn't pulled out of it—he had died in the Infirmary before morning, and they had said it was the pneumonia that did it.

So Rusty was safe—and Rusty could make plans.

Up till now, his plans were going through okay. He had never applied for parole—believing it better to sweat out another six months, so he could go free without anybody hanging onto his tail. When they sprung him, he had taken the first bus to Hainesville. He knew where to go because Mike had told him about Helen working in this restaurant.

He hadn't been conning her as to his need for her in the deal. He needed her all right. He needed help, needed her to front for him, so he wouldn't have to look around on his own and arouse curiosity when he asked questions of strangers. That part was straight enough.

But, all along, he had believed what Mike told him about Helen—that she was a good-looking doll, the kind of dame you read about in the paperback books. He had coked himself up on the idea of finding the dough *and* going away with her, of having a real ball.

Well, that part was out.

He made a face in the darkness as he remembered the clammy fat of her, the wheezing and the panting and the clutching. No, he couldn't take much more of that. But he had to go through with it, it was part of the plan. He needed her on his side, and that was the best way to keep her in line.

But now he'd have to decide on the next move. If they found the dough, how could he be sure of her, once they made the split? He didn't want to be tied to this kitchen mechanic, and there had to be a way.

"Darling, are you awake?"

Her voice! And calling him "darling." He shuddered, then controlled himself.

"Yeah." He doused the cigarette in an ash tray.

"Do you feel like talking now?"

"Sure."

"I thought maybe we'd better make plans."

"That's what I like, a practical dame." He forced a smile into his voice. "You're right, baby. The sooner we get to work the better." He sat up and turned to her. "Let's start at the beginning—with what Mike told me, before he died. He said they'd never find the money, they couldn't—because Pete still had it."

For a moment Helen Krauss was silent. Then she said, "Is that all?"

"*All?* What more do you want? It's plain as the nose on your face, isn't it? The dough is hidden with Pete Taylor's body."

He could feel Helen's breath on his shoulder. "Never mind the nose on my face," she said. "I know where that is. But for two years, all the cops in the county haven't been able to find Pete Taylor's body." She sighed. "I thought you really had something, but I guess I was wrong. I should of known."

Rusty grabbed her by the shoulders. "Don't *talk* like that! We've got the answer we need. All we got to do now is figure where to look."

"*Sure.* Real easy!" Her tone dripped sarcasm.

"Think back, now. Where did the cops look?"

"Well, they searched our place, of course. We were living in a rented house, but that didn't stop them. They tore up the whole joint, including the cellar. No dice there."

"Where else?"

"The sheriff's department had men out for a month, searching the woods around Norton's Center. They covered all the old barns and deserted farm-houses too, places like that. They even dragged the lake. Pete Taylor was a bachelor—he had a little shack in town and one out at the lake, too. They ripped them both apart. Nothing doing."

Rusty was silent. "How much time did Mike have between picking up Pete and coming back home again?"

"About three hours."

"Hell, then he couldn't have gone very far, could he? The body must be hid near town."

"That's just how the police figured. I tell you, they did a job. They dug up the ditches, drained the quarry. It was no use."

"Well, there's got to be an answer somewhere. Let's try another angle. Pete Taylor and your husband were pals, right?"

"Yes. Ever since we got married, Mike was thick with him. They got along great together."

"What did they do? I mean, did they drink, play cards or what?"

"Mike wasn't much on the sauce. Mostly, they just hunted and fished. Like I say, Pete Taylor had this shack out at the lake."

"Is that near Norton's Center?"

"About three miles out." Helen sounded impatient. "I know what you're thinking, but it's no good. I tell you, they dug things up all around there.

They even ripped out the floorboards and stuff like that."

"What about sheds, boathouses?"

"Pete Taylor didn't have anything else on his property. When Mike and him went fishing, they borrowed a boat from the neighbors down the line." She sighed again. "Don't think I haven't tried to figure it out. For two years, I've figured, and there just isn't any answer."

Rusty found another cigarette and lit it. "For fifty-six grand, there's got to be an answer," he said. "What happened the day Pete Taylor was killed? Maybe there's something you forgot about."

"I don't know what happened, really. I was at home, and Mike had the day off, so he went downtown to bum around."

"Did he say anything before he left? Was he nervous? Did he act funny?"

"No—I don't think he had anything planned, if that's what you mean. I think it was just one of those things—he found himself in the car with Pete Taylor and all this money, and he just decided to do it.

"Well, they figured it was all planned in advance. They said he knew it was payroll day, and how Pete always went to the bank in his car and got the money in cash. Old Man Huggins at the factory was a queer duck, and he liked to pay that way. Anyway, they say Pete went into the bank, and Mike must have been waiting in the parking lot behind.

"They think he sneaked over and stole Pete's car keys, so, when he came out with the guard, Pete couldn't get started. Mike waited until the guard left, then walked over and noticed Pete, as if it was an accident he happened to be there, and asked what the trouble was.

"Something like that must have happened, because the guy in the parking lot said they talked, and then Pete got into Mike's car and they drove off together. That's all they know, until Mike came home alone almost three hours later."

Rusty nodded. "He came home to you, in the car, alone. What did he say?"

"Nothing much. There wasn't time, I guess. Because the squad car pulled up about two minutes after he got in the house."

"So fast? Who tipped them off?"

"Well, naturally the factory got worried when Pete never showed with the payroll. So Old Man Huggins called the bank, and the bank checked with the cashier and the guard, and somebody went out and asked around in the parking lot. The attendant told about how Pete had left in Mike's car. So they came around here, looking for him."

"Did he put up any struggle?"

"No. He never even said a word. They just took him away. He was in the bathroom, washing up."

"Much dirt on him?" Rusty asked.

"Just his hands, is all. They never found anything they could check up on in their laboratories, or whatever. His shoes were muddy, I think. There was a big fuss because his gun was missing. That was the worst part, his taking the gun with him. They never found it, of course, but they knew he'd owned one, and it was gone. He said he'd lost it months beforehand but they didn't believe him."

"Did *you?*"

"I don't know."

"Anything else?"

"Well, he had a cut on his hand. It was bleeding a little when he came in. I noticed it and asked him about it. He was halfway upstairs, and he said something about rats. Later in court, he told them he'd caught his hand in the window-glass, and that's why there was blood in the car. One of the windows was cracked. They analyzed the blood, it wasn't his type. It checked with Pete Taylor's blood-type record."

Rusty took a deep drag. "But he didn't tell you that when he came home. He said a big rat bit him."

"No—he just said something about rats, I couldn't make out what. In court, the doctor testified he'd gone upstairs and cut his hand open with a razor. They found his razor on the washstand and it was bloody."

"Wait a minute," Rusty said slowly. "He started to tell you some thing about rats. Then he went upstairs and opened up his hand with a razor. Now its beginning to make sense, don't you see? A rat did bite him, maybe when he was getting rid of the body. But if anyone knew that, they'd look for the body some place where there were rats. So he covered up by opening the wound with his razor."

"Maybe so," Helen Krauss said. "But where does that leave us? Are we going to have to search every place with rats in it around Norton's Center?"

"I hope not," Rusty answered. "I hate the damned things. They give me the creeps. Used to see them in the Service, big fat things hanging around the docks. . . ." He snapped his fingers. "Just a second. You say, when Pete and Mike went fishing, they borrowed a boat from the neighbors. Where did the neighbors keep their boat?"

"They had a boathouse."

"Did the cops search there?"

"I don't know—I guess so."

"Maybe they didn't search good enough. Were the neighbors on the property that day?"

"No."

"Are you sure?"

"Sure enough. They were a city couple from Chicago, name of Thomason. Two weeks before the payroll robbery, they got themselves killed in an auto accident on the way home."

"So nobody was around at all, and Mike knew it."

"That's right." Helen's voice was suddenly hoarse. "It was too late in the season anyway, just like now. The lake was deserted. Do you think . . . ?"

"Who's living in the neighbors' place now?" Rusty asked.

"No one, the last I heard. They didn't have any kids, and the real estate man couldn't sell it. Pete Taylor's place is vacant, too. Same reason."

"It adds up—adds up to fifty-six thousand dollars, if I'm right. When could we go?"

"Tomorrow, if you like. It's my day off. We can use my car. Oh, darling, I'm so excited!"

She didn't have to tell him. He could feel it, feel her as she came into his arms. Once more, he had to force himself, had to keep thinking about something else, so that he wouldn't betray how he felt.

He had to keep thinking about the money, and about what he'd do after they found it. He needed the right answer, fast.

He was still thinking when she lay back, and then she suddenly surprised him by asking, "What are you thinking about, darling?"

He opened his mouth and the truth popped out. "The money," he said. "All that money. Twenty-eight gees apiece."

"Does it have to be apiece, darling?"

He hesitated—and then the right answer came. "Of course not—not unless you want it that way." And it wouldn't be. It was still fifty-six thousand, and it would be his after they found it.

All he had to do was rub her out.


If Rusty had any doubts about going through with it, they vanished the next day. He spent the morning and afternoon with her in her room, because he had to. There was no sense in letting them be seen together here in town or anywhere around the lake area.

So he forced himself to stall her, and there was only one way to do that. By the time twilight came, he would have killed her anyway, money or no money, just to be rid of her stinking fat body.

How could Mike have ever figured she was good-looking? He'd never know, any more than he'd ever known what had gone on in the little jerk's head when he suddenly decided to knock off his best friend and steal the dough.

But that wasn't important now—the important thing was to find that black metal box.

Around four o'clock he slipped downstairs and walked around the block. In ten minutes, she picked him up at the corner in her car.

It was a good hour's drive to the lake. She took a detour around Norton Center, and they approached the lake shore by a gravel road. He wanted her to cut the lights, but she said there was no need, because nobody was there anyway. As they scanned the shore Rusty could see she was telling the truth—the lake was dark, deserted, in the early November night.

They parked behind Pete Taylor's shack. At sight of it, Rusty realized that the body couldn't possibly be hidden there. The little rickety structure wouldn't have concealed a dead fly for long. Helen got a flashlight from the car. "I suppose you want to go straight to the boathouse," she said. "It's down this way, to the left. Be careful—the path is slippery."

It was treacherous going in the darkness. Rusty followed her, wondering if now was the time. He could pick up a rock and bash her head in while she had her back to him.

No, he decided, better wait. First see if the dough was there, see if he could find a good place to leave her body. There must be a good place—Mike had found one.

The boathouse stood behind a little pier running out into the lake. Rusty tugged at the door. It was padlocked. "Stand back," he said. He picked up a stone from the bank. The lock was flimsy, rusty with disuse. It broke easily and fell to the ground.

He took the flashlight from her, opened the door and peered in. The beam swept the interior, piercing the darkness. But it wasn't total darkness. Rusty saw the glow of a hundred little red cigarette butts winking up at him, like eyes.

Then, he realized, they *were* eyes. "Rats," he said. "Come on, don't be afraid. Looks like our hunch was right."

Helen moved behind him, and she wasn't afraid. But he had really been talking to himself. He didn't like rats. He was glad when the rodents scattered and disappeared before the flashlight's beam. The sound of footsteps sent them scampering off into the corners, into their burrows beneath the boathouse floor.

The floor! Rusty sent the beam downward. It was concrete, of course. And underneath . . . ?

"Damn it!" he said. "They *must* have been here."

They had—because the once-solid concrete floor was rubble. The pick-axes of the sheriff's men had done a thorough job. "I *told* you," Helen Krauss sighed. "They looked everywhere."

Rusty swept the room with light. There was no boat, nothing stored in corners. The beam bounced off bare walls.

He raised it to the flat roof of the ceiling and caught only the reflection of mica from tar-paper insulation.

"It's no use," Helen told him. "It couldn't be this easy."

"There's still the house," Rusty said. "Come on." He turned and walked out of the place, glad to get away from the rank, fetid animal odor. He turned the flashlight toward the roof.

Then he stopped. "Notice anything?" he said.

"What?"

"The roof. It's higher than the ceiling."

"So what?"

"There could be space up there," Rusty said.

"Yes, but . . ."

"Listen."

She was silent—both of them were silent. In the silence, they could hear the emerging sound. It sounded at first like the patter of rain on the roof, but it wasn't raining, and it wasn't coming from the roof. It was coming from directly underneath—the sound of tiny, scurrying feet between roof and ceiling. The rats were there. The rats and what else?

"Come on," he muttered.

"Where are you going?"

"Up to the house—to find a ladder."

He didn't have to break in, and that was fine. There was a ladder in the shed, and he carried it back. Helen discovered a crowbar. She held the flashlight while he propped the ladder against the wall and climbed up. The crowbar pried off the tar-paper in strips. It came away easily, ripping out from the few nails. Apparently the stuff had been applied in a hurry. A man with only a few hours to work in has to do a fast job.

Underneath the tar-paper, Rusty found timbers. Now the crowbar really came in handy. The boards groaned in anguish, and there were other squeaking sounds as the rats fled down into the cracks along the side walls. Rusty was glad they fled, otherwise he'd never have had the guts to crawl up there through the opening in the boards and look around. Helen handed him the flashlight, and he used it.

He didn't have to look very far.

The black metal box was sitting there right in front of him. Beyond it lay the thing.

Rusty knew it was Pete Taylor, because it had to be, but there was no way of identification. There wasn't a shred of clothing left, or a shred of flesh, either. The rats had picked him clean, picked him down to the bones. All that was left was a skeleton—a skeleton and a black metal box.

Rusty clawed the box closer, opened it. He saw the bills, bulging in stacks. He smelled the money, smelled it even above the sickening fetor. It smelled good, it smelled of perfume and tenderloin steak and the leathery seat-cover aroma of a shiny new car.

"Find anything?" Helen called. Her voice was trembling.

"Yes," he answered, and his voice was trembling just a little too. "I've got it. Hold the ladder, I'm coming down now."

He was coming down now, and that meant it was time—time to act. He handed her the crowbar and the flashlight, but kept his fingers on the side of the black metal box. He wanted to carry that himself. Then, when he put it down on the floor, and she bent over to look at it, he could pick up a piece of concrete rubble and let her have it.

It was going to be easy. He had everything figured out in advance—everything except the part about handing her the crowbar.

That's what she used to hit him with when he got to the bottom of the ladder. . . .

He must have been out for ten minutes, at least. Anyway, it was long enough for her to find the rope somewhere. Maybe she had kept it in the car. Wherever she got it, she knew how to use it. His wrists and ankles hurt almost as much as the back of his head, where the blood was starting to congeal.

He opened his mouth and discovered that it did no good. She had gagged him tightly with a handkerchief. All he could do was lie there in the rubble on the boathouse floor and watch her pick up the black metal box.

She opened it and laughed.

The flashlight was lying on the floor. In its beam, he could see her face quite plainly. She had taken off her glasses, and he discovered the lenses lying shattered on the floor.

Helen Krauss saw what he was staring at and laughed again.

"I don't need those things any more," she told him. "I never did. It was all part of the act, like letting my hair go black and putting on all this weight. For two years now, I've put on this dumb slob routine, just so nobody'd notice me. When I leave town, nobody's going to pay any attention either. Sometimes it's smart to play dumb, you know?"

Rusty made noises underneath the gag. She thought that was funny, too.

"I suppose you're finally beginning to figure it out," she said. "Mike never meant to pull off any payroll job. Pete Taylor and I had been cheating on him for six months, and he had just begun to suspect. I don't know who told him, or what they said.

"He never said anything to me about it beforehand—just went downtown with his gun to find Pete and kill him. Maybe he meant to kill me too. He never even thought about the money at the time. All he knew was that it would be easy to pick Pete up on payroll day.

"I guess he knocked Pete out and drove him down here, and Pete came to before he died and kept saying he was innocent. At least, Mike told me that much when he did come back.

"I never got a chance to ask where he'd taken Pete or what he'd done with the money. The first thing I did, when Mike came home and said what he'd done, was to cover up for myself. I swore it was all a pack of lies, that Pete and I hadn't done anything wrong. I told him we'd take the money and go away together. I was still selling him on that when the cops came.

"I guess he believed me—because he never cracked during the trial. But I didn't get a chance again to ask where he hid the dough. He couldn't write me from prison, because they censor all the mail. So my only out was to wait—wait until he came back, or someone else came. And that's how it worked out."

Rusty tried to say something, but the gag was too tight.

"Why did I conk you one? For the same reason you were going to conk me. Don't try to deny it—that's what you intended to do, wasn't it? I know the way creeps like you think." Her voice was soft.

She smiled down at him. "I know how you get to thinking when you're a prisoner—because I've been a prisoner myself, for two years—prisoner in this big body of mine. I've sweated it out for that money, and now I'm leaving. I'm leaving here, leaving the dumb waitress prison I made for myself. I'm going to shed forty pounds and bleach my hair again and go back to being the old Helen Krauss—with fifty-six grand to live it up with."

Rusty tried just once more. All that came out was a gurgle. "Don't worry," she said, "they won't find me. And they won't find you for a long, long time. I'm putting that lock back on the door when I go. Besides, there's nothing to tie the two of us together. It's clean as a whistle."

She turned, and then Rusty stopped gurgling. He hunched forward and kicked out with his bound feet. They caught her right across the back of the knees, and she went down. Rusty rolled across the rubble and raised his feet from the ground, like a flail. They came down on her stomach, and she let out a gasp.

She fell against the boathouse door, and it slammed shut, her own body tight against it. Rusty began to kick at her face. In a moment the flashlight rolled off into the rubble and went out, so he kicked in the direction of the gasps. After a while, the moaning stopped, and it was silent in the boathouse.

He listened for her breathing and heard no sound. He rolled over to her and pressed his face against something warm and wet. He shivered and drew back, then pressed again. The unbattered area of her flesh was cold.

He rolled over to the side and tried to free his hands. He worked the rope-ends against the jagged edges of rubble, hoping to feel the strands fray and part. His wrists bled, but the rope held. Her body was wedged against the door, holding it shut—holding him here in the rank darkness.

Rusty knew he had to move her, had to get the door open fast. He had to get out of here. He began to butt his head against her, trying to move her—but she was too solid, too heavy, to budge. He banged into the money box and tried to gurgle at her from under the gag, tried to tell her that she must get up and let them out, that they were both in prison together now, and the money didn't matter. It was all a mistake, he hadn't meant to hurt her or anyone, he just wanted to get out.

But he didn't get out.

After a little while, the rats came back.

# A TASTE OF PARADISE

*Bill Pronzini*

J an and I met the Archersons at the Hotel Kolekole in Kailua Kona, on
the first evening of our Hawaiian vacation. We'd booked four days on
the Big Island, five on Maui, four on Kauai, and three and a half at Waikiki
Beach on Oahu. It would mean a lot of shunting around, packing and
unpacking, but it was our first and probably last visit to Hawaii and we had
decided to see as many of the islands as we could. We'd saved three years
for this trip—a second honeymoon we'd been promising ourselves for a
long time—and we were determined to get the absolute most out of it.

Our room was small and faced inland; it was all we could afford at a
luxury hotel like the Kolekole. So in order to sit and look at the ocean, we
had to go down to the rocky, black-sand beach or to a roofed but open-
sided lanai bar that overlooked the beach. The lanai bar was where we met
Larry and Brenda Archerson. They were at the next table when we sat
down for drinks before dinner, and Brenda was sipping a pale green drink in
a tall glass. Jan is naturally friendly and curious and she asked Brenda what
the drink was—something called an Emerald Bay, a specialty of the hotel
that contained rum and crème de menthe and half a dozen other ingredi-
ents—and before long the four of us were chatting back and forth. They
were about our age, and easy to talk to, and when they invited us to join
them we agreed without hesitation.

It was their first trip to Hawaii too, and the same sort of dream vacation
as ours: "I've wanted to come here for thirty years," Brenda said, "ever since
I first saw Elvis in *Blue Hawaii*." So we had that in common. But unlike us,
they were traveling first-class. They'd spent a week in one of the most
exclusive hotels on Maui, and had a suite here at the Kolekole, and would
be staying in the islands for total of five weeks. They were even going to
spend a few days on Molokai, where Father Damien had founded his lepers'
colony over a hundred years ago.

Larry told us all of this in an offhand, joking way—not at all flaunting the fact that they were obviously well-off. He was a tall, beefy fellow, losing his hair as I was and compensating for it with a thick brush moustache. Brenda was a big-boned blond with pretty gray eyes. They both wore loud Hawaiian shirts and flower leis, and Brenda had a pale pink flower—a hibiscus blossom, she told Jan—in her hair. It was plain that they doted on each other and plain that they were having the time of their lives. They kept exchanging grins and winks, touching hands, kissing every now and then like newlyweds. It was infectious. We weren't with them ten minutes before Jan and I found ourselves holding hands too.

They were from Milwaukee, where they were about to open a luxury catering service. "Another lifelong dream," Brenda said. Which gave us something else in common, in an indirect way. Jan and I own a small restaurant in Coeur d'Alene, Carpenter's Steakhouse, which we'd built into a fairly successful business over the past twenty years. Our daughter Lynn was managing it for us while we were in Hawaii.

We talked with the Archersons about the pros and cons of the food business and had another round of drinks which Larry insisted on paying for. When the drinks arrived he lifted his mai tai and said, "*Aloha nui kakou,* folks."

"That's an old Hawaiian toast," Brenda explained. "It means to your good health, or something like that. Larry is a magnet for Hawaiian words and phrases. I swear he'll be able to write a tourist phrasebook by the time we leave the islands."

"Maybe I will too, *kuu ipo.*"

She wrinkled her nose at him, then leaned over and nipped his ear. "*Kuu ipo* means sweetheart," she said to us.

When we finished our second round of drinks Larry asked, "You folks haven't had dinner yet, have you?"

We said we hadn't.

"Well then, why don't you join us in the Garden Court. Their mahimahi is out of this world. Our treat—what do you say?"

Jan seemed willing, so I said, "Fine with us. But let's make it Dutch treat."

"Nonsense. I invited you, that makes you our guests. No arguments, now—I never argue on an empty stomach."

The food was outstanding. So was the wine Larry selected to go with it, a rich French chardonnay. The Garden Court was open-sided like the lanai bar and the night breeze had a warm, velvety feel, heavy with the scents of hibiscus and plumeria. The moon, huge and near full, made the ocean look as though it were overlaid with a sheet of gold.

"Is this living or is this living?" Larry said over coffee and Kahlúa.

"It's a taste of paradise," Jan said.

"It *is* paradise. Great place, great food, great drinks, great company. What more could anybody want?"

"Well, I can think of one thing," Brenda said with a leer.

Larry winked at me. "That's another great thing about the tropics, Dick. It puts a new spark in your love life."

"I can use a spark," I said. "I think a couple of my plugs are shot."

Jan cracked me on the arm and we all laughed.

"So what are you folks doing tomorrow?" Larry asked. "Any plans?"

"Well, we thought we'd either drive down to the Volcanoes National Park or explore the northern part of the island."

"We're day-tripping up north ourselves—Waimea, Waipio Valley, the Kohala Coast. How about coming along with us?"

"Well . . ."

"Come on, it'll be fun. We rented a Caddy and there's plenty of room. You can both just sit back and relax and soak up the sights."

"Jan? Okay with you?"

She nodded, and Larry said, "Terrific. Let's get an early start—breakfast at seven, on the road by eight. That isn't too early for you folks? No? Good, then it's settled."

When the check came I offered again to pay half. He wouldn't hear of it. As we left the restaurant, Brenda said she felt like going dancing and Larry said that was a fine idea, how about making it a foursome? Jan and I begged off. It had been a long day, as travel days always are, and we were both ready for bed.

In our room Jan asked, "What do you think of them?"

"Likable and fun to be with," I said. "But exhausting. Where do they get all their energy?"

"I wish I knew."

"Larry's a little pushy. We'll have to make sure he doesn't talk us into anything we don't want to do." I paused. "You know, there's something odd about the way they act together. It's more than just being on a dream vacation, having a good time, but I can't quite put my finger on it . . ."

"They're like a couple of kids with a big secret," Jan said. "They're so excited they're ready to burst."

We've been married for nearly thirty years and we often have similar impressions and perceptions. Sometimes it amazes me just how closely our minds work.

"That's it," I said. "That's it exactly."


The trip to the northern part of the island was enjoyable, if wearying. Larry and Brenda did most of the talking, Larry playing tour guide and unraveling an endless string of facts about Hawaii's history, geography, flora, and fauna. We spent a good part of the morning in the rustic little town of Waimea, in the saddle between Kohala Mountain and the towering Mauna Kea—the seat of the Parker Ranch, the largest individually owned cattle ranch in the United States. It was lunchtime when we finished rubbing elbows with Hawaiian cowboys and shopping for native crafts, and Brenda suggested we buy sandwich fixings and a bottle of wine and find someplace to have a picnic.

Larry wanted to hike out to the rim of the Waipio Valley and picnic there, but the rest of us weren't up to a long walk. So we drove up into the mountains on the Kawaihae road. When the road leveled out across a long plateau we might have been in California or the Pacific Northwest: rolling fields, cattle, thick stands of pine. In the middle of one of the wooded sections, Larry slowed and then pulled off onto the verge.

"Down there by that stream," he said. "Now that's a perfect spot for a picnic."

Brenda wasn't so sure. "You think it's safe? Looks like a lot of brush and grass to wade through. . . ."

He laughed. "Don't worry, there aren't any wild animals up here to bother us."

"What about creepy-crawlies?"

"Nope. No poisonous snakes or spiders on any of the Hawaiian islands."

"You sure about that?"

"I'm sure, *kuu ipo*. The guidebooks never lie."

We had our picnic, and all through it Larry and Brenda nuzzled and necked and cast little knowing glances at each other. Once he whispered something in her ear that made her laugh raucously and say, "Oh, you're wicked!" Their behavior had seemed charming last night, but today it was making both Jan and me uncomfortable. Fifty-year-old adults who act like conspiratorial teenagers seem ludicrous after you've spent enough time in their company.

Kawaihae Bay was beautiful, and the clifftop view from Upolu Point was breathtaking. On the way back down the coast we stopped at a two-hundred-year-old temple built by King Kamehameha, and at the white-sand Hapuna Beach where Jan fed the remains of our picnic to the dozens of stray cats that lived there. It was after five when we got back to Kailua Kona.

The Archersons insisted again that we have dinner with them and wouldn't take no for an answer. So we stayed at the Kolekole long enough to change clothes and then went out to a restaurant that specialized in luau-style roast pork. And when we were finished eating, back we went to the hotel and up to their suite. They had a private terrace and it was the perfect place, Brenda said, to watch one of the glorious Hawaiian sunsets.

Larry brought out a bottle of Kahlúa, and when he finished pouring drinks he raised his glass in another toast. "To our new *aikane*, Jan and Dick."

"*Aikane* means good friends," Brenda said.

Jan and I drank, but my heart wasn't in it and I could tell that hers wasn't either. The Archersons were wearing thin on both of us.

The evening was a reprise of yesterday's: not too hot, with a soft breeze carrying the scent of exotic flowers. Surfers played on the waves offshore. The sunset was spectacular, with fiery reds and oranges, but it didn't last long enough to suit me.

Brenda sighed elaborately as darkness closed down. "Almost the end of another perfect day. Time goes by so quickly out here, doesn't it, Jan?"

"Yes it does."

Larry said, "That's why you have to get the most out of each day in paradise. So what'll we do tomorrow? Head down to see the volcanoes, check out the lava flows?"

"There's a road called Chain of Craters that's wonderful," Brenda said. "It goes right out over the flows and at the end there's a place where you can actually walk on the lava. Parts of it are still *hot!*"

I said, "Yes, we've been looking forward to seeing the volcano area. But since you've already been there, I think we'll just drive down by ourselves in the morning—"

"No, no, we'll drive you down. We don't mind seeing it all again, do we, Brenda?"

"I sure don't. I'd love to see it again."

"Larry, I don't mean this to sound ungrateful, but Jan and I would really like some time to ourselves—"

"Look at that moon coming up, will you? It's as big as a Halloween pumpkin."

It was, but I couldn't enjoy it now. I tried again to say my piece, and again he interrupted me.

"Nothing like the moons we get back home in Wisconsin," he said. He put his arm around Brenda's shoulders and nuzzled her neck. "Is it, pet? Nothing at all like a Wisconsin moon."

She didn't answer. Surprisingly, her face scrunched up and her eyes glistened and I thought for a moment she would burst into tears.

Jan said, "Why, Brenda, what's the matter?"

"It's my fault," Larry said ruefully. "I used to call her that all the time, but since the accident . . . well, I try to remember not to but sometimes it just slips out."

"Call her what? Pet?"

He nodded. "Makes her think of her babies."

"Babies? But I thought you didn't have children."

"We don't. Brenda, honey, I'm sorry. We'll talk about something else . . ."

"No, it's all right." She dried her eyes on a Kleenex and then said to Jan and me, "My babies were Lhasa apsos. Brother and sister—Hansel and Gretel."

"Oh," Jan said, "dogs."

"Not just dogs—the sweetest, most gentle . . ." Brenda snuffled again. "I miss them terribly, even after six months."

"What happened to them?"

"They died in the fire, the poor babies. We buried them at Shady Acres. That's a nice name for a pet cemetery, don't you think? Shady Acres?"

"What kind of fire was it?"

"That's right, we didn't tell you, did we? Our house burned down six months ago. Right to the ground while we were at a party at a friend's place."

"Oh, that's *awful*. A total loss?"

"Everything we owned," Larry said. "It's a good thing we had insurance."

"How did it happen?"

"Well, the official verdict was that Mrs. Cooley fell asleep with a lighted cigarette in her hand."

I said, "Oh, so there was someone in the house besides the dogs. She woke up in time and managed to get out safely, this Mrs. Cooley?"

"No, she died too."

Jan and I looked at each other.

"Smoke inhalation, they said. The way it looked, she woke up all right and tried to get out, but the smoke got her before she could. They found her by the front door."

"Hansel and Gretel were trapped in the kitchen," Brenda said. "She was so selfish—she just tried to save herself."

Jan made a throat-clearing sound. "You sound as though you didn't like this woman very much."

"We didn't. She was an old witch."

"Then why did you let her stay in your house?"

"She paid us rent. Not much just a pittance."

"But if you didn't like her—"

"She was my mother," Brenda said.

Far below, on the lanai bar, the hotel musicians began to play ukuleles and sing a lilting Hawaiian song. Brenda leaned forward, listening, smiling dreamily. "That's 'Maui No Ka Oi,'" she said. "One of my all-time favorites."

Larry was watching Jan and me. He said, "Mrs. Cooley really was an awful woman, no kidding. Mean, carping—and stingy as hell. She knew how much we wanted to start our catering business but she just wouldn't let us have the money. If she hadn't died in the fire . . . well, we wouldn't be here with you nice folks. Funny the way things happen sometimes, isn't it?"

Neither Jan nor I said anything. Instead we got to our feet, almost as one.

"Hey," Larry said, "you're not leaving?"

I said yes, we were leaving.

"But the night's young. I thought maybe we'd go dancing, take in one of the Polynesian revues—"

"It's been a long day."

"Sure, I understand. You folks still have some jet lag too, I'll bet. Get plenty of sleep and call us when you wake up, then we'll all go have breakfast before we head for the volcanoes."

They walked us to the door. Brenda said, "Sleep tight, you lovely people," and then we were alone in the hallway.

We didn't go to our room; instead we went to the small, quiet lobby bar for drinks we both badly needed. When the drinks came, Jan spoke for the first time since we'd left the Archersons. "My God," she said, "I had no idea they were like that—so cold and insensitive under all that bubbly charm. Crying over a pair of dogs and not even a kind word for her mother.

They're actually glad the poor woman is dead."

"More than glad. And much worse than insensitive."

"What do you mean?"

"You know what I mean."

"You don't think they—"

"That's just what I think. What we both think."

"Her own mother?"

"Yes. They arranged that fire somehow so Mrs. Cooley would be caught in it, and sacrificed their dogs so it would look even more like an accident."

"For her money," Jan said slowly. "So they could start their catering business."

"Yes."

"Dick . . . we can't just ignore this. We've got to *do* something."

"What would you suggest?"

"I don't know, contact the police in Milwaukee . . ."

"And tell them what that can be proven? The Archersons didn't admit anything incriminating to us. Besides, there must have been an investigation at the time. If there'd been any evidence against them, they wouldn't have gotten Mrs. Cooley's money and they wouldn't be here celebrating."

"But that means they'll get away with it, with cold-blooded murder!"

"Jan, they already have. And they're proud of it, proud of their own cleverness. I'll tell you another thing I think. I think they contrived to tell us the story on purpose, with just enough hints so we'd figure out the truth."

"Why would they do that?"

"The same reason they latched onto us, convinced themselves we're kindred spirits. The same reason they're so damned eager. They're looking for somebody to share their secret with."

"Dear God."

We were silent after that. The tropical night was no longer soft; the air had a close, sticky feel. The smell of hibiscus and plumeria had turned cloyingly sweet. I swallowed some of my drink, and it tasted bitter. Paradise tasted bitter now, the way it must have to Adam after Eve bit into the forbidden fruit.

The guidebooks do lie, I thought. There are serpents in this Eden, too.

Early the next morning, very early, we checked out of the Kolekole and took the first inter-island flight to Honolulu and then the first plane home.

# BITS

*Mat Coward*

M any things led to the killing of Ian Unwin, but the beginning was when Tony Shaw's leather jacket was stolen in a pub near King's Cross. He'd stupidly left it unattended for about two minutes, while he crossed the uncrowded lounge bar to buy some cigarettes from a machine by the Gents. When he got back, his jacket was gone and with it his wallet, chequebook, cheque guarantee card, ATM card, credit cards, union membership card—the lot, the whole pack.

Tony made all the right phone calls, cancelled everything, and so was very annoyed when his next current account statement showed that several of the missing cheques had been used.

He left the town hall half an hour early that afternoon, and asked to see the manager at his local bank. After a longish wait, a woman—a girl really, she looked about twelve—appeared from behind a mirror-glassed door, wearing an expression which hovered between irritation and nervousness.

"Can I help you, please?"

"Are you the manager?"

"I'm your Personal Branch Banker," said the girl, her intonation suggesting that the words held no individual meaning for her.

Tony, wondering how she could be his Personal Branch Banker when she hadn't even asked his name yet, explained about the cheques which had been cashed after he'd reported them stolen.

His Personal Branch Banker took down his details, including home and work phone numbers, and then spent ten minutes fiddling at a computer which she had obviously not been trained to use. Eventually she must have elicited an answer of some sort, for she turned back to Tony and said, "Mr. Shaw, is it?"

Tony said it still was.

"Um—actually, Mr. Shaw, are you aware that your account currently shows an unauthorised negative balance of nine hundred pounds?"

"Oh, for Christ's sake," he groaned, and began explaining it all again.


A week later he'd heard nothing, and so flexi-timed another half hour for a return match. The Personal Branch Banker had changed sex, was now a twelve-year-old boy, and had never heard of Mr. Shaw or his fugitive cheques. Once more, Tony went through the story, but it wasn't until six weeks, eleven letters and seven phone calls to head office later that the stain on his account was expunged. The penultimate conversation included the following exchange:

*Senior Account Supervisor (London):* Mr. Shaw, the cheques in question appear to bear the signature "D. Duck." Is that your normal form of signature, can you confirm?

*Tony:* My normal form of signature is "A. L. Shaw."

*Senior Account Supervisor (London):* Ah, right. OK, yeah.

Over the next few months, Tony thought about The Donald Duck Business quite a lot. Thinking about things quite a lot was one of the things he did most. He enjoyed thinking, sorting, planning, puzzling things out. He lived alone, had no noticeable family, either immediate or extended, and one of the reasons he liked living alone was so that he had time to think about things.

He made a list, indexed it on his List of Lists, and filed it in his List Box. The list said:

1. Seeing the manager was a waste of time. No one sees their bank managers these days—indeed, don't even have managers to see.

2. Everything is computers these days. Nobody actually knows anyone. Not like when I was a kid.

3. I have never met my landlord, Mr. Chipping. I met his agent once, when I moved in, and all dealings since have been by post or by messages on answering machines.

4. I have never actually met most of the people with whom I am in regular contact at work. They work in different buildings, in different parts of the borough, and even many of those in the same building communicate by phone, fax, or internal mail.

5. Although I am only forty, the world I inhabit now is already a different planet to the one I was born on. What will it be like when I am sixty?

6. The world today exists in bits. The old cow was right when she said,

"There is no such thing as society." Modern urban life for the upper working/lower-middle class (i.e. most of us) is fragmented, automated, alienated.

7. From what I have heard, it is worse in the suburbs. Here in West Hampstead, people do at least occasionally say "Hi" to each other, in passing. Out in Metroland, apparently, nobody knows their neighbours, nobody talks to anybody, nobody notices anything—or if they do notice, they don't give a toss.

He named the file "Bits." He found what it told him of life faintly shocking, rather sad in a generalised way, but not personally discomfiting. Tony had given up on life—on LIFE, anyway—long ago; not out of bitterness or depression or frustration, but just because he had discovered that his wants and ambitions were modest ones.

He would be quite happy—really, perfectly content—to spend the rest of his days sitting in a comfortable armchair, with a book, a glass of whisky, a cigarette, and the knowledge that he would always have somewhere warm to sleep.

Not that Tony was a hermit. He lived a fairly solitary life, true, but he didn't actively shun other people—he just wasn't addicted to them. He preferred human company to be rationed, on his terms. Most of the time he was happy at home, listening to blues on his CD, watching the telly, or reading (SF or fantasy mostly, but only the good stuff). Once a week, however—or more, he was no slave to routine—he would visit a pub. There were several decent ones in walking distance.

And once or twice a year, in one of these casually cheerful places, he would get off with a woman. The last few had been, he readily acknowledged to himself, just a bit on the ropy side. He was no great catch, after all—an ordinary bloke, ordinary looking—and though at one time he had been able to impress young girls with his quiet, worldly maturity, he found that the present young generation had little interest in sex. They all worked in banks.

Never mind: he got by. He wasn't a superstud, and he wasn't celibate. He was fine, he got by.

Tony had no close friends, as such; had never seen the need for them. Instead, he had drinking companions—not rowdy, big boozers, more like playing-the-quiz-machine, doing-the-crossword-in-the-evening-paper, moaning-about-the-tube companions. The sort of people who drift in and out of the margins of each other's lives, and only notice that one of their number isn't around any more during nostalgically drunken evenings of "Whatever happened to old wossname . . . ?"

Work didn't come into it. He'd been in the same department since leaving school at fifteen, so his salary and conditions of service were quite acceptable. He didn't mind the job particularly, it wasn't hard or dangerous or painfully boring, but he was always glad to get away from it. And he did have a dream.

Tony Shaw dreamed of ER/VR: Early Retirement/Voluntary Redundancy. As municipal government throughout the nation disintegrated, Tony dreamed of his fiftieth birthday, when his eternally cost-cutting employers would gratefully relieve him and themselves of the burden of his employment. At fifty, he would be free, with a pension and a small lump sum, and a reasonable expectation of enough remaining years in which to enjoy them. Quietly; securely.

Even then, though, at the back of his mind, was a sharp splinter of perfect self-knowledge: in common, he imagined, with many people whose ambitions were small, his ruthlessness in pursuing them could be, if necessary, unlimited. After all, he didn't ask for much—he was surely entitled to the little he did ask for?

Tony found that thought comforting; then, and later.


Five years after the Donald Duck Business, something terrible happened to Tony's plans. The council announced that the current round of ER/VR would be the last. Management had decided that their staff reduction exercises had reached a point where the cost of further redundancies would be greater than the cost of maintaining existing staffing levels.

Tony was still only forty-five. There was no way he could escape now. And, according to the memo he read and re-read, no way he could escape *ever*.

There *had* to be! That was all, there just *had* to be. One thing was certain, he couldn't carry on spending eight hours a day away from his chair, his book, his whisky, seven days a week, forty-six weeks a year, for the next twenty years!

Impossible. He'd been dreaming of early retirement for almost half his working life. If the realisation of his dream, his modest dream, was not to be given to him, then he would have to find a way to take it.

He'd have to, that's all.

Almost wild with anger—in a rare, scorching rage—Tony Shaw literally ran from his office. It wasn't quite half-ten in the morning, but he didn't tell anyone where he was going, he didn't leave any messages, he didn't open the rest of his post or switch off his terminal. He just ran: to the lift, out of the door, down the street, into the Underground.

And when he stopped running, he was in a pub near Hampstead station.

He was, at least, in sufficient command of his senses to have come to this pub, and not to the one he preferred, further up the hill, but which he had had to abandon a few weeks earlier. That was the pub where Michelle drank.

She probably wouldn't be there so early in the day, but he couldn't take the risk. Michelle had become a real nuisance, a one-night stand that had turned into something perilously close to "a relationship." That was what she called it; that was what she wanted.

Tony was always honest with his women. He never pretended to be looking for love, never pretended to be interested in anything but a brief interlude of mutually refreshing sex. It wasn't his fault, then, that Michelle had failed to understand the rules of engagement—or of non-engagement.

She was a good bit younger than him (mid-thirties, he guessed, though she didn't say, and he never asked) and considerably better-looking than he'd lately been used to. Tony had enjoyed being with her, once, even twice, but somehow she'd got it into her head that they were a couple. Michelle's skin was thick as well as pretty, and no amount of straight talking rid her of her troublesome illusions. When Tony would gently but firmly explain that, sorry, he didn't feel the same way about her as she apparently felt about him, she'd just smile and say, "That's OK. I know how hard men find it to talk about their emotions. It's your upbringing."

Thus it was that Tony now sat in a pub he didn't much care for, trying to find a way round a problem which was even more threatening than the Michelle situation.

It didn't take him long. All he had to do, after all, was give his subconscious a bit of a stir, and then decide if he could stomach what came to the surface.

Halfway though his second pint, he decided he could.

Which meant that he had lists to see to: to begin with, one to steal and one to make.

The stolen list—the details of all those who had been accepted for the current, final round of ER/VR—was not hard to come by. In fact, he didn't even have to leave his office; just press a few keys on his computer, and make an educated guess or two.

When the system had been installed, the computer company woman who trained the council staff in its use had told everybody the same thing: "Give yourself a password that isn't easy to guess, something random. Not your name, for instance." But she had taken a shine to Tony, who was a good pupil, and had added to him, confidentially, "Six months from now, ninety-five per cent of the passwords in this building will be user's names. It's always the same—people forget their original term, and end up thinking *What the hell, there's nothing confidential here, anyway.* You see if I'm not right."

She was right.

Back home, a printout of the stolen list safely in his pocket, Tony made another list. He headed it OPERATION POD, in honour of one of his all-time favorite SF films:

1. Male, obviously.
2. Roughly same age (few years either side might not matter).
3. Good deal—big pension and lump sum—so, long service.
4. Home owner, preferably paid off mortgage.
5. No visible family.
6. Suburban address.
7. Good sick record, so not visiting doctor, etc. . . . often enough to be known.

Comparing the two lists quickly eliminated most of the retirers, but left six possibles; six potential hosts, as Tony thought of them.


The next stage of selection required some footslogging, not just paper shuffling.

In truth, Ian Unwin looked good to Tony right from the start, but he nonetheless worked methodically through his short list, with the aid, naturally, of another list of criteria:

1. Physical appearance: similar, or easily adapted to (i.e. long hair doesn't matter, but baldness is no good; slight weight gain or loss would be feasible, but height must be close).
2. Position of house (definitely not flat or maisonette, bungalow best of all). As few neighbours as possible.

3. *Must have garden*—must not be overlooked by neighbours' windows.

4. Host's routine, weekends, evenings, etc. . . . Make sure, as far as possible, no regular visitors (including lovers, relatives), and no regular outings—hobbies, groups, church, etc.

All this took time; he could have spent forever on it, of course, checking and double-checking, being ultra-cautious. But he didn't have forever. As it was, Tony used up his remaining fortnight of annual leave watching and eliminating. And in the end, as he had suspected at the beginning, it was Ian Unwin who passed all the tests most satisfactorily.

The clincher came on his third secret visit to the Ruislip cul-de-sac, bordering a park, in which Ian lived. Ian's only next-door neighbour had had a For Sale sign in the garden on Tony's first visit. That sign now read "Sold."

"Well then, Ian," said Tony to the silent street. "You're it."


Tony handed in his notice at work—having now, he explained to his boss, given up all hope of ever securing a decent ER/VR deal.

Sonia, the friendly, overworked young woman who had been his supervisor for the last eighteen months, was only too pleased to give him the reference he asked for, and to make it one that glowed like the sun above. A quiet guy, not very matey, but that was his business. He was always pleasant enough, and everyone knew he was a good worker.

"Got something lined up, Tony?" she asked, having made the appropriate noises about how much he'd be missed.

"Well, you know," he said. "Fingers crossed."

"Local government?"

He made a wry face. "No thanks! A book shop, as it happens. Old schoolmate, looking for a manager. While *he* takes early retirement, if you're into irony."

She smiled. "A book shop, how lovely! I quite envy you. Local?"

"No. Nottingham, in fact. Cheap property, clean air. Good beer. I fancied a real change." He grinned; he could quite fancy her, if it wasn't for the obvious complications. "Mid-life crisis, I expect."

Sonia laughed. "So it really is goodbye, then."

"Looks like it," Tony agreed.

He had to have a leaving do, of course. Avoiding it would have involved too much fuss. A photocopied note in the internal mail advertised his availability for farewell drinks in the pub opposite the town hall on his last

154    *Bits*

Friday. Everyone attended—because he wasn't disliked—but none took their coats off, because none could really call him a friend. Souvenir photos were taken (and taken great pains with, by the office's resident camera bore), and a presentation cheque (topped up by Sonia, to prevent it appearing insultingly small) was duly presented.

Tony gave the same story about the Nottingham book shop to a few pub acquaintances, and, by letter, to his landlord. He was a little put out when the landlord rang to ask for a forwarding address, but couldn't very well refuse without seeming suspicious.

"Better make it care of the shop for now, Mr. Chipping," he said, reaching for a guide to the second-hand book shops of England with his spare hand. "Hang on, I've got it here somewhere."


While working out his notice, he'd got to know Ian Unwin. This was essential, perhaps a little risky, but certainly not difficult. They turned out to have quite a bit in common. Ian, like Tony, was a loner. More so, if anything, really rather withdrawn, and Tony soon spotted one of the reasons why: Ian was an unadmitted homosexual.

"Great," thought Tony. "He'll be glad of some sympathetic company. Discussing books, playing chess." But he was careful to make it clear to Ian that he was a confirmed, if unprejudiced, heterosexual, so as not to arouse in the other any fears of being confronted with a decision about himself.

Their friendship proceeded very nicely, initially in lunch-hour pub sessions, and later at the bungalow in Ruislip; and after a month or so, when Tony felt he knew as much about Ian as he was ever likely to learn, or to need, he killed him.

That, too, was delightfully simple.

"Look, mate, sorry about this, but I really think I'm too pissed to make that last bus. You do realise that's our second bottle of Scotch we're half way through?"

"No probs," said Ian—with some difficulty; though he didn't know it, he'd drunk at least four times as much as Tony. "Spare room, sofa, bath, whatever you like."

"Good man," said Tony. "In which case . . ." and he filled his host's glass to the top, one more time.

That was all it took. Getting Ian's unconscious frame through the hall and into the bath was hard work, but Tony was both fit and determined. Dragging the drowned body back out of the bath and out through the kitchen door was more exhausting than he'd anticipated, but in the end it was done.

As he dug the grave in the secluded, maturely hedged garden (first place the police would look, of course, but in this instance they wouldn't be look- ing—no disappearance, no inquiry), Tony comforted himself with the thought that, from what he knew of his late friend, Ian would probably rather be dead, given the choice. He'd had no life to speak of, and seemed to harbour no hopes of ever finding one. Couldn't even admit what he was looking for, poor sod.

"So all I've really done," Tony thought, patting the earth back into place and covering the spot with a garden bench, "is put to sleep a sad old dog who had no use for his life, and in the process secure for myself—a deserv- ing and appreciative person—everything my own modest heart has ever longed for. A comfortable house full of books, and nothing to do all day but read them."

The first potential crisis came quite soon: some kind of chesty, throaty thing that just wouldn't let go.

Well, why not? If anyone was entitled to be somewhat under the weather, it was him. He'd been through a lot. He'd been under a consider- able strain.

Living as someone else was a little strange, Tony found, even though he had prepared himself for it so well. Bound to be, really. Not his fault, just one of those things. Even so, he eventually surrendered to the inevitable, and nervously, reluctantly, made an appointment with his—with Ian's—GP.

In the event, he could hardly contain his triumphant laughter as he left the doctor's surgery, clutching a prescription. *Bits!* The whole world was in bits! Even if there had been any risk of the doctor spotting him as an impostor, the question hadn't arisen—because the doctor had *never once taken her eyes off her computer screen!* Not even when she'd asked him if he smoked, and he'd said, "Yes, if you must know."

All the same, he took the prescription to a pharmacist a couple of bus stops away, just to be on the safe side, but really: how could a scheme like his fail, in a world like this?

Other minor alarms, potentially tricky encounters with petty officialdom, came and went, but Tony didn't panic. He always kept an emergency plan in reserve, but never needed it; and, as time went on, he began to realise that he had actually done it. He had never wanted much from life, and now he'd got it all.

Got it, and held it.


Tony was aware of a slight change in his personality. Cautiously, always cautiously, but undeniably, he was . . . well, yes, he was coming out of his shell.

The suburbs, it transpired, were not as cold and unwelcoming as he had been led to believe. Or at least, not in this cul-de-sac they weren't. Not, anyway, since his—Ian's—next-door neighbour had been replaced by June Welsh.

Never having played the romantic role, it had taken Tony a while to realise that June's almost daily poppings-round—to ask about refuse collections, to get the name of a reliable newsagent, to borrow a screwdriver— were more frequent than might be considered normal.

After they had slept together for the first time—at her place; he hadn't completely abandoned his defences—thoughts of Michelle, the clinging nuisance from his former life, drifted into his mind. But this was different. Well, *he* was different: a different name, a different life. Perhaps it was natural that he should want different things now. Want more, even.

And June was definitely different. Not as obviously attractive as Michelle, older for one thing, about Tony's age; but more of a woman, in other ways. A woman of some refinement. Not posh, not stuck-up, but thoughtful.

Quiet, like him. She was a divorcee—of a few year's standing, he gathered. Her husband had obviously hurt her (she didn't say how, and he didn't ask), and she had an air about her of emotional convalescence. And she was clearly keen on Tony.

He began to wonder if, after all, there was any real reason why he should continue to confine himself to one-night stands. Maybe, at his time of life, safe in his new existence, a steady lover might be just the thing.

He could even justify it on security grounds, without too much casuistry. A regular sexual outlet would certainly reduce the temptation to put his secret at risk through unwise pick-ups in local pubs where, for all he knew, someone might dimly recall that his face didn't fit his name. His sexual lifestyle had previously been a matter of choice, of personal taste, but now—in the post-Ianian period—other considerations had to take precedence.

And so June and Tony's second quiet, companionable coupling, a week after the less significant first, took place in Ian Unwin's handsome double bed (the bed in which Ian himself had been conceived, he had told Tony, by his now long-dead parents), and after that things took their course.

Life settled down. Marriage was never spoken of. No need, thought Tony, when the holy estate of next door neighbourness was already so ideal.

There were nasty moments, inevitably. He did not think of himself as a naturally dishonest man, and living a lie, in the most literal sense of the cliche, did not come easily to him. When June told him, her grey-blond head on his chest, "Ian, you just can't imagine how happy I am we found each other," he longed to say: "It's Tony. Call me Tony."

The answering machine incident was unfortunate. He had left Ian's message on the tape, and kept the machine on at all times, as one more barrier against danger. The phone rarely rang. Tony did nothing to encourage calls, and clearly Ian—despite his, in retrospect, rather pathetic investment—was not the sort who had come home daily to a spool full of urgency.

When the phone did ring that time, just as he was letting June in through the front door, it made his heart jump.

She listened to the outgoing message (there was no incoming message; a wrong number, or a frustrated salesman, presumably) with her head cocked, and then said, "Your voice sounds really weird on that. It's not like you at all."

He shrugged. "I bet even Frank Sinatra would sound like a prat on one of those things." They laughed, and the moment soon passed, but from then on Tony kept the machine's monitor volume set at zero.


Three-quarters of a year of growing happiness. Not just contentment; he was sure he knew the difference now—this was happiness.

He had his leisure, his security, his house to grow old in, his books, Ian's lump sum and pension. He had his whisky (here on the table beside him right now), he had everything he'd always dreamed of—and as if all the above wasn't more than enough, he had love as well.

Then, one night, Tony Shaw saw something on the television that revealed to him the shocking discovery that life wasn't only unfair, it was outrageously unreasonable. That no matter how modest a man's wishes, he could still never be allowed to enjoy them in peace.

There had been a row, a minor tiff. So minor, indeed, that it had ended not in shouting, but with a peck on the cheek, and the suggestion that "It might be better if we eat separately tonight, Ian, love. I'll see you in the morning."

Tony sat now, vaguely looking at the TV, planning the exact wording of the telephonic apology he would shortly make, when a face on the screen suddenly commanded his full attention.

It was unmistakably his face, in one of the photographs, the clear, professional-quality photographs, taken at his town hall leaving do.

It was quickly replaced by a moving picture of Michelle. Clinging, thick-skinned, telegenic Michelle. Tony zapped up the sound.

" . . . leaving his fiancée, Michelle Knight, fearing the worst. Michelle: the most awful thing must be just not knowing?"

He killed the sound again. He didn't need to hear what had happened, it was already unfolding in his mind:

1. Michelle, convinced that he would never leave her without a word, had called at his flat. Somehow made contact with the landlord, been told that letters forwarded to Nottingham had been returned NOT KNOWN AT THIS ADDRESS.

2. Had gone to his former workplace, where his puzzled boss, Sonia, had helpfully unearthed a copy of the farewell photo.

3. Had received little help from the police, who were not interested in disappearances of healthy, adult men when there were no suggestions of suspicious circumstances.

4. Had approached the production company responsible for *Lost And Found*, where her good looks, her obvious sincerity, and her romantic fantasies had struck a chord with a researcher bored with stories of missing dads and runaway teenagers.

5. And the rest was history.

And even as this list (file under *End of the World*) unfurled behind his eyes, the greater part of Tony's mind was filled with just two thoughts:

1. Is June sitting next door, watching this programme?

2. And if she is, what the hell am I going to do about it?

# COME DOWN
# FROM THE HILLS

*John F. Suter*

Arlan Boley backed his backhoe down the ramp from the flatbed, cut the motor, and climbed off. It was early in the morning in the dry season of late August, but the dew was just starting to rise. Boley knew that the oppressiveness of the air would pass, but he hated it all the same.

"You want me to do the first one along about here?" he asked. He brushed at his crinkly blond hair where a strand of cobweb from an overhanging branch had caught.

Sewell McCutcheon, who was hiring Boley's services for the morning, walked to the edge of the creek and took a look. He picked up a dead sycamore branch and laid it perpendicular to the stream. "One end about here." He walked downstream about fifteen feet and repeated the act with another branch. "Other end here."

Boley glanced across the small creek and, without looking at McCutcheon, asked, "How far out?"

The older man grinned, the ends of his heavy brown moustache lifting. "We do have to be careful about that." He reached into a pocket of his blue-and-white coveralls and took out a twenty-five-foot reel of surveyor's tape. He laid it on the ground, stooped over to remove heavy shoes and socks, and rolled the coveralls to his knees.

He unreeled about a foot of tape and handed the end to Boley. "Stand right at the edge and hold that," he said, picking up a pointed stake about five feet long.

While Boley held the tape's end, McCutcheon stepped down the low bank and entered the creek. The dark brown hair on his sinewy legs was plastered against the dead-white skin from the knees down. When he reached the other side, he turned around. "She look square to you?"

"A carpenter couldn't do better."

McCutcheon looked down. "Fourteen and a quarter feet. Midway's seven feet, one and a half inches. I don't know about you, Boley, but I hate fractions."

He started back, reeling up tape as he came. "Seven feet, three inches from her side. I'll just give her a little more than half, then she can't complain. Not that she won't."

He plunged the stake in upright at the spot. Then he waded ashore, went to the other boundary, and repeated the performance.

"That's the first one. When you finish," he told Boley, "come down just opposite the house and we'll mark off the second one."

"How deep?" Boley asked.

"Take about two feet off the bottom," McCutcheon said. "Water's low now. When she comes back up, it'll make a good pool there. Trout ought to be happy with it."

"I'll be gettin' to 'er, then," Boley said, going back to his machine. He was already eyeing the spot where he would begin to take the first bite with the scoop. He began to work within minutes. He had moved enough dirt with his backhoe in the past to know what he was doing, even with the added presence of the water that soaked the muck. There was also an abundance of gravel in the piles he was depositing along the bank.

When he judged that he had finished the hole, he lifted the scoop until it was roughly level with the seat. Then he swung the machine around and ran it down the creek toward his next worksite.

The pebble-bottomed stream, one typical of West Virginia, was known as Squirrel Creek. It divided two farms of nearly flat land at an altitude between one and two thousand feet. On the eastern side was McCutcheon's well-kept eighty acres. McCutcheon, a recent widower, planned well and worked hard, aided by his son and daughter-in-law. Both sides of the stream were lined with trees whose root systems kept the banks from crumbling and silting the creek bed. This was deliberate on McCutcheon's part, happenstance on his neighbor's.

When Boley came down opposite McCutcheon's white frame two-story, he cut the motor and walked over to where the farmer was sitting on the steps of his porch. The house was on a small rise, with a high foundation that would protect it in the event of an unusually heavy flash flood. Because of this, Boley had to look up a few inches to talk to McCutcheon.

"See anything of her?" he asked.

"Not yet," the farmer answered.

"Maybe this isn't gonna bother her."

McCutcheon rubbed his moustache. "*Everything* about this stream bothers that woman, Arly. One of the biggest trout I ever hooked in there was givin' me one helluva fight one day. I was tryin' to play him over to this side, but I hadn't yet managed it. Then, all of a sudden, outa nowhere came the old woman, screechin' her head off. 'What d'you mean ketchin' *my* fish?' she squawks. And with that she wades right out into the water, grabs the line with both hands, and flops that trout out on the ground at her side of the creek. Whips out a knife I'da never guessed she had and cuts the line. Then off to the house with my catch."

"Well," said Boley, "it was on her half of the creek, wasn't it? Property line down the middle? That why you've been measurin'?"

"Oh, sure," the farmer replied. "I recognize that. But that's not the way she looks at it. Had the fish been over here, she'd still have done it."

"I'd better get at it while it's quiet," Boley said, mentally thankful for his own Geneva's reasonableness.

As he walked to his machine, he heard McCutcheon say, "She must be away somewhere."

Later, Boley finished piling the last of the scooped silt and rocks on the bank of the stream. McCutcheon would later sort out the rocks and use the silt in his garden.

Paid for his work, Boley put the backhoe on the flatbed and fastened it securely. He turned around to head out, when he glanced over the creek toward the brown-painted cottage on the other side. A battered red half-ton pickup was just pulling up to the front of the house, barely visible through the tangle of bushes between stream and house.

A rangy older woman with dyed jet-black hair jumped from the truck and began to force her way toward the creek.

"Arlan Boley!" she screamed. A crow's voice contained more music. "What're you doin' over there?"

Boley put the truck in gear and pushed down the accelerator. He had no wish to talk to Alice Roberts. Leave that to McCutcheon.

Six days later, Boley and his family went into town. While Geneva and the two children were making some minor purchases for the opening of school, Boley went to the courthouse to the sheriff's office.

He had just finished paying his first-half taxes and was pocketing the receipt when he was tapped on the shoulder.

"Guess I'll have to wait 'til spring now before I can get you for non-payment," a voice said.

Boley recognized the voice of his old friend, the sheriff. "Hi, McKee," he said, turning. "You want that place of mine so bad, make me an offer. I might surprise you."

"No, thanks," McKee replied. "More'n I could handle." He nodded toward the clerk's window. "You payin' with what you got from Sewell McCutcheon?"

"Some. It took a little extra." He looked at McKee with curiosity. "What's the big deal? All I did was scoop him two holes in the creek for trout to loll around in from now on."

"You did more than that, Boley. You might have provided him with a fortune. Or part of one."

Boley nudged McKee's shoulder with his fist, feeling the hardness still existing in McKee's spare frame. "Don't tell me he panned that muck and found gold."

"You're not far off the mark."

Boley's eyes widened. He noticed a tiny lift at the ends of McKee's lips and a small deepening of the lines in the sheriff's tanned face. "Well, get to it and tell me," he said.

"Maybe you heard and maybe you didn't," McKee said, "but a state geologist's been usin' a vacant office here in the courthouse for the last ten days. Been workin' in the lower end of the county tryin' to see if there's a coal seam worth explorin' by that company that owns some of the land. Anyway, today McCutcheon walked in lookin' for him. Said he needed an opinion on an object in his pocket."

"And he got his interview?"

McKee nodded. "It seems he pulled out a fair-sized rock. First glance, could have been quartz or calcite. Kinda dull—but somehow different. This state fellow thought at first it was another pebble, then he took a good look and found it wasn't."

"So what *did* he find it was?"

"A diamond."

Boley had been half anticipating the answer, but he had tried to reject it. His jaw dropped. "No kidding!"

"No kidding."

"McCutcheon's probably turning over every rock out of that stream."

The sheriff dipped his chin. "I'll bet. Geologist said it's what they call an alluvial diamond, and the probability of findin' more is very small. Said it was formed millions of years ago when these mountains were as high as the Himalayas or higher. Somewhere in all that time, water eroded away whatever surrounded this one, and it might have even washed down here from someplace else. Come down from the hills, you might say."

An odd feeling crossed Boley's mind. Several times in the past, fragments of an old ersatz folk song had made themselves recognizable at the fringe of an unpleasant situation. "Just come down from the hills" was in one of the verses.

"What's the matter?" McKee asked.

"Nothing. How big is this rock? What's it worth?"

"A little bigger than the last joint on my thumb, not as big as the whole thumb. Worth? The man told McCutcheon there's no way of knowin' until it's cut. And it might be flawed."

Boley stared into the distance. "I'd better get on home and start seein' what's in the bottom of that run that goes through my property. Everybody in the country'll be doin' the same thing wherever there's water." He paused. "Or does anybody else know?"

"Only McCutcheon, that geologist, and the two of us," McKee said. "There's sort of an agreement to keep our mouths shut. You never know who would get drawn in here, if the word got out. Don't you even tell Geneva."

"What's McCutcheon done with the thing?"

"I suggested that he should put it in a safety-deposit box."

"It's what I'd do. I hope he has," Boley said.

The quirk around McKee's mouth had gone. "You know Alice Roberts?"

"Miner's widow across the creek from McCutcheon?"

"That's the one."

"No. I've seen her. She evidently knows who I am. I don't think I want to know her."

"Not good company," McKee said. "I wonder if she's heard about this. Do me a favor, would you? Drop by McCutcheon's place before long. You have a good excuse—checkin' up on the job you did. See what you can find out, but don't let on what you know."

Boley gave him a thoughtful look. "Seems to me you know a lot already."

❦   ❦   ❦

The following evening, Boley left home on the pretext that he wanted to look at some land where he might be asked to make a ditch for a farmer who wanted to lay plastic pipe from his well pump to a new hog house. Instead, Boley went to McCutcheon's.

He found the farmer sitting alone on his porch. The sun had not quite set. His son and daughter-in-law had gone into town.

"Hello, Sewell," Boley said, walking to the foot of the steps. "Water cleared yet where I dug 'er out?"

"If it ain't by now, it never will," McCutcheon said. "Come up."

Boley went up and sat in a cane-bottomed rocker like the farmer's. "Ever since I dug it out, I've been wonderin' why you did that," he said. "After all, you have a pretty good farm pond at the back. Fed by three springs, stocked with bass and blue gills, isn't it?"

McCutcheon smiled. "That's right. Bass and blue gills. But no trout. Running water's for trout. I like variety."

"You put all that gunk on your garden yet?"

"Oh, yeah. We just took a bunch of rakes and dragged all the rocks and pebbles out, let the muck dry some, then shoveled 'er into a small wagon, towed 'er to the garden, and that was it."

Boley looked at the gravel drive leading from the house to the main road. "I guess you can bust up the rocks and fill in some potholes when you get more."

McCutcheon seemed uninterested. "I suppose. I have a small rock pile out there. Don't know what I'll do with 'em."

Boley decided that the other man was keeping his secret. He wondered if the son and daughter-in-law knew. And if they could keep quiet. To change the subject, he said, "Anybody ever want to buy your land, Sewell?"

The farmer nodded. "Every now and then some developer comes by. Thing is, this isn't close to the lake and the recreation area, and they don't want to offer much."

"It's a good bit for the three of you to handle."

"Maybe it will be later," McCutcheon agreed. "That's when I'll think again."

Boley jerked his head toward the Roberts property. "I'd think they'd get that over there for the price they want."

"Funny old gal," McCutcheon said. "Her husband was a miner, died of black lung. No children. He never had time to work the property. Thirty-nine acres, came down from his old man. Alice like to wore herself out years ago, tryin' to make somethin' of it, then gave up. Except she thinks the place is worth like the middle of New York City—*and* that the creek belongs to her, clear to where it touches my land. You understand any better?"

"I see the picture," Boley answered, "but I don't understand the last part."

"Neither do I," McCutcheon admitted. "How about a cold beer?"

"Fine," Boley said.

McCutcheon went into the house to get it. He had been gone for several minutes when Boley heard footsteps coming around the house from the rear. He turned and saw Alice Roberts at the foot of the steps. She began to talk in a loud voice. "So. Both of you'll be here together—the two of you who took that diamond out've my crick. And how many more we haven't heard about yet."

Boley stood up. "What diamond? I don't know what you're talkin' about, Mrs. Roberts."

She continued up the steps. Boley guessed her to be in her early sixties, but her vigor was of her forties.

"Don't you lie to me, mister!" she growled, sitting in the chair he had just vacated. "You know all about it. I saw you here the day it came out of the water. What cut is he giving you?"

Boley leaned against a porch post. "I'm not gettin' any cut of any kind, lady. I've been paid for diggin' some dirt and rocks out of the water for McCutcheon. I don't see where any diamond comes into it."

McCutcheon reappeared at the door, carrying two cans of cold beer. He gave one to Boley. "Alice," he said, "I didn't know you were here. Could I get you some cola?"

"The only thing you can get me is the diamond you stole from my crick."

McCutcheon glanced quickly at Boley, who continued to look puzzled. "There's some mistake, Alice. I never took anything of yours. Did you lose a diamond in the water?"

"No, I did not lose *anything* in the water," she snapped. "You found out a big diamond was in my crick and your crony fished it out. I want it."

"I made two fishin' holes in my side of the water," McCutcheon said. "I got some rich dirt for my garden and a heap of rocks. You can have every rock in that pile, if you like."

She got to her feet. "I'll take you up on that. There might be more diamonds in there that you missed. I'll go get the pickup." She went down the steps at a speed that awed Boley.

He turned to McCutcheon. "What was that all about?"

The farmer began to talk in a low tone. "Water's down more and she can get across on steppin' stones, so she'll be back in a hurry." He proceeded to tell Boley the same story McKee had. Boley did not admit to its familiarity. Instead, he said, "How did she find out?"

"Beats me," McCutcheon answered. "But if you don't want a bad case of heartburn, you'd better leave right now. I'm used to it. It won't bother me."

"The diamond—"

"Is in the bank."


Boley was unable to tell McKee about this for several days. He had necessary work at home, getting in apples from his small orchard. He was also getting in field corn for a very sick neighbor.

After a little more than a week, he went to the courthouse. On the walk outside he was stopped by a friend. Harry Comstock, a quiet, balding man with thick glasses, drew maps for Border States, Inc. Border States harvested timber and was as efficient as the businesses that got everything from slaughtered pigs except the squeal. At times the company leased land for its operations; at others, it drew on its own land. Some of their holdings abutted the land owned by McCutcheon and Alice Roberts.

"Boley!" Comstock said. "Got a minute?"

"One or two."

"Won't keep you." Comstock squinted in the sun. "Didn't you do some work on Squirrel Creek for Sewell McCutcheon right recently?"

"Yeah. Scooped out a couple of fishin' holes for him," Boley said, hoping no more information was asked for.

"Well, you must have started something. Or maybe it's just coincidence. You know what happened yesterday? He came to the office and made a deal to buy fifty more acres from us to add to his land. All rights."

"Whereabouts?"

"Beginning at the creek and going east five acres, then back upstream."

"I'll bet it costs him," Boley said.

Comstock shook his head. "Not too much. Stuff in there's mostly scrub. Company's been wishing this sort of thing might happen."

Boley began to speak, but Comstock went on. "What makes it *real* interesting is that that wild old Alice Roberts came barging in about an hour later and bought twenty acres on the opposite side of the creek. Only hers is two acres west, the rest upstream. Again, all rights. What's goin' on?"

Boley looked blank. "Beats me. Did Alice Roberts pay for hers now?"

"In cash."

Boley studied the pavement. "That's the funny part, Harry. I can't give you any answers, most of all about that."

He went into the courthouse and sought McKee. The sheriff was in.

After McKee had closed his office door, Boley ran through all that had happened, including the recent land purchases.

"I figure what they're doin' is buyin' more land along that stream so they can hunt for more diamonds without Border States gettin' into it," he finished.

McKee's head was cocked to one side. "What it really sounds like is that Alice intended to go up there and buy up land on both sides of the water and cut Sewell off. He beat her to enough of it that she didn't want to push, or she would have stirred up Border States."

"Oh, well," said Boley. "It's none of our business."

"I hope you're right," said McKee, his voice dry and astringent. "I wish you'd keep your eyes and ears open, anyway. When there's somethin' in dispute that might be valuable, I always feel I might be on the hot seat. Somebody'll be in this jail out of this, is my guess."


The following morning, Boley had left home in his four-wheel-drive jeep to help an acquaintance assess the feasibility of gathering bittersweet from a difficult location in the man's woods. With autumn coming, the colorful plant was easily saleable for decorations to tourists passing through town.

He had completed the trip and was starting home after returning the man to his house. Looking down the long corridor of trees before him he couldn't see the highway. The lane swung to the right for a few hundred feet before meeting the paved road. He slowed and made the curve, then stopped abruptly. The lane was blocked by a familiar battered red pickup. Standing beside it was Alice Roberts.

He climbed from the jeep. "Mrs. Roberts. What do you want?"

The woman was expressionless. "Mornin', Boley. I want you to get back in your jeep and follow me."

Boley considered several replies. He answered evenly, "I'm afraid I can't do that. If you have work for me, there are some people ahead of you."

"I never said anything about that," she rasped. "How do you think I found where you were?"

"I suppose you called, and my wife told you."

"I didn't call, but she told me." She moved aside and opened the truck door.

Boley stared. Inside, very pale and very straight, sat Geneva.

There was a movement beside him and Boley's eyes dropped. Alice Roberts was holding a double-barrel shotgun in her hands.

"Woman," he said, "shotgun or no shotgun, if you've hurt Geneva, I'll stomp you to bits."

"Don't get excited, Boley," she replied. "Nobody's hurt—yet. Now, you get behind that wheel and follow me."

Forcing himself to be calm, Boley did as he was told. He watched Alice Roberts climb into the truck and prop the gun between the door and her left side. Then she started, turned, and drove out.

Boley followed, driving mechanically. He paid little attention to direction or time. Rage threatened to take control, but he refused to let it. He might need all of his wits.

He wasn't entirely surprised when he saw that they had reached McCutcheon's farm and were pulling into the drive leading to the front.

The truck stopped directly before the steps to the front porch. With her surprising agility, Alice Roberts came down from the driver's seat carrying the shotgun, darted around the front of the pickup, and opened the other door to urge Geneva out.

Boley pulled up behind the truck and got out. He walked over to his wife and put his arm around her quivering shoulders.

"Arly. What's this all about?" she whispered.

"I'm not sure I know," he murmured.

"Quit talkin'!" snapped the woman. "Just behave yourselves and nobody'll get hurt. Now get up there."

She followed them up to the porch and banged on the screen door. "McCutcheon! You in there? Come out!"

There was no answer. She repeated her demands.

Finally a voice came faintly through the house. "Come on around to the west side."

Boley took Geneva's arms and urged her down from the porch, Alice Roberts' footsteps impatient behind them. They went around the house to the right. Waiting for them, leaning against a beech tree, was Sewell McCutcheon.

The farmer's eyes rounded with surprise. "This is more than I expected," he said. "Why the gun, Alice?"

"To convince you I mean business. If I pointed it at *you*, you might think I was foolin'. I hear these folks got two kids, so you'll think a bit more about it. There's shells in both these chambers."

"What do you want, Alice?"

"I want to see that diamond. I want to look at it. I want to hold it."

"We'd have to go to the bank. It's in a safety-deposit box."

Alice lifted the gun. "You're a liar, Sewell McCutcheon. How do I know? I went to the bank yesterday and asked to rent a box the same size as yours. And what did the girl say? 'We don't have a box rented to Mr. McCutcheon.' Now you get that diamond out here."

McCutcheon looked from one to another of the three. "All right. You go sit on the porch. I have to go in the house. You can't ask me to give my hidin' place away to you."

"I could, but I won't," Alice answered. "And don't you try to call anybody or throw down on me with your own gun."

McCutcheon's only answer was a nod. He went rapidly up to the side door and into the house. Boley led Geneva up to a swing that hung near the front end of the porch and sat down on it with her.

Alice followed. "If you're thinkin' about those other two who live here, fergit it. They went off down to Montgomery earlier." She leaned against a stack of firewood McCutcheon had put up to season.

After what seemed to Boley to be an interminable time, the farmer reappeared. He carried a cylindrical plastic medicine container about two inches long and an inch in diameter.

"We'd best go down into the sun," he said. "You can get a better idea."

He led the way down into the yard toward the stream, out of the shade of the trees surrounding the house. He stopped, opened the container, and shook something into his right palm. He offered it to Alice.

"Here it is."

She plucked it from his hand and peered at it.

"Why, it looks just like a dirty quartz pebble or some of them other rocks," she muttered. "This is a diamond? An uncut one?"

"It is. It's real," McCutcheon answered. "I can prove it, too."

She stared at it, letting the sun shine on it. "Well, some ways you look at it—A real, honest-to-God diamond, pulled outa my crick! McCutcheon, all my life I've wanted one nice thing to call my own."

The farmer pulled at his moustache. "Well, Alice, I'm sorry for you, but it came off my property. It came outa my side."

She raised her eyes to his. "How about you get it cut? Cut in two parts. Let me have half."

McCutcheon reached over and removed the stone from her hand. "Alice, you've been too much trouble to me over the years. Threatenin' these people with a shotgun is just too much."

"Shotgun!" she yelled. "I'll give you shotgun!"

She raised the gun swiftly, reversing it, and grasping the barrels with both hands, she clubbed McCutcheon across the back of the head. He fell to the ground, bleeding.

Stooping, she pried his fingers open and took the stone from them. "I'm not gonna let you take it!" she cried, running to the creek. When she reached the bank, she drew back her arm and threw the diamond as hard as she could into the woods upstream from her house. "Now," she yelled, "it's where it belongs! I might be forever findin' it, but you ain't gonna get it!"

Boley retrieved the gun where she had dropped it. "Go inside and call the sheriff," he told Geneva. "Say we need paramedics for Sewell."


When the sheriff's car and the ambulance came, McCutcheon was unconscious. Alice Roberts sat by the creek, ignoring everything until they took her to the car in handcuffs.

Boley explained the morning's events to McKee, who had come with a deputy. The sheriff heard him out. "Sounds like we've got her for kidnaping and assault, at least."

Alice Roberts, in the police car, heard them. "Kidnaping?" she said. "They's only old empty shells in that gun."

McKee leaned in the window. "But they didn't know that, Alice." To Boley, he said, "And don't you back off on the charge."

"I won't," Boley promised. "I'm just glad it's over."

McKee gave him an odd look. "If you think that, you've got another think comin'. Let's do today's paperwork, then come see me late tomorrow afternoon."

❦   ❦   ❦

When Boley arrived at his office late the next day, the sheriff closed the door and waved him to a seat. "Things are pretty much as I figured," he said.

"How's McCutcheon?" Boley asked. "And what about Alice?"

"Sewell's not too bad." McKee sat down. "He's gettin' a good goin' over for concussion, but that's about it. Alice is still locked up, which is where I want her." He leaned across the desk. "How's it feel to be a cat's-paw?"

Boley was startled. "There's some kind of set-up in this?"

McKee sat back. "I'll run it past you. Some of this I can't prove and we'll just have to wait and see what happens. Anyway, you know same as I do that one of this county's big hopes is to attract people with money to buy up some of this land. Build themselves a place where they can come week-ends or for the summer. The trouble is, we have only one good-sized lake and one nice recreation area. There are lots of other good places, but developers want to pick 'em up for peanuts."

"Alice Roberts, poor soul, has a place that looks like the devil's back yard. But it wouldn't take a lot to make it presentable, and it lays well. Sewell's place looks good. Given the right price, he'd quit and retire."

"I'm beginning to get an idea," Boley said. "McCutcheon decided to start a diamond rush, is that it? Where'd he get the stone?"

"You dug it out for him," McKee replied. "Until then, everything was just what it seemed. You dug two fishin' holes. Then he did find the diamond, and all that hush-hush commenced."

"I'd say he called Alice over and had a talk. Showed her how they could put on an act, building things up to her sluggin' him, so his discovery would really hit the papers."

Boley said, "So they bought that land from Border States hoping to resell and clean up. But where did Alice get the money?"

"Maybe she had some put back. But I'd bet Sewell made her a loan."

"The diamond. Is it real?"

McKee grinned. "It's real. The state man wouldn't lie about that."

"You want me to press the kidnap charge."

"I do. And I've had the hospital keep McCutcheon sedated, partly to keep him from droppin' the assault charge. You hang on until I suggest you drop it."

Boley was still puzzled. "What about the diamond? She threw it into the woods. I saw her."

"You saw her throw something into the woods. Remember I said you might mistake it for dirty quartz or calcite? That's probably what Sewell let her throw away." McKee's amusement grew. "Another reason for keepin' her locked up—I want McCutcheon to have time to go over there and 'find' that stone again." He added a postscript. "Or maybe they'll leave it as an inducement for whoever buys Alice's place."

# THE WRONG HANDS

*Peter Robinson*

"Is everything in order?" the old man asked, his scrawny fingers clutching the comforter like talons.

"Seems to be," said Mitch.

Drawing up the will had been a simple enough task. Mr. Garibaldi and his wife had the dubious distinction of outliving both their children, and there wasn't much to leave.

"Would you like to sign it now?" he asked, holding out his Mont Blanc.

The old man clutched the pen the way a child holds a crayon and scribbled his illegible signature on the documents.

"There . . . that's done," said Mitch. And he placed the papers in his briefcase.

Mr. Garibaldi nodded. The movement brought on a spasm and such a coughing fit that Mitch thought the old man was going to die right there and then.

But he recovered. "Will you do me a favor?" he croaked when he'd got his breath back.

Mitch frowned. "If I can."

With one bent, shrivelled finger, Mr. Garibaldi pointed to the floor under the window. "Pull the carpet back," he said.

Mitch stood up and looked.

"Please," said Mr. Garibaldi. "The carpet."

Mitch walked over to the window and rolled back the carpet. Underneath was nothing but floorboards.

"One of the boards is loose," said the old man. "The one directly in line with the wall socket. Lift it up."

Mitch felt and, sure enough, part of the floorboard was loose. He lifted it easily with his fingernails. Underneath, wedged between the joists, lay a package wrapped in old newspaper.

"That's it," said the old man. "Take it out."

Mitch did. It was heavier than he had expected.

"Now put the board back and replace the carpet."

After he had done as he was asked, Mitch carried the package over to the bed.

"Open it," said Mr. Garibaldi. "Go on, it won't bite you."

Slowly, Mitch unwrapped the newspaper. It was from December 18, 1947, he noticed, and the headline reported a blizzard dumping twenty-eight inches of snow on New York City the day before. Inside, he found a layer of oilcloth wrapped around the object. When he had folded back that too, the gun gleamed up at him. It was old, he could tell that, but it looked in superb condition. He hefted it into his hand, felt its weight and balance, pointed it towards the wall as if to shoot.

"Be careful," said the old man. "It's loaded."

Mitch looked at the gun again, then put it back on the oilcloth. His fingers were smudged with oil or grease, so he took a tissue from the bedside table and wiped them off as best he could.

"What the hell are you doing with a loaded gun?" he asked.

Mr. Garibaldi sighed. "It's a Luger," he said. "First World War, probably. Old, anyway. A friend gave it to me many years ago. A German friend. I've kept it ever since. Partly as a memento of him and partly for protection. You know what this city's been getting like these past few years. I've maintained it, cleaned it, kept it loaded. Now I'm gonna die I want to hand it in. I don't want it to fall into the wrong hands."

Mitch set the Luger down on the bed. "Why tell me?" he asked.

"Because it's unregistered and I'd like you to hand it over for me." He shook his head and coughed again. "I haven't got long left. I don't want no cops coming round here and giving me a hard time."

"They won't give you a hard time." More like give you a medal for handing over an unregistered firearm, Mitch thought.

"Maybe not. But . . ." Mr. Garibaldi grabbed Mitch's wrist with his talon. The fingers felt cold and dry, like a reptile's skin. Mitch tried to pull back a little, but the old man held on, pulled him closer, and croaked, "Sophie doesn't know. It would make her real angry to know we had a gun in the house the last fifty years and I kept it from her. I don't want to end my days with my wife mad at me. Please, Mr. Mitchell. It's a small favor I ask."

Mitch scratched the side of his eye. True enough, he thought, it *was* a small favor. And it might prove a profitable one, too. Old firearms were worth something to collectors, and Mitch knew a cop who had connections. All he had to say was that he had been entrusted with this gun by a client, who had brought it to his office, that he had put it in the safe and called the police immediately. What could be wrong with that?

"Okay," he said, rewrapping the gun and slipping it in his briefcase along with the will. "I'll do as you ask. Don't worry. You rest now. Everything will be okay."

Mr. Garibaldi smiled and seemed to sink into a deep sleep.


Mitch stood on the porch of the Garibaldi house and pulled on his sheep-skin-lined gloves, glad to be out of the cloying atmosphere of the sickroom, even if it was minus ninety or something outside.

He was already wearing his heaviest overcoat over a suit and a wool scarf, but still he was freezing. It was one of those clear winter nights when the ice splinters underfoot and the breeze off the lake seems to numb you right to the bone. Reflected street lamps splintered in the broken mirror of the sidewalk, the colour of Mr. Garibaldi's jaundiced eyes.

Mitch pulled his coat tighter around his scarf and set off, cracking the iced-over puddles as he went. Here and there, the remains of last week's snow had frozen into ruts, and he almost slipped and fell a couple of times on the uneven surface.

As he walked, he thought of old Garibaldi, with no more than a few days left to live. The old man must have been in pain sometimes, but he never complained. And he surely must have been afraid of death? Maybe dying put things in perspective, Mitch thought. Maybe the mind, facing the eternal, icy darkness of death, had ways of dealing with its impending extinction, of discarding the dross, the petty and the useless.

Or perhaps not. Maybe the old man just lay there day after day running baseball statistics through his mind; or wishing he'd gone to bed with his neighbour's wife when he had the chance.

As Mitch walked up the short hill he cursed the fact that you could never get a decent parking spot in these residential streets. He'd had to park in the lot behind the drugstore, the next street over, and the quickest way there was through a dirt alley just about wide enough for a garbage truck to pass through.

It happened as he cut through the alley. And it happened so fast that, afterwards, he couldn't be quite sure whether he felt the sharp blow to the back of his head before his feet slipped out from under him, or after.

When Mitch opened his eyes again, the first thing he saw was the night sky. It looked like a black satin bedsheet with some rich woman's diamonds spilled all over it. There was no moon.

He felt frozen to the marrow. He didn't know how long he had been lying there in the alley—long enough to die of exposure, it felt like—but when he checked his watch, he saw he had only been out a little over five minutes. Not surprising no one had found him yet. Not here, on a night like this.

He lay on the frozen mud and took stock. Despite the cold, everything hurt—his elbow, which he had cracked trying to break his fall; his tailbone; his right shoulder; and, most of all, his head—and the pain was sharp and spiky, not at all numb like the rest of him. He reached around and touched the sore spot on the back of his head. His fingers came away sticky with blood.

He took a deep breath and tried to get to his feet, but he could only manage to slip and skitter around like a newborn lamb, making himself even more dizzy. There was no purchase, nothing to grip. Snail-like, he slid himself along the ice towards the rickety fence. There, by reaching out and grabbing the wooden rails carefully, he was able to drag himself to his feet.

At first, he wished he hadn't. His head started to spin and he thought it was going to split open with pain. For a moment, he was sure he was going to fall again. He held on to the fence for dear life and vomited, the world swimming around his head. After that, he felt a little better. Maybe he wasn't going to die.

The only light shone from a street lamp at the end of the alley, not really enough to search by, so Mitch used the plastic penlight attached to his key ring to look for his briefcase. But it wasn't there. Stepping carefully on the ribbed ice, still in pain and unsure of his balance, Mitch extended the area of his search in case the briefcase had skidded off somewhere on the ice when he fell. It was nowhere to be found.

Almost as an afterthought, as the horrible truth was beginning to dawn on him, he felt for his wallet. Gone. So he'd been mugged. The blow had come *before* the fall. And they'd taken his briefcase.

Then Mitch remembered the gun.

The next morning was a nightmare. Mitch had managed to get himself home from the alley without crashing the car, and after a long, hot bath, a glass of Scotch, and four extra-strength Tylenol, he began to feel a little better. He seemed to remember his mother once saying you shouldn't go to sleep after a bump on the head—he didn't know why—but it didn't stop him that night.

In the morning he awoke aching all over.

When he had showered, taken more Tylenol, and forced himself to eat some bran flakes, he poured a second cup of strong black coffee and sat down to think things out. None of his thoughts brought any comfort.

He hadn't gone to the cops. How could he, given what he had been carrying? Whichever way you looked at it, he had been in possession of an illegal, unregistered firearm when he was mugged. Even if the cops had been lenient, there was the Law Society to reckon with, and like most lawyers, Mitch feared the Law Society far more than he feared the cops.

Maybe he could have sort of skipped over the gun in his account of the mugging. After all, he was pretty sure that it couldn't be traced either to him or to Garibaldi. But what if the cops found the briefcase, and the gun was still inside it? How could he explain that?

Would that be worse than if the briefcase turned up and the gun was gone? If the muggers took it, then chances were someone might get shot with it. Either way, it was a bad scenario for Mitch, and it was all his fault. Well, maybe *fault* was too strong a word—he couldn't help getting mugged—but he still felt somehow responsible.

All he could do was hope that whoever took the gun would get rid of it, throw it in the lake, before anyone came to any harm.

Some hope.

Later that morning, Mitch remembered Garibaldi's will. That had gone, too, along with the briefcase and the gun. And it would have to be replaced.

There's only one true will—copies have no legal standing—and if you lose it you could have a hell of a mess on your hands. Luckily, he had Garibaldi's will on his computer. All he had to do was print it out again and hope to hell the old guy hadn't died during the night.

He hadn't. Puzzled, but accepting Mitch's excuse of a minor error he'd come across when proofreading the document, Garibaldi signed again with a shaking hand.

"Is the gun safe?" he asked afterwards. "You've got it locked away in your safe?"

"Yes," Mitch lied. "Yes, don't worry, the gun's perfectly safe."

Every day Mitch scanned the paper from cover to cover for news of a shooting or a gun found abandoned somewhere. He even took to buying the *Sun*, which he normally wouldn't even use to light a fire at the cottage, because it covered far more local crime than the *Globe and Mail* or the *Toronto Star*. Anything to do with a gun was sure to make it into the *Sun*.

But it wasn't until three weeks and three days after the mugging—and two weeks after Mr. Garibaldi's death "peacefully, at home"—that the item appeared. And it was big enough news to make the *Globe and Mail*.

> Mr. Charles McVie was shot dead in his home last night during the course of an apparent burglary. A police spokesperson says Mr. McVie was shot twice, once in the chest and once in the groin, while interrupting a burglar at his Beaches mansion shortly after midnight last night. He died of his wounds three hours later at Toronto East General Hospital. Detective Greg Hollins, who has been assigned the case, declined to comment on whether the police are following any significant leads at the moment, but he did inform our reporter that preliminary tests indicate the bullet was most likely fired from an old 9mm semiautomatic weapon, such as a Luger, unusual and fairly rare these days. As yet, police have not been able to locate the gun. Mr. McVie, 62, made his fortune in the construction business. His wife, Laura, who was staying overnight with friends in Windsor when the shooting occurred, had no comment when she was reached early this morning.

The newspaper shook in Mitch's hands. It had happened. Somebody had died because of him. But while he felt guilt, he also felt fear. Was there really no way the police could tie the gun to him or Mr. Garibaldi? Thank God the old man was dead, or he might hear about the shooting and his conscience might oblige him to come forward. Luckily, his widow, Sophie, knew nothing.

With luck, the old Luger was in the deepest part of the lake for sure by now. Whether anyone else had touched it or not, Mitch knew damn well that he had, and that his greasy fingerprints weren't only all over the handle and the barrel, but they were on the wrapping paper, too. The mug-gers had probably been wearing gloves when they robbed him—it was a cold night—and maybe they'd had the sense to keep them on when they saw what was in the briefcase.

Calm down, he told himself. Even if the cops did find his fingerprints on the gun, they had no way of knowing whose they were. He had never been fingerprinted in his life, and the cops would have no reason to subject him to it now.

They couldn't connect Charles McVie to either Mr. Garibaldi or to Mitch.

Except for one thing.

Mitch had done McVie's will two years ago, after his marriage to Laura, his second wife.


Mitch had known that Laura McVie was younger than her husband, but even that knowledge hadn't prepared him for the woman who opened the door to him three days after Charles McVie's funeral.

Black became her. Really became her, the way it set off her creamy com-plexion, long blond hair, Kim Basinger lips, and eyes the colour of a blue-jay's wing.

"Yes?" she said, frowning slightly.

Mitch had put on his very best, most expensive suit, and he knew he looked sharp. He didn't want her to think he was some ambulance chaser come after her husband's money.

As executor, Laura McVie was under no obligation to use the same lawyer who had prepared her husband's will to handle his estate. Laura might have a lawyer of her own in mind. But Mitch *did* have the will, so there was every chance that if he presented himself well she would choose him to handle the estate too.

And there was much more money in estates—especially those as big as McVie's—than there was in wills.

At least, Mitch thought, he wasn't so hypocritical as to deny that he had mixed motives for visiting the widow. Didn't everyone have mixed motives? He felt partly responsible for McVie's death, of course, and a part of him genuinely wanted to offer the widow help.

After Mitch had introduced himself, Laura looked him over, plump lower lip fetchingly nipped between two sharp white teeth, then she flashed him a smile and said, "Please come in, Mr. Mitchell. I was wondering what to do about all that stuff. I really could use some help." Her voice was husky and low-pitched, with just a subtle hint of that submissive tone that can drive certain men wild.

Mitch followed her into the high-ceilinged hallway, watching the way her hips swayed under the mourning dress.

He was in. All right! He almost executed a little jig on the parquet floor.


The house was an enormous heap of stone overlooking the ravine. It had always reminded Mitch of an English vicarage, or what he assumed an English vicarage looked like from watching PBS. Inside, though, it was bright and spacious and filled with modern furniture—not an antimacassar in sight. The paintings that hung on the white walls were all contemporary abstracts and geometric designs, no doubt originals and worth a small fortune in themselves. The stereo equipment was state of the art, as were the large-screen TV, VCR, and laser-disc player.

Laura McVie sat on a white sofa and crossed her legs. The dress she wore was rather short for mourning, Mitch thought, though he wasn't likely to complain about the four or five inches of smooth thigh it revealed. Especially as the lower part was sheathed in black silk stockings and the upper was bare and white.

She took a cigarette from a carved wooden box on the coffee table and lit it with a lighter that looked like a baseball. Mitch declined the offer to join her.

"I hope you don't mind," she said, lowering her eyes. "It's my only vice."

"Of course not." Mitch cleared his throat. "I just wanted to come and tell you how sorry I was to hear about the . . . the tragic accident. Your husband was—"

"It wasn't an accident, Mr. Mitchell," she said calmly. "My husband was murdered. I believe we should face the truth clearly and not hide behind euphemisms, don't you?"

"Well, if you put it like that . . ."

She nodded. "You were saying about my husband?"

"Well, I didn't know him well, but I *have* done some legal work for him—specifically his will—and I am aware of his circumstances."

"My husband was very rich, Mr. Mitchell."

"Exactly. I thought . . . well . . . there are some unscrupulous people out there, Mrs. McVie."

"Please, call me Laura."

"Laura. There are some unscrupulous people out there, and I thought if there was anything I could do to help, perhaps give advice, take the burden off your hands . . . ?"

"What burden would that be, Mr. Mitchell?"

Mitch sat forward and clasped his hands on his knees. "When someone dies, Mrs.—Laura—there are always problems, legal wrangling and the like. Your husband's affairs seem to be in good order, judging from his will, but that was made two years ago. I'd hate to see someone come and take advantage of you."

"Thank you," Laura said. "You're so sweet. And why shouldn't you handle the estate? Someone has to do it. I can't."

Mitch had the strangest feeling that something was going awry here. Laura McVie didn't seem at all the person to be taken advantage of, yet she seemed to be swallowing his line of patter.

That could only be, he decided, because it suited her, too. And why not? It would take a load off her mind.

"That wasn't the main reason I came, though," Mitch pressed on, feeling an irrational desire to explain himself. "I genuinely wanted to see if I could help in any way."

"Why?" she asked, blue eyes open wide. "Why should you? Mr. Mitchell, I've come to learn that people do things for selfish motives. Self-interest rules. Always. I don't believe in altruism. Nor did my husband. At least we were agreed on that." She turned aside, flicked some ash at the ashtray, and missed. In contrast to everything else in the place, the tin ashtray looked as if it had been stolen from a lowlife bar. "So you want to help me?" she said. "For a fee, of course."

Mitch felt embarrassed and uncomfortable. The part of him that had desperately wanted to make amends for his part in Charles McVie's death was being thwarted by the frankness and openness of the widow. Yes, he could use the money—of course he could—but that really *wasn't* his only reason for being there, and he wanted her to know that. How could he explain that he really wasn't such a bad guy?

"There are expenses involved in settling an estate," Mitch went on. "Of course there are. But I'm not here to cheat you."

She smiled at him indulgently. "Of course not."

Which definitely came across as, "As *if you could.*"

"But if you'll allow me to—"

She shifted her legs, showing more thigh. "Mr. Mitchell," she said. "I'm getting the feeling that you really do have another reason for coming to see me. If it's not that you're after my husband's money, then what are you after?"

Mitch swallowed. "I . . . I feel . . . You see, I—"

"Come on, Mr. Mitchell. You can tell me. You'll feel better."

The voice that had seemed so submissive when Mitch first heard it now became hypnotic, so warm, so trustworthy, so easy to answer. And he had to tell someone.

"I feel partly responsible for your husband's death," he said, looking into her eyes. "Oh, I'm not the burglar, I'm not the killer. But I think I inadvertently supplied the gun."

Laura McVie looked puzzled. Now he had begun, Mitch saw no point in stopping. If he could only tell this woman the full story, he thought, then she would understand. Perhaps she would even be sympathetic towards him. So he told her.

When he had finished, Laura stood up abruptly and walked over to the picture window with its view of a back garden as big as High Park. Mitch sat where he was and looked at her from behind. Her legs were close together and her arms were crossed. She seemed to be turned in on herself. He couldn't tell whether she was crying or not, but her shoulders seemed to be moving.

"Well?" he asked, after a while. "What do you think?"

She let the silence stretch a moment, then dropped her arms and turned around slowly. Her eyes did look moist with tears. "What do I think?" she said. "I don't know. I don't know what to think. I think that maybe if you'd reported the gun stolen, the police would have searched for it and my husband wouldn't have been murdered."

"But I would have been charged, disbarred."

"Mr. Mitchell, surely that's a small price to pay for someone's life? I'm sorry. I think you'd better go. I can't think straight right now."

"But I—"

"Please, Mr. Mitchell. Leave." She turned back to the window again and folded her arms, shaking.

Mitch got up off the sofa and headed for the door. He felt defeated, as if he had left something important unfinished, but there was nothing he could do about it. Only slink off with his tail between his legs feeling worse than when he had come. Why hadn't he just told her he was after handling

McVie's estate. Money, pure and simple. Self-interest like that she would have understood.

Two days later, and still no developments reported in the McVie investigation, Laura phoned.

"Mr. Mitchell?"

"Yes."

"I'm sorry about my behaviour the other day. I was upset, as you can imagine."

"I can understand that," Mitch said. "I don't blame you. I don't even know why I told you."

"I'm glad you did. I've had time to think about it since then, and I'm beginning to realize how terrible you must feel. I want you to realize that I don't blame you. It's not the gun that commits the crime, after all, is it? It's the person who pulls the trigger. I'm sure if the burglar hadn't got that one, he'd have got one somewhere else. Look, this is very awkward over the telephone; do you think you could come to the house?"

"When?"

"How about this evening. For dinner?"

"Fine," said Mitch. "I'm really glad you can find it in your heart to forgive me."

"Eight o'clock?"

"Eight it is."

When he put down the phone, Mitch jumped to his feet, punched the air, shouted, "Yes!"

"Dinner" was catered by a local Italian restaurant, Laura McVie not being, in her own words, "much of a cook." Two waiters delivered the food, served it discreetly, and took away the dirty dishes.

Mostly, Mitch and Laura made small talk in the candlelight over the pasta and wine, and it wasn't until the waiters had left and they were alone, relaxing on the sofa, each cradling a snifter of Courvoisier XO Cognac, with mellow jazz playing in the background, that the conversation became more intimate.

Laura was still funereally clad, but tonight her dress, made of semi-transparent layers of black chiffon—more than enough for decency—fell well below knee-height. There was still no disguising the curves, and the rustling sounds as she crossed her legs made Mitch more than a little hot under the collar.

Laura puckered her lips to light a cigarette. When she had blown the smoke out, she asked, "Are you, married?"

Mitch shook his head.

"Ever been?"

"Nope."

"Just didn't meet the right girl, is that it?"

"Something like that."

"You're not gay, are you?"

He laughed. "What on earth made you think that?"

She rested her free hand on his and smiled. "Don't worry. Nothing made me think it. Nothing in particular. Just checking, that's all."

"No," Mitch said. "I'm not gay."

"More cognac?"

"Sure." Mitch was already feeling a little tipsy, but he didn't want to spoil the mood.

She fetched the bottle and poured them each a generous measure. "I didn't really *love* Charles, you know," she said when she had settled down and smoothed her dress again. "I mean, I respected him, I even liked him, I just didn't love him."

"Why did you marry him?"

Laura shrugged. "I don't know, really. He asked me. He was rich and seemed to live an exciting life. Travel. Parties. I got to meet all kinds of celebrities. We'd only been married two years, you know. And we'd only known one another a few weeks before we got married. We hadn't even . . . you know. Anyway, I'm sorry he's dead . . . in a way."

"What do you mean?"

Laura leaned forward and stubbed out her cigarette. Then she brushed back a long blond tress and took another sip of cognac before answering. "Well," she said, "now that he's dead, it's all mine, isn't it? I'd be a hypocrite and a fool if I said that didn't appeal to me. All this wealth and no strings attached. No responsibilities."

"What responsibilities were there before?"

"Oh, you know. The usual wifely kind. Charles was never, well . . . let's say he wasn't a very passionate lover. He wanted me more as a showpiece than anything else. Something to hang on his arm that looked good. Don't get me wrong, I didn't mind. It was a small price to pay. And then we were forever having to entertain the most boring people. Business acquaintances. You know the sort of thing. Well, now that Charles is gone, I won't have to do that anymore, will I? I'll be able to do what I want. Exactly what I want."

Almost without Mitch knowing it, Laura had edged nearer towards him as she was speaking, and now she was so close he could smell the warm, acrid smoke on her breath. He found it curiously intoxicating. Soon she was close enough to kiss.

She took hold of his hand and rested it on her breast. "It's been a week since the funeral," she said. "Don't you think it's time I took off my widow's weeds?"


When Mitch left Laura McVie's house the following morning, he was beginning to think he might be onto a good thing. Why stop at being estate executor? he asked himself. He already knew that, under the terms of the will, Laura got everything—McVie had no children or other living relatives—and *everything* was somewhere in the region of five million dollars.

Even if he didn't love her—and how could you tell if you loved someone after just one night?—he certainly felt passionately drawn to her. They got on well together, thought alike, and she was a wonderful lover. Mitch was no slouch, either. He could certainly make up for her late husband in that department.

He mustn't rush it, though. Take things easy, see what develops. . . . Maybe they could go away together for a while. Somewhere warm. And then . . . well . . . five million dollars.

Such were his thoughts as he turned the corner, just before the heavy hand settled on his shoulder and a deep voice whispered in his ear, "Detective Greg Hollins, Mr. Mitchell. Homicide. I think it's about time you and I had a long talk."


Relieved to be let off with little more than a warning after cooperating with the police, Mitch turned up at Laura's the next evening as arranged. This time, they skipped the dinner and drinks preliminaries and headed straight for her bedroom.

Afterwards, she lay with her head resting on his shoulder, smoking a cigarette.

"My God," she said. "I missed this when I was married to Charles."

"Didn't you have any lovers?" Mitch asked.

"Of course I didn't."

"Oh, come on. I won't be jealous. I promise. Tell me."

She jerked away, stubbed out the cigarette on the bedside ashtray, and said, "You're just like the police. Do you know that? You've got a filthy mind."

"Hey," said Mitch. "It's me. Mitch. Okay?"

"Still . . . They think I did it, you know."

"Did what?"

"Killed Charles."

"I thought you had an alibi."

"I do, idiot. They think the burglary was just a cover. They think I hired someone to kill him."

"Did you?"

"See what I mean? Just like the cops, with your filthy, suspicious mind."

"What makes you think they suspect you?"

"The way they talked, the way they questioned me. I think they're watching me."

"You're just being paranoid, Laura. You're upset. They always suspect someone in the family at first. It's routine. Most killings are family affairs. You'll see, pretty soon they'll drop it."

"Do you really think so?"

"Sure I do. Just you wait and see."

And moments later they were making love again.


Laura seemed a little distracted when she let him in the next night. At first, he thought she had something on the stove, but then he remembered she didn't cook.

She was on the telephone, as it turned out. And she hung up the receiver just as he walked into the living room.

"Who was that?" he asked. "Not reporters, I hope?"

"No," she said, arms crossed, facing him, an unreadable expression on her face.

"Who, then?"

Laura just stood there. "They've found the gun," she said finally.

"They've what? Where?"

"In your garage, under an old tarpaulin."

"I don't understand. What are you talking about? When?"

She looked at her watch. "About now."

"How?"

Laura shrugged. "Anonymous tip. You'd better sit down, Mitch." Mitch collapsed on the sofa.

"Drink?"

"A large one."

Laura brought him a large tumbler of scotch and sat in the armchair opposite him.

"What's all this about?" he asked, after the whiskey had warmed his insides. "I don't understand what you're saying. How could they find the gun in my garage? I told you what happened to it."

"I know you did," said Laura. "And I'm telling you where it ended up. You're really not that bright, are you, Mitch? How do *you* think it got there?"

"Someone must have put it there."

"Right."

"One of the muggers? But . . . ?"

"What does it matter? What matters is that it will probably have your fingerprints on it. Or the wrapping will. All those greasy smudges. And even if it doesn't, how are you going to explain its presence in your garage?"

"But why would the cops think I killed Charles?"

"We had a relationship. We were lovers. Like I told you, I'm certain they've been watching me, and they can't fail to have noticed that you've stayed overnight on more than one occasion."

"But that's absurd. I hadn't even met you before your husband's death."

"Hadn't you?" She raised her eyebrows. "Don't you remember, honey, all those times we met in secret, made love cramped in the back of your car because we didn't even dare be seen signing in under false names in the Have-a-Nap Motel or wherever? We had to keep our relationship very, very secret. Don't you remember?"

"You'd tell them that?"

"The way they'll see it is that the relationship was more important to you than to me. You became obsessed by jealousy because I was married to someone else. You couldn't stand it anymore. And you thought by killing my husband you could get both me and my money. After all, you did prepare his will, didn't you? You knew all about his finances."

Mitch shook his head.

"I *would* like to thank you, though," Laura went on. "Without you, we had a good plan—a very good one—but *with* you we've got a perfect one."

"What do you mean?"

"I mean you were right when you suggested I had a lover. I do. Oh, not you, not the one I'm handing over to the police, the one who became so obsessed with me that it unhinged him and he murdered my husband. No. I've been very careful with Jake. I met him on the Yucatán Peninsula when Charles and I were on holiday there six months ago and Charles went down with Montezuma's revenge. I know it sounds like a cliché, but it was love at first sight. We hatched the plan very quickly and we knew we had to keep our relationship a total secret. Nobody must suspect a thing. So we never met after that vacation. There were no letters or postcards. The only contact we had was through public telephones."

"And what happens now?"

"After a decent interval—after you've been tried and convicted of my husband's murder—Jake and I will meet and eventually get married. We'll sell up here, of course, and live abroad. Live in luxury. Oh, please don't look so crestfallen, Mitch. Believe me, I *am* sorry. I didn't know you were going to walk into my life with that irresistible little confession, now, did I? I figured I'd just ride it out, the cops' suspicions and all. I mean, they might suspect me, but they couldn't prove anything. I *was* in Windsor staying with an old university friend. They've checked. And now they've got you in the bargain. . . ." She shrugged. "Why would they bother with little old me? I just couldn't look a gift horse in the mouth. You'll make a wonderful fall guy. But because I like you, Mitch, I'm at least giving you a little advance warning, aren't I? The police will be looking for you, but you've still got time to make a break, leave town."

"What if I go to them, tell them everything you've told me?"

"They'll think you're crazy. Which you are. Obsession does that to people. Makes them crazy."

Mitch licked his lips. "Look, I'd have to leave everything behind. I don't even have any cash on me. Laura, you don't think you could—"

She shook her head. "Sorry, honey. No can do. Nothing personal."

Mitch slumped back in the chair. "At least tell me one more thing. The gun. I still don't understand how it came to be the one that killed your husband."

She laughed, showing the sharp white teeth. "Pure coincidence. It was beautiful. Jake happens to be . . ."

❧     ❧     ❧

". . . a burglar by profession, and a very good one. He has worked all over the States and Canada, and he's never been caught. We thought that if I told him about the security system at the house, he could get around it cleverly and . . . Of course, he couldn't bring his own gun here from Mexico, not by air, so he had to get one. He said that's not too difficult when you move in the circles he does. The kind of bars where you can buy guns and other stolen goods are much the same anywhere, in much the same sort of neighborhoods. And he's done jobs in Toronto before.

"As luck would have it, he bought an old Luger off two inexperienced muggers. For a hundred bucks. I just couldn't believe it when you came around with your story. There couldn't be two old Lugers kicking around the neighborhood at the same time, could there? I had to turn away from you and hold my sides, I was laughing so much. It made my eyes water. What unbelievable luck!"

"I'm so glad you think so," said Mitch.

"Anyway, when I told Jake, he agreed it was too good an opportunity to miss, so he came back up here, dug the gun up from where he had buried it, safe in its wrapping, and planted it in your garage. He hadn't handled it without gloves on and he thought the two young punks he bought it from had been too scared to touch it, so the odds were, after you told me your story, that your fingerprints would still be on it. As I said, even if they aren't . . . It's still perfect."

Only tape hiss followed, and Detective Hollins flipped off the machine. "That it?" he asked.

Mitch nodded. "I left. I thought I'd got enough."

"You did a good job. Jesus, you got more than enough. I was hoping she'd let something slip but I didn't expect a full confession and her accomplice's name in the bargain."

"Thanks. I didn't have a lot of choice, did I?"

The last two times Mitch had been to see Laura, he had been wearing a tiny but powerful voice-activated tape recorder sewn into the lining of his suit jacket. It had lain on the chair beside the bed when they made love, and he had tried to get her to admit she had a boyfriend, as Hollins had suspected. He had also been wearing it the night she told him the police were about to find the Luger in his garage.

The recorder was part of the deal. Why he got off with only a warning for not reporting the theft of an unregistered firearm.

"What'll happen to her now?" he asked Hollins.

"With any luck, both her and her boyfriend will do life," said Hollins. "But what do you care, after the way she treated you? She's a user. She chewed you up and spat you out."

Mitch sighed. "Yeah, I know," he said. "But it could have been worse, couldn't it?"

"How?"

"I could've ended up married to her."

Hollins stared at him for a moment, then he burst out laughing. "I'm glad you've got a sense of humor, Mitchell. You'll need it, what's coming your way next."

Mitch shifted uneasily in his chair. "Hey, just a minute, Hollins. We made a deal. You assured me there'd be no charges over the gun."

Hollins nodded. "That's right. We did make a deal. And I never go back on my word."

Mitch shook his head. "Then I don't understand. What are you talking about?"

"Well, there's this woman from the Law Society waiting outside, Mitchell. And she'd *really* like to talk to you."

# THE HIGH COST OF LIVING

*Dorothy Cannell*

"They're not coming!" Cecil said for the fourth time, peering out into the rain-soaked night. The gale had whipped itself into a frenzy, buffeting trees and shaking the stone house like a dog with a rag doll. On that Saturday evening the Willoughbys—Cecil and his sister, Amanda—were in the front room, waiting for guests who were an hour late. The fire had died down and the canapés on their silver tray were beginning to look bored.

"They're not coming!" mimicked Amanda from the sofa, thrusting back her silver-blond hair with an irritable hand. "Repeating oneself is an early sign of insanity . . . remember?"

Her eyes, and those of her brother, shifted ceilingward.

"Cecil, I regret not strangling you at birth. Stop hovering like a leper at the gate. Every time you lift the curtain an icy blast shoots up my skirt."

A shrug. "I've been looking forward to company. The Thompsons and Bumbells lack polish, but it doesn't take much to break the monotony in this morgue."

"Really, Pickle Face!" Amanda eyed a chip in her pearl-pink manicure with disfavor. "Is that kind?"

"Speaking of kind"—Cecil let the curtain drop and adjusted his gold-rimmed spectacles—"I didn't much care for that crack about insanity. I take exception to jibes at Mother."

"Amazing!" Amanda wielded an emery board, her eyes on the prying tongues of flame loosening the wood fibers and sending showers of sparks up the chimney. "Where did I get the idea that but for the money, you would have shoved the old girl in a cage months ago? Don't hang your head. All she does is eat and—"

"You always were vulgar."

"And you always were forty-five, Cecily dear. How you love to angst, but spare me the bit about this being Mother's house and our being a pair of hyenas feasting off decaying flesh. That woman is not our mother. Father remarried because we motherless brats drove off every housekeeper within a week."

"Mary was good to us." Drawing on a cigarette with a shaking hand, Cecil sank into a chair.

"Brother, you have such a way with words. Mary had every reason to count her blessings. She acquired a roof over her head and a man to keep her warm in bed. Not bad for someone who was always less bright than a twenty-watt bulb."

"I still think some respect . . ." The cigarette got flung into the fire.

"Sweet Cecily"—Amanda buffed away at her nails—"you have deception refined to an art. I admit to living in Stepmother's house because it's free. Come on! These walls don't have ears. The only reason Mad Mary isn't shut up in a cracker box is because we're not wasting her money on one."

"I won't listen to this."

"Your sensitivity be damned. You'd trade her in for a used set of golf clubs any day of the week. Who led the way, brother, to see what could be done about opening up Father's trust? Who swore with his hand on the certificates of stock that Mary was *non compos mentis*? Spare me your avowals of being here to keep Mary company in her second childhood." Amanda tossed the emery board aside. "You wanted a share in Daddy's pot of gold while still young enough to fritter it away."

Cecil grabbed for the table lighter and ducked a cigarette toward the flame. "I believe he would have wished—"

"And I wish him in hell." Amanda tapped back a yawn. "Leaving his money tied up in that woman for life . . ."

"Mary was halfway normal when Father died. Her sister was the fly in the ointment in those days. Always meddling in money matters."

"Hush, brother dear." Amanda prowled toward the window and gave the curtain a twitch. "Is the storm unnerving you? I'm amazed we haven't had the old lady down to look for her paper dolls. For the record, I've done my turn of nursemaid drill this week. Mrs. Bridger didn't come in the last couple of days, and if I have to carry another tray upstairs I will need locking up."

Her brother stared into the fire.

"No pouting." Peppermint-pink smile. "Beginning to think, dear Cecily, that the world might be a better place if we treated old people the way we do our dogs? When they become a bother, shouldn't we put them out of everyone's misery? Nothing painful! I hate cruelty. A whiff of a damp rag and then deep, deep sleep. . . . Oh, never mind! Isn't that the doorbell?"

Cecil stopped cringing to listen. "Can it be the Thompsons or the Bumbells?"

"Either them or the Moonlight Strangler." Amanda's voice chased him from the room. Hitching her skirt above the knee, she perched on the sofa arm. From the hall came voices.

"Terrible night! Sorry we're late. Visibility nil." A thud as the wind took the front door. Moments later an arctic chill preceded Cecil and the Thompsons into the room. Mrs. Thompson was shivering like a blancmange about to slide off the plate. Her husband, as thin as she was stout, was blue around the gills.

"Welcome." Amanda, crisp and sprightly, stepped forward. "I see you've let Cecil rob you of your coats. What sports to turn out on such a wicked night."

Mr. Thompson thawed. This was one hell of a pretty woman. He accepted a brandy snifter and a seat by the fire. His wife took sherry and stretched her thick legs close to the flames. That popping sound was probably her varicose veins.

"The Bumbells didn't make it." Norman Thompson spoke the obvious. "I told Gerty you wouldn't expect us, but she would have it that you'd be waiting and wondering."

"Our phone was dead," Gerty Thompson defended herself. "Heavens above!" Cheeks creasing into a smile. "Only listen to that wind and rain rattling the windows. Almost like someone trying to get in. I won't sleep tonight if it keeps up."

"She could sleep on a clothesline," came her husband's response.

"Refills?" Cecil hovered with the decanters.

Gerty held out her glass without looking at him. Staring at the closed door, she gave a squeaky gasp. "There's someone out in the hall. I saw the doorknob turn." Sherry slopped from glass.

Norman snorted. "You've been reading too many spookhouse thrillers."

"I tell you I saw—"

The door opened a wedge.

"Damn! Not now." Almost dropping the decanter, Cecil grimaced at Amanda. "Did you forget her sleeping pills?"

An old lady progressed unsteadily into the room. Both Thompsons thought she looked like a gray flannel rabbit. She had pumice-stone skin and her nightdress was without color. Wisps of wintry hair escaped from a net and she was clutching something tightly to her chest. A child terrified of having her treasures snatched away.

"How do you do?" Gerty felt a fool. She had heard that old Mrs. Willoughby's mind had failed. On prior occasions when she and Norman had been guests here, the poor soul had not been mentioned, let alone seen. Meeting her husband's eye, she looked away. Amanda wore a faint smirk, as though she had caught someone drinking his finger bowl. Most uncomfortable. Gerty wished Norman would say something. He was the one who had thought the Willoughbys worth getting to know. The old lady remained marooned in the center of the room. A rag doll. One nudge and she would fold over. Why didn't someone say something?

Cecil almost tripped on the hearth rug. "Gerty and Norman, I present my stepmother, Mary Willoughby. She hasn't been herself lately. Not up to parties, I'm afraid. You never did like them did you, Mother?" Awkwardly he patted Mrs. Willoughby's shoulder, then propelled her toward the Thompsons.

Gerty began shivering worse than when she was on the door-step. "What's that you're holding, dear?" She had to say something—anything. The old lady's eyes looked dead.

An unreal laugh from Cecil. "A photo of her twin sister, Martha. They were very close; in fact, it was after Martha passed on last year that Mother began slipping. She always was the more dependent of the two. They lived together here after my father was taken."

"Sad, extremely sad." Mr. Thompson would have liked to sit back down, but while the old lady stood there . . .

Nudging Cecil aside, Amanda slid an arm around Mrs. Willoughby. "Nighty-night, Mary, dear!" she crooned. "Up the bye-bye stairs we go."

"No." The old lady's face remained closed, tight as a safe. But her voice rose shrill as a child's. A child demanding the impossible. "I want Martha. I won't go to sleep without Martha."

"Poor lost soul!" Ready tears welled in Gerty Thompson's eyes. "What can we do? There must be something."

"Mind our own business," supplied her husband. He was regretting not keeping his relationship with the Willoughbys strictly business. They had been a catch as investors, money having flowed from their pockets this last year.

The old lady did not say another word. But everyone sensed it would take a tow truck to remove her from the room.

"I give up," Amanda said. "Let's skate the sweet lamb over to that chair in the bookcase corner. She won't want to be too near the fire and get over-heated. I expect she feels crowded and needs breathing space. Look, she's coming quite happily now, aren't you, Mary?"

"Ah!" Gerty dabbed at her eyes with a cocktail napkin as Amanda tossed a rug over Mrs. Willoughby's knees. "She didn't want to be sent upstairs and left out of things. Being with the ones she loves is all she has left, I suppose."

"Yes, we are devoted to Mother," responded Amanda.

Mrs. Willoughby rocked mindlessly, her pale lips slack, the photo of her dead sister locked in her bony hands.

The others regrouped about the fire. Cecil poured fresh drinks and Amanda produced the tray of thaw-and-serve hors d'oeuvres. Rain continued to beat against the windows and the mantel clock ticked on self-consciously.

"We could play bridge, or do I hear any suggestions from the floor?" Amanda popped an olive into her mouth, eyes on Norman Thompson.

"How about . . ." Gerty's face grew plumper and she fussed with the pleats of her skirt. Everyone waited with bated breath, for her to suggest Monopoly. ". . . How about a séance? Don't look at me like that, Norman. You don't have to be a crazy person to believe in the Other Side. And the weather couldn't be more perfect!"

Amanda set her glass down on the coffee table. "What fun! My last gentleman friend suspected me of having psychic powers when I knew exactly what he liked in the way of . . . white wine."

Cecil broke in. "I don't like dabbling in the Unseen. We wouldn't throw our doors open to a bunch of strangers were they alive—"

"Coward!" His sister wagged a finger at him. "How can you disappoint Gerty and Norman?"

Mr. Thompson forced a smile.

Gerty was thrilled. "Everything's right for communication. This house—with the wind wrapped all about it! What could be more ghostly? And those marvelous ceiling beams and that portrait of the old gentleman with side whiskers . . ." While she enthused the others decided the game table in the window alcove would serve the purpose. Amanda fetched a brass candlestick.

"Perfect!" Fearless leader Gerty took her seat. "All other lights must be extinguished and the curtains tightly drawn."

"I trust this experiment will not unsettle Mrs. Willoughby." Norman Thompson glanced over at the old lady seated in the corner.

"Let's get this over." Cecil was tugging at his collar.

"Lead on, Gerty." Amanda smiled.

"Very well. Into the driver's seat. All aboard and hold on tight! Everyone at his own risk. Are we holding hands? Does our blood flow as one? Feel it tingling through the veins—or do I mean the arteries? I can never remember."

"My dear, lay an egg or get off the perch," ordered her husband.

Gerty ignored him. She was drawing upon the persona of her favorite fictional medium, the one in that lovely book *Ammie Come Home*. "Keep those eyes closed. No peeking! Let your minds float . . . drift, sway a little."

"I can't feel a damn thing," said Norman. "My leg's gone to sleep."

"The change in temperature! We're moving into a different atmosphere. We are becoming lighter. Buoyant! Are we together, still united in our quest? The spirits don't like ridicule, Norman."

"They'll have to lump it."

Amanda wiggled a foot against his. *Let's see if the old coyote is numb from the waist down.*

"Is anybody out there?" Madame Gerty cooed. "We are all friends here. With outstretched arms we await your coming."

Sounds of heavy breathing . . . the spluttering of the fire and a muffled snoring from the bookcase corner.

"Is there a message?" Gerty called. Only the wind and rain answered. The room was still, except for Norman, who was trying to shake his leg free of the cramp—or Amanda's teasing foot. The clock struck eleven. From outside, close to the front wall of the house, came the blistering crack of lightning. The whole house took a step backward. The table lurched toward the window. For a moment they all imagined themselves smashing through the glass to be swept away by the wind. Gerty went over with her chair, dragging Cecil down with her. The candle, still standing, went out.

It was agreed to call a halt to the proceedings.

"We must try another time." Gerty hoisted herself onto one knee and reached for her husband's hand. "I am sure someone was trying to reach me."

Amanda shivered. "My God, this place is an igloo."

"The fire's out." Cecil righted the chairs.

"Well, get it going again! I'm freezing solid. Someone stick a cigarette between my lips so I can inhale some heat."

"The trouble with your generation is, you have been much indulged. A little cold never hurt anyone. Leave those logs alone. They must last all winter. I am not throwing money on a woodpile."

The voice cracked through the room like another bolt of lightning, turning the Willoughbys—brother and sister—into a pair of dummies in a shop window. Norman Thompson sat down without meaning to, while Gerty resembled a fish trying to unswallow the hook. Otherwise the only movement came from the old lady in the corner. Even seated, she appeared to have grown. Her eyes burned in the parchment face. Glancing at the photo in her hands, she laid it down on the bookcase, tossed off her blanket, and stood up. "There has been a great deal of waste in this house lately." The voice dropped to a whisper but carried deep into the shadows.

"This extravagance will stop. When one is old, people tend to take advantage. It appears I must come out of retirement, get back in harness and pull this team."

Her face as ashen as her hair, Amanda stood hunched like an old woman. She and Cecil looked like brother and sister for once. They wore matching looks of horror—the way they had worn matching coats as children. As for the Thompsons, they resembled a pair of missionaries who, having wandered into a brothel, are unable to find the exit.

"Norman, dear, I think we should be running along; it is getting late. . . ."

"We can get our own coats. . . . Good night!" Husband and wife backed out the door. Never again would Gerty Thompson lift the mystic veil.

"Good night," echoed the voice of Mary Willoughby. "A pedestrian pair . . ." A pause, filled by the banging of the front door. "In future the decision as to who comes into this house is mine. I certainly do not enjoy entertaining in my nightdress, and more to the point . . ." The pale lips flared back. "You, Amanda and Cecil, are uninvited guests here. Don't forget. Whether you go or stay will depend on how we all get on together. A pity, but I don't think either of you can afford to live anywhere else at present. Gambling is your vice, Cecil. The corruption of the weak and indolent. I remember how you never wanted a birthday cake because you'd have to share it. As for you, Amanda, all you're good for is painting your nails and throwing up your skirts." A smile that turned the parchment face colder. "Neither of you are talking and I won't say much more tonight. I don't want to strain my voice. Tomorrow I will telephone lawyer Henry Morbeck and invite him out here—for the record. Your year of playing Monopoly is over. Your father left me control of his money and I want it back in my hands. The capital will come to you both one day, but bear in mind you may have quite a wait." Smoothing a hand over her forehead, Mrs. Willoughby removed the hair net and dropped it in the grate. "Good night, children. Don't stay up late; I won't have electricity wasted."

She was gone. They stood listening to her footsteps mounting the stairs. Finally a door on the second floor closed.

"It's not her!" Amanda pummeled a fist into her palm. "That creature—that monster—is not Mary."

Cecil grabbed for a cigarette, then could not hold his hand steady to light it. "That fool Thompson woman and her fun-and-games séances. She unearthed this horror. We're talking possession. Someone else looked out of Mother's eyes. Something has appropriated her voice."

"We have to think." Amanda hugged herself for warmth. "We gave it entrée now we must find a way to be rid of it before it sucks the life out of us all. It will bleed the bank accounts dry. We'll be paupers at the mercy of an avenging spirit. We're to be made to pay for every unkind word and deed Mary has experienced at our hands."

"What do you suggest?" Cecil still had not lit the cigarette. "Do we tell the bank manager that should Mary Willoughby ask to see him, she is really a ghost in disguise?"

"We'll talk to Dr. Denver." Amanda was pulling at her nails. "He saw the condition Mother was in last week. He'll know something is crazy. He'll come up with a diagnosis of split personality or . . . some newfangled disorder. Who cares, so long as he declares her incompetent."

"He won't." With a wild laugh Cecil broke his cigarette into little pieces and tossed them onto the dead fire. "He'll opt for a miracle, and why shouldn't he? Is anything less believable than the truth?"

"Do you never stop kidding yourself?" The words were screamed. "We all know who she is, and we know why she has come back. So if you can't answer the question how to be rid of her, kindly shut up. I'll die of cold if I remain in this ice chest. Let's go to bed."

"I'll sleep in a chair in your room," offered Cecil.

"Some protection you'd be. At the first whisper of her nightdress down the hall you'd turn into a giant goose bump." Amanda opened the door. "Remember, she's seeing Morbeck tomorrow."

❧    ❧    ❧

They huddled up the stairs like sheep, making more than usual of saying good night before separating into their rooms. After a while the murmur of footsteps died away and the lights went out, leaving the house to itself and the rasping breath of the storm. The stair treads creaked and settled, while the grandfather clock in the hall tocked away the minutes . . . the hours. The house listened and waited. Only the shadows moved until, at a little after three, came the sound of an upstairs door opening . . . then another. . . .

Early the next morning Dr. Denver received a phone call at his home.

"Doctor, this is Amanda Willoughby!" Hysteria threatened to break through her control. "There's been the most dreadful accident. It's Mother! She's fallen down the stairs. God knows when it happened . . . sometime during the night! We think she may have been sleepwalking! She was very worked up earlier in the evening. . . . Please, please hurry!"

The doctor found the door of Stone House open and entered the hall, pajama legs showing under his raincoat. Dripping water and spilling instruments from his bag, he brushed aside the brother and sister to kneel by the gray-haired woman sprawled at the foot of the stairs.

"Oh, Lord!" Cecil pressed his knuckles to his eyes. "I can't bear to look. I've never seen anyone dead before. This bloody storm. If she screamed, we would have thought it the wind! I did hear a . . . thump around three A.M. but thought it must be a tree going down in the lane. . . ."

"These Victorian staircases are murder." The doctor raised one of Mrs. Willoughby's eyelids and dangled a limp wrist between his fingers. "One wrong step and down you go."

Amanda's eyes were bright with tears. "Our one hope, Dr. Denver, is that she died instantly."

"My dear girl." He straightened up. "Mrs. Willoughby is not dead."

"What?" Cecil staggered onto a chair that wasn't there and had to grip the banister to save himself from going down. His sister looked ready to burst into mad laughter.

"Your stepmother is in a coma; there is the possibility of internal injuries and the risk of shock." The doctor folded away his stethoscope. "Shall we say I am cautiously optimistic? Her heart has always been strong. Mr. Willoughby, fetch your sister a brandy. And how about taking this photo. Careful, old chap, the glass is smashed."

"She was holding on to it for dear life when she fell . . . I suppose," Cecil said in an expressionless voice.

Dr. Denver stood up. "Get a new frame and put it by her bed. Amazing what the will to live can accomplish. Ah, here comes the ambulance. . . ."

Two weeks later the setting was a hospital corridor. "Often the way with these will-o'-the-wisp old ladies!" Henry Morbeck, lawyer, ignored the no-smoking sign and puffed on his pipe. "They harbor constitutions of steel. Had a word with Dr. Denver this morning and he gave me to understand that barring any major setbacks, Mrs. Willoughby will live."

Amanda tapped unvarnished nails against her folded arms. "Did he tell you she has joined the ranks of the living dead?"

Mr. Morbeck puffed harder on his pipe. "I understand your frustration. She remains unconscious, even though the neurologists have been unable to pinpoint a cause. Small comfort to say that such cases . . . happen. The patient lapses into a coma from which not even the most advanced medical treatment can rouse him."

"They say Mary could linger for years." Cecil's voice barely rose above a whisper. "She looked older, but she is only in her early sixties. What do you think, Henry?" Desperate for some crumb of doubt.

"My friend, I am not a doctor. And remember, doctors are not God. With careful nursing and prayers for a miracle . . . well, let's wait and see." Mr. Morbeck cleared his throat and got down to business. "Since this hospital does not provide chronic patient care, the time comes to find the very best nursing home. Such places are extraordinarily expensive, but not to worry. Mrs. Willoughby is secure. Your far-seeing father provided for such a contingency as this."

Silence.

"The bank, as co-trustee, is empowered to arrange for her comfort and care no matter what the cost. The house and other properties will be sold."

"Oh, quite, quite." Cecil knew he was babbling. "We had hoped to take Mother back to Stone House and care for her ourselves."

"I love nursing." Amanda knew she was begging.

"Out of the question." The lawyer tapped out his pipe in a plant stand and left it stuck there. "Your devotion to Mrs. Willoughby is inspiring, but you must now leave her and the finances in the hands of the professionals. Take comfort that the money is there. She keeps her dignity and you are not burdened. You have my assurance I will keep in close touch with the bank." He pushed against a door to his left. "I'll go in with you and . . . take a look at her."

The three of them entered a white, sunlit room. The woman in the railed bed could have been a china doll hooked up to a giant feeding bottle.

"She would seem at peace," Mr. Morbeck said.

There must be something we can do, Amanda thought. It always sounds so easy. Someone yanks out the plug and that's that.

Nothing to pull, Cecil thought wearily. She's existing on her own. No artificial support system, other than the IV and no damned doctor is going to starve a helpless old woman.

She has no business being alive, Amanda thought as she gripped the rail. She should be ten feet under, feeding the grubs instead of feeding off us. "Cecil, let's get out of here." She didn't care what the lawyer thought. "And if I ever suggest coming back, have me committed."

Alone with the patient, Mr. Morbeck quelled a shiver and clasped the leaden hand. "Mary Willoughby, are you in there?" His voice hung in the air like a bell pull, ready to start jangling again if anyone breathed on it. And Mary Willoughby was breathing—with relish. Had Mr. Morbeck been a man of imagination he would have thought the pale lips smiled mischievously. Eager to be gone, he turned and saw that the woman in the photo by the bed seemed to be laughing back. Mary's twin sister, Martha. Or was it . . . ? Mr. Morbeck had always had trouble telling the two of them apart.

# MY HEART CRIES FOR YOU

*Bill Crider*

I met Ethel Ann Adams on Valentine's Day and we met cute, just like in the movies. I was in the flower department at Kroger, thinking I might buy some flowers to send to the woman who'd just ditched me two days before for a man who drove a BMW. I thought maybe she'd feel sorry for me and give me another chance. I don't know. Anyway, I was standing there looking at the roses when Ethel Ann ran into me with her grocery cart.

She didn't knock me far, not more than a foot, and I figured the bruises would go away in a week or two, so I told her not to worry about it. To forget it. I was fine.

If she'd been good-looking, it might've been a different story, but she wasn't the kind of woman I was interested in at all. She was short and chunky, about five-three and 140 pounds. Solid. She had black hair like wires—curly wires, the kind inside a sofa cushion. Those were on her head. Her mustache was black, too, but the hairs weren't curly. They were too short.

She wouldn't leave me alone, though. She acted like she'd done me irreparable harm and it was her duty to make it all right.

"Here, let me help ya," she said. She had a voice like a stevedore. "I'll pick up ya packages."

She scuttled around like a crab with Saint Vitus's Dance and picked up the cereal box and the granola bars and the Hamburger Helper, then stuffed them back on top of my basket.

"Ya okay now?" she said.

"I'm fine," I said, always the gentleman. "I'll be just fine, thanks."

"Good, good. I'm glad. Ya buying some posies for your chick?"

She really said things like that: Posies. Chick.

"No," I said. "I was thinking of sending some to my mother." My mother had been dead for ten years, but how do you say you were thinking of sending flowers to someone who'd just dumped you?

"Ya got a chick?"

"I beg your pardon?"

"Ya got a chick? A babe? A hotsie-totsie?"

She really said that. Hotsie-totsie.

"No," I said, rather coldly I'm afraid.

"A nice-looking hunk like you? All alone on the most romantic day of the year? I can't believe it."

I am rather nice-looking, I have to admit. A slight natural wave in my hair, a nice smile (thanks to extensive orthodontic work in my youth), and a trim body (thanks to a three-times-a-week jog of up to three miles).

"Ya got cute buns too."

Buns. I ask you.

"I betcha wouldn't believe I don't have a fella myself."

"Uh . . ."

"Yeah, I know. Hard to believe. But true." She tried to look wistful, but instead looked only dyspeptic. She had on a horrible pair of knit stretch pants that did nothing to help the effect.

"Look," she said. "Why don't you and me get together? I mean, it's a real shame, two hot numbers like us, all alone on the most important romantic day of the year."

She stood there and looked up at me with her black eyes way back in her head under the heavy ridges of her brows. The brows were black and straight, like her mustache. I had heard of the supermarket as being one of the hot places to meet dates nowadays but this was too much. Hot numbers. I mean, give me a break.

Still, there I was. Ditched not two days before by the light of my life, who said she thought I lacked ambition and "charisma." I had told *her* that I liked selling shoes, and that you didn't need charisma to do that. She had laughed at me and said she could tell I'd never amount to anything and that she was going to start dating somebody named Chris. "He drives a BMW," she said. "Not a tacky old Subaru." I told her that Subarus had even better repair records than BMWs, but it didn't do any good.

So call it temporary insanity. Call me irresponsible. Or call me a masochist, which is probably more like it. I was punishing myself for losing somebody who liked a car better than she liked me. Anyway, for whatever reason, I looked into Ethel Ann's pitchy black eyes and said, "Why not?"

She told me her name then, and I told her mine, which is Wayne G. (for

Garfield, but I never tell anyone that, not since that cat in the comic pages) Cook, and we agreed that she would come by and pick me up later at my apartment.

"I got a nice car," she said. "You'll like it. Plus I like to drive. We'll have a few drinks, tell a few jokes, see what develops."

Then she leered at me, a truly frightening sight, and icy fingers ran up and down my spine. Not the Old Black Magic kind. The kind that you get when you're reading Stephen King on a dark and stormy night, except that she was even scarier. . . .

But I'd given my word and that was that. I finished my shopping, without buying any roses, checked out, and went home to get ready.

She arrived right on time, wearing a red skirt with a white blouse that just sort of hung on her flat chest. She had a white envelope in her hand. "Here," she said, sticking the envelope at me. "I got ya a valentine."

I hadn't gotten her one, of course. The thought never even entered my mind, and if it had I would have rejected it instantly. I took the envelope.

"Aren't ya gonna ask me in?" she said.

I opened the door a little wider and she walked through. My living room is nothing to brag about, not being much larger than most people's second bedroom, but it is at least tidy.

She walked over and sat down on the couch while I tore at the envelope. When I got it open, I pulled out the card. It was in the shape of a heart (not a real one, of course, but a valentine one, which has absolutely no relationship to the human heart that I can see) with eyes and a mouth drawn on it. The mouth was turned down in a frown, and there were tiny tears in the corners of the eyes.

I opened the card. Inside it was written in red letters, *My heart cries for you.*

Cute, huh?" Ethel Ann said.

"Very," I said. I put the card down on my coffee table.

"So where ya wanta go?" she said. "Find a nice spot, hoist a few brewskis?"

Brewskis. Of course.

"I was thinking more along the lines of a movie," I said. The idea of what Ethel Ann might be like after a couple of brewskis frankly terrified me.

"Aww ri-i-i-i-ght!" she said. There's this new one out I've been wanting to see over at the Plaza Town Eight."

"Fine," I said. "What is it?"

"It's a new one for Valentine's Day. I EAT YOUR HEART. It's about these teenagers, see, who have this Valentine's party and this maniac or something—"

"I can't wait," I said.


She was right about one thing, at least. I loved her car. It was a perfectly restored 1957 Chevrolet.

"Original factory paint," she said. "It was a bitch to find the purple, too, believe me."

"I can imagine."

"The white for the top was easy, though. I wanted to go with red, but the guy who did the work wouldn't go for it. Some people got no taste at all."

"Too right," I said.

The movie was worse than I'd thought it might be. It wasn't so much the actual movie, though the sight of entrails and brains and exploding teenage skulls didn't really do much for me. No, the worst thing was the way Ethel Ann behaved.

She belched.

I suppose that could be my fault. After all, I did ask if she wanted something to drink to go with her popcorn (two large tubs, buttered), and carbonated water does that to some people.

She didn't have to do it so often, however. I think some of it must have been deliberate.

Also, she laughed raucously every time some semi-innocent victim lost one of his or her vital body parts or got skewered with a tree limb, broken boat paddle, lug wrench, or whatever.

Everyone else cringed, gagged, or simply looked away. Not Ethel Ann. She brayed like a mule. Or is it donkeys that bray? Well, you get the idea.

And then she . . . there's simply no delicate way to put this, really. She . . . broke wind.

Loudly.

At a time when the audience sat in absolute silence as the maniac crept quietly up on yet another teenage beauty who had thoughtlessly rejected him and who in fact had laughed when he sent her a valentine.

Just as he raised his arms high, prepared to bring the jagged mop handle down into her chest as she lay sleeping on a sofa, just as the quiet in the theater had grown almost unbearable, Ethel Ann broke wind.

It was like a gunshot, but more drawn out, if you understand what I mean. Heads turned.

Giggles began.

Ethel Ann joined in the giggles, looked at me, and pointed her finger, shaking her head sadly as if to say, "He does that all the time."

The giggles turned to laughter as I tried, without much luck, to melt through the bottom of my seat.

It was, beyond any doubt, the worst evening of my life. I can't recall ever being more repelled or disgusted. People were still giving me surreptitious glances as we left the theater. Then they would look away quickly and laugh, sometimes putting their hands over their mouths as if they didn't want me to see.

Ethel Ann wasn't bothered in the least. "That was great, huh? I don't know when I've seen so much guts on the screen."

I didn't say anything. I just wanted to get home, lock my door, and get away from her. Thank God, I would never have to see her again.

Exactly three months later, Ethel Ann Adams and I were united in what is loosely referred to as holy matrimony.

It was a lovely service, and the bride wore white. She hadn't lost any weight over the intervening months, and she looked a little like a sow stuffed into a wedding gown. Her little piggy eyes watched me from under her veil as we repeated our vows.

I managed not to throw up as I kissed her. The hairs of her little mustache pricked me under my nose.

It all came about because of her brother.

The day after Valentine's, he'd come by my apartment. It was late afternoon, and I'd just gotten in from a hard day of trying to make women's feet fit into shoes that were generally ill-made and about a size too small for the feet that were being forced into them.

I wasn't in a good mood, and Ethel Ann's brother didn't cheer me up.

He stood there in my doorway wearing a lavender silk shirt and a pair of jeans so tight that you could see the outlines of certain personal portions of his anatomy. The jeans were bell bottoms, so when he told me that he was Ethel Ann's brother, I wasn't surprised. He didn't mention that he had chosen what we call these days an "alternate life-style," but then, he didn't have to. I could just tell.

His name was Raymond and I asked him to come in. I didn't know what else to do with him.

"This is such a *sweet* little place," he said, pirouetting around to get a good look at it. "Ethel Ann said that you were charming and handsome, and she certainly didn't exaggerate. She has a tendency to do that, you know." He posed there with one hand on his hip and another in the air. "Is it all right if I sit?"

"Look," I said. "I just got in from work, and I'm not feeling too well. I'm not sure what you want, but if it's about your sister, well, I'm sorry, but I don't really think I want to see her again."

I hoped that was all it was. I hoped that Ethel Ann wasn't a recruiting service for her brother. I didn't feel like fighting him off. I really didn't.

"Oh, my dear boy," he said. "It's not at all what you think, I'm sure. Not at all. Why, you wouldn't be able to guess in a million, trillion years what I want. I'm *sure* you wouldn't."

"Why don't you tell me, then," I said.

"All right, I will, if you insist on rushing me into it. I had hoped that we might discuss the matter in a civilized manner, you know. Not rushing into it like a pair of primitives."

"I'm sorry," I said. "I'm tired, and I need my rest. If you have something to say, please say it."

"Very well. It's simple, really." He waved the hand that was in the air. "I want you to marry Ethel Ann. And then to kill her."

I just looked at him for a second or two. Then I asked him to sit down.


It was all very simple, really. I hadn't realized that Ethel Ann's father was Ronald H. Adams, the richest man in town, an oil millionaire from one of the big booms of the twenties. He was quite old now, and, according to Raymond, on his last legs.

"The old dear is going to kick off any day now," is the way Raymond put it.

As far as Raymond was concerned, that was just fine, since there was no love lost between the two of them, and that was just the problem: Raymond was cut out of the will.

"Almost, dear boy. *Almost.* Should my sweet, ingenuous sister die first, predecease me as they say in the legal offices, then the money goes to me. Not that there is much of a chance of that in the natural order of things. Ethel Ann is as healthy as a horse." He sighed. "Still, there are ways."

"Why me?" I said. "I'm just a shoe salesman. There are professionals for that kind of thing." It wasn't that I had anything against the idea. If ever anyone deserved to go, it was Ethel Ann Adams.

"Oh, *please*," he said. "Are you suggesting that I get some sort of *hitman*? That is so *common*."

Common. Well, he was probably right. I wondered how he and his sister got to be so different. Ethel Ann would have gone to a hitman in a minute. Less, probably.

"Besides, dear boy, don't you read the newspapers? Every single hitman in this city is a policeman working undercover. The last three people who have hired hitmen around here have wound up in prison."

"That's right," I said. "Not a nice place. You could get raped in there."

"I didn't say it didn't have its attractive side," he said. "It's just that I don't want to spend my *life* there."

"What about *my* life?"

"It would have to look like an accident, of course. There could be no question of your involvement. No hint of scandal could ever touch you."

"If that were possible, which I don't for a minute say it is, what's in it for me?"

"Why, money, of course; money, dear boy."

Of course.

It turned out that Raymond had managed to find out a good deal about me in the course of the day. As soon as he discovered that his sister had managed to find an actual *date*, he got the name and started to work. The idea had been in his head for weeks.

And I was the ideal subject, as it turned out. A man who had been recently rejected by a woman and who had a history of such rejection.

"How did you find that out?" I said.

"It was easy," he said, but he wouldn't elaborate. I didn't argue. It was true. The latest was just one of a continuing series. All of them for more or less the same reasons.

"And that's the problem we can solve," Raymond said. "You can show them that they were all wrong. You can show them that you are virtually *filled* with drive and ambition. That you can marry the richest woman in town and obtain a great deal of money in the process."

"If they can stop laughing," I said.

Raymond smiled. "People seldom laugh at rich people very long." He sounded as if he knew whereof he spoke.

"How much?" I said.

He told me. It was more than I'd ever dreamed of.

"And my share?"

"Let's say . . . half."

"Let's say sixty percent."

"Done," he said, and stuck out a soft pink hand.

"I don't suppose we could put this in writing," I said.

He tittered. I don't think I'd ever heard anyone titter before, but that was what he did. There's no other way to describe it. "I don't suppose we could," he said. "You'll just have to trust me, dear heart."

"I'll think about it," I said, and I did.

It took a lot of thought. I'd never even thought of killing anyone before, and it took some getting used to. On the other hand, I'd never had the chance to become a millionaire before. And, let's face it, there was never anyone on the face of the earth that I could more cheerfully kill than Ethel Ann Adams.

Raymond had given me his number. I called him back two days later. "I'll do it," I told him. "For sixty-five percent."

"Greedy, greedy," he simpered. "But all right. Sixty-five percent."

"I may need a little help."

"We'll talk about it. After the marriage."

"I've been thinking about that part. Why do I have to marry her?"

"Opportunity, of course," he said. "You'll be close to her at all times. Who knows what might come up? She might climb a ladder. Slip in the bath. And you'll be right there."

"We'll talk later," I said.

After I hung up, I called Ethel Ann and, God help me, asked her for a date.


I won't try to tell you what the marriage was like. If you have the nasty habit of imagining the bedroom scenes played out in other people's lives, then feel free to go ahead, but such events are far beyond my own poor powers of description. Suffice it to say that those scenes were as horrible as I had anticipated they might be, and in some ways even worse. I'd prefer not to think about it.

I called Raymond after a month. He said the time was "not ripe as yet, dear boy," and that his father still had a while to live. There was no rush.

I called after another month had dragged its way past, and after that I called every week. Raymond didn't seem in a great hurry. "Remember," he said, "if anything happens too soon after the wedding, there are bound to be nasty rumors and suspicions. Caeser's wife, dear boy. Caesar's wife."

I wasn't worried about Caesar's wife. I was worried about mine. She snored like a riveter. She ate like a horse. She wallowed in the bed like a wounded rhino.

She couldn't cook, and she refused to allow me to do so, though I am fairly competent in the kitchen. "It wouldn't be right to let ya do it," she said. "I'll take care of the meals."

So we subsisted on a diet of Budget Gourmet frozen dinners, along with occasional treats such as Mrs. Paul's fish sticks and Pepperidge Farms croissant pizza.

And she was a far worse housekeeper than cook. If she used a tissue, she left it in the chair or couch. Or she tossed it aside on the rug. She never dusted, and she was too lazy even to put such dishes as we used in the dishwasher. Powder covered the washstand in the bathroom. Mildew grew rampant in the shower and in the pile of towels that began to accumulate in a corner by the shower stall.

My formerly tidy apartment into which we had moved was becoming a slum area. It was almost unrecognizable.

I tried to avoid taking her out in public. She looked far worse than when we first met. As she put it, "Now that I got ya, I can afford to let myself go."

And go she did. Up by twenty or more pounds. She quit using makeup. "Too much trouble, sweetie. Bring me another brewski."

Ah, yes, the beer. Four six-packs a day at the very least. She guzzled the stuff.

Still, her father doted on her. We visited him twice a week, every week. He was a frail old man with a pink scalp and a few strands of white hair. Hands like claws.

After every visit, I called Raymond.

"Now, now," he said. "Don't be in a rush. If you're so eager for the money, just let the old man die. Then your wife will have it all."

"I don't want her to have it. I want her out of the way. Besides, if she dies then, I'll be suspected for sure. No one knows how I can stand her anyway."

"Just smile mysteriously if they ask," he said. "And don't worry."

I did worry, though, and finally I couldn't take it anymore. It was just after Ethel Ann threw up on the carpet—"Too many brewskis, I guess, honey"—and then passed out on the couch leaving me to clean up the mess.

I called Raymond. "This is it," I told him. "Now, tonight."

"Wait—" he said.

I hung up the phone.

Looking at Ethel Ann there on the couch, her mouth open, the snoring rattling the windows in the apartment, I knew I could do it. Oddly enough, I'd worried about that earlier. When it came right down to it, could I actually kill another person?

The answer was yes if the person was Ethel Ann.

I didn't think much about how to do it. I concocted some wild story about rapists and killers and went to the kitchen for a knife. I didn't have a gun, or I would have used that.

I'd slit her throat, then leave. Go to a movie. Make sure I was noticed. Then come home and find her dead. I would be the grieving husband. No one would ever know.

In my current state, it even sounded logical.

I got out the knife and tested the edge with the ball of my thumb, a stupid error, since I always kept my knives sharp.

I cut a deep gash in my thumb.

Blood was running everywhere. I got a towel from under the sink and wrapped my thumb. The bitch was going to pay for this. I rarely use foul language, but that was the way I thought of her then. The bitch.

Even then I might have done it if I hadn't stepped in the vomit. I should have cleaned it up first, I know, but I forgot. In my haste I put my foot right in the middle of it.

What a vile feeling that is, knowing what you've stepped in even though at the same time you're surprised. I brought one hand up and the other hand down. The sharp blade of the knife just missed the towel and sliced neatly into the palm of my hand. Neatly and fairly deeply. I hardly felt it at first.

Later, I felt it, of course.

I managed to get the towel around my hand and stop the blood. I knew the cut was bad. Somehow I didn't think the police would buy my story about the movies now. I left Ethel Ann lying there and went to the Emergency Room instead.

I said I'd been chopping lettuce, but no one really cared.

I bled a little on the seat covers of Ethel Ann's '57 Chevy. That was the only satisfaction I got.

❧   ❧   ❧

The next time I vowed to be much more careful. And to plan better.

I waited until just the right moment, after she had drunk her daily allotment of brewskis—*beers*; after her daily allotment of beers. Then I offered to take her to the movies.

"Ya mean it? We don't hardly go out much no more."

"I mean it," I said. *"Nightmare on Elm Street V."*

*"Aww ri-i-i-i-ght!"*

*She got ready in mere moments, ready to see Freddy.*

"Where's the car?" she said as we got to the street. "Has the car been stole?"

"No, no," I said. "I just had to park across the street. It's right over there." I pointed, and sure enough the car was there, right where I'd parked it. "Just a minute, before we cross," I said. "My shoelace is untied." I knew it was untied because I'd never tied it. I bent down.

My plan was simple. We lived on a fairly busy street. We were standing between two parked cars. I would wait until I heard a car coming, rise up fast, and bump Ethel Ann in her gigantic rear end.

She, in turn, would stumble in front of the oncoming car and be crushed to jelly.

It should have worked, but what happened was rather different.

Apparently, she moved. So, when I made my move, she wasn't where she should have been. That, in itself, wouldn't have been so bad.

The bad thing was that, while pretending to tie my shoe, I had actually done so. But in trying to keep an eye out for the oncoming car, tie the shoe and judge Ethel Ann's position, I had managed to tie my shoelaces together.

I raised up, took a half step, which was all the step I could take with my shoes tied to one another, and pitched forward into the street.

I have to give the driver full credit. He was much more alert than I would have thought he might be.

He almost managed to stop.

One of the doctors in the Emergency Room asked if I had been in before. He thought I looked familiar.

I didn't answer him. I just lay there and suffered.

Three cracked ribs. Numerous contusions and abrasions, most of them coming from skidding along the concrete street. Several gashes that required stitches.

Aside from that, I was just fine. Ethel Ann couldn't wait to get me home.

"Oh, he is my ittle itsy boogums," she said, "I take care wuv itsy boogums."

Itsy boogums. Good God.

She kept me in bed and fed me Budget Gourmet, potato chips, ice cream, and brewskis—*beers.*

She kept the television set on all the time: *The Love Connection. The New Hollywood Squares. Divorce Court. The People's Court. Superior Court.* A few more weeks of convalescing, and I might have been able to pass the bar in most states. *The New Newlywed Game* was the worst. The only thing the announcer didn't ask the contestants—if indeed they should be dignified by that word—was whether they liked to grease their mates with salad oil before they "made whoopie." (I was beginning to learn where Ethel Ann picked up her expressions.) Of course, he might have asked them that on an earlier show.

"I wonder if any of 'em ever made whoopie in bed with broke ribs?" Ethel Ann said one day. Then she leered at me. Then . . . frankly, I don't want to talk about it.

After more than a week, I was able to go back to work. It was a frightening experience. At odd moments I found myself wondering what Chuck Woolery was prying out of some woman about her date with the sleazoid of her choice, or whether the audience would vote for date number one, number two, or number three.

Occasionally, I would crave a brewski.

When I was getting about as scared of myself as I was of my wife, I called Raymond from work. "We've got to meet," I said.

He didn't like it, but he agreed. He was afraid of being seen with me.

We met on my lunch hour, in the third row of a movie theater, a place that showed third-run films for a dollar admission.

The theater was practically deserted, which was a good thing, since Raymond had no idea of protective coloration. He would have stood out in any crowd. It wasn't that he looked like his sister—quite the contrary. He was taller, and much thinner. Where her hair curled, his waved. Where she was coarse, he was refined. Except in the matter of proper dress.

It was too dark in the theater for me to tell what color his pants were, but his shirt was shocking pink. He was wearing an ascot of some dark color, and it was covered with tiny pink hearts.

My heart cries for you, I thought for some reason.

He sat down beside me. "I simply *adore* Paul Newman," he said. "He's just so *butch* with that little mustache."

So is Ethel Ann, I thought.

"But really, dear boy, we shouldn't meet like this. It's much too dangerous. What if someone should see us?"

My reputation would be ruined, I thought.

"I don't know why you're so *eager*," he went on. "If you could only be patient, I'm sure—"

"I can't wait," I said. "I think something's happening to me. Living with your sister is doing something to me. I . . . I can't explain it, but I don't think I like it."

He shook his head without taking his eyes off Paul Newman, who was stalking around a pool table in full color. "I know what you mean," he said. "I went out on my own early in life for much the same reason."

"Then *why*—" I stopped and started over, realizing I had raised my voice considerably. "Then why did you do this to me?"

"To be quite frank, I thought my father would have died by now. Surely you've *seen* him?"

I admitted that I had.

"Then you know what I mean. The strength of that man amazes me."

"But couldn't I kill her now and remain a grieving widower until you get the money? Why do I have to suffer like this?"

He managed to take his eyes off the screen and look at me. "I should think that would be quite evident," he said.

"It's sure as hell not—it's surely not evident to *me*."

He sighed theatrically. "Should she die too soon, too long before dear Father's own crisis, then he would have time to change his will. Don't you see? Why the old fool might do something *drastic*, like leaving his money to the Friends of the Earth or the Save the Whales Club. Not that I don't think that whales are quite *sweet* in their own way, but really I would much prefer to see the money go to a worthier cause. Such as myself." Then he gave me the old up and under. "And you, of course."

"Of course."

"So wait. Persevere." He pronounced it with the accent on the next-to-last syllable, so that it rhymed with *ever*. "You will be rewarded in the end."

"I'll try," I said.

He looked at me kindly. "Please do, dear boy. Please do. For both our sakes."

I left the movie then. Raymond said he thought he'd stay. "That Tom Cruise is just simply *gorgeous*," he said as I stepped into the aisle.

I looked back, and he was leaning forward in his seat. Drooling, probably.

Months went by.

Slowly.

So slowly.

Ethel Ann and I continued to visit her father. It was after one such visit that Ethel Ann said, "The old guy's lookin' better, don't ya think, hon?"

My pace faltered. She had confirmed my own suspicious. He *did* look better. Healthier, somehow.

"He's fillin' out, did ya notice? His color's better, too. He says his authuritis"—as God is my witness, that's what she said—"is better, even. He can open and close his hands real good."

I must have shuddered then.

"What's 'a matter?" Ethel Ann said. "Is my sugar booger cold?"

Sugar booger Holy shi—I mean, good grief.

It was a few weeks later that I noticed that I was eager to get home after work in time for *Wheel of Fortune*.

"That Vanna's such a doll," Ethel Ann was fond of saying. "If we ever have a kid"—she leered hopefully—"a girl kid, let's name her Vanna."

"I . . . uh . . . it's a lovely name," I said.

"And that Pat Sajak? A doll. Just a doll. Lucky for you ya got me when ya did. I could really go for I guy like that."

"Be quiet," I said. "You made me miss what letter that idiot asked for."

"It was an *m*," she said. "I thought it was a pretty good guess, myself."

"Hush," I said. "I'll miss the next one, too."

And it wasn't long after that when I realized that I was getting used to the filthy apartment. I tossed my towel on the floor right by Ethel Ann's, though I still used one more often than she did.

"After all, I hardly done a thing today," she said. "Why bathe?"

Why, indeed?

The dirty dishes piled up, the Budget Gourmet containers accumulated in the trash can, and there was actual grit on the kitchen floor. I saw roaches creeping and scuttling across the cabinets.

And at work I wondered: Who will sit in the center square on *New Hollywood Squares* today? And I wondered: Why didn't that fool take door number three yesterday? Anybody would have taken door number three. And I wondered: How could that nincompoop not have written down his answer in the form of a question? Does he have a death wish?

Worst of all was the time I thought, Gee, I wish I had me a brewski. It made my palms sweat, and my hands slipped on the smooth brown leather of the shoe I was trying to force onto the foot of a woman who obviously should have asked for a much larger size.

"What's the matter with you, fella?" she said. "Trying to feel me up?"

"You wish," I said. It slipped out. Honestly.

"What did you say, buster?"

"I . . . uh . . . said this *shoe* ish sized wrong. I'm shorry."

She looked at me with a great deal of suspicion, but she let it pass. She didn't buy any shoes, though.

I knew then that it couldn't go on any longer. I didn't care if Mr. Adams left his considerable fortune to Morris the Cat or the Liberace Museum. Something terrible was happening to me, and the longer I lived with Ethel Ann, the worse it got. I was crazy to have gone along with Raymond in the first place. For my own sanity, Ethel Ann had to go. And she had to go soon.

I didn't say anything about it to Raymond. There was no need for him to know, and I was sure he would have objected. He would have had good reason. Only two days before, Mr. Adams had gotten so much better that he had asked the doctor for an exercise program.

There was no doubt in my mind that he would live to be a hundred.

This time I made sure that nothing could go wrong. I planned everything carefully, even went over it in a practice run of sorts. This time was for keeps.

I waited until the perfect night—dark, cloudy, a little drizzle. I asked Ethel Ann if she'd like to take a drive.

"Gee, I don't know, hon. On *Lifestyles of the Rich and Famous* tonight, Robin Leach is gonna give us a tour of one of Wayne Newton's places."

"No kidding? Well—No. *No.* We really ought to get out more. All we do is watch the tube—the television set. A little drive is what we need. And you know?" I smiled at her in what I hoped was a provocative manner. "A drive in the cool night air just might give me some hot ideas."

She jumped off the couch. Well, actually, she more or less rolled off. At her size and weight, which must have been nearing 190 by then, jumping was more or less out of the question. "Why didn't ya say so the first time, sport? Lemme get some shoes on."

She did, and we left.

"Let me drive," I said. "I like to drive the Chevy."

"Fine by me, kiddo. That way I can snuggle-bunny on you."

Snuggle-bunny. Give me strength.

We drove around town for a while, nowhere in particular, listening to the radio. Ethel Ann had put a really good stereo in the old car, and a good set of speakers. Unfortunately, she usually insisted on playing her Slim Whitman tapes, but tonight she had forgotten them in her haste to get out to the car and make snuggle-bunnies.

Then I headed out toward Mount Granton.

She caught on fast. "I know where y're goin', big boy," she said. "Thinkin' about makin' a little time, huh?" She wormed her way even closer to me. "Well, I'll tell ya, ya got a good chance."

I held my gorge down and kept driving. Mount Granton was a popular spot for parking and engaging in sexual activity. It had quite a good view of the city, actually, and at night the lights could look quite attractive if you were in the right mood. Of course, on such a rainy night as this, there wouldn't be many couples there. The view was terrible, it was cold, and these days most people simply preferred to stay at home and do it in bed.

Or at least, so I hoped.

Near the top, there was a small turnout. As we neared it, I said, "Gosh, honey, I think there's something wrong with one of our tires."

There was, too. I'd let a great deal of the air out of it when I came home that afternoon. Not enough to be really bothersome, but enough to be noticeable if someone called your attention to it.

"It's in the back on my side, I think," I said. She raised her head as if that would help her to sense it. "Ya may be right," she said. "It's kinda bump-ing."

And that was true, too, not that I'd planned it. Just a little luck for a change. Things were at last about to go my way.

It was about time, after all.

"Why don't I pull up here," I said. "I can get out and check it." I gave a delicate cough. "I wish I didn't feel like I was coming down with a cold."

"If ya are, ya better not get your tootsics wet. I'll check it out for ya."

"How very thoughtful," I said.

I pulled into the turnout very carefully, just the way I had practiced it. Just the right angle. I stopped the car. Not a single automobile had passed us on the way up.

Goodbye, Ethel Ann, I thought. Or maybe I said it aloud. She laughed. "I'll be right back, ya big jerk."

That's what *you* think, my dear.

I could visualize myself talking to the police officer, tears of sorrow welling in my eyes. "It . . . it was terrible, officer. I suppose my foot slipped off the brake—God knows how!—just as she was crossing behind the car. It struck her, and the railing—the railing there is so low! There was nothing I could do to save her! Oh, my sweet darling!"

And at that point I would break down in body-shaking sobs, the drizzle in the night air blending with the tears that flowed down my innocent cheeks.

As a plan, it was perfect.

The execution of it, however, was flawed.

In order to be sure that I struck her hard enough, I was going to have to do a bit more than let the car roll backward. I was going to have to put it into reverse and give her a good, solid bump.

Even at that, I might have succeeded had I not been overly eager. I should have waited until she got right in the middle, but I didn't. I let her take one step behind the car, and shifted gears. She saw the backup lights and stepped back to the side.

I got my foot off the gas and back on the brake, but the surface was extremely slick, possibly oily. The guardrail was no help at all.

I remember hearing it splinter, my foot still frozen to the brake. I remember the rear end of the car tilting out over the ledge and the hood rearing up in the air.

I remember looking out the window at Ethel Ann's horror-stricken face.

And that's all I remembered for quite some time.


When I woke up in the hospital, all I could think of was how cold it seemed and how thirsty I felt.

I tried to move, I think, but that proved to be impossible. I was encased in casts and had one leg suspended in some sort of medieval torture device. The pain was excruciating.

I fainted.

When I came out of it again, I felt better, though not much. There was a nurse in my room. I tried to say something to her, but I found I couldn't talk. It was as if my tongue had swollen until it filled my entire mouth. So I just lay there. Then I went to sleep.

I woke up more and more often, and the nurses and doctors seemed to be encouraged by my progress. Ethel Ann was there most of the time. I tried not to look at her.

One day she asked me how I was feeling. I surprised myself by being able to answer. After that we talked a little.

I had been in the hospital for three weeks. In another three I might be able to go home, if I behaved myself and was a good little boy.

"My itsy boogums will be good," she said. "I will take care wuv my itsy boogums."

It hardly bothered me.

I got better and was able to watch the tube. I watched all the game shows that came on, which meant that I got to see a few I'd missed because of work, like *The Price Is Right*. I also got to see *Donahue*, and by the time I was ready to go home I knew I'd miss him when I had to go back to work, even if he was a little bit wimpy.

Then one day Ethel Ann came in crying. "What's the matter?" I said. "Have you talked to the doctor? He didn't say anything that he told you not to tell me, did he?"

And then an even more terrible thought struck me. "Ethel Ann—your father. He's not . . . he didn't . . ."

She looked at me and I could see that she wasn't sad at all. She was actually smiling, but the tears were running down her face and she was sobbing. "It's Daddy," she said. "It's Daddy."

I was out of traction by then, almost ready to go home. Just the casts here and there. One arm (the left) and one leg (the right), plus wrappings around my ribs (broken again, five this time). I sort of fell back in the bed in a collapse.

The old man was dead.

She was trying to keep a good face on things, but the tears gave it all away. He was dead, and that was that. If I killed Ethel Ann now, everyone would suspect me.

I tried to do the right thing. "I . . . I'm sorry," I said.

Ethel Ann wiped the back of her hand across her eyes and pulled at her nose with her fingers. "Don't be sorry," she said. "It's just that I'm so happy."

"Happy?" I said.

"That Daddy's doing so well."

"Uh . . . well?"

"Yeah. I was gonna surprise ya when ya got out of the hospital. He's been just gettin' better and better ever' day. Strong as an ox. I just found out he's gonna run in the WonTon Marathon."

"He's . . . going to run . . . in a marathon?"

She rubbed her face, which made it look redder than ever. "Ain't it great? It's like, you know, a miracle. The doctor says he may live another hundred years."

Something came over me. I don't know what. I just knew that I had to do it then, no matter what. I came off the bed at her.

At least that's what I tried to do. I remember the leg with the cast hitting the floor and skidding. I remember the sound of the bedpan clattering across the floor. I remember falling.

I remember Ethel Ann telling the doctor, "He was so excited about my news that he tried to get up. I didn't know it would make him do that, honest I didn't."

And the doctor saying, "It's not your fault; don't worry."


So I had to stay in the hospital for a while longer, and watch a bit more television. I got real good at *The Wheel of Fortune*. Did a little more study for the bar exam with Judge Wapner. Ate hospital food.

Eventually I got to go back to the apartment. What it looked like after more than a month of Ethel Ann's care and hers alone, I can hardly tell you. There were piles of dirty clothes on the couch. The roaches had moved to the coffee table. There were coffee cups on top of the TV set. With cold coffee in them. Some of them had mold growing on the top of the coffee. It was yellowish, with green around the edges.

Ethel Ann shoved the dirty clothes from the couch to the floor and installed me on the Hide-A-bed. "This'll be fun," she said. "We can watch a lotta TV."

And we did. And we drank brewskis. And we ate Budget Gourmet. Drank Diet Pepsi. Ate ice cream. And watched TV.

Finally all the casts were gone. I could walk almost as well as I had before. I could have worked at the shoe store, but I had long since been replaced. They were very sorry, but that was all.

One day when Ethel Ann was out for more junk food, I called Raymond. I named the movie theater where we'd met before and gave him a time. I told Ethel Ann that I had to get out for exercise and some fresh air.

"Is it the Glade I've been spraying? I could change brands."

I assured her that the house smelled fine. It smelled like a gymnasium built in a pine forest, but I didn't say that part.

"What, then? Exercise? That stuff'll kill ya."

I assured her that I wouldn't be long, and I went.

Raymond showed up on time. He was a little bit put out that the movie was *Crimes of the Heart*. "Honestly, Diane Keaton should never have let herself go like that, even to get the part. And Jessica Lange? My dear, she should at least have used a little makeup."

I wasn't interested in his criticisms of the movie. I had Siskel and Ebert for that. And Harris and Reed. I had another thing entirely on my mind, I told him.

"Yes, it's really too bad that it turned out this way," he said. "It seemed like such a good idea at the time," he said.

"That's all you've got to say?"

"I'm sorry, dear boy. What else *can* I say?"

"How could you ever have come up with such a harebrained scheme in the first place?" I said.

"I've often wondered. I don't think I ever took it really seriously. I did hope to get the money, but I suppose that will never happen, not now. *C'est la vie*."

"*C'est la vie?*"

"French, dear boy. It means—"

"I know what it means," I said. "What about me?"

"You?"

"Me. The man married to your sister. What about me?"

"Well," he said, "there's always divorce."

"Divorce," I said.

"I suppose she'd never agree to it. Well, one has to make the best of things."

I looked at him. It was dark, but I think he was laughing at me, quietly.

So I killed him.

It was quite easy, much easier than all my attempts with Ethel Ann. I simply stepped across him to the aisle then looked back and bent down.

"That's a lovely ascot," I said.

He simpered. "Thank you. It's pure silk. You don't think the color is a trifle . . . much?"

"Chartreuse? Don't be silly." I reached out my fingers to touch it.

And before he knew it, I had it off, twisted around his neck, and tight, so tight that he could only gargle. On the screen, Sissy Spacek was trying to hang herself, and the two or three other customers were more interested in her troubles than in Raymond's. I sat in the seat behind him and slowly strangled the life out of him. Then I left him there.

When I got back to the apartment, Ethel Ann met me at the door. She had an envelope in her hand. "Do ya know what day this is?" she said.

"No," I said. "I don't believe I do."

"That's what happens when ya spend all ya time inside. I guess gettin' out is good for ya sometimes. Anyhow, it's a special day for us." She handed me the envelope.

Then I knew, of course. How sentimental. I hadn't really suspected her of being so sentimental.

She walked toward the kitchen. "I'll get us some brewskis to help us celebrate," she said. "Open it up. It's special."

I opened the envelope, though I already suspected what I would find inside. I was right. A duplicate of the valentine she'd given me exactly one year before.

I looked at the face on the heart, the downturned mouth, the tears.

I looked up at the apartment, the filth, the roaches, the coffee cups, the clothes in piles, the plates full of crusts and crumbs.

I opened the card.

*My heart cries for you.*

I saw Ethel Ann heading toward me with the brewskis.

And cries, I thought.

And cries.

# INSIDE JOB

*Ed Gorman*

As you might imagine, I was pretty nervous when the morning finally arrived.

Electric shave so I wouldn't cut myself. New aftershave called "Impact." New blue button-down oxford shirt. And my very best blue pin-striped suit. (Oh, yes: And my newest cordovan loafers, the ones with the discreet little tassles, my old cordovans having tassles the size of golf balls.)

There. All ready to go.

Walked to the door, took a last fond look at my apartment (I really had worked hard at fixing it up) and started out the door when I looked down and saw Tasha looking up. Beautiful, elegant Tash. I picked her up far enough to nuzzle her nose against mine but not so far that she'd get any fur on me. She meowed her appreciation and I set her down again.

There. *Now* I was all ready to go.

The bank was downtown, across from a small square where nearby office workers brought sack lunches and lounged on blankets when the temperature, as today, was in the low eighties and when the breezes were so sweet and soft they made you a little crazy.

I got there an hour early, took a park bench directly across from the front doors of the bank, and proceeded to go through the entire operation.

A beat cop walked past several times, each pass with a smile larger than the last one. The soft breezes had made him just as crazy as they had the rest of us.

I studied the bank. Built in the twenties of native stone, rising fourteen stories into the midwestern sky, First National is notable mainly for the pagan religion it celebrates. Or seems to, anyway. Gargoyles are everywhere on the face of the bank, peering down ominously on the human beings below. When I was a boy growing up here, I used to dream that the gargoyles, bat-like, flew from their perches at night and chased people through alleys and dark buildings.

The cop stopped by again. "Couldn't ask for a better day."

"You sure couldn't."

His blue eyes narrowed a little as he looked first at my brown leather attaché case and then at the glass doors of the bank and then back at my attaché case again.

"On your lunch hour, huh?" the cop said.

Easy enough to figure out what he was thinking. I'd be thinking the same thing myself.

"No. Just kind of relaxing."

"Oh. I see." Staring at my attaché case again.

I smiled. "Meeting somebody, actually."

"Oh."

"Girlfriend. Well, not girlfriend. But a friend of mine who's a girl." I laughed. "I mean, I wish she really were my girlfriend."

He had relaxed again. Looked at me now instead of my attaché case. Or the front doors of the bank.

"Lookit that butterfly," he said. "Half as big as my fist."

"Beautiful."

He tapped the sole of my shoe with his nightstick. "Good luck with that friend of yours who's a girl."

"Thanks."

He strolled on.


Came the time. Twenty-six minutes later.

All sorts of terrible things happening to my digestive tract, I crossed the busy street, attaché case in hand, and entered the bank.

Having been middle-class all my life, banks, especially ones as splendidly appointed as this one with its church-like arches and vast vaulting windows, intimidate me.

I feel unworthy. Especially when I remember how little I have in my checking account.

Feeling unworthy, I crossed the bank to the tellers' windows that ran along the east wall. Each window had a line at least six people deep. Noon hours were busy times.

I got behind a tall man in a buckskin jacket and a ten-gallon cowboy hat. His expensive running shoes didn't really go with the rest of his outfit but I figured he probably wouldn't want any fashion tips from me.

Eight minutes later, Mimsy glanced up from the paperwork of her last transaction. Her blue gaze smote me.

"Good afternoon," she said, her lovely smile parting her soft, sweet lips.

I nodded. My voice had apparently gone out for lunch. For a terrible, never-ending moment there, I literally couldn't speak.

"Remember me?" I said, finally.

"Sure. You're Mr. McFall. You're in here almost every day. Until lately, I mean."

"Right. I—came in today because I've got something for you."

I had already taken it from my attaché case. I slid it across the counter, beneath the three brass bars of her cage, into her perfect hands.

She picked it up. Looked it over. "An envelope." The smile again. "This really is mysterious."

"Open it."

"Mmm. Smells good."

"I overheard you talking the other day—about your twenty-fifth birth-day coming up and I just thought—"

By now, she had it open and was tugging the big splashy card from it.

She read the sentiments on the card and said, "It's beautiful. Thank you very much, Mr. McFall. I'm really flattered."

"That's not all."

I handed her a second envelope. This one much smaller than the first.

She opened it up, extricated the card, looked inside.

"This is very, very nice. I've always wanted to see what that restaurant looked like."

"Well, you're about to find out."

"But I only have an hour for lunch and I—"

"I have a table reserved. They're waiting for us right now."

A certain impishness shone in her electric blue eyes. "What if I'd said no?"

"Then I'd have had myself two delicious lunches."

"You're crazy," she laughed. "But in a nice way. I'll meet you at the front door in five minutes."

My God, I could scarcely believe it. All those nights of tossing and turn-ing, all those nights of planning my reaction when she turned me down, all those nights of dreaming about Mimsy Williams in my arms as I told her I loved her—

But she had said yes.

Yes.


Even though there were at least two dozen elegantly dressed and coiffed ladies in the expensive restaurant, none of them was as intriguing, in her easy unpretentious way, as Mimsy in her white blouse and blue skirt and artfully mussed strawberry blonde hair.

After much debate, we both settled on food that sounded awfully fancy but was basically a hamburger with white sidewalls and a few other options.

"Are you going steady?" she said after the waiter had left.

"No. I'm completely unattached at the moment. And, frankly, I'm hoping you are, too."

"A) I am unattached at the moment. And B) I meant are you going steady with your attaché case?"

I smiled. "I probably should have left it with the hat check girl, huh?"

"Just as long as you don't start dancing with it out on the floor there."

At night, patrons used the small floor space to our right for dancing.

The waiter brought our drinks. Two Coca-Colas.

"So what do you do?" she asked. "Besides tote your attaché case around?"

"I'm an actor."

"A thespian?"

"Thanks for not saying lesbian."

"I was going to but I figured you'd probably heard that before."

"About 10,000 times," I said.

"How come you're in the Midwest?"

I shrugged. "Re-charging my batteries, I guess. When I first went to LA ten years ago, I got a lot of series work. One- and two-line parts, mostly, but there was a lot of it. I just figured this was how you worked your way up." I stopped. "But here I go, the typical actor's lunch. Talking about himself."

"No. Go on. Please. Unless you want to hear all about my life as a bank teller. Which, believe me, you don't."

"Well, anyway, those one- and two-line parts that were supposed to lead somewhere? They didn't. I did a lot of dinner theater and some commercials but I could never do better than make a very marginal living. So, on my thirty-fifth birthday last year, I came back home to look for meaningful employment."

"And you found it?"

"Afraid not. Employers take one look at my résumé and see 'Actor' and I'm all done. Out here 'actor' has a very strange sound to it."

"So you haven't been able to find a job?"

"Oh, no, I found one, all right. The only one that suits my talents."

"Uh-huh? So what's your job?"

"I'm a phone solicitor. 'Hello, Mrs. Adams, Acme Siding will be in your neighborhood next week and be offering—'"

"—a free inspection—"

" '—and a 20 percent discount if you act now.' "

"God, I hate people like you."

"Thank you."

"I mean, nothing personal."

"I know. My calling has not exactly made me a lot of friends." I smiled. "I used to think I got rejected a lot when I was trying out for acting parts. That was nothing compared to this. People slamming phones and swearing at you and—"

"That's probably why you need your security blanket—that attaché case."

"You're probably right. But actually, I've got another present for you. That's why I brought my trusty attaché case along."

"Now you've really got me interested."

"But I like suspense. So we won't open the case until after we finish eating."

At which point, as if on cue, the waiter arrived with our upwardly mobile hamburgers.

We ate. And we were comfortable enough to do it heartily. No mincing little bites, either. Big, hungry bites.

When we were each halfway through the luncheon fare, she said, "Where've you been?"

"You mean you really noticed that I haven't been there for awhile? At your window I mean?"

"Sure. I told you that already. I've missed you." For the first time her composure seemed to slip a little. She seemed just the tiniest bit awkward. "It always made me feel better when I saw you there."

"Well, thank you."

"Especially since Don told me about Susan."

"Don being—"

"—my old boyfriend."

"And Susan being—"

"—his new girlfriend."

"Ah."

"But it was for the best. I mean, I was heartbroken at first, after he told me about her and everything, but after awhile I realized that we would have made lousy mates anyway." She smiled that smile. "So I was kind of hoping, when I saw you at my window I mean, that someday you'd get up the nerve to ask me—Well, ask me to go have some lunch. The way you did today." She paused. "I thought maybe I'd scared you off somehow."

"Are you kidding?"

"Either that, or I thought it might have had something to do with the robbery. Believe it or not, there are customers who won't come back to the bank since it happened."

"Afraid they'll run into a robbery in progress?"

"Exactly." She looked at me a most curious way. "That's kind of funny."

"What is?"

"I didn't realize it before but you stopped coming to my window right after I got stuck up."

"Really?"

The same curious took. "Really."

"Boy," I said, "isn't this a great lunch?"

"Did I upset you just then?"

"Upset me? Why would you upset me?"

"Talking about the robbery and all. Some people hate to talk about stuff like that."

"I'm not upset at all. I'm fine. Really."

She finished her hamburger. Now, oddly enough, we both seemed a little awkward with each other.

I wasn't sure how to say it.

"Have you ever made a very serious mistake?" I said.

"Sure."

"I mean, a really *serious* one."

"I'm sure I have."

I raised my attaché case. Set it on the table.

"Well, a few weeks ago I made a profoundly serious mistake."

"Oh, damn," she said. "It is you, isn't it?"

"Huh?"

"You are the man who stuck me up, aren't you?"

"How did you know?"

"Your attaché case. The Richard Nixon mask was a nice touch. But you shouldn't have used your own attaché case. I knew right away when I saw it today. At the bank, I mean. It's the same case you used when you robbed my teller window."

I sighed. "I knew I'd screw it up somehow. I mean, I just wasn't cut out to be a bank robber. Too many things can go wrong and I've never been worth a damn at detail. And anyway—"

We sat silent for a long moment.

"Anyway, it was wrong, stealing the money. That's why I brought it back."

"You did?"

I tapped the attaché case. "Every dollar of it is in here. When I got home, I just kept thinking of your face and how much—well, how much I've come to like seeing you every day and—well, how could I ever ask you out if I was a bank robber?"

"Why'd you want the money, anyway?"

I shrugged. "Grub stake in LA. Go back and give acting one more try. But—it was crazy all the way around. I don't want to go back to LA and I don't want to be a bank robber." I pushed the attaché case toward her. "Could you sneak the money back into the bank and pretend you just found it lying there?"

She suddenly looked miserable. "I could have if I hadn't been such a good citizen." She nodded to two men in dark suits standing by the maitre d'. "Those are the two detectives who're in charge of the case. Remember when I said I'd meet you at the front door in five minutes? Well, having seen your attaché case, I called them and said that the man who'd robbed me had just asked me out to lunch. I didn't know it was you. They said they'd meet me here. They're tried to come over here twice now but I gave them a little signal to wait. I wanted to talk to you first for awhile." She paused and said, "No, wait a minute. I can take the money back. Sure I can. And just say I found it sitting on my cage. Give me the attaché case before they get here."

I was just about to say something when I saw her wave and smile at the two detectives who were now starting toward us. As she waved and smiled, she eased the attaché case off the table to the floor next to her chair.

"Good afternoon," she said.

They both looked like businessmen, which seems to be the preferred style for police officers today.

"Hello, Mimsy."

She shook her head and laughed. "I know what you two are thinking, but he's not the one. Detectives Manheim and Toler, this is my boyfriend Michael McFall."

The two detectives looked properly confused.

"He was gone—the robber, I mean—when I went to meet him at the front door. Poof, gone." She snapped her fingers. "And luckily for me, Michael had stopped in to say hello so I had a lunch date after all."

"So you don't know where the robber went?"

She shrugged, "Must've gotten scared and took off. That's all I can think of." She then gave a detailed description of a short, stocky man with dark hair. In contrast to my own slender blond six-two.

"Sorry for the false alarm. I was going to call you, but then I decided you'd want to talk to me anyway—to get his description and all."

She gave them an innocent look that nobody could resist. Nobody with any soul, anyway.

They sighed and looked a little frustrated, maybe even a little irritated, but what could they say?

"You see or hear from the suspect again, please call us right away," said Detective Manheim. Then he offered me his best professional smile. "Nice to meet you, Mr. McFall."

I nodded to both men and watched as they walked away.

When I turned back to Mimsy, she was writing something down on a small square of white paper.

"My unlisted phone number and address. Why don't you bring a pizza over around seven? There's a John Wayne movie on cable that I just love. *The Searchers*."

"That's one of my favorite movies," I said, as I got up, went around and pulled her chair out for her.

We paid the bill and walked outside.

The stroll back to the bank was leisurely and pleasureful.

"God, it feels so good," she said. "Finding each other, I mean."

"I know," I said, giving her hand a gentle squeeze.

I walked her around to the employees' entrance and there I kissed her goodbye. Temporarily.

"Seven o'clock," I said.

"You've got my address."

As indeed I had.

She went inside.


I suppose you can figure the rest out for yourself. I couldn't—not at first—but then I guess I'm a pretty naive guy when you come right down to it.

She wasn't there at seven because there wasn't any such address. Nor any such phone number.

Nor was she at work in the morning. Or the following morning. Or the morning after that.

Yesterday I got a card from her, stamped *Buenos Aires*.

*Dear Michael,*

*I just want you to know that, deep down, I'm not really a bad person.*

*And I also want you to know that this is the first really impulsive thing I've ever done in my life.*

*But the bank was so b-o-r-i-n-g.*

*Yrs. Mimsy*

It's enough to make a fellow cynical. It really is.

# DEADLY FANTASIES

*Marcia Muller*

M s. McCone, I know what you're thinking. But I'm not paranoid. One of them—my brother or my sister—*is* trying to kill me!"

"Please, call me Sharon." I said it to give myself time to think. The young woman seated across my desk at All Souls Legal Cooperative certainly sounded paranoid. My boss, Hank Zahn, had warned me about that when he'd referred her for private investigative services.

"Let's go over what you've told me, to make sure I've got it straight," I said. "Six months ago you were living here in the Mission district and working as a counselor for emotionally disturbed teenagers. Then your father died and left you his entire estate, something in the neighborhood of thirty million dollars."

Laurie Newingham nodded and blew her nose. As soon as she'd come into my office she'd started sneezing. Allergies, she'd told me. To ease her watering eyes she'd popped out her contact lenses and stored them in their plastic case; in doing that she had spilled some of the liquid that the lenses soaked in over her fingers, then nonchalantly wiped them on her faded jeans. The gesture endeared her to me because I'm sloppy, too. Frankly, I couldn't imagine this freshly scrubbed young woman—she was about ten years younger than I, perhaps twenty-five—possessing a fortune. With her trim, athletic body, and tanned, snub-nosed face, and carelessly styled blond hair, she looked like a high school cheerleader. But Winfield Newingham had owned much of San Francisco's choice real estate, and Laurie had been the developer's youngest—and apparently favorite—child.

I went on, "Under the terms of the will, you were required to move back into the family home in St. Francis Wood. You've done so. The will stipulated that your brother Dan and sister Janet can remain there as long as they wish. So you've been living with them, and they've both been acting hostile because you inherited everything."

"Hostile? One of them wants to *kill* me! I keep having stomach cramps, throwing up—you know."

"Have you seen a doctor?"

"I *hate* doctors! They're always telling me there's nothing wrong with me, when I know there is."

"The police, then?"

"I like them a whole lot less than doctors. Besides, they wouldn't believe me." Now she took out an inhaler and breathed deeply from it.

Asthma, as well as allergies, I thought. Wasn't asthma sometimes psychosomatic? Could the vomiting and other symptoms be similarly rooted?

"Either Dan or Janet is trying to poison me," Laurie said, "because if I die, the estate reverts to them."

"Laurie," I said, "why did your father leave everything to you?"

"The will said it was because I'd gone out on my own and done something I believed in. Dan and Janet have always lived off him; the only jobs they've ever been able to hold down have been the ones Dad gave them."

"One more question: why did you come to All Souls?" My employer is a legal services plan for people who can't afford the going rates.

Laurie looked surprised. "I've *always* come here, since I moved to the Mission and started working as a counselor five years ago. I may be able to afford a downtown law firm, but I don't trust them, any more now than I did when I inherited the money. Besides, I talked it over with Dolph, and he said it would be better to stick with a known quantity."

"Dolph?"

"Dolph Edwards. I'm going to marry him. He's director of the guidance center where I used to work—still work, as a volunteer."

"That's the Inner Mission Self-Help Center?"

She nodded. "Do you know them?"

"Yes." The center offered a wide range of social services to a mainly Hispanic clientele—including job placement, psychological counseling, and short term financial assistance. I'd heard that recently their programs had been drastically cut back due to lack of funding—as all too often happens in today's arid political climate.

"Then you know what my father meant about my having done something I believed in," Laurie said. "The center's a hopeless mess, of course; it's never been very well organized. But it's the kind of project I'd like my money to work for. After I marry Dolph I'll help him realize his dreams effectively—and in the right way."

I nodded and studied her for a moment. She stared back anxiously. Laurie was emotionally ragged, I thought, and needed someone to look out for her. Besides, I identified with her in a way. At her age, I'd also been the cheerleader type, and I'd gone out on my own and done something I believed in, too.

"Okay," I said. "What I'll do is talk with your brother and sister, feel the situation out. I'll say you've applied for a volunteer position here, counseling clients with emotional problems, and that you gave their names as character references."

Her eyes brightened and some of the lines of strain smoothed. She gave me Dan's office phone number and Janet's private line at the St. Francis Wood house. Preparing to leave, she clumsily dropped her purse on the floor. Then she located her contact case and popped a lens into her mouth to clean it; as she fitted it into her right eye, her foot nudged the bag, and the inhaler and a bottle of time-release vitamin capsules rolled across the floor. We went for them at the same time, and our heads grazed each other's.

She looked at me apologetically. One of her eyes was now gray, the other a brilliant blue from the tint of the contact. It was like a physical manifestation of her somewhat schizoid personality: down to earth wholesomeness warring with what I had begun to suspect was a dangerous paranoia.

Dan Newingham said, "Why the hell does Laurie want to do that? She doesn't have to work any more, even as a volunteer. She controls all the family's assets."

We were seated in his office in the controller's department of Newingham Development, on the thirty-first floor of one of the company's financial district buildings. Dan was a big guy, with the same blond good looks as his sister, but they were spoiled by a petulant mouth and a body whose bloated appearance suggested an excess of good living.

"If she wants to work," he added, "there're plenty of positions she could fill right here. It's her company, dammit, and she ought to take an interest in it."

"I gather her interests run more to social service."

"More to the low life, you mean."

"In what respect?"

Dan got up and went to look out the window behind the desk. The view of the bay was blocked by an upthrusting jumble of steel and plate glass—

the legacy that firms such as Newingham Development had left a once old-fashioned and beautiful town.

After a moment, Dan turned. "I don't want to offend you, Ms. . . . McCone, is it?"

I nodded.

"I'm not putting down your law firm, or what you're trying to do," he went on, "but when you work on your end of the spectrum, you naturally have to associate with people who aren't quite . . . well, of our class. I wasn't aware of the kind of people Laurie was associating with during those years she didn't live at home, but now . . . her boyfriend, that Dolph, for instance. He's always around; I can't stand him. Anyway, my point is, Laurie should settle down now, come back to the real world, learn the business. Is that too much to ask in exchange for thirty million?"

"She doesn't seem to care about the money."

Dan laughed harshly, "Doesn't she? Then why did she move back into the house? She could have chucked the whole thing."

"I think she feels she can use the money to benefit people who really need it."

"Yes, and she'll blow it all. In a few years there won't *be* any Newingham Development. Oh, I know what was going through my father's mind when he made that will: Laurie's always been the strong one, the dedicated one. He thought that if he forced her to move back home, she'd eventually become involved in the business and there'd be real leadership here. Laurie can be very single-minded when she wants things to go a certain way, and that's what it takes to run a firm like this. But the sad thing is, Dad just didn't realize how far gone she is in her bleeding heart sympathies."

"That aside, what do you think about her potential for counseling our disturbed clients?"

"If you really want to know, I think she'd be terrible. Laurie's a basket case. She has psychosomatic illnesses, paranoid fantasies. She needs counseling herself."

"Can you describe these fantasies?"

He hesitated, tapping his fingers on the window frame. "No, I don't think I care to. I shouldn't have brought them up."

"Actually, Mr. Newingham, I think I have an inkling of what they are. Laurie told her lawyer that someone's trying to poison her. She seemed obsessed with the idea, which is why we decided to check her references thoroughly."

"I suppose she also told her lawyer who the alleged poisoner is?"

"In a way. She said it was either you or your sister Janet."

"God, she's worse off than I realized. I suppose she claims one of us wants to kill her so he can inherent my father's estate. That's ridiculous—I don't need the damned money. I have a good job here, and I've invested profitably." Dan paused, then added, "I hope you can convince her to get into an intensive therapy program before she tries to counsel any of your clients. Her fantasies are starting to sound dangerous."


Janet Newingham was the exact opposite of her sister: a tall brunette with a highly stylized way of moving and speaking. Her clothes were designer, her jewelry expensive, and her hair and nails told of frequent attention at the finest salons. We met at the St. Francis Wood house—a great pile of stone reminiscent of an Italian villa that sat on a double lot near the fountain that crowned the area's main boulevard. I had informed Laurie that I would be interviewing her sister, and she had agreed to absent herself from the house; I didn't want my presence to trigger an unpleasant scene between the two of them.

I needn't have worried, however. Janet Newingham was one of those cool, reserved women who may smolder under the surface but seldom displays anger. She seated me in a formal parlor overlooking the strip of park that runs down the center of St. Francis Boulevard and served me coffee from a sterling silver pot. From all appearances, I might have been there to discuss the Junior League fashion show.

When I had gotten to the point of my visit, Janet leaned forward and extracted a cigarette from an ivory box on the coffee table. She took her time lighting it, then said, "*Another* volunteer position? It's bad enough she kept on working at that guidance center for nothing after they lost their federal funding last spring, but this . . . I'm surprised; I thought nothing would ever pry her away from her precious Dolph."

"Perhaps she feels it's not a good idea to stay on there, since they plan to be married."

"Did she tell you that? Laurie's always threatening to marry Dolph, but I doubt she ever will. She just keeps him around because he's her one claim to the exotic. He's one of these social reformers, you know. Totally devoted to his cause."

"And what is that?"

"Helping people. Sounds very sixties, doesn't it. That center is his *raison d'être*. He founded it, and he's going to keep it limping along no matter what. He plays the crusader role to the hilt, Dolph does: dresses in Salvation Army castoffs, drives a motorcycle. You know the type."

"That's very interesting," I said, "but it doesn't have much bearing on Laurie's ability to fill our volunteer position. What do you think of her potential as a counselor?"

"Not a great deal. Oh, I know that's what she's been doing these past five years, but recently Laurie's been . . . a very disturbed young woman. But you know that. My brother told me of your visit to his office, and that you had already heard of her fantasy that one of us is trying to kill her."

"Well, yes. It's odd—"

"It's not just odd, it's downright dangerous. Dangerous for her to walk around in such a paranoid state, and dangerous for Dan and me. It's our reputations she's smearing."

"Because on the surface you both appear to have every reason to want her out of the way."

Janet's lips compressed—a mild reaction, I thought, to what I'd implied. "On the surface, I suppose that is how it looks," she said. "But as far as I'm concerned Laurie is welcome to our father's money. I had a good job in the public relations department at Newingham Development; I saved and invested my salary well. After my father died, I quit working there, and I'm about to open my own public relations firm."

"Did the timing of your quitting have anything to do with Laurie's inheriting the company?"

Janet picked up a porcelain ashtray and carefully stubbed her cigarette out. "I'll be frank with you, Ms. McCone: it did. Newingham Development had suddenly become not a very good place to work; people were running scared—they always do when there's no clear managerial policy. Besides . . ."

"Besides?"

"Since I'm being frank, I may as well say it. I did not want to work for my spoiled little bitch of a sister who's always had things her own way. And if that makes me a potential murderer—"

She broke off as the front door opened. We both looked that way. A man wearing a shabby tweed coat and a shocking purple scarf and aviator sunglasses entered. His longish black hair was windblown, and his sharp features were ruddy from the cold. He pocketed a key and started for the stairway.

"Laurie's not here, Dolph," Janet said.

He turned. "Where is she?"

"Gone shopping."

"Laurie hates to shop."

"Well, that's where she is. You'd better come back in a couple of hours." Janet's tone did little to mask her dislike.

Nor did the twist of his mouth mask *his* dislike of his fiancée's sister. Without a word he turned and strode out the door.

I asked, "Dolph Edwards?"

"Yes. You can see what I mean."

Actually, I hadn't seen enough of him, and I decided to take the opportunity to talk to him while it was presented. I thanked Janet Newingham for her time and hurried out.

Dolph's motorcycle was parked at the curb near the end of the front walk, and he was just revving it up when I reached him. At first his narrow lips pulled down in annoyance, but when I told him who I was, he smiled and shut the machine off. He remained astride it while we talked.

"Yes, I told Laurie it would be better to stick with All Souls," he said when I mentioned the context in which I'd first heard of him. "You've got good people there, and you're more likely to take Laurie's problem seriously than someone in a downtown law firm."

"You think someone *is* trying to kill her, then?"

"I know what I see. The woman's sick a lot lately, and those two"—he motioned at the house—"hate her guts."

"You must see a great deal of what goes on here," I said. "I noticed you have a key."

"Laurie's my fiancée," he said with a puritanical stiffness that surprised me.

"So she said. When do you plan to be married?"

I couldn't make out his eyes behind the dark aviator glasses, but the lines around them deepened. Perhaps Dolph suspected what Janet claimed: that Laurie didn't really intend to marry him. "Soon," he said curtly.

We talked for a few minutes more, but Dolph could add little to what I'd already observed about the Newingham family. Before he started his bike he said apologetically, "I wish I could help, but I'm not around them very much. Laurie and I prefer to spend our time at my apartment."

�֍    ✕    ✕

I didn't like Dan or Janet Newingham, but I also didn't believe either was trying to poison Laurie. Still, I followed up by explaining the situation to my former lover and now good friend Greg Marcus, lieutenant with the SFPD homicide detail. Greg ran a background check on Dan for me, and came up with nothing more damning than a number of unpaid parking tickets. Janet didn't even have those to her discredit. Out of curiosity, I asked him to check on Dolph Edwards, too. Dolph had a record of two arrests involving political protests in the late seventies—just what I would have expected.

At that point I reported my findings to Laurie and advised her to ask her brother and sister to move out of the house. If they wouldn't, I said, she should talk to Hank about invalidating that clause of her father's will. And in any case she should also get herself some psychological counseling. Her response was to storm out of my office. And that, I assumed, ended my involvement with Laurie Newingham's problems.

But it didn't. Two weeks later Greg called to tell me that Laurie had been taken ill during a family cocktail party and had died at the St. Francis Wood house, an apparent victim of poisoning.

I felt terrible, thinking of how lightly I had taken her fears, how easily I'd accepted her brother and sister's claims of innocence, how I'd let Laurie down when she'd needed and trusted me. So I waited until Greg had the autopsy results and then went to the office at the Hall of Justice.

"Arsenic," Greg said when I'd seated myself on his visitor's chair. "The murderer's perfect poison: widely available, no odor, little if any taste. It takes the body a long time to eliminate arsenic, and a person can be fed small amounts over a period of two or three weeks, even longer, before he or she succumbs. According to the medical examiner, that's what happened to Laurie."

"But why small amounts? Why not just one massive dose?"

"The murderer was probably stupid enough that he figured if she'd been sick for weeks we wouldn't check for poisons. But why he went on with it after she started talking about someone trying to kill her . . ."

"He? Dan's your primary suspect, then?"

"I was using 'he' generically. The sister looks good, too. They both had extremely strong motives, but we're not going to be able to charge either until we can find out how Laurie was getting the poison."

"You say extremely strong motives. Is there something besides the money?"

"Something connected to the money; each of them seems to need it more badly than they're willing to admit. The interim management of Newingham Development has given Dan his notice; there'll be a hefty severance payment, of course, but he's deeply in debt—gambling debts, to the kind of people who won't accept fifty-dollars-a-week installments. The sister had most of her savings tied up in one of those real estate investment partnerships; it went belly up, and Janet needs to raise additional cash to satisfy outstanding obligations to the other partners."

"I wish I'd known about that when I talked with them. I might have prevented Laurie's death."

Greg held up a cautioning hand. "Don't blame yourself for something you couldn't know or foresee. That should be one of the cardinal rules of your profession."

"It's one of the rules, all right, but I seem to keep breaking it. Greg, what about Dolph Edwards?"

"He didn't stand to benefit by her death. Laurie hadn't made a will, so everything reverts to the brother and sister."

"No will? I'm surprised Hank didn't insist she make one."

"According to your boss, she had an appointment with him for the day after she died. She mentioned something about a change in circumstances, so I guess she was planning to make the will in favor of her future husband. Another reason we don't suspect Edwards."

I sighed. "So what you've got is a circumstantial case against one of two people."

"Right. And without uncovering the means by which the poison got to her, we don't stand a chance of getting an indictment against either."

"Well . . . the obvious means is in her food."

"There's a cook who prepares all the meals. She, a live-in maid, and the family basically eat the same things. On the night she died, Laurie, her brother and sister, and Dolph Edwards all had the same hors d'oeuvres with cocktails. The leftovers tested negative."

"And you checked what she drank, of course."

"It also tested negative."

"What about medications? Laurie probably took pills for her asthma.

She had an inhaler—"

"We checked everything. Fortunately, I caught the call and remembered what you'd told me. I was more than thorough. Had the contents of the bedroom and bathroom inventoried, anything that could have contained poison was taken away for testing."

"What about this cocktail party? I know for a fact that neither Dan nor Janet liked Dolph. And according to Dolph, they both hated Laurie. He wasn't fond of them, either. It seems like an unlikely group for a convivial gathering."

"Apparently Laurie arranged the party. She said she had an announcement to make."

"What was it?"

"No one knows. She died before she could tell them."

Three days later Hank and I attended Laurie's funeral. It was in an old-fashioned churchyard in the little town of Tomales, near the bay of the same name northwest of San Francisco. The Newinghams had a summer home on the bay, and Laurie had wanted to be buried there.

It was one of those winter afternoons when the sky is clear and hard, and the sun is as pale as if it were filtered through water. Hank and I stood a little apart from the crowd of mourners on the knoll, near a windbreak of eucalyptus that bordered the cemetery. The people who had traveled from the city to lay Laurie to rest were an oddly assorted group: dark-suited men and women who represented San Francisco's business community; others who bore the unmistakable stamp of high society; shabbily dressed Hispanics who must have been clients of the Inner Mission Self-Help Center. Dolph Edwards arrived on his motorcycle; his inappropriate attire—the shocking purple scarf seemed several shades too festive—annoyed me.

Dan and Janet Newingham arrived in the limousine that followed the hearse and walked behind the flower-covered casket to the graveside. Their pious propriety annoyed me, too. As the service went on, the wind rose. It rustled the leaves of the eucalyptus trees and brought with it dampness and the odor of the nearby bay. During the final prayer, a strand of my hair escaped the knot I'd fastened it in and blew across my face. It clung damply there, and when I licked my lips to push it away, I tasted salt—whether from the sea air or tears, I couldn't tell.

As soon as the service was concluded, Janet and Dan went back to the limousine and were driven away. One of the Chicana women stopped to speak to Hank; she was a client, and he introduced us. When I looked around for Dolph, I found he had disappeared. By the time Hank finished chatting with his client, the only other person left at the graveside besides us and the cemetery workers was an old Hispanic lady who was placing a single rose on the casket.

Hank said, "I could use a drink." We started down the uneven stone walk, but I glanced back at the old woman, who was following us unsteadily.

"Wait," I said to Hank and went to take her arm as she stumbled.

The woman nodded her thanks and leaned on me, breathing heavily.

"Are you all right?" I asked. "Can we give you a ride back to the city?" My old MG was the only car left beyond the iron fence.

"Thank you, but no," she said. "My son brought me. He's waiting down the street, there's a bar. You were a friend of Laurie?"

"Yes." But not as good a friend as I might have been, I reminded myself. "Did you know her through the center?"

"Yes. She talked with my grandson many times and made him stay in school when he wanted to quit. He loved her, we all did."

"She was a good woman. Tell me did you see her fiancé leave?" I had wanted to give Dolph my condolences.

The woman look puzzled.

"The man she planned to marry—Dolph Edwards."

"I thought he was her husband."

"No, although they planned to marry soon."

The old woman sighed. "They were always together. I thought they were already married. But nowadays who can tell? My son—Laurie helped his own son, but is he grateful? No. Instead of coming to her funeral, he sits in a bar. . . ."

I was silent on the drive back to the city—so silent that Hank, who is usually oblivious to my moods, asked me twice what was wrong. I'm afraid I snapped at him, something to the effect of funerals not being my favorite form of entertainment, and when I dropped him at All Souls, I refused to have the drink he offered. Instead I went downtown to City Hall.

꙳  ꙳  ꙳

When I entered Greg Marcus's office a couple of hours later, I said without preamble, "The Newingham case: you told me you inventoried the contents of Laurie's bedroom and bathroom and had anything that could have contained poison taken away for testing?"

". . . Right."

"Can I see the inventory sheet?"

He picked up his phone and asked for the file to be brought in. While he waited, he asked me about the funeral. Over the years, Greg has adopted a wait-and-see attitude toward my occasional interference in his cases. I've never been sure whether it's because he doesn't want to disturb what he considers to be my shaky thought processes, or that he simply prefers to leave the hard work to me.

When the file came, he passed it to me. I studied the inventory sheet, uncertain exactly what I was looking for. But something was missing there. What? I flipped the pages, then wished I hadn't. A photo of Laurie looked up at me, brilliant blue eyes blank and lifeless. No more cheerleader out to save the world—

Quickly I flipped back to the inventory sheet. The last item was "handbag, black leather, & contents." I looked over the list of things from the bathroom again and focused on the word "unopened."

"Greg," I said, "what was in Laurie's purse?"

He took the file from me and studied the list. "It should say here, but it doesn't. Sloppy work—new man on the squad."

"Can you find out?"

Without a word he picked up the phone receiver, dialed, and made the inquiry. When he hung up he read off the notes he'd made. "Wallet. Checkbook. Inhaler, sent to lab. Vitamin capsules, also sent to lab. Contact lens case. That's all."

"That's enough. The contact lens case is a two-chambered plastic receptacle holding about half an ounce of fluid for the lenses to soak in. There was a brand-new, unopened bottle of the fluid on the inventory of Laurie's bathroom."

"So?"

"I'm willing to bet the contents of that bottle will test negative for arsenic; the surface of it might or might not show someone's fingerprints, but not Laurie's. That's because the murderer put it there *after* she died, but *before* your people arrived on the scene."

Greg merely waited.

"Have the lab test the liquid in that lens case for arsenic. I'm certain the results will be positive. The killer added arsenic to Laurie's soaking solution weeks ago, and then he removed that bottle and substituted the unopened one. We wondered why slow poisoning, rather than a massive dose; it was because the contact case holds so little fluid."

"Sharon, arsenic can't be ingested through the eyes—"

"Of course it can't! But Laurie had the habit, as lots of contact wearers do—you're not supposed to, of course; it can cause eye infections—of taking her lenses out of the case and putting them into her mouth to clean them before putting them on. She probably did it a lot because she had allergies and took the lenses off to rest her eyes. That's how he poisoned her, a little at a time over an extended period."

"Dan Newingham?"

"No. Dolph Edwards."

Greg waited, his expression neither doubting nor accepting.

"Dolph is a social reformer," I said. "He founded that Inner Mission Self-Help Center; it's his whole life. But its funding has been cancelled and it can't go on much longer. In Janet Newingham's words, Dolph is intent on keeping it going 'no matter what.'"

"So? He was going to marry Laurie. She could have given him plenty of money—"

"Not for the center. She told me it was a 'hopeless mess.' When she married Dolph, she planned to help him, but in the 'right way.' Laurie has been described to me by both her brother and sister as quite single-minded and always getting what she wanted. Dolph must have realized that too, and knew her money would never go for his self-help center."

"All right, I'll take your word for that. But Edwards still didn't stand to benefit. They weren't married, she hadn't made a will—"

"They *were* married. I checked that out at City Hall a while ago. They were married last month, probably at Dolph's insistence when he realized the poisoning would soon have a fatal effect."

Greg was silent for a moment. I could tell by the calculating look in his eyes that he was taking my analysis seriously. "That's another thing we slipped up on—just like not listing the contents of her purse. What made you check?"

"I spoke with an old woman who was at the funeral. She thought they were married and made the comment that nowadays you can't tell. It got me thinking. . . . Anyway, it doesn't matter about the will because under

California's community property laws, Dolph inherits automatically in the absence of one."

"It seems stupid of him to marry her so soon before she died. The husband automatically comes under suspicion—"

"But the poisoning started long *before* they were married. That automatically threw suspicion on the brother and sister."

"And Dolph had the opportunity."

"Plenty. He even tried to minimize it by lying to me: he said he and Laurie didn't spend much time at the St. Francis Wood House, but Dan described Dolph as being around all the time. And even if he wasn't he could just as easily have poisoned her lens solution at his own apartment. He told another lie to you when he said he didn't know what the announcement Laurie was going to make at the family gathering was. It could only have been the announcement of their secret marriage. He may even have increased the dosage of poison, in the hope she'd succumb before she could reveal it."

"Why do you suppose they kept it secret?"

"I think Dolph wanted it that way. It would minimize the suspicion directed at him if he just let the fact of the marriage come out after either Dan or Janet had been charged with the murder. He probably intended to claim ignorance of the community property laws, say he'd assumed since there was no will he couldn't inherit. Why don't we ask him if I'm right?"

Greg's hand moved toward his phone. "Yes—why don't we?"


When Dolph Edwards confessed to Laurie's murder, it turned out that I'd been absolutely right. He also added an item of further interest: he hadn't been in love with Laurie at all, had had a woman on the Peninsula whom he planned to marry as soon as he could without attracting suspicion.

It was too bad about Dolph; his kind of social crusader had so much ego tied up in their own individual projects that they lost sight of the larger objective. Had Laurie lived, she would have applied her money to any number of worthy causes, but now it would merely go to finance the lifestyles of her greedy brother and sister.

But it was Laurie I felt worst about. And it was a decidedly bittersweet satisfaction that I took in solving her murder, in fulfilling my final obligation to my client.

# DEATH SCENE

*Helen Nielsen*

The woman who had driven in with the black Duesenberg fascinated Leo Manfred. She stood well, as if she might be a model or a dancer. Her ankles were arched and her calves firm. Leo wriggled out from under the car he was working on in order to examine her more closely.

She was dressed all in white—white hat with a wide, schoolgirl brim; white dress, fitted enough to make her body beckon him further; white shoes with high, spiked heels.

But it was more than the way she dressed and the way she stood. There was something strange about her, almost mysterious, and mystery didn't go well in the grease-and-grime society of Wagner's Garage. Leo got to his feet.

Carl Wagner, who was half again Leo's thirty years, and far more interested in the motor he'd uncovered than in any woman, blocked the view of her face. But her voice, when she spoke, was soft and resonant.

"Mr. Wagner," she said, "can you tell me when my automobile will be ready?"

Automobile—not car. Leo's active mind took note.

By this time Wagner was peering under the hood with the enthusiasm of a picnicker who had just opened a boxed banquet.

"It's a big motor, Miss Revere," he answered, "and every cylinder has to be synchronized. Your father's always been very particular about that."

"My father—" She hesitated. There was the ghost of a smile. It couldn't be seen, but it was felt—the way some perfumes, Leo reflected, are felt. "My father is very particular, Mr. Wagner. But it's such a warm day, and I don't feel like shopping."

Carl Wagner wasted neither words nor time. The fingers of one hand went poking into the pocket of his coveralls and dug up a set of keys at the same instant that he glanced up and saw Leo.

"My helper will take you home," he said. "You can tell your father that we'll deliver the car just as soon as it's ready."

If Leo Manfred had believed in fate, he would have thought this was it; but Leo believed in Leo Manfred and a thing called opportunity.

Women were Leo's specialty. He possessed a small black book containing the telephone numbers of more than 57 varieties; but no one listed in his book was anything like the passenger who occupied the backseat of the boss's new Pontiac as it nosed up into the hills above the boulevard.

Leo tried to catch her face in the rearview mirror. She never looked at him. She stared out of the window or fussed with her purse. Her face was always half lost beneath the shadow of the hat. She seemed shy, and shyness was a refreshing challenge.

At her direction, the Pontiac wound higher and higher, beyond one new real estate development after another, until, at the crest of a long private driveway, it came to a stop at the entrance of a huge house. Architecturally, the house was a combination of Mediterranean and late Moorish, with several touches of early Hollywood. Not being architecturally inclined, Leo didn't recognize this; but he did recognize that it must have cost a pretty penny when it was built, and that the gardener toiling over a pasture-size lawn couldn't have been supplied by the Department of Parks and Beaches.

And yet, there was a shabbiness about the place—a kind of weariness, a kind of nostalgia, that struck home as Leo escorted his passenger to the door.

"I know this house!" he exclaimed. "I've seen pictures of it. It has a name—" And then he stared at the woman in white, who had been given a name by Carl Wagner. "Revere," he remembered aloud. "Gordon Revere."

"Gavin Revere," she corrected.

"Gavin Revere," Leo repeated. "That's it! This is the house that the big film director Gavin Revere built for his bride, Monica Parrish. It's called—"

The woman in white had taken a key out of her purse.

"Mon-Vere," she said.

Leo watched her insert the key into the lock of the massive door and then, suddenly, the answer to the mystery broke over him.

"If you're Miss Revere," he said, "then you must be the daughter of Monica Parrish. No wonder I couldn't take my eyes off you."

"Couldn't you?"

She turned toward him, briefly, before entering the house. Out of her purse she took a dollar bill and offered it; but Leo had glimpsed more than a stretch of long, drab hall behind her. Much more.

"I couldn't take money," he protested, "not from you. Your mother was an idol of mine. I used to beg dimes from my uncle—I was an orphan—to go to the movies whenever a Monica Parrish was playing."

Leo allowed a note of reverence to creep into his voice.

"When you were a very small boy, I suppose," Miss Revere said.

"Eleven or twelve," Leo answered. "I never missed a film your mother and father made—"

The door closed before Leo could say more; and the last thing he saw was that almost smile under the shadow of the hat.


Back at the garage, Carl Wagner had questions to answer.

"Why didn't you tell me who she was?" Leo demanded. "You knew."

Wagner knew motors. The singing cylinders of the Duesenberg were to him what a paycheck and a beautiful woman, in the order named, were to Leo Manfred. He pulled his head out from under the raised hood and reminisced dreamily.

"I remember the first time Gavin Revere drove this car in for an oil change," he mused. "It was three weeks old, and not one more scratch on it now than there was then."

"Whatever happened to him?" Leo persisted.

"Polo," Wagner said. "There was a time when everybody who was anybody had to play polo. Revere wasn't made for it. Cracked his spine and ended up in a wheelchair. He was in and out of hospitals for a couple of years before he tried a comeback. By that time everything had changed. He made a couple of flops and retired."

"And Monica Parrish?"

"Like Siamese twins," Wagner said, "Their careers were tied together. Revere went down, Parrish went down. I think she finally got a divorce and married a Count Somebody—or maybe she was the one who went into that Hindu religion. What does it matter? Stars rise and stars fall, Leo, but a good motor . . ."

Twelve cylinders of delight for Carl Wagner; but for Leo Manfred, a sweet thought growing in the fertile soil of his rich, black mind.

"I'll take the car back when it's ready," he said.

And then Wagner gave him one long stare and a piece of advice that wasn't going to be heeded.

"Leo," he said, "stick to those numbers in your little black book."


For a man like Leo Manfred, time was short. He had a long way to travel to get where he wanted to go, and no qualms about the means of transportation. When he drove the Duesenberg up into the hills, he observed more carefully the new developments along the way. The hills were being whittled down, leveled off, terraced, and turned into neat pocket-estates as fast as the tractors could make new roads and the trucks haul away surplus dirt. Each estate sold for $25,000 to $35,000, exclusive of buildings, and he would have needed an adding machine to calculate how much the vast grounds of Mon-Vere would bring on the open market.

As for the house itself—he considered that as he nosed the machine up the steep driveway. It might have some value as a museum or a landmark—Mon-Vere Estates, with the famous old house in the center. But who cared about relics anymore? Raze the house and there would be room for more estates. It didn't occur to Leo that he might be premature in his thinking.

He had showered and changed into his new imported sports shirt; he was wearing his narrowest trousers, and had carefully groomed his mop of near-black hair. He was, as the rearview mirror reassured him, a handsome devil, and the daughter of Gavin Revere, in spite of a somewhat ethereal quality, was a woman—and unless all his instincts, which were usually sound, had failed him, a lonely woman. Celebrities reared their children carefully, as if they might be contaminated by the common herd, which made them all the more susceptible to anyone with nerve and vitality.

When Leo rang the bell of the old house, it was the woman in white who answered the door, smiling graciously and holding out her hand for the keys. Leo had other plans. Wagner insisted that the car be in perfect order, he told her. She would have to take a test drive around the grounds. His job was at stake—he might get fired if he didn't obey the boss's orders.

With that, she consented, and while they drove Leo was able to communicate more of his awe and respect and to make a closer evaluation of the property, which was even larger than he had hoped. Not until they returned and were preparing to enter the garage did he manage to flood the motor and stall the car.

"It must be the carburetor," he said. "I'll have a look."

Adjusting the carburetor gave him additional time and an opportunity to get his hands dirty. They were in that condition when a man's voice called out from the patio near the garage.

"Monica? What's wrong? Who is that man?"

Gavin Revere was a commanding figure, even in a wheelchair. A handsome man with a mane of pure white hair, clear eyes, and strong features. The woman in white responded to his call like an obedient child.

When the occasion demanded, Leo could wear humility with the grace of his imported sports shirt. He approached Revere in an attitude of deep respect. Mr. Revere's car had to be in perfect condition. Would he care to have his chair rolled closer so that he could hear the motor? Would he like to take a test drive? Had he really put more than 90,000 miles on that machine himself?

Revere's eyes brightened, and hostility and suspicion drained away. For a time, then, he went reminiscing through the past, talking fluently while Leo studied the reserved Monica Revere at an ever-decreasing distance. When talk wore thin, there was only the excuse of his soiled hands. The servants were on vacation, he was told, and the water in their quarters had been shut off. The gardener, then, had been a day man.

Leo was shown to a guest bath inside the house—ornate, dated, and noisy. A few minutes inside the building was all he needed to reassure himself that his initial reaction to the front hall had been correct: the place was a gigantic white elephant built before income taxes and the high cost of living. An aging house, an aging car—props for an old man's memories.

Down the hall from the bathroom he found even more interesting props. One huge room was a kind of gallery. The walls were hung with stills from old Revere-Parrish films—love scenes, action scenes, close-ups of Monica Parrish. Beauty was still there—not quite lost behind too much makeup; but the whole display reeked of an outdated past culminating in a shrine-like exhibition of an agonized death scene—exaggerated to the point of the ridiculous—beneath which, standing on a marble pedestal, stood a gleaming Oscar.

Absorbed, Leo became only gradually aware of a presence behind him. He turned. The afternoon light was beginning to fade, and against it, half-shadow and half-substance, stood Monica Revere.

"I thought I might find you here," she said. She looked toward the death scene with something like reverence in her eyes. "This was his greatest one," she said. "He comes here often to remember."

"He" was pronounced as if in reference to a deity.

"He created her," Leo said.

"Yes," she answered softly.

"And now both of them are destroying you."

It was the only way to approach her. In a matter of moments she would have shown him graciously to the door. It was better to be thrown out trying, he thought. She was suddenly at the edge of anger.

"Burying you," Leo added quickly. "Your youth, your beauty—"

"No, please," she protested.

Leo took her by the shoulders. "Yes, please," he said firmly. "Why do you think I came back? Wagner could have sent someone else. But today I saw a woman come into that garage such as I'd never seen before. A lovely, lonely woman—"

She tried to pull away, but Leo's arms were strong. He pulled her closer and found her mouth. She struggled free and glanced back over her shoulder toward the hall.

"What are you afraid of?" he asked. "Hasn't he ever allowed you to be kissed?"

She seemed bewildered.

"You don't understand," she said.

"Don't I? How long do you think it takes for me to see the truth? A twenty-five-year-old car, a thirty-year-old house, servants on 'vacation.' No, don't deny it. I've got to tell you the truth about yourself. You're living in a mausoleum. Look at this room! Look at that stupid shrine!"

"Stupid!" she gasped.

"Stupid," Leo repeated. "A silly piece of metal and an old photograph of an overdone act by a defunct ham. Monica, listen. Don't you hear my heart beating?" He pulled her close again. "That's the sound of life, Monica—all the life that's waiting for you outside these walls. Monica—"

There was a moment when she could have either screamed or melted in his arms. The moment hovered—and then she melted. It was some time before she spoke again.

"What is your name?" she murmured.

"Later," Leo said. "Details come later."


The swiftness of his conquest didn't surprise Leo. Monica Revere had been sheltered enough to make her ripe for a man who could recognize and grasp opportunity.

The courtship proved easier than he dared hope. At first they met, somewhat furtively, at small, out-of-the-way places where Monica liked to sit in a half-dark booth or at candlelit tables. She shunned popular clubs and bright lights, and this modesty Leo found both refreshing and economical.

Then, at his suggestion, further trouble developed with the Duesenberg, necessitating trips to Mon-Vere, where he toiled over the motor while Gavin Revere, from his wheelchair watched, directed, and reminisced. In due time Leo learned that Revere was firmly entrenched at Mon-Vere. "I will leave," he said, "in a hearse and not before—"which, when Leo pondered on it, seemed a splendid suggestion.

A man in a wheelchair. The situation posed interesting possibilities, particularly when the grounds on which he used the chair were situated so high above the city—so remote, so rugged, and so neglected. The gardener had been only for the frontage. Further inspection of the property revealed a sad state of disrepair in the rear, including the patio where Revere was so fond of sunning himself and which overlooked a sheer drop of at least two hundred feet to a superhighway someone had thoughtfully constructed below. Testing the area with an old croquet ball found in the garage, Leo discovered a definite slope toward the drop, and only a very low and shaky stucco wall as an obstacle.

Turning from a minute study of this shaky wall, Leo found Monica, mere yards away, watching him from under the shadow of a wide-brimmed straw hat. He rose to the occasion instantly.

"I hoped you would follow me," he said. "I had to see you alone. This can't go on, Monica. I can't go on seeing you, hearing you, touching you—but never possessing you. I want to marry you, Monica—I want to marry you now."

Leo had a special way of illustrating "now" that always left a woman somewhat dazed. Monica Revere was no exception. She clung to him submissively and promised to speak with Gavin Revere as soon as she could.

Two days later, Leo was summoned to a command performance in the gallery of Mon-Vere. The hallowed stills surrounded him; the gleaming Oscar and the grotesque death scene formed a background for Gavin Revere's wheelchair. Monica stood discreetly in the shadows. She had pleaded the case well. Marriage was agreeable to Gavin Revere—with one condition.

"You see around us the mementos of a faded glory," Revere said. "I know it seems foolish to you, but aside from the sentimental value, these relics indicate that Monica has lived well. I had hoped to see to it that she always would; but since my accident I am no longer considered a good insurance risk. I must be certain that Monica is protected when I leave this world, and a sick man can't do that. If you are healthy enough to pass the physical examination and obtain a life insurance policy for fifty thousand dollars, taken out with Monica Revere named as beneficiary, I will give my consent to the marriage. Not otherwise.

"You may apply at any company you desire," he added, "provided, of course, that it is a reputable one. Monica, dear, isn't our old friend, Jeremy Hodges, a representative for Pacific Coast Mutual? See if his card is in my desk."

The card was in the desk.

"I'll call him and make the appointment, if you wish," Revere concluded, "but if you do go to Hodges, please, for the sake of an old man's pride, say nothing of why you are doing this. I don't want it gossiped around that Gavin Revere is reduced to making deals."

His voice broke. He was further gone than Leo had expected—which would make everything so much easier. Leo accepted the card and waited while the appointment was made on the phone. It was a small thing for Leo to do—to humor an old man not long for this world.

While he waited, Leo mentally calculated the value of the huge ceiling beams and hardwood paneling, which would have to come out before the wreckers disposed of Gavin Revere's faded glory.

Being as perfect a physical specimen as nature would allow, Leo had no difficulty getting insurance. Revere was satisfied. The marriage date was set, and nothing remained except discussion of plans for a simple ceremony and honeymoon.

One bright afternoon on the patio, Leo and Monica—her face shaded by another large-brimmed hat—and Gavin Revere in his wheelchair, discussed the details. As Revere talked, recalling his own honeymoon in Honolulu, Monica steered him about. The air was warm, but a strong breeze came in from the open end of the area where the paving sloped gently toward the precipice.

At one point, Monica took her hands from the chair to catch at her hat, and the chair rolled almost a foot closer to the edge before she recaptured it. Leo controlled his emotion. It could have happened then, without any action on his part. The thought pierced his mind that she might have seen more than she pretended to see the day she found him at the low wall. Could it be that she too wanted Gavin Revere out of the way?

Monica had now reached the end of the patio, and swung the chair about.

"Volcanic peaks," Revere intoned, "rising like jagged fingers pointing Godward from the fertile, tropical Paradise . . ."

Monica, wearied, sank to rest on the shelf of the low wall. Leo wanted to cry out.

"A veritable Eden for young lovers," Gavin mused. "I remember it well . . ."

Unnoticed by Monica, who was busy arranging the folds of her skirt, the old wall had cracked under her weight and was beginning to bow outward toward the sheer drop. Leo moved forward quickly. This was all wrong— Monica was his deed to Mon-Vere. All those magnificent estates were poised on the edge of oblivion.

The crack widened.

"Look out—"

The last words of Leo Manfred ended in a kind of eerie wail, for in lunging forward, he managed somehow—probably because Gavin Revere, as if on cue, chose that instant to grasp the wheels of the chair and push himself about—to collide with the chair and thereby lose his balance at the very edge of the crumbling wall.

At the same instant, Monica rose to her feet to catch at her wind-snatched hat, and Leo had a blurred view of her turning toward him as he hurtled past in his headlong lunge into eternity.

At such moments, time stands as still as the horrible photos in Gavin Revere's gallery of faded glory; and in one awful moment Leo saw what he had been too self-centered to see previously—Monica Revere's face without a hat and without shadows. She smiled in a serene, satisfied sort of way; and in some detached manner of self-observation he was quite certain that his own agonized features were an exact duplication of the face in the death scene.

Leo Manfred was never able to make an accurate measurement; but it was well over two hundred feet to the busy superhighway below.


In policies of high amounts, the Pacific Coast Mutual always conducted a thorough investigation. Jeremy Hodges, being an old friend, was extremely helpful. The young man, he reported, had been insistent that Monica Revere be named his sole beneficiary; he had refused to say why. "It's a personal matter," he had stated. "What difference does it make?" It had made no difference to Hodges, when such a high commission was at stake.

"It's very touching," Gavin Revere said. "We had known the young man such a short time. He came to deliver my automobile from the garage. He seemed quite taken with Monica."

Monica stood beside the statuette, next to the enlarged still of the death scene. She smiled softly.

"He told me that he was a great fan of Monica Parrish when he was a little boy," she said.

Jeremy handed the insurance check to Gavin and then gallantly kissed Monica's hand.

"We are all fans . . . and little boys . . . in the presence of Monica Parrish," he said. "How do you do it, my dear? What is your secret? The years have taken their toll of Gavin, as they have of me, but they never seem to touch you at all."

It was a sweet lie. The years had touched her—about the eyes, which she liked to keep shaded, and the mouth, which sometimes went hard—as it did when Jeremy left and Gavin examined the check.

"A great tragedy," he mused. "But as you explained to me at rehearsal, my dear, it really was his own idea. And we can use the money. I've been thinking of trying to find a good script."

Monica Parrish hardly listened. Gavin could have his dreams; she had her revenge. Her head rose proudly.

"All the critics agreed," she said. "I was magnificent in the death scene."

# GOODBYE, SUE ELLEN

*Gillian Roberts*

I don't want a lifetime supply of chewing gum! I want *stock*!" Ellsworth Hummer looked around the conference table, pausing to glare at each of the other directors of Chatworth Chewing Gum, Incorporated.

Neither Peter Chatworth (Shipping), Jeffrey Chatworth (Advertising), Oliver Chatworth (Product Control), Agatha Chatworth (Accounting), nor Henry Chatworth (Human Resources) glared back. Instead, each adopted a rather sorrowful expression. Then they turned their collective attention to the chairperson of the board, Sue Ellen Chatworth Hummer.

Sue Ellen looked at her red-faced husband. "We've told you before, honey," she said in her sweetest voice, "Daddy didn't want it that way. This is the Chatworth *family* business."

"I'm family now, aren't I?"

His response was a mildly surprised widening of six pairs of disgustingly similar Chatworth eyes.

"You're my *husband* now, honey, but you're a Hummer, not a Chatworth," Sue Ellen said, purring. "Besides, you should be happy. After all, you're president of the company."

Ellsworth Hummer's blood percolated. She made it sound like playing house—You be the mommy and I'll be the daddy. Only Sue Ellen's game was, You play the president and I'll be the chairperson for real. His title was meaningless as long as Sue Ellen held the stock in her name only.

He'd received the position as an extra wedding gift from his bride, six months earlier, but all it had yielded so far was a lot of free chewing gum. And now, for the sixth time in as many months, the board had voted him down, denied him any real control, any stock, any say.

Ellsworth stood up. The chair he'd been on toppled backwards and landed with a soft thunk on the thick Persian carpet. "I'm sick of Daddy and his rules!" he shouted. "Sick of Chatworths, one and all! Sick of chewing gum!"

"You can't truly mean that." Cousin Peter sounded horrified.

"I do!" Ellsworth shouted.

"But, honey," Sue Ellen said, "chewing gum has kept the Chatworths alive. Chewing gum is our life! How can you possibly be sick of it?"

"What's more," Ellsworth said, "I am not interested in anything else you have to say, or in any of the business on the agenda today or in the future." And he left, slamming the heavy door behind him, cursing the fate that had brought him so far, and yet not far enough.

Once home, he settled into the lushly panelled room Sue Ellen had redecorated for him. She called it his "study," although she'd been unable to tell him what important documents he was supposed to study in there, so he used the room to study the effects of alcohol on the human nervous system. It was the most hospitable room in the rambling, semidecrepit mansion Sue Ellen had inherited. The place had gone to seed after Mrs. Chatworth's death and Sue Ellen had been too busy being his bride—she said—to begin renovations yet. So Ellsworth spent a great deal of time in his study. Now he poured himself a brandy and considered his options. Sue Ellen owned the house. Sue Ellen owned the company. And Sue Ellen owned him. That was not at all the way things were supposed to have worked out.

Divorce was not an option. He had signed a prenuptial agreement because, long ago, Sue Ellen's daddy had reminded her that she'd better not forget that husbands were outsiders, not family. All a split would get him was a one-way ticket back to his mother's shack or, God help us all, to a nine-to-five job. Ellsworth shuddered at the thought of either possibility.

There was only one logical solution. Aside from what she made as chairperson of the present-day company, Sue Ellen was rich in trust funds and the fruits of earlier chewing gum sales, and he was Sue Ellen's legal heir. Ergo, Sue Ellen had to die.

He sighed, not with distaste for the idea itself, but for the work and effort involved in it. This was not how he'd envisioned the happily-everafter part. He sighed again, and squared his shoulders. He was equal to the task and would do whatever was necessary to achieve his destiny.

All he'd been gifted with at birth was a well-designed set of features and a great deal of faith in himself. His mother, poor in every other way, was rich in hope. Her favorite phrase had always been, "You'll go far, Ellsworth."

And as soon as it was possible, he had.

He'd kept on going, farther and farther, until he finally found the perfect ladder on which to climb to success: Sue Ellen Chatworth, a plain and docile young woman who had spent her life trying to atone for having been born a female.

The elder Chatworths, including the much revered Daddy himself, had never paid attention to Sue Ellen. She was regarded as a bit of an error, a botched first try at producing a son. All their attention was focused on the point in the future when they would be blessed with their rightful heir.

After two heirless decades, during which time the daughter of the house attempted invisibility and was by and large raised by the servants, it finally dawned on the Chatworths that Sue Ellen and chewing gum were to be their only products.

Upon realizing this, Mrs. Chatworth quietly died of shame.

Given that Mr. Chatworth's entire existence was devoted to chewing gum, he was naturally made of more resilient material than his spouse had been. He came home from his wife's funeral and looked toward the horizons. As soon, he made it clear, as a decent period of mourning was over, he'd start afresh with a new brood mare.

But before he found a woman with the look of unborn sons in her, Ellsworth Hummer appeared and became the first human being to take Sue Ellen seriously. She was, understandably, dazzled. Her father took a dimmer view of the courtship.

He was not for a moment enchanted when Ellsworth appeared at his office door and formally asked for Sue Ellen's hand. "Blackgaurd!" he shouted. "Fortune hunter!"

Ellsworth merely grinned. "Now, now," he said. "You won't be losing a daughter. You'll be gaining a son at long last."

Mr. Chatworth was unused to either irony or defiance in even the most minute dosages. His veins expanded dangerously. His face became mauve, a color Ellsworth had never particularly cared for. Short of breath, he waved his fist at the young man on the other side of his desk. "You'll get *nothing*! I'll change my will!" he shouted. "If you and that daughter of mine, that—"

"Sue Ellen," Ellsworth prompted him. "Sue Ellen's her name, Pop."

Mr. Chatworth was now the color of a fully mature eggplant. "I'll see that you don't get what you want if it's the last thing I—"

"We were thinking of having the wedding in about two weeks," Ellsworth said mildly. "I'd like you to give your daughter away, of course."

"You'll marry over my dead body!" Mr. Chatworth shouted. And then he toppled, face-down, onto his desk and ceased this life thereby, as ever, proving himself correct and having the last word on the subject.

Grateful that the gods and high blood pressure had conspired to pave his way, Ellsworth sailed into marriage and a chewing gum empire. But a mere six months later, he recognized that his triumph was hollow. A sham. All he'd truly gotten was married. Very. And Sue Ellen thought that meant something, wanted to be close to him, seemed unable to comprehend that she was merely a means to an end, to the stock, to the money.

At each of the six monthly board meetings, Ellsworth wheedled, cajoled, charmed, argued, and pontificated about the necessity of his being given some real control. During six months' worth of non-board meeting days, Ellsworth suggested, hinted, insinuated, and said outright how much more of a man he'd feel if Sue Ellen would only treat him as an equal.

"Oh, honey," Sue Ellen would giggle from her pillow, "you're more than enough of a man for me already!"

Today's board meeting had been his last attempt. Now there was no remedy left except Sue Ellen's death.

But how?

Every eye in the impossibly tight-knit family would be on him. He needed a rock-solid alibi. No amateurish hacking or burying in the cellar would work. The cousins detested him as actively as he disliked them. He had to remain above suspicion.

"Hi, Ellsworth," Sue Ellen said brightly, interrupting his dark and private thoughts. "You working in here or something?"

"What work would I be doing?" he said. "What real work do I have to do?"

"Still sulking? Oh, my, honey, you don't want to be so glum about everything. After all, we've got each other and our health."

He was not cheered by being reminded of those truisms. "You and your cousins take care of all your business?" he asked tartly.

She nodded.

"Anything special?"

She lit a cigarette. "Oh, the company picnic plans and . . . you know, this and that. Ellsworth, honey, you yourself said you weren't and never would be interested in the kind of stuff that concerns the board, and I respect that." She inhaled deeply.

"Those cigarettes will kill you," he muttered. But too slowly, he added to himself. Much too slowly.

"Aren't you the most considerate groom a girl could have?" she chirruped. "I know I have to stop, but maybe in a bit. Not right now. I'm a little too tense to think about it."

"Your family would make anybody tense," he said. "I hate them."

"Yes. I know that. But I like them." She had been leaning on the edge of his desk, but now she stood straight, then bent to stub out her cigarette in his otherwise unused ashtray. "I'm going to visit Cousin Tina this afternoon," she said. "She's been feeling poorly."

There was nothing newsworthy about either Tina's health or the weekly visit. Sue Ellen saw her crotchety cousin every Saturday afternoon. "Goodbye, Sue Ellen," he said.

"See you," she answered with a wave.

Studying the effects of more brandy, Ellsworth listened as his wife's car pulled out, beginning its way over the mountain pass to her cousin's. And he smiled, because Sue Ellen had just helped him decide the method of her death. She would meet her end in a tragic crash going down that mountain. A little tinkering with the brakes and the car would be too far gone after plummeting over the side for anyone to bother investigating.

Ellsworth had one week left before he became a widower. For seven days, he was almost polite to his wife, providing her with fond final memories of him. He kissed her goodbye on the morning of the last day.

"Goodbye, Sue Ellen," he said, and he repeated the words to himself several times during the day as he lay dreaming of how he'd spend the Chatworth fortune. He smiled as he dozed, waiting for the police to arrive and announce the accident.

"Ellsworth!" The voice was agitated, feminine and definitely Sue Ellen's. He opened one eye and saw her. The dull, drab, infinitely boring, and incredibly rich Sue Ellen was intact.

"You'll never believe what happened to me!"

"Try me," he said slowly.

"I was going over the pass and suddenly I didn't have any brakes! I just screamed and panicked and knew that I was going to die!"

Ellsworth sat up. So far, it was exactly as he'd planned it. Except for this part, with her standing here, very much alive. "What did you do, Sue Ellen?" For once, he was honestly interested in what she had to say.

"Don't laugh, but I lost my head and screamed for my daddy. 'Daddy! Daddy! Help me!' like a real idiot, I guess, or something. But then, like magic, suddenly I could hear him, clear as day, a voice from beyond shouting and impatient with me the way he always was. It was mystical almost, Ellsworth, like he was right there with me screaming, 'Don't be such an all-around idiot, girl, and don't *bother* me! Get a grip and leave me out of this!' It almost makes you believe, doesn't it?" She looked bedazzled.

"Well, what good is it to be told to get a grip?" Ellsworth asked.

"What good? Well, I always did what my Daddy said. So I got a grip—on the steering wheel. I stopped waving my arms and being crazy, that's what. And to tell you the truth, I think that's what my . . . my heavenly *vision* meant, because what else could I have gripped? That message from my dear daddy saved me, because I hung on, racing around those curves until finally I was on flat ground again, and then I just ran the car into Cousin Tina's barn to stop it." She finally drew a breath.

Ellsworth tilted his head back and glowered upward. He felt strongly that supernatural intervention—even of the bad-tempered kind—violated all the rules.

Sue Ellen's bright smile flashed and then faded almost immediately. "I pretty much wrecked it, though," she said.

"The barn?"

"That, too. I meant the car. I think they're both totaled. I have Cousin Tina's car right now."

Ellsworth mentally deducted the cost of a car and Tina's new barn from the inheritance he'd receive as soon as he came up with a second, more reliable plan for her disposal.

He was appalled by how few really good ways there were to safely murder anyone. He studied mystery magazines and books about criminals and was depressed and discouraged by the fact that the murderer was too often apprehended. It seemed to him that the most successful homicides were those semi-random drive-by shootings that seemed to happen in great uninvestigated clusters, but they were so urban, and Ellsworth and Sue Ellen lived nestled in rural rolling hills, not a street corner within shooting distance. Gang warfare would be too much of a stretch in the sticks.

The problem was, once the crime grew more deliberate and focused, there were horrifyingly accurate ways of identifying the culprit, right down to matching his DNA from the merest bit of him. It was Ellsworth's opinion that forensic science had gone entirely too far.

However, accidents in the home seemed more likely to pass muster. People clucked their tongues and shook their heads and moved on without undue attention or speculation. So one Monday morning, before he left for another day of sitting and staring at his office walls, Ellsworth carefully greased the bottom of the shower with Sue Ellen's night cream. Then he dropped the jar and left. Sue Ellen was fond of starting her day a bit later than he began his. She was "not a morning person" in her own clichéd words, and she required a steamy hot shower to "get the old motor turning over." This time, he hoped to get more than the old motor and the clichés twirling. He was confident she'd slip and either be scalded to death, die of head injuries, or cover the drain in her fall and drown. That sort of thing happened all the time and didn't even make headlines.

This plan had some latitude, and he liked it.

He was downstairs, drinking coffee and reading the morning paper, when the old pipes of the house signaled that Sue Ellen's shower was going full blast.

"Yes!" he said, raising his buttered toast like a flag. "Yes!" Soon he would call the police and explain how he'd found his wife's body in the shower, too late, alas, to save her.

And then he heard the scream. Yes, yes! He waited for the thud or the gurgle.

Instead, he heard a torrent of words.

Words were wrong. Words did not compute. Whole long strings of words were not what a slipping, sliding, fatally wounded woman would utter.

The words came closer, toward the top of the stairs. Two voices. Ellsworth tensed.

"I don't care if you're new!" Sue Ellen was behaving in a shrill and unlady-like manner, to put it mildly. Her daddy would not have approved. "Some-body must have told you my routine. I *need* my morning shower!"

"But, miss, I wanted to make it nice. It was all greasy in there."

"That's ridiculous! It was cleaned yesterday afternoon. That's when it's always done. Well after I'm through."

"Messy. Greasy. But it's nice now."

And then the voices softened. Sue Ellen had a temper when crossed, but it was morning and she wasn't "up to speed" as she would undoubtedly say, so she made peace and retreated to her unslick, horribly safe shower.

Ellsworth refused to be discouraged. He decided to poison her instead, and he chose the family's Memorial Day gathering as the occasion. With forty relatives on his patio, there would be safety in numbers.

Cousin Lotta, according to Sue Ellen, was bringing her famous potato salad, just as she had every other year. Ellsworth had never tasted it, but he decided its recipe could nonetheless be slightly altered. He'd offer to help bring out the covered dishes. It wouldn't be difficult to make an addition in the kitchen.

The plan was brilliant. Many Chatworths would be sickened, but Sue Ellen, her portion hand-delivered by him and specially spiced, would be sickened unto death. And if anyone came under suspicion, it would be Lotta.

He sang all through the morning of the party. In his pocket were small vials of dangerous this and lethal that to be sprinkled over the potatoes, and a special bonus vial for his best beloved.

"I'll bring out the food," he told his wife later in the day.

"Oh, thank you." She spoke listlessly and looked pastier than ever. Her makeup barely clung to her skin. Unwholesome, he thought. Definitely unappetizing. "I'm feeling a bit woozy. I'd be glad to just sit a while longer. Thank you."

It was amazing how easy it was to doctor the salad with no one noticing.

Except that Sue Ellen didn't want to eat. "I'm not really feeling very well," she murmured.

Ah, but unfortunately, left to her own devices, she eventually *would* feel better, he thought. Or was she suspicious? He felt a moment's panic, then relaxed. She was merely being her usual uncooperative, dim self. "It's hunger," he insisted. "You know how you get when you forget to eat for too long. You need something in your stomach. Sit right there—I'll prepare a plate for you."

"Oh, no, I don't think . . . I really do feel quite odd."

"You're overexcited by this wonderful party, these wonderful people," he said. "Relax and let me take care of you."

He watched happily as she ate Gert's ribs and Mildred's pickled beans and Lotta's quietly augmented potato salad. He had known that if pressed, Sue Ellen wouldn't dare hurt her cousins' feelings by refusing to eat their offerings. He could see the headlines in tomorrow's papers. "Tragedy Stalks Chatworth Barbecue: Chewing Gum Heiress Bites Potato Salad and the Dust."

Maybe he'd give the reporters Sue Ellen's wedding portrait. She looked almost good in it. "Goodbye, Sue Ellen," he whispered.

Suddenly, she stood up, horror and pain distorting her features, and she ran, clutching her mouth, toward the woodsy spot behind the house. He followed until he heard the sounds of her being violently ill. And then, slump-shouldered, he walked back to the party.

"Stomach virus," the doctor said later. "Comes on all of a sudden, just like that. Going around. Let her rest a few days. She's plumb cleaned out inside."

"I told you I felt awful," Sue Ellen murmured from her bed.

A few of the cousins also felt poorly. Too poorly to drive home, in fact, and Ellsworth spent the night in his study, trying to lock out the noises of people being sick all over the house.

He could not believe that of all the world, he alone was a failure at murder. He went upstairs and stared at Sue Ellen. She managed a faint wave of greeting.

"I'm so ashamed," she said. "Getting sick in front of everybody like that. Ruining the party. I could just die!"

Fat chance, he thought as he watched her drift back to sleep.

Finally, Sue Ellen regained her strength and began to visit her cousins again. They had a new source of conversation besides each other and chewing gum these days. Now they could review the Day the Chatworths Got the Stomach Flu. They also had a new project. While in residence, several of the cousins had noticed that the house could use some modern-ization and loving care. Sue Ellen had also become aware of needed work while she was on the mend. "Falling apart," she would now say.

"Not at all! It's a fortress! They built strong and sturdy places back then," Ellsworth insisted. The sort of remodeling she had in mind would cost a fortune—*his* fortune. Even talking about prospective expenses felt like being robbed, or having a favorite part of his body amputated.

Nonetheless, Ellsworth did not have any more of a vote in the future of his dwelling or his inheritance than he did in the chewing gum empire, which is to say he had none. The house was going to be thoroughly redone. Sue Ellen had developed a yen to "do it right," to use her unoriginal phrase. She wanted someday to be featured in *Architectural Digest*. The prospective tab was astronomical. Ellsworth suffered each planned purchase as a physi-cal pain to his heart, and eventually he refused to listen.

"Let me tell you about what we're going to do up in the—" Sue Ellen would say.

"Not now. I don't understand house things, anyway. Besides, I'm busy," he'd answer.

And he was. He was constantly, frantically, obsessively busy with plans for shortening both the span of his wife's life and the duration of her spending spree. He had failed with the car, with the shower, and with the poison. His mother had always said that bad things come in threes. Perhaps that included bungled murder attempts.

People were dying all over the world. Was it asking too much for Sue Ellen to join them?

But their town had no subway for her to fall under. Their house had no large windows for her to crash through. Sue Ellen seldom drank or took even prescription drugs, and when she did, she was careful. A faked suicide was ridiculous, since she was so unrelentingly cheerful—aside from a bit of a temper tantrum now and then, of course.

He thought he would go crazy formulating a new plan. He read accounts of perfect crimes, but couldn't find one that didn't hinge on intricate coincidences or isolation or strange habits of the deceased that had earned them a slew of enemies, all of whom could be suspects.

One evening, over dessert, Sue Ellen and Cousin Tina chattered away as Ellsworth mulled over murder and watched the women with disgust.

Sue Ellen lit a cigarette.

"You ought to stop smoking," Tina said. "It'll kill you."

"But not for years." Ellsworth had not meant to say it out loud.

Cousin Tina's spoon stopped midway to her mouth and she looked intently at Ellsworth.

"Sweet Ellsy," Sue Ellen said, "trying to keep me from worrying about my dreadful habit. But Tina's right. I should stop."

Ellsworth watched his wife's plain little face disappear behind a smoke screen and he suddenly smiled.

The next day Ellsworth carefully disconnected the positive battery contact in the upstairs smoke alarm. The change was nearly invisible. Nobody, even a fire marshal, would notice—and if he did, it would be chalked up to mischance. Ellsworth lit a match, held it up to the alarm, and smiled as nothing whatsoever happened. And then he waited until the time was right.

The time was perfect three nights later, when Sue Ellen stood in the living room in her stocking feet, contemplating her brandy snifter. They had just come back from an early dinner with Cousin Peter and his wife. They dined out frequently these days as half the house, including the kitchen, was pulled apart and chaotic. Besides, it was the housekeeper's evening off, and neither Sue Ellen nor Ellsworth was much good at figuring out what to do in a servantless pinch.

"I'm exhausted," Sue Ellen said. "Between the office and the remodeling, I feel like I'm spinning. Can't wait till we get past these practical things and to the fun stuff, like new furniture and wallpaper and things. I just hate even talking about the plumbing and the wiring and the replastering and—"

"Then don't," Ellsworth said. "Why don't you toddle up to bed instead, and get yourself some well-deserved rest?"

"You mean you're just as bored as I am about all that retrofitting and rewiring stuff?" Sue Ellen asked with a yawn. "I thought men liked that kind of hardware store thing. Why just today—"

"Tell me tomorrow," he said. "You must be completely exhausted."

Thirty minutes later, he tiptoed upstairs. Sue Ellen lay, snoring softly, in the pink and repulsively ruffled chamber she insisted on calling the master bedroom, although it made the theoretical master ill. It was symbolic of the many ways in which he was ignored and undervalued. Sue Ellen's pet husband. He looked down at his sleeping wife and felt not a single pang at what he was about to do. Her brandy snifter sat, drained, on her bedside table, next to an ashtray with one stubbed-out cigarette.

Ellsworth took a fresh cigarette from her pack and lit it, then placed it carefully on the pillow next to her. Then he tiptoed out, leaving the door open, the better to let the currents of air flow up the staircase and fan the fire.

He stretched out on his study's sofa and waited. When the smoke reached all the way to him, he would rush to save his bride but, tragically, it would be too late.

Just as everybody had told her—even her own relatives—smoking would be the death of her.

Ellsworth grinned to himself. "Goodbye, Sue Ellen," he said, and closed his eyes.

The howl hurled down the stairwell, directly into his skull. How had she awakened? Smoke wasn't supposed to do that to people—in fact, it was supposed to do just the opposite. The sounds from upstairs were loud and harsh and he closed his eyes again. In five minutes he'd go up far enough to burn his jacket. Then he'd call the fire department.

"Ellsworth! Ellsworth! Wake up!" The voice reached him from outside the study, but then, there she was. Without so much as a singed hair and in her nightgown.

The scream continued from upstairs.

"The house is on fire!" she said. "Upstairs. I already called the fire department." She helped him up. "You look so confused," she said. "You must have been sleeping very soundly." Then together they went and stood outside on the lawn.

"Sue Ellen," he said slowly, "somebody is still up there."

She shook her head. "There's only the two of us home tonight."

"But I heard screaming. In fact, I can still hear it."

"Screaming?" She looked puzzled for a moment, then she chuckled. "I tried to tell you! The contractor said our old alarm was unsafe. He made me light up directly under it and puff into it and he was right, Ellsworth. It didn't even make a peep. That's incredibly dangerous! So he put in these new electronic ones, and now we have them all over the place." She looked back at the flaming roof. "Had," she said. "We had electronic ones."

They both sighed. But then Sue Ellen brightened. "We should look at the bright side, though. Maybe we lost some of the house and a lot of time and hard work, but we have our *lives*. Isn't it lucky that contractor was so sharp? And what a miracle—he put the new ones in today and they saved our lives tonight! It really makes you think, doesn't it?"

Ellsworth nodded dully. The thoughts it made him think were unbearable and endless, and only the whine of approaching fire engines finally distracted him.

"Oh, Ellsworth," Sue Ellen shrieked, "I'm a mess! The whole fire department will see me in my nightgown. I could just die!"

"*Stop saying that!*" he shouted.

He began to smoke himself shortly thereafter, needing to do something besides pace the floor through the long nights. He searched wildly for a solution to his problem. He considered hazardous sports, but they made him nervous and Sue Ellen was, by her own admission, rather a klutz.

He pondered whether a fish bone could be wedged down somebody else's throat.

He considered disguising himself as a robber and shooting Sue Ellen dead as he entered the house. But he couldn't figure but how to arrange a good alibi for the time since the only people he knew in town were her doting relatives.

He wept a great deal, lost weight, and bit at his bottom lip until he had a series of small sores there.

Then one fine Sunday, thirty-two days after Ellsworth had first decided that Sue Ellen must go, Sue Ellen herself provided him with the answer. "Oh," she gasped with excitement as she peered out of his study's window. They had been sleeping in the small room, living in much too close surrounds while the upstairs was repaired. "Look," she said. "We have a perfect day for it."

"For what?" he asked, although he had long since lost all interest in his wife's babble.

"For the board meeting!"

"What does the weather have to do with anything?" he asked. "Besides, it's Sunday."

"You left that last meeting, honey, so you didn't hear. We decided to have the next one on the river. Picnic lunch and all. Kind of combining business and pleasure."

"Well, then," he grumbled, "since I am finished with your kind of business, in that case, I'll see you tonight." The fact that it was time for another monthly meeting was incredibly depressing. *Tempus fugit* but Sue Ellen didn't. An entire month gone and nothing had changed. Nothing whatsoever. He was still Ellsworth Hummer, possessor of nothing except a meaningless title, and the status quo might last forever.

"Nonsense!" Sue Ellen said. "We need you there. Oh, I know you had your little snit, but you are still the company president. Don't ruin everything. Besides, it'll be fun." She pursed her mouth and burst into an ancient and boring song, "'Cruising down the river . . . on a Sunday afternoon—' I can't remember any more of the words," she said.

Wait a second, he thought. Rivers were good things. People drowned in them. And with a little help, so would Sue Ellen, this very day. "Goodie," he said. "A family picnic. What a treat."

He whistled as he drove. The river, he knew, turned and curved romantically between banks laden with trees. If he could get a head start and place their canoe beyond a curve, away from the relatives, he could push Sue Ellen into the water and hold her there long enough to finally do the job. A few minutes were all that were required—probably even less. A person could only hold her breath for so long. Then he'd release her, flounder around, and call for help. Her whole family would witness his desperate attempts to save her.

After a hearty lunch, Peter asked whether they wanted to hold the business meeting now or later.

"Later," Ellsworth said. "Always later and later."

"Ah," Peter said. "Are we then to take it you haven't had a change of heart toward chewing gum concerns or board matters? Is that how it still is?"

"I have the same heart I always had. Why change it?" Ellsworth said with a mean smile.

The seven board members headed for the river and climbed into canoes. Agatha said she'd rather paddle by herself, and the rest, including Ellsworth and Sue Ellen, divided up into pairs.

Ellsworth was younger and stronger than his fellow board members, so it was easy and fairly quick to get himself a wide lead and to station his canoe in the arc of a blind curve. He could hear the cousins laugh and call to one another just beyond the trees. This was good, because he'd be able to summon them quickly.

"Isn't this nice?" Sue Ellen said dreamily. "Wasn't this a great idea?"

He nodded and grinned.

"I'm so glad we had today together this way," she said. "For once you don't seem angry about the business or how we're running it."

"Well . . ." Ellsworth said, positioning himself. "Things change. People learn. Finally, I think I really understand what can be and what can't be and what must be. So goodbye, Sue Ellen."

Her Chatworth eyes opened wide. "Why, Ellsworth—" she began.

Quickly, he stood up in the canoe, but Sue Ellen instantly followed his lead, and her motions overturned the boat, throwing them both into the water.

The dive into the river was unplanned, but it didn't discourage Ellsworth. However, the hard clap on his head from Sue Ellen's oar definitely did.

As he sank, he heard her shouting. For help, he hoped. But then, he could hear nothing more as the pressure on his head grew heavier and heavier. Was little Sue Ellen really that strong? he wondered.

Then that and all other concerns left him forever.

Sue Ellen shivered as she climbed into Cousin Aggie's canoe.

Cousins Peter and Jeremy smiled at her from their boats and then Jeremy finally released his oar from Ellsworth's submerged head. "Went well, don't you think?" Jeremy said as he righted the overturned canoe and, with help from Henry, pulled the inert form into it.

"Exactly as planned," Peter said. "Ellsworth was wrong, you know."

"Dead wrong," Aggie said with a chuckle. "He should have stayed at that last meeting, don't you think?"

"He should have given chewing gum another chance," Henry said.

"He blew it," Aggie said. Her voice took on a chillingly Ellsworth-like quality as she mimicked him. "'I have the same heart I always had. Why change it?'" She shook her head. "No turning back after that."

"We have a *good* board and we work well together. Look how smoothly this decision was implemented," Peter said. "Quite a pity that he never learned to appreciate our strengths or how the system works."

"Your daddy was right, Sue Ellen," Oliver of Product Control said. "The family can handle everything by itself, just like he always said."

"We'd best get back to report the unfortunate accident," Jeremy said.

"Yes," Sue Ellen agreed. "But first, I have to tell you one thing I surely can't tell the police. I'm positive that Ellsworth knew just what we were going to do and that he *approved*. He knew that he didn't fit in. He didn't belong. But in the end he understood. The last few weeks, he's been so kind to me, so concerned, so *serene*, you know? Why, it's almost like he knew the plan and accepted it. Especially today. Because just before I toppled us into the water, you know what he said, real sweetly? He said that he understood what must be—honest and truly, just like that, he said it. And then he said, 'Goodbye, Sue Ellen.' Makes you wonder, doesn't it?"

And with contented strokes she and her cousins and uncles and aunt paddled back to shore. Once she looked over at her late husband, nestled in his canoe.

"Goodbye," Sue Ellen whispered.

# DEATH AND DIAMONDS

*Sue Dunlap*

The thing I like most about being a private investigator is the thrill of the game. I trained in gymnastics as a kid. I love cases with lots of action. But, alas, you can't always have what you love." Kiernan O'Shaughnessy glanced down at her thickly bandaged foot and the crutches propped beside it.

"Kicked a little too much ass, huh?" The man in the seat beside her at the Southwest Airlines gate grinned. There was an impish quality to him. Average height, sleekly muscled, with the too-dark tan of one who doesn't worry about the future. He was over forty but the lines around his bright green eyes and mouth suggested quick scowls, sudden bursts of laughter, rather than the folds of age setting in. Amid the San Diegans in shorts and T-shirts proclaiming the Zoo, Tijuana, and the Chargers, he seemed almost formal in his chinos and sports jacket and the forest green polo shirt. He crossed, then recrossed his long legs and glanced impatiently at the purser standing guard at the end of the ramp.

The gate waiting area was jammed with tanned families ready to fly from sunny San Diego to sunnier Phoenix. The rumble of conversations was broken by children's shrill whines and exasperated parents barking their names in warning.

*"We are now boarding all passengers for Southwest Airlines flight twelve forty-four to Oakland, through gate nine."*

A mob of the Oakland-bound crowded closer to their gate, clutching their blue plastic boarding passes.

Beside Kiernan the man sighed. But there was a twinkle in his eyes. "Lucky them. I hate waiting around like this. It's not something I'm good at. One of the reasons I like flying Southwest is their open seating. If you move fast you can get whatever seat you want."

"Which seat is your favorite?"

"One-B or one-C. So I can get off fast. *If* they ever let us *on*."

The Phoenix-bound flight was half an hour late. With each announcement of a Southwest departure to some other destination, the level of grumbling in the Phoenix-bound area had grown till the air seemed thick with frustration, and at the same time old and overused, as if it had held just enough oxygen for the scheduled waiting period, and now, half an hour later, served only to dry out noses and to make throats raspy and tempers short.

The loudspeaker announced the Albuquerque flight was ready for boarding. A woman in a rhinestone-encrusted denim jacket raced past them toward the Albuquerque gate. Rhinestones. Hardly diamonds, but close enough to bring the picture of Melissa Jessup to Kiernan's mind. When she'd last seen her, Melissa Jessup had been dead six months, beaten and stabbed, her corpse left outside to decompose. Gone were her mother's diamonds, the diamonds her mother had left her as security. Melissa hadn't been able to bring herself to sell them, even to finance her escape from a life turned fearful and the man who preferred them to her. It all proved, as Kiernan reminded herself each time the memory of Melissa invaded her thoughts, that diamonds are *not* a girl's best friend, that Mother (or at least a mother who says "don't sell them") does *not* know best, and that a woman should never get involved with a man she works with. Melissa Jessup had done all those things. Her lover had followed her, killed her, taken her mother's diamonds, and left not one piece of evidence. Melissa's brother had hired Kiernan, hoping that with her background in forensic pathology she would find some clue in the autopsy report, or that once she could view Melissa's body she would spot something the local medical examiner had missed. She hadn't. The key that would nail Melissa's killer was not in her corpse, but with the diamonds. Finding those diamonds and the killer with them had turned into the most frustrating case of Kiernan's career.

She pushed the picture of Melissa Jessup out of her mind. This was no time for anger or any of the emotions that the thought of Melissa's death brought up. The issue now was getting this suitcase into the right hands in Phoenix. Turning back to the man beside her, she said, "The job I'm on right now is baby-sitting this suitcase from San Diego to Phoenix. This trip is not going to be 'a kick.'"

"Couldn't you have waited till you were off the crutches?" he said, looking down at her bandaged right foot.

"Crime doesn't wait." She smiled, focusing her full attention on the conversation now. "Besides, courier work is perfect for a hobbled lady, don't you think, Mr.—uh?"

He glanced down at the plain black suitcase, then back at her. "Detecting all the time, huh?" There was a definite twinkle in his eyes as he laughed. "Well, this one's easy. Getting my name is not going to prove whether you're any good as a detective. I'm Jeff Siebert. And you are?"

"Kiernan O'Shaughnessy. But I can't let that challenge pass. Anyone can get a name. A professional investigator can do better than that. For a start, I surmise you're single."

He laughed, the delighted laugh of the little boy who's just beaten his parent in rummy. "No wedding ring, no white line on my finger to show I've taken the ring off. Right?"

"Admittedly, that was one factor. But you're wearing a red belt. Since it's nowhere near Christmas, I assume the combination of red belt and green turtleneck is not intentional. You're color-blind."

"Well, yeah," he said buttoning his jacket over the offending belt. "But they don't ask you to tell red from green before they'll give you a marriage license. So?"

"If you were married, your wife might not check you over before you left each morning, but chances are she would organize your accessories so you could get dressed by yourself, and not have strange women like me commenting on your belt."

*"This is the final call for boarding Southwest Airlines flight twelve forty-four to Oakland at gate nine."*

Kiernan glanced enviously at the last three Oakland-bound passengers as they passed through gate 9. If the Phoenix flight were not so late, she would be in the air now and that much closer to getting the suitcase in the right hands. Turning back to Siebert, she said, "By the same token, I'd guess you have been married or involved with a woman about my size. A blonde."

He sat back down in his seat, and for the first time was still.

"Got your attention, huh?" Kiernan laughed. "I really shouldn't show off like that. It unnerves some people. Others, like you, it just quiets down. Actually, this was pretty easy. You've got a tiny spot of lavender eyeshadow on the edge of your lapel. I had a boyfriend your height and he ended up sending a number of jackets to the cleaners. But no one but me would think to look at the edge of your lapel, and you could have that jacket for years and not notice that."

"But why did you say a blonde?"

"Blondes tend to wear violet eyeshadow."

He smiled, clearly relieved.

*"Flight seventeen sixty-seven departing gate ten with service to Phoenix will begin boarding in just a few minutes. We thank you for your patience."*

He groaned. "We'll see how few those minutes are." Across from them a woman with an elephantine carry-on bag pulled it closer to her. Siebert turned to Kiernan, and giving her that intimate grin she was beginning to think of as *his look*, Siebert said, "You seem to be having a good time being a detective."

The picture of Melissa Jessup popped up in her mind. Melissa Jessup had let herself be attracted to a thief. She'd ignored her suspicions about him until it was too late to sell her mother's jewels and she could only grab what was at hand and run.

Pulling her suitcase closer, Kiernan said, "Investigating can be a lot of fun if you like strange hours and the thrill of having everything hang on one maneuver. I'll tell you the truth—it appeals to the adolescent in me, particularly if I can pretend to be something or someone else. It's fun to see if I can pull that off."

"How do I know you're not someone else?"

"I could show you ID, but, of course, that wouldn't prove anything." She laughed. "You'll just have to trust me, as I am you. After all, *you* did choose to sit down next to me."

"Well, that's because you were the best-looking woman here sitting by herself."

"Or at least the one nearest the hallway where you came in. And this is the only spot around where you have room to pace. You look to be a serious pacer." She laughed again. "But I like your explanation better."

Shrieking, a small girl in yellow raced in front of the seats. Whooping gleefully, a slightly larger male version sprinted by. He lunged for his sister, caught his foot on Kiernan's crutch and sent it toppling back as he lurched forward, and crashed into a man at the end of the check-in line. His sister skidded to a stop. "Serves you right, Jason. Mom, look what Jason did!"

Siebert bent over and righted Kiernan's crutch. "Travel can be dangerous, huh?"

"Damn crutches! It's like they've got urges all their own," she said. "Like one of them sees an attractive crutch across the room and all of a sudden it's gone. They virtually seduce underage boys."

He laughed, his green eyes twinkling impishly. "They'll come home to you. There's not a crutch in the room that holds a *crutch* to you."

She hesitated a moment before saying, "My crutches and I thank you." This was, she thought, the kind of chatter that had been wonderfully seductive when she was nineteen. And Jeff Siebert was the restless, impulsive type of man who had personified freedom then. But nearly twenty years of mistakes—her own and more deadly ones like Melissa Jessup's—had shown her the inevitable end of such flirtations.

Siebert stood up and rested a foot against the edge of the table. "So what else is fun about investigating?"

She shifted the suitcase between her feet. "Well, trying to figure out people, like I was doing with you. A lot is common sense, like assuming that you are probably not a patient driver. Perhaps you've passed in a no-passing zone, or even have gotten a speeding ticket."

He nodded, abruptly.

"On the other hand," she went on, "sometimes I know facts beforehand, and then I can fake a Sherlock Holmes and produce anything-but-elementary deductions. The danger with that is getting cocky and blurting out conclusions before you've been given evidence for them."

"Has that happened to you?"

She laughed and looked meaningfully down at her foot. "But I wouldn't want my client to come to that conclusion. We had a long discussion about whether a woman on crutches could handle his delivery."

"Client?" he said, shouting over the announcement of the Yuma flight at the next gate. In a normal voice, he added, "In your courier work, you mean? What's in that bag of your client's that so very valuable?"

She moved her feet till they were touching the sides of the suitcase. He leaned in closer. He was definitely the type of man destined to be trouble, she thought, but that little-boy grin, that conspiratorial tone, were seductive, particularly in a place like this where any diversion was a boon. She wasn't surprised he had been attracted to her; clearly, he was a man who liked small women. She glanced around, pleased that no one else had been drawn to this spot. The nearest travelers were a young couple seated six feet away and too involved in each other to waste time listening to strangers' conversation. "I didn't pack the bag. I'm just delivering it."

He bent down with his ear near the side of the suitcase. "Well, at least it's not ticking." Sitting up, he said, "But seriously, isn't that a little dangerous? Women carrying bags for strangers, that's how terrorists have gotten bombs on planes."

"No!" she snapped. "I'm not carrying it for a lover with an M-1. I'm a bonded courier."

The casual observer might not have noticed Siebert's shoulders tensing, slightly, briefly, in anger at her rebuff. Silently, he looked down at her suitcase. "How much does courier work pay?"

"Not a whole lot, particularly compared to the value of what I have to carry. But then there's not much work involved. The chances of theft are minuscule. And I do get to travel. Last fall I drove a package up north. That was a good deal since I had to go up there anyway to check motel registrations in a case I'm working on. It took me a week to do the motels, and then I came up empty." An entire week to discover that Melissa's killer had not stopped at a motel or hotel between San Diego and Eureka. "The whole thing would have been a bust if it hadn't been for the courier work."

He glanced down at the suitcase. She suspected he would have been appalled to know how visible was his covetous look. Finally he said, "What was in that package, the one you delivered?"

She glanced over at the young couple. No danger from them. Still Kiernan lowered her voice. "Diamonds. Untraceable. That's really the only reason to go to the expense of hiring a courier."

"Untraceable, huh?" he said, grinning. "Didn't you even consider taking off over the border with them?"

"Maybe," she said slowly, "if I had known they were worth enough to set me up for the rest of my actuarial allotment, I might have."

*"We will begin preboarding Southwest Airlines flight seventeen sixty-seven with service to Phoenix momentarily. Please keep your seats until preboarding has been completed."*

She pushed herself up and positioned the crutches under her arms. It was a moment before he jerked his gaze away from the suitcase and stood, his foot tapping impatiently on the carpet. All around them families were hoisting luggage and positioning toddlers for the charge to the gate. He sighed loudly. "I hope you're good with your elbows."

She laughed and settled back on the arm of the seat.

His gaze went back to the suitcase. He said, "I thought couriers were handcuffed to their packages."

"You've been watching too much TV." She lowered her voice. "Handcuffs play havoc with the metal detector. The last thing you want in this business is buzzers going off and guards racing in from all directions. I go for the lowkey approach. Always keep the suitcase in sight. Always be within lunging range."

He took a playful swipe at it. "What would happen if, say, that bag were to get stolen?"

"Stolen!" She pulled the suitcase closer to her. "Well, for starters, I wouldn't get a repeat job. If the goods were insured, that might be the end of it. But if it were something untraceable"—she glanced at the suitcase—"it could be a lot worse." With a grin that matched his own, she said, "You're not a thief, are you?"

He shrugged. "Do I look like a thief?"

"You look like the most attractive man here." She paused long enough to catch his eye. "Of course, looks can be deceiving." She didn't say it, but she could picture him pocketing a necklace carelessly left in a jewelry box during a big party, or a Seiko watch from under a poolside towel. She didn't imagine him planning a heist, but just taking what came his way.

Returning her smile, he said, "When you transport something that can't be traced, don't they even provide you a backup?"

"No! I'm a professional. I don't need backup."

"But with your foot like that?"

"I'm good with the crutches. And besides, the crutches provide camouflage. Who'd think a woman on crutches carrying a battered suitcase had anything worth half a mi—Watch out! The little girl and her brother are loose again." She pulled her crutches closer as the duo raced through the aisle in front of them.

"*We are ready to begin hoarding Southwest Airlines flight number seventeen sixty-seven to Phoenix. Any passengers traveling with small children or those needing a little extra time may begin boarding now.*"

The passengers applauded. It was amazing, she thought, how much sarcasm could be carried by a nonverbal sound.

She leaned down for the suitcase. "Preboarding. That's me."

"Are you going to be able to handle the crutches and the suitcase?" he asked.

"You're really fascinated with this bag, aren't you?"

"Guilty." He grinned. "Should I dare to offer to carry it? I'd stay within lunging range."

She hesitated.

In the aisle a woman in cerise shorts, carrying twin bags, herded twin toddlers toward the gate. Ahead of her an elderly man leaned precariously on a cane. The family with the boy and girl were still assembling luggage.

He said, "You'd be doing me a big favor letting me preboard with you. I like to cadge a seat in the first row on the aisle."

"The seat for the guy who can't wait?"

"Right. But I got here so late that I'm in the last boarding group. I'm never going to snag one-B or one-C. So help me out. I promise," he said, grinning, "I won't steal."

"Well . . . I wouldn't want my employer to see this. I assured him I wouldn't need any help. But . . ." She shrugged.

"No time to waver now. There's already a mob of preboarders ahead of us." He picked up the bag. "Some heavy diamonds."

"Good camouflage, don't you think? Of course, not everything's diamonds."

"Just something untraceable?"

She gave him a half wink. "It may not be untraceable. It may not even be valuable."

"And you may be just a regular mail carrier," he said, starting toward the gate.

She swung after him. The crutches were no problem, and the thickly taped right ankle looked worse than it was. Still, it made things much smoother to have Siebert carrying the suitcase. If the opportunity arose, he might be tempted to steal it, but not in a crowded gate at the airport with guards and airline personnel around. He moved slowly, staying right in front of her, running interference. As they neared the gate, a blond man carrying a jumpy toddler hurried in front of them. The gate phone buzzed. The airline rep picked it up and nodded at it. To the blond man and the elderly couple who had settled in behind him, Kiernan, and Siebert, he said, "Sorry, folks. The cleaning crew's a little slow. It'll just be a minute."

Siebert's face scrunched in anger. "What's 'cleaning crew' a euphemism for? A tire fell off and they're looking for it? They've spotted a crack in the engine block and they're trying to figure out if they can avoid telling us?"

Kiernan laughed. "I'll bet people don't travel with you twice."

He laughed. "I just hate being at someone else's mercy. But since we're going to be standing here awhile, why don't you do what you love more than diamonds, Investigator: tell me what you've deduced about me."

"Like reading your palm?" The crutches poked into her armpits; she shifted them back, putting more weight on her bandaged foot. Slowly she surveyed his lanky body, his thin agile hands, con man's hands, hands that were never quite still, always past *ready*, coming out of *set*. "Okay. You're traveling from San Diego to Phoenix on the Friday evening flight, so chances are you were here on business. But you don't have on cowboy boots, or a Stetson. You're tan, but it's not that dry tan you get in the desert. In fact, you could pass for a San Diegan. I would have guessed that you travel for a living, but you're too impatient for that, and if you'd taken this flight once or twice before you wouldn't be surprised that it's late. You'd have a report to read, or a newspaper. No, you do something where you don't take orders, and you don't put up with much." She grinned. "How's that?"

"That's pretty elementary, Sherlock," he said with only a slight edge to his voice. He tapped his fingers against his leg. But all in all he looked only a little warier than any other person in the waiting area would as his secrets were unveiled.

"*Southwest Airlines flight number seventeen sixty-seven with service to Phoenix is now ready for preboarding.*"

"Okay, folks," the gate attendant called. "Sorry for the delay."

The man with the jittery toddler thrust his boarding pass at the gate attendant and strode down the ramp. The child screamed. The elderly couple moved haltingly, hoisting and readjusting their open sacks with each step. A family squeezed in in front of them, causing the old man to stop dead and move his bag to the other shoulder. Siebert shifted from foot to foot.

Stretching up to whisper in his ear, Kiernan said, "It would look bad if you shoved the old people out of your way."

"How bad?" he muttered, grinning, then handed his boarding pass to the attendant.

As she surrendered hers, she said to Siebert, "Go ahead, hurry. I'll meet you in one-C and D."

"Thanks." He patted her shoulder.

She watched him stride down the empty ramp. His tan jacket had caught on one hip as he balanced her suitcase and his own. But he neither slowed his pace nor made an attempt to free the jacket; clutching tight to her suitcase, he hurried around the elderly couple, moving with the strong stride of a biker. By the time she got down the ramp the elderly couple and a family with two toddlers and an infant that sucked loudly on a pacifier crowded behind Siebert.

Kiernan watched irritably as the stewardess eyed first Siebert, then her big suitcase. The head stewardess has the final word on carry-on luggage, she knew. With all the hassle that was involved with this business anyway, she didn't want to add a confrontation with the stewardess. She dropped the crutches and banged backward into the wall, flailing for purchase as she slipped down to the floor. The stewardess caught her before she hit bottom. "Are you okay?"

"Embarrassed," Kiernan said, truthfully. She hated to look clumsy, even if it was an act, even if it allowed Siebert and her suitcase to get on the plane unquestioned. "I'm having an awful time getting used to these things."

"You sure you're okay? Let me help you up," the stewardess said. "I'll have to keep your crutches in the hanging luggage compartment up front while we're in flight. But you go ahead now; I'll come and get them from you."

"That's okay. I'll leave them there and just sit in one of the front seats," she said, taking the crutches and swinging herself on board the plane. From the luggage compartment it took only one long step on her left foot to get to row 1. She swung around Siebert, who was hoisting his own suitcase into the overhead bin beside hers, and dropped into seat 1-D, by the window. The elderly couple was settling into seats 1-A and 1-B. In another minute Southwest would call the first thirty passengers, and the herd would stampede down the ramp, stuffing approved carry-ons in overhead compartments and grabbing the thirty most prized seats.

"That was a smooth move with the stewardess," Siebert said, as he settled into his coveted aisle seat.

"That suitcase is just about the limit of what they'll let you carry on. I've had a few hassles. I could see this one coming. And I suspected that you"— she patted his arm—"were not the patient person to deal with that type of problem. You moved around her pretty smartly yourself. I'd say that merits a drink from my client."

He smiled and rested a hand on hers. "Maybe," he said, leaning closer, "we could have it in Phoenix."

For the first time she had a viscerally queasy feeling about him. Freeing her hand from his, she gave a mock salute. "Maybe so." She looked past him at the elderly couple.

Siebert's gaze followed hers. He grinned as he said, "Do you think they're thieves? After your loot? Little old sprinters?"

"Probably not. But it pays to be alert." She forced a laugh. "I'm afraid constant suspicion is a side effect of my job."

The first wave of passengers hurried past. Already the air in the plane had the sere feel and slightly rancid smell of having been dragged through the filters too many times. By tacit consent they watched the passengers hurry on board, pause, survey their options, and rush on. Kiernan thought fondly of that drink in Phoenix. She would be sitting at a small table, looking out a tinted window; the trip would be over, the case delivered into the proper hands; and she would feel the tension that knotted her back releasing with each swallow of scotch. Or so she hoped. The whole frustrating case depended on this delivery. There was no fallback position. If she screwed up, Melissa Jessup's murderer disappeared.

That tension was what normally made the game fun. But this case was no longer a game. This time she had allowed herself to go beyond her regular rules, to call her former colleagues from the days when she had been a forensic pathologist, looking for some new test that would prove culpability. She had hoped the lab in San Diego could find something. They hadn't. The fact was that the diamonds were the only "something" that would trap the killer, Melissa's lover, who valued them much more than her, a man who might not have bothered going after her had it not been for them. Affairs might be brief, but diamonds, after all, are forever. They would lead her to the murderer's safe house, and the evidence that would tie him to Melissa. *If* she was careful.

She shoved the tongue of the seat belt into the latch and braced her feet as the plane taxied toward the runway. Siebert was tapping his finger on the armrest. The engines whirred, the plane shifted forward momentarily, then flung them back against their seats as it raced down the short runway.

The FASTEN SEAT BELT sign went off. The old man across the aisle pushed himself up and edged toward the front bathroom. Siebert's belt was already unbuckled. Muttering, "Be right back," he jumped up and stood hunched under the overhead bin while the old man cleared the aisle. Then Siebert headed full-out toward the back of the plane. Kiernan slid over and watched him as he strode down the aisle, steps firmer, steadier than she'd have expected of a man racing to the bathroom in a swaying airplane. She could easily imagine him hiking in the redwood forest with someone like her, a small, slight woman. The blond woman with the violet eyeshadow. She in jeans and one of those soft Patagonia jackets Kiernan had spotted in the L.L. Bean catalog, violet with blue trim. He in jeans, turtleneck, a forest green down jacket on his rangy body. Forest green would pick up the color of his eyes and accent his dark, curly hair. In her picture, his hair was tinted with the first flecks of autumn snow and the ground still soft like the spongy airplane carpeting beneath his feet.

When he got back he made no mention of his hurried trip. He'd barely settled down when the stewardess leaned over him and said, "Would you care for something to drink?"

Kiernan put a hand on his arm. "This one's on my client."

"For that client who insisted you carry his package while you're still on crutches? I'm sorry it can't be Lafite-Rothschild. Gin and tonic will have to do." He grinned at the stewardess. Kiernan could picture him in a bar, flashing that grin at a tall redhead, or maybe another small blonde. She could imagine him with the sweat of a San Diego summer still on his brow, his skin brown from too many days at an ocean beach that is too great a temptation for those who grab their pleasures.

"Scotch and water," Kiernan ordered. To him, she said, "I notice that while I'm the investigator, it's you who are asking all the questions. So what about you, what do you do for a living?"

"I quit my job in San Diego and I'm moving back to Phoenix. So I'm not taking the first Friday night flight to get back home, I'm taking it to get to my new home. I had good times in San Diego: the beach, the sailing, Balboa Park. When I came there a couple years ago I thought I'd stay forever. But the draw of the desert is too great. I miss the red rock of Sedona, the pines of the Mogollon Rim, and the high desert outside Tucson." He laughed. "Too much soft California life."

It was easy to picture him outside of Show Low on the Mogollon Rim with the pine trees all around him, some chopped for firewood, the ax lying on a stump, a shovel in his hand. Or in a cabin near Sedona lifting a hatch in the floorboards.

The stewardess brought the drinks and the little bags of peanuts, giving Jeff Siebert the kind of smile Kiernan knew would have driven her crazy had she been Siebert's girlfriend. How often had that type of thing happened? Had his charm brought that reaction so automatically that for him it had seemed merely the way women behave? Had complaints from a girlfriend seemed at first unreasonable, then melodramatic, then infuriating? He was an impatient man, quick to anger. Had liquor made it quicker, as the rhyme said? And the prospect of unsplit profit salved his conscience?

He poured the little bottle of gin over the ice and added tonic. "Cheers."

She touched glasses, then drank. "Are you going to be in Phoenix long?"

"Probably not. I've come into a little money and I figure I'll just travel around, sort of like you do. Find someplace I like."

"So we'll just have time for our drink in town then?"

He rested his hand back on hers. "Well, now I may have reason to come back in a while. Or to San Diego. I just need to cut loose for a while."

She forced herself to remain still, not to cringe at his touch. *Cut loose*— what an apt term for him to use. She pictured his sun-browned hand wrapped around the hilt of a chef's knife, working it up and down, up and down, cutting across pink flesh till it no longer looked like flesh, till the flesh mixed with the blood and the organ tissue, till the knife cut down to the bone and the metal point stuck in the breastbone. She pictured Melissa Jessup's blond hair pink from the blood.

She didn't have to picture her body lying out in the woods outside Eureka in northern California. She had seen photos of it. She didn't have to imagine what the cracked ribs and broken clavicle and the sternum marked from the knife point looked like now. Jeff Siebert had seen that too, and had denied what Melissa's brother and the Eureka sheriff all knew— knew in their hearts but could not prove—that Melissa had not gone to Eureka camping by herself as he'd insisted, but had only stopped overnight at the campground she and Jeff had been to the previous summer because she had no money and hadn't been able to bring herself to sell the diamonds her mother had left her. Instead of a rest on the way to freedom, she'd found Siebert there.

Now Siebert was flying to Phoenix to vanish. He'd pick up Melissa's diamonds wherever he'd stashed them, and he'd be gone.

"What about your client?" he asked. "Will he be meeting you at the airport?"

"No. No one will meet me. I'll just deliver my goods to the van, collect my money, and be free. What about you?"

"No. No one's waiting for me either. At least I'll be able to give you a hand with that bag. There's no ramp to the terminal in Phoenix. You have to climb down to the tarmac there. Getting down those metal steps with a suitcase and two crutches would be a real balancing act."

All she had to do was get it into the right hands. She shook her head. "Thanks. But I'll have to lug it through the airport just in case. My client didn't handcuff the suitcase to me, but he does expect I'll keep hold of it."

He grinned. "Like you said, you'll be in lunging range all the time."

"No," she said firmly. "I appreciate your offer, Jeff; the bag weighs a ton. But I'm afraid it's got to be in my hand."

Those green eyes of his that had twinkled with laughter narrowed, and his lips pressed together. "Okay," he said slowly. Then his face relaxed almost back to that seductively impish smile that once might have charmed her, as it had Melissa Jessup. "I want you to know that I'll still find you attractive even if the bag yanks your shoulder out of its socket." He gave her hand a pat, then shifted in his seat so his upper arm rested next to hers.

The stewardess collected the glasses. The plane jolted and began its descent. Kiernan braced her feet. Through his jacket, she felt the heat of his arm, the arm that had dug that chef's knife into Melissa Jessup's body. She breathed slowly and did not move.

To Kiernan he said, "There's a great bar right here in Sky Harbor Airport, the Sky Lounge. Shall we have our drink there?"

She nodded, her mouth suddenly too dry for speech.

The plane bumped down, and in a moment the aisles were jammed with passengers ignoring the stewardess's entreaty to stay in their seats. Siebert stood up and pulled his bag out of the overhead compartment and then lifted hers onto his empty seat. "I'll get your crutches," he said, as the elderly man across the aisle pushed his way out in front of him. Siebert shook his head. Picking up both suitcases, he maneuvered around the man and around the corner to the luggage compartment.

Siebert had taken her suitcase. *You don't need to take both suitcases to pick up the crutches.* Kiernan stared after him, her shoulders tensing, her hands clutching the armrests. Her throat was so constricted she could barely breathe. For an instant she shared the terror that must have paralyzed Melissa Jessup just before he stabbed her.

"Jeff!" she called after him, a trace of panic evident in her voice. He didn't answer her. Instead, she heard a great thump, then him muttering and the stewardess's voice placating.

The airplane door opened. The elderly man moved out into the aisle in front of Kiernan, motioning his wife to go ahead of him, then they moved slowly toward the door.

Kiernan yanked the bandage off her foot, stepped into the aisle. "Excuse me," she said to the couple. Pushing by them as Siebert had so wanted to do, she rounded the corner to the exit.

The stewardess was lifting up a garment bag. Four more bags lay on the floor. So that was the thump she'd heard. A crutch was beside them.

She half beard the stewardess's entreaties to wait, her mutterings about the clumsy man. She looked out the door down onto the tarmac.

Jeffrey Siebert and the suitcase were gone. In those few seconds he had raced down the metal steps and was disappearing into the terminal. By the time she could make it to the Sky Lounge he would be halfway to Show Low, or Sedona.

Now she felt a different type of panic. *This* wasn't in the plan. She couldn't lose Siebert. She jumped over the bags, grabbed one crutch, hurried outside to the top of the stairs, and thrust the crutch across the hand rails behind her to make a seat. As the crutch slid down the railings, she kept her knees bent high into her chest to keep from landing and bucking forward onto her head. Instead the momentum propelled her on her feet, as it had in gymnastics. In those routines, she'd had to fight the momentum; now she went with it and ran, full-out.

She ran through the corridor toward the main building, pushing past businessmen, between parents carrying children. Siebert would be running ahead. But no one would stop him, not in an airport. People run through airports all the time. Beside the metal detectors she saw a man in a tan jacket. Not him. By the luggage pickup another look-alike. She didn't spot him till he was racing out the door to the parking lot.

Siebert ran across the roadway. A van screeched to a halt. Before Kiernan could cross through the traffic, a hotel bus eased in front of her. She skirted behind it. She could sense a man following her now. But there was no time to deal with that. Siebert was halfway down the lane of cars. Bent low, she ran down the next lane, the hot dusty desert air drying her throat.

By the time she came abreast of Siebert, he was in a light blue Chevy pickup backing out of the parking slot. He hit the gas, and, wheels squealing, drove off.

She reached toward the truck with both arms. Siebert didn't stop. She stood watching as Jeffrey Siebert drove off into the sunset.

There was no one behind her as she sauntered into the terminal to the Sky Lounge. She ordered the two drinks Siebert had suggested, and when they came, she tapped "her" glass on "his" and took a drink for Melissa Jessup. Then she swallowed the rest of the drink in two gulps.

By this time Jeff Siebert would be on the freeway. He'd be fighting to stay close to the speed limit, balancing his thief's wariness of the highway patrol against his gnawing urge to force the lock on the suitcase. Jeffrey Siebert was an impatient man, a man who had nevertheless made himself wait nearly a year before leaving California. His stash of self-control would be virtually empty. But he would wait awhile before daring to stop. Then he'd jam a knife between the top and bottom of the suitcase, pry and twist it till the case fell open. He would find diamonds. More diamonds. Diamonds to take along while he picked up Melissa Jessup's from the spot where he'd hidden them.

She wished Melissa Jessup could see him when he compared the two collections and realized the new ones he'd stolen were fakes. She wished she herself could see his face when he realized that a woman on crutches had made it out of the plane in time to follow him to point out the blue pickup truck.

Kiernan picked up "Jeff's" glass and drank more slowly. How sweet it would be if Melissa could see that grin of his fade as the surveillance team surrounded him, drawn by the beepers concealed in those fake diamonds. He'd be clutching the evidence that would send him to jail. Just for life, not forever. As Melissa could have told him, only death and diamonds are forever.

# A TICKET OUT

*Brendan DuBois*

Then there are the nights when I can't sleep, when the blankets seem wrapped around me too tight, when the room is so stuffy that I imagine the air is full of dust and age, and when my wife Carol's sighs and breathing are enough to make me tremble with tension. On these nights I slip out of bed and put on my heavy flannel bathrobe, and in bare feet I pad down the hallway—past the twins' bedroom—and go downstairs to the kitchen. I'm smart enough to know that drinking at night will eventually cause problems, but I ignore what my doctor tells me and I mix a ginger and Jameson's in a tall glass and go to the living room and look out the large bay window at the stars and the woods and the hills. Remembering what we had planned, what we had stolen, the blood that had been spilled, the tears and the anguish, I sip at my drink and think, well, it wasn't what we wanted to do. We weren't stealing for drugs or clothes or to impress the chunky, giggly girls Brad and I went to high school with. We were stealing for a ticket, for a way out. In the end, only one of us got out. That thought doesn't help me sleep at all.

It began on an August day in 1976, about a month before Brad Leary and I were going in as seniors to our high school. That summer we worked at one of the shoe mills in Boston Falls, keeping a tradition going in each of our families. Brad's father worked in one of the stitching rooms at Devon Shoe while my dad and two older brothers worked on the other side of the Squamscott River at Parker Shoe. My dad was an assistant bookkeeper, which meant he wore a shirt and tie and earned fifty cents more an hour than the "bluecollar boys" that worked among the grinding and dirty machinery.

Brad and I worked in the packing room, piling up cardboard boxes of shoes and dodging the kicks and punches from the older men who thought we were moving too slow or too sloppily. We usually got off at three, and after buying a couple of cans of 7-Up or Coke and a bag of Humpty Dumpty potato chips we biked away from the mills up Mast Road to the top of Cavalry Hill, which looked over the valley where Boston Falls was nestled. Well, maybe nestled's too nice a word. It was more tumbled in than nestled in.

On that day, we both wore the standard uniform of the summer, dark-green T-shirts, bluejeans, and sneakers. We were on an exposed part of the hill, past the town cemetery, looking down at the dirty red-brick mill buildings with the tiny windows that rose straight up from both sides of the Squamscott River. Steam and smoke fumes boiled away from tall brick stacks and neither of us really had gotten used to the pungent, oily smell that seemed to stay right in the back of the throat. The old timers never mind the smell. They sniff and say, "Aah," and say, "Boys, that's the smell of money." We weren't so dumb that we didn't know if Devon Shoe and Parker Shoe and the lumberyard shut down, Boston Falls would crumple away like a fall leaf in November.

But Brad never liked the smell.

"God," he said, popping open his can of soda. "It seems worse today."

"Wind's out of the south," I replied. "Can't be helped."

Our bikes were on their sides in the tall grass. There was a low buzz of insects and Brad took a long swallow from his soda, water beading up on the side of the can. It was a hot day. Brad's long hair was combed over to one side in a long swoop and I was jealous of him because my dad made me keep my hair about two inches long, with no sideburns. But then again, Brad wore thick glasses and my vision was perfect.

"Brad," I said, "we're in trouble."

He tossed his empty soda can over his shoulder. "How are you doing?"

"With the sixty from last week, I got four hundred and twelve."

"Idiot. You should have four hundred and fifteen like me. Where's the other three?"

"I had to buy a dress shirt for Aunt Sara's funeral last week. I tore my last good one in June and Mom's been bugging me."

"Mothers." Brad hunched forward and rested his chin on his knee.

"State says we need at least a thousand for the first year."

"Yeah."

"And we can't get part-time jobs this winter, there won't be any around."

"Yeah."

"So what do we do?"

"I'm thinking. Shut up, will you?"

I let it slide, knowing what he was thinking. We were both six hundred dollars' short for the first-year tuition at the state college. My dad had made some brave noises about helping out when the time came, but six months ago my oldest brother Tom had wrapped his '68 Chevy around a telephone pole and now he was wired up to a bed in a hospital in Hanover and my parents' bank account was shrinking every month. But at least my father had offered to help. Brad's father usually came home drunk from the mill every night, sour-mad and spoiling for a fight. I'd slept over Brad's house only once, when we were both fourteen and had just become friends. It was a Friday night and by midnight Brad's father and mother were screaming and swinging at each other with kitchen knives. Brad and I snuck out to the backyard with our blankets and pillows and we never talked about it again. But one day Brad came to school with his face lumpy and swollen from bruises, and I knew he must have told his father he wanted to go to college.

"Monroe," he said, finally speaking up.

"Go ahead."

"We're special people, aren't we?"

"Hunh?"

"I mean, compared to the rest of the kids at school, we're special, right? Who's at the top of the class? You and me, right?"

"Right."

"So we're special, we're better than they are."

"Oh, c'mon—"

"Face it, Monroe. Just sit there and face it, will you? That's all I ask right now. Just face it."

Well, he was somewhat right, but then you have to understand our regional high school, Squamscott High. Kids from Boston Falls, Machias, and Albion go there, and those other towns are no better off than ours. And in our state there's little aid for schools, so the towns have to pay the salaries and supplies. Which means a school building with crumbling plaster ceilings. Which means history books that talk about the promise of the Kennedy administration and science books that predict man will go into space one day. Which means teachers like Mr. Hensely, who stumbles into his afternoon history classes, his breath reeking of mouthwash, and Miss

Tierney, the English teacher, not long out of college, who also works Saturday and Sunday mornings as a waitress at Mona's Diner on Front Street.

"All right, Brad," I said. "I guess we're special. We study hard and get good marks. We like books and we want to go places."

"But we're trapped here, Monroe," he said. "All we got here is Boston Falls, the Mohawk Cinema, Main Street—and the Wentworth Shopping Plaza ten miles away. And a lot of brick and smoke and trees and hills. Here, straight As and straight Fs will get you the same thing."

"I know. The lumberyard or Parker or Devon Shoe."

"Or maybe a store or a gas station. We're too smart for that, damn it."

"And we're too broke for college."

"That we are," he said, resting his head on his knees. "That we are."

He remained silent for a while, a trait of Brad's. We'd been friends since freshman year, when we were the only two students who were interested in joining the debate team—which lasted a week because no one else wanted to join. We shared a love of books and a desire to go to college, but no matter how many hours we spent together there was always a dark bit of Brad I could never reach or understand. It wasn't something dramatic or apparent, just small things. Like his bedroom. Mine had the usual posters of cars and rocketships and warplanes, but his had only one picture—a framed photograph of Joseph Stalin. I was pretty sure no one else in Brad's family recognized the picture—I got the feeling he told his father the man had been a famous scientist. When I asked Brad why Stalin of all people, he said, "The man had drive, Monroe. He grew up in a peasant society and grabbed his ticket. Look where it took him."

Brad wanted to become a lawyer and I wanted to write history books.

"Feel it," he said, his voice low, rocking back and forth. "Feel how it's strangling us?"

I felt it. If we didn't go to State, then next summer we'd be on that slippery slope where we couldn't get off, a life at the mill, a life of praying and hoping for a nickel-an-hour wage increase, of waiting for the five o'clock whistle. A life where we would find our friends and amusement at the Legion Hall, Drake's Pub, or Pete's Saloon, where we would sit comfortable on the bar stools, swapping stories about who scored what winning touchdown at what state tournament, sipping our beers and feeling ourselves and our tongues getting thick with age and fear. Just getting along, getting older and slower, the old report cards with the perfect marks hidden away in some desk drawer, buried under old bills, a marriage certificate, and insurance policies.

"We gotta get out," I said.

"We do. And I know how." Brad had gotten to his feet, brushing potato-chip crumbs from his pants. "Monroe, we're going to become thieves."

The next day we were at Outland Rock, tossing pebbles into the river. We were upstream from the mills and the waters flowed fast and clean. About another mile south, after the river passed through town, the waters were slow and slate-grey, clogged with chemical foam and wood chips and scraps of leather. Outland Rock was a large boulder that hung over the river bank. We were too lazy to swim, so we sat and tossed pebbles into the river, watching the wide arcs of the ripples rise up and fade away.

"What are we going to steal?" I asked. "Gold? Diamonds? The bank president's Cadillac?"

Brad was on his stomach, his feet heading up to the bank, his head over the water. "Don't screw with me, Monroe. I'm serious."

I shook my head, tossing another rock in. "Okay, so you're serious. Answer the question."

"Cash." He had a stick in his hand, a broken piece of pine, and he stirred it in the water like he was casting for something. "Anything else can be traced. We steal cash and we're set."

The day was warm and maybe it was the lazy August mood I was in—the comfortable, hazy feeling that the day would last forever and school and September would never come—but I decided to go along with him.

"Okay, cash. But you gotta realize what we're working with."

He looked up at me, his eyes unblinking behind the thick glasses. "Go ahead, Monroe."

"Our parents still won't let us drive by ourselves, so we're stuck with our bikes. Unless you want to steal a car to get out of town—which doubles the danger. So whatever we go after has to be in Boston Falls."

"I hadn't thought of that."

"There's another thing," I said. "We can't go into the National Bank or Trussen's Jewelers in broad daylight and rob 'em. In an hour they'd be looking for two kids our age and they wouldn't have a hard time tracking us down." I lay back on the rock, the surface warm against my back, and closed my eyes, listening to some birds on the other side of the river and the swish-swish as Brad moved the stick back and forth in the water.

"Burglary," he said. I sat up, shading my face with one hand. "Burglary?"

"Yeah. We find someone who's got a lot of cash and break into their house. Do it when no one's home and they'll blame it on some drifters or something."

Somewhere a dog barked. "Do you realize we're actually talking about stealing, Brad? Not only is it a crime, but it's wrong. Are you thinking about that?"

He turned to me and his face changed—I had the strange feeling I knew what he'd look like in ten years.

"Don't get soft on me, Monroe. In another three weeks we'll be back at school. If we don't get more money this summer we're done for. 'Wrong.' Isn't it wrong that you and me have to grow up in a place like this? Isn't it wrong that we have to live alongside people who haven't read a book in years? Don't you think it's wrong that for lack of a few measly bucks we have to rot here?"

He bent over the rock and pointed. "Look." In the shallow water I saw a nesting of mussels, their shells wide open. "There you have," he continued, "the population of Boston Falls, New Hampshire. Sitting still, dumb and happy and open, letting everything go by them, ready to snap at anything that comes within reach." He pushed his stick into one of the mussels and it snapped shut against the wood. He pulled the stick out, the mussel hanging onto the stick, dripping water. "See how they grab the first thing that comes their way?"

He slammed the end of the stick onto the rock and the mussel exploded into black shards.

"We're not going to grab the first thing that comes our way, Monroe. We're going to plan and get the hell out of here. That will take cash, and if that means stealing from the fat, dumb mussels in this town, that's what we'll do."

On the ride home, Brad slowed and stopped and I pulled my rusty five-speed up next to him. A thick bank of rolling grey clouds over the hills promised a thunderstorm soon. Our T-shirts were off and tied around our waists. I was tanned from working in our garden all summer but Brad was thin and white, and his chest was a bit sunken, like he'd been punched hard there and never recovered.

"Look there," he said. I did and my stomach tightened up.

A dead woodchuck was in the middle of the road, its legs stiff. Two large black grackles hopped around the swollen brown body, their sharp beaks at work.

"So it's a burglary," I said. "Whose house?"

He shrugged his bony shoulders. "I'll find the right one. I'll go roaming."

Roaming. It was one of Brad's favorite things to do. At night, after everyone at his house was asleep, he would sneak out and roam around the dark streets and empty back yards of Boston Falls. The one time I'd gone with him, I thought he was just being a Peeping Tom or something, but it wasn't that simple. He just liked watching what people did, I think, and he moved silently from one lighted window to another. I didn't like it at all. I wasn't comfortable out on the streets or in the fields at night and I couldn't shake off the feeling that I was trespassing.

Brad rolled his bike closer to the dead woodchuck. "Are you in, Monroe? We're running out of time."

Thunder boomed from the hills and I glanced up and saw a flash of lightning. "We better get going if we're going to beat the storm."

"I said, are you with me?"

The wind shifted, blowing the leaves on the trees in great gusts. "Brad, we gotta get moving."

"You get moving," he said, his lips tense. "You get moving wherever you're going. I'm staying here for a bit."

I pedaled away as fast as I could, pumping my legs up and down, thinking, I'll save a bit here and there, maybe deliver some papers, maybe just work an extra summer—there's got to be another way to get the money.


A week later. Suppertime at my house. My brothers Jim and Henry had eaten early and gone out, leaving me alone with my parents. My brother Tom was still in the hospital in Hanover. My parents visited him every Saturday and Sunday, bringing me along when I wasn't smart enough to leave the house early. I guess you could say I loved my brother, but the curled over, thin figure with wires and tubes in the noisy hospital ward didn't seem to be him any more.

We sat in the kitchen, a plastic tablecloth on the table, my mother, looking worn and tired, still wearing her apron. My dad wore his shirt and tie. His crewcut looked sweaty and he smelled of the mill. On his right shirt pocket was a plastic pen holder that said Parker Does It Right with four pens. Supper was fried baloney, leftover mashed potatoes, and canned yellow string beans. I tried to talk about what went on at the mill that day—a pile of boxes stuffed full of leather hiking boots had fallen and almost hit me—but my parents nodded and said nothing and I finally concentrated on quietly cleaning my plate. The fried baloney left a puddle of grease that flowed into the lumpy white potatoes.

My father looked over at Mom and she hung her head, and he seemed to shrug his shoulders before he said, "Monroe?"

"Yes?"

He put his knife and fork down and folded his hands, as if we were suddenly in church.

"At work today they announced a cutback." He looked at me and then looked away, as if someone had walked past the kitchen window. "Some people are being laid off and the rest of us are having a pay cut."

"Oh." The baloney and potatoes were now very cold.

"Tom is still very sick, and until he—gets better, we still have to pay the bills. With the cutback—well, Monroe, we need the money you've saved."

I looked at my mother, but she didn't look up. "Oh," I said, feeling dumb, feeling blank.

"I know you've got your heart set on college, but this is a family emergency—that has to come first, a family has to stick together. Jim and Henry have agreed to help—"

"With what?" I said, clenching my knife and fork tight. "They don't save anything at all."

"No, but they're giving up part of their paychecks. All we ask is that you do your part."

Then Mom spoke up. "There's always next year," she said. "Not all of your friends are going to college, are they? You'll be with them next summer."

Dad gave me a weak smile. "Besides, I never went to college, and I'm doing all right. Monroe, it's just temporary, until things improve with Tom."

Until he gets better or until he dies, I thought. I didn't know what to say next, so I finished eating and went down the hallway to my bedroom and got the dark-brown passbook from First Merchants of Boston Falls and brought it back and gave it to my father.

Back in my bedroom, I lay on the bed, staring up at the models of airplanes and rocketships hanging from thin black threads attached to the ceiling. I looked at my textbooks and other books on the bookshelves I made myself. I curled up and didn't think of much at all and after a while I fell asleep.

❧    ❧    ❧

There was a tapping at my window and I threw the top sheet off and went over, lifting up the window screen. I stood there in my shorts, looking at Brad on the back lawn. My glow-in-the-dark clock said it was two in the morning.

"What is it?" I whispered.

"I found it," he whispered back, leaning forward so his head was almost through the open window. "I found the place."

"Whose house is it?"

"Mike Willard's."

"Mike? The ex-marine?"

"That's right," Brad said. "I've watched him two nights in a row. He goes into his bedroom and underneath his bed he's got this little strongbox—before shutting off the light and going to bed he opens it up and goes through it. Monroe, he's got tons of money in there. Wads as big as your fist."

"You saw it?"

"Of course I did. I was in a tree in his yard. He must've been saving up all his life. You never saw so much money."

The night air was warm but goosebumps traveled up and down my arms. "How do we do it?"

"Easy. He lives out on Tanner Avenue. We can get to it by cutting through the woods. His house has hedges all around. It'll be a cinch."

I chewed on my lip. "When?" I asked.

Brad grinned at me. I could almost smell the sense of excitement. "Tomorrow. It's Saturday—your parents will be in Hanover and Mike goes to the Legion Hall every afternoon. We'll do it while he's there."

I didn't argue. "Fine," I said.


The next afternoon we were in a stand of trees facing a well mowed back yard. Tall green hedges flanked both sides of the yard and the two-story white house with the tall gables was quiet. Beside me, Brad was hunched over, peering around a tree trunk. We heard a door slam and saw Mike Willard walk down his drive and down the street. His posture was straight as a pine, his white hair cut in a crewcut.

"Let's give him a few minutes," Brad said. "Make sure he didn't forget anything."

I nodded. My heart was pounding so hard I wondered if Brad could hear it. I knew what we were doing was wrong, I knew it wouldn't be right to steal Mike Willard's money, but money was all I could think of. Wads as big as my fist, Brad had said.

"Go time," Brad said, and he set off across the yard. I followed. There were no toys or picnic tables or barbecue sets in Mike Willard's back yard, just a fine lawn, as if he mowed it every other day. Up on the back porch I had the strange feeling we should knock or something. I was scared Mike would come back and yell, "Boys, what the hell do you want?" or that a mailman would walk up the drive and ask if Mike was home. I almost hoped a mailman would come, but Brad picked up a rock and went to the door and it was too late. He smashed a pane of glass—the sound was so loud it seemed like every police cruiser within miles would be sent around—then he reached in and unlocked the door, motioning me to follow him inside. A small voice told me to stay outside and let him go in alone, but I followed him into the kitchen, my sneakers crunching on the glass.

The kitchen smelled clean and everything was shiny and still. There weren't even any dishes in the sink.

"God, look how clean it is," I said.

"Tell me about it. My mom should keep our house so clean."

The kitchen table was small and square, with only two chairs. There was one placemat out, a blue woven thing with stars and anchors, and I thought of Mike Willard coming home every night to this empty house, opening a can of spaghetti maybe and eating alone at his table. I looked at Brad and wanted to say, 'Come on, let's not do it,' because I got a bad feeling at the thought of Mike coming home and finding he'd been robbed, that someone had been in his house, but Brad looked at me hard and I followed him down the hallway.

The bedroom was small and cramped, with neatly labeled cardboard boxes piled on one side of the room and a long bureau on the other, on the other side of the bed. The labels on the boxes read CHINA 34, IWO 45, OCC., and things like that. Brad pointed at the walls, where pictures and other items were hanging. "Look, there's Mike there, I think. I wonder where it was taken. Guadalcanal, maybe?"

The faded black-and-white picture showed a group of young men standing in a jungle clearing, tired-looking, in uniforms and beards, holding rifles and automatic weapons. There was no name on the picture but I recognized a younger Mike Willard, hair short and ears sticking out, standing off to one side.

I heard a board creak. "Shh!" I said. "Did you hear that?"

"Yeah. This is an old house, Monroe."

"Well, let's get going," I said, rubbing my palms against my jeans. They were very sweaty.

"What's the rush?" Brad said, his eyes laughing at me from behind his glasses. "Old Mike's down at the Legion, telling the boys how he won the big one back in 'forty-five. Look here."

Below an American flag and a furled Japanese flag was a sheathed curved sword resting on two wooden pegs. Brad took it down and slid it out of its scabbard. He ran a thumb across the blade and took a few swings through the air. "I wonder if Mike bought it or got it off some dead Jap."

By now I was glancing out the window, wondering if anyone could see us. Brad put the sword down and climbed onto the bed. "Hold on a sec," he said.

The bed was a brown four-poster. Brad reached under the pillows and pulled out a handgun, large and oily-looking. "A forty-five. Can you believe it? Old Mike sleeps with a forty-five under his pillow."

"Brad, stop fooling around," I said. "Let's get the box and go." But I could tell he was enjoying himself too much.

"Hold it, I just want to see if it works. He moved his hand across the top of the gun and part of it slid back and forth with a loud click-clack. "There," he said. "Just call me John Wayne. This sucker's ready to fire. I might take it with me when we leave."

He took the gun and stuck it in his waistband, then reached over and pulled a dull-grey strongbox with a simple clasp lock from under the bed. My mouth felt dry and suddenly I was no longer nervous. I was thinking of all the money.

Brad rubbed his hands across the box. "Look, partner. In here's our ticket out."

Then Mike Willard was at the bedroom door, his face red, and I could smell the beer from where I was standing, almost five feet away. "You!" he roared. "What the hell are you doing in here? I'm gonna beat the crap out of you, boys!"

I backstepped quickly, tripping over the cardboard boxes and falling flat on my butt, wondering what to do next, wondering what I could say. Brad scampered across the other side of the bed, pulling out the gun and saying in a squeaky voice, "Hold it." Mike Willard swore and took two large steps, grabbing the sword and swinging it at Brad. I closed my eyes and there was a loud boom that jarred my teeth. There was a crash and an awful grunt, and another crash, then a sharp scent of smoke that seemed to cut right through me.

When I opened my eyes, Brad was sitting across from me, the gun in his lap, both of his hands pressed against his neck. He was very pale and his glasses had been knocked off—without them he looked five years younger.

"It hurts," he said. And then I saw the bright redness seep through his fingers and trickle down his bare arms.

"God," I breathed.

"I can't see," he said. "Where's Mike?"

I got up, weaving slightly, and saw Mike's feet sticking out from the other side of the bed. I crawled across the bed and peered over. Mike was on his back, his arms splayed out, his mouth open like he was still trying to yell, but his eyes were closed and there was a blossom of red spreading across his green workshirt. I stared at him for what seemed hours but his chest didn't move. When I looked up, Brad was resting his back against the bed. Both of his arms were soaked red and I gazed at him, almost fascinated by the flow of blood down his thin wrists. His face was now the color of chalk.

"Wait, I'll get a towel," I said.

"No, you idiot. If I take my hands away, I'm dead. An artery's gone. Listen. Take the box and call an ambulance."

"I think Mike's dead, Brad."

"Shut up," he said, his teeth clenched. "Just grab the box, hide it, and get help! We're juveniles—nothing's going to happen to us! Get going!" I grabbed the box and was out of the house, running through the woods, the strongbox tight against my chest. The air was fresh and smelled wonderful, and I ran all the way home.

Three days later Mike Willard was buried with full military honors and a Marine Corps honor guard at Cavalry Hill Cemetery. I learned from his front-page obituary that his wife died five years earlier and he had a daughter who lived in Jamaica Plain, Massachusetts. I also learned that Mike had been in the Marines since he was seventeen, stationed in China in the 1930s and in the Pacific in the 1940s, island-hopping, fighting the Japanese. Then after occupation duty and a year in Korea, he pulled embassy duty until he retired. His nickname had been Golden Mike, for in all his years on active duty he'd never been wounded, never been shot or scratched by shrapnel. The newspaper said he'd come home early that day to dig out a magazine clipping to show some friends at the Legion Hall. To settle a bet.

I kept the strongbox hidden in the attic. Despite the temptation and the worries and the urging, I didn't open it until that day in May after my college acceptance letter came, followed by a bill for the first year's tuition. Then I went up with a chisel and hammer and broke open the lock. The wads of money were in there, just as Brad had said, thick as my fist. They were buried under piles of fragile, yellowed letters, some newspaper and magazine clippings, and a few medals. The money was banded together by string, and in the dim light of the attic I wasn't sure of what I had. I bicycled over to Machias, to a coin shop, and the owner peered over his half-glasses and looked up at me, the money spread over his display case.

"Interesting samples," he said. He wore a dark-green sweater and his hair was white. "Where did you get them?"

"From my uncle," I lied. "Can you tell me what they're worth?"

"Hmm," he said, lifting the bills up to the light. "Nineteen thirties, it looks like. What you have here is Chinese money from that time, what old soldiers and sailors called 'LC,' or local currency. It varied from province to province, and I'd say this is some of it."

He put the bills back on the counter. "Practically worthless," he said. I thanked him and rode back to Boston Falls. That afternoon I burned some of the paper money along with my acceptance letter and tuition bill. I didn't go to college that fall and ended up never going at all.

My ginger and Jameson is gone and I continue looking out at the stars, watching the moon rise over the hill, Cavalry Hill. And even though it's miles away, I imagine I can see the white stone markers up there, marking so many graves.

In the end I stayed in Boston Falls and took a job at a bank. I worked a little and now I'm an assistant branch manager. Some years ago I married Carol, a teller I helped train, and now we're out of Boston Falls, in Machias.

It's just over the line, but I get some satisfaction from getting that far.

Upstairs I still have the old strongbox with some of the money, and though I don't look at it all that often I feel like I have to have something, something I can tell myself I got from that day we broke into Mike Willard's house. I have to have something to justify what we did, and what I did. Especially what I did.

After running all that distance home, I stashed the strongbox in the attic, and as I came downstairs my parents came home. Dad patted me on the back and Mom started supper and I thought of the strongbox upstairs and the blood and the acrid smoke and Mike Willard on his back and Brad holding onto his neck like that. I knew no one had seen me. Mom offered me some lemonade and I took it and went to the living room and watched television with my dad, cheering on the Red Sox as they beat the Yankees—all the while waiting and waiting, until finally the sirens went by.

Brad was buried about a hundred feet from Mike Willard a day later. On the day of his funeral, I said I was sick and stayed home, curled up in a ball on my bed, not thinking, not doing anything, just knowing that I had the box and the money.

I put down my empty glass and open the back door, hoping the fresh air will clear my head so I can go back upstairs and try to sleep. Outside there's a slight breeze blowing in from Boston Falls, and like so many other nights I go down the porch steps and stand with my bare feet cool on the grass, the breeze on my face bringing with it the stench of the mills from Boston Falls. The smell always seems to stick in the back of my throat, and no matter how hard I try I can never get the taste of it out.

# Speaking of Greed

*Lawrence Block*

The doctor shuffled the pack of playing cards seven times, then offered them to the soldier, who sat to his right. The soldier cut them, and the doctor picked up the deck and dealt two cards down and one up to each of the players—the policeman, the priest, the soldier, and himself.

The game was poker, seven-card stud, and the priest, who was high on the board with a queen, opened the betting for a dollar, tossing in a chip to keep the doctor's ante comfortable. The soldier called, as did the doctor and the policeman.

Over by the fireplace, the room's other occupant, an elderly gentleman, dozed in an armchair.

The doctor gave each player a second up-card. The policeman caught a king, the priest a nine in the same suit with his queen, the soldier a jack to go with his ten. The doctor, who'd had a five to start with, caught another five for a pair. That made him high on the board, but he took a look at his hole cards, frowned, and checked his hand. The policeman checked as well, and the priest gave his Roman collar a tug and bet two dollars.

The soldier said, "Two dollars? It's a dollar limit until a pair shows, isn't it?"

"Doctor has a pair," the priest pointed out.

"So he does," the soldier agreed, and flicked a speck of dust off the sleeve of his uniform. "Of course he does, he was high with his fives. Still, it's one of the anomalies of the game, isn't it? Priest gets to bet more, not because his own hand just got stronger, but because his opponent's did. What are you so proud of, Priest? Queens and nines? Four hearts?"

"I hope I'm not too proud," the priest said. "Pride's a sin, after all."

"Well, I'm proud enough to call you," the soldier said. The doctor and the policeman also called, and the doctor dealt another round. Now the policeman was high with a pair of kings. He too was in uniform, and wordlessly he tossed a pair of chips into the center of the table.

The priest had caught a third heart, the seven. He thought for a long moment before tossing four chips into the pot. "Raise," he said softly.

"Priest, Priest, Priest," said the soldier, checking his own cards. "Have you got your damned flush already? If you had two pair, well, I just caught one of your nines. But if I'm chasing a straight that's doomed to lose to the flush you've already got . . ." The words trailed off, and the soldier sighed and called.

So did the doctor, and the policeman looked at his kings and picked up four chips, as if to raise back, then tossed in two of them and returned the others to his stack.

On the next round, three of the players showed visible improvement. The policeman, who'd had a three with his kings, caught a second three for two pair. The priest added the deuce of hearts and showed a four flush on board. The soldier's straight got longer with the addition of the eight of diamonds.

The doctor, who'd had a four with his pair of fives, acquired a ten.

The policeman bet, the priest raised, the soldier grumbled and called. The doctor called without grumbling. The policeman raised back, and everyone called.

"Nice little pot," the doctor said, and gave everyone a down card.

The betting limits were a dollar until a pair showed, then two dollars until the last card, at which time you could bet five dollars. The policeman did just that, tossing a red chip into the pot. The priest picked up a red chip to call, thought about it, picked up a second red chip, and raised five dollars. The soldier said something about throwing good money after bad.

"There's no such thing," the doctor said.

"As good money?"

"As bad money."

"It turns bad," said the soldier, "as soon as I throw it in. I was straight in five and got to watch everybody outdraw me. Now I've got a choice of losing to Policeman's full house or Priest's heart flush, depending on which one's telling the truth. Unless you're both full of crap."

"Always a possibility," the doctor allowed.

"The hell with it," the soldier said, and tossed in a red chip and five white chips. "I call," he said, "with no expectation of profit."

The doctor was wearing green scrubs, with a stethoscope peeping out of his pocket. He looked at his cards, looked at everyone else's cards, and called. The policeman raised. The priest looked troubled, but took the third and final raise all the same, and everybody called.

"Full," the policeman said, and turned over a third three. "Threes full of kings," he said, but the priest was shaking his head, even as he turned over his hole cards, two queens and a nine.

"Queens full," said the priest.

"Oh, hell," said the soldier. "A full house masquerading as a flush. Not that I have a right to complain—the flush would have beaten me just as handily. Got it on the last card, didn't you, Priest? All that raising, and you went in with two pair and a four flush."

"I had great expectations," the priest admitted.

"The Lord will provide and all that," said the soldier, turning over his up-cards. The priest, beaming, reached for the chips.

The doctor cleared his throat, turned over his hole cards. Two of them were fives, matching the pair of fives he'd had on board.

"Four fives," the policeman said reverently. "Beats your boat, Priest."

"So it does," said the priest. "So it does."

"Had them in the first four cards," the doctor said.

"You never bet them."

"I never had to," said the doctor. "You fellows were doing such a nice job of it, I saw no reason to interfere." And he reached out both hands to gather in the chips.

"Greed," said the priest.

The policeman was shuffling the cards, the doctor stacking his chips, the soldier looking off into the middle distance, as if remembering a battle in a long-forgotten war. The priest's utterance stopped them all.

"I beg your pardon," said the doctor. "Just what have I done that's so greedy? Play the hand so as to maximize my gains? That, it seems to me, is how one is intended to play the game."

"If you're not trying to win," said the soldier, "you shouldn't be sitting at the table."

"Maybe Priest feels you were gloating," the policeman suggested. "Salivating over your well-gotten gains."

"Was I doing that?" The doctor shrugged. "I wasn't aware of it. Still, why play if you're not going to relish your triumph?"

The priest, who'd been shaking his head, now held up his hands as if to ward off everyone's remarks. "I uttered a single word," he protested, "and intended no judgment, believe me. Perhaps it was the play of the hand that prompted my train of thought, perhaps it was a reflection on the entire ethos of poker that put it in motion. But, when I spoke the word, I was thinking neither of your own conduct, Doctor, or of our game itself. No, I was contemplating the sin of greed, of avarice."

"Greed is a sin, eh?"

"One of the seven deadly sins."

"And yet," said the soldier, "there was a character in a film who argued famously that greed is good. And isn't the profit motive at the root of much of human progress?"

"A man's reach should exceed his grasp," the policeman said, "but it's the desire for what one can in fact grasp that makes one reach out in the first place. And isn't it natural to want to improve one's circumstances?"

"All the sins are natural," said the priest. "All originate as essential impulses and become sins when they overstretch their bounds. Without sexual desire the human race would die out. Without appetite we'd starve. Without ambition we'd graze like cattle. But when desire becomes lust, or appetite turns to gluttony, or ambition to greed—"

"We sin," the doctor said.

The priest nodded.

The policeman gave the cards another shuffle. "You know," he said, "that reminds me of a story."

"Tell it," the others urged, and the policeman put down the deck of cards and sat back in his chair.


Many years ago (said the policeman) there were two brothers, whom I'll call George and Alan Walker. They came from a family that had had some money and respectability at one time, and their paternal grandfather was a physician, but he was also a drunk, and eventually patients stopped going to him, and he wound up with an office on Railroad Avenue, where he wrote prescriptions for dope addicts. Somewhere along the way his wife ran off, and he started popping pills, and the time came when they didn't combine too well with what he was drinking, and he died.

He had three sons and a daughter, and all but the youngest son drifted away. The one who stayed—call him Jack—married a girl whose family had also come down in the world, and they had two boys, George and Alan.

Jack drank, like his father, but he didn't have a medical degree, and thus he couldn't make a living handing out pills. He wasn't trained for anything, and didn't have any ambition, so he picked up day work when it came his way, and sometimes it was honest and sometimes it wasn't. He got arrested a fair number of times, and he went away and did short time on three or four occasions. When he was home he slapped his wife around some, and was generally free with his hands around the house, but no more than you'd expect from a man like that living a life like that.

Now everybody can point to individuals who grew up in homes like the Walkers' who turned out just fine. Won scholarships, put themselves through college, worked hard, applied themselves, and wound up pillars of the community. No reason it can't happen, and often enough it does, but sometimes it doesn't, and it certainly didn't for George and Alan Walker. They were discipline problems in school and dropped out early, and at first they stole hubcaps off cars, and then they stole cars.

And so on.

Jack Walker had been a criminal himself, in a slipshod amateurish sort of way. The boys followed in his footsteps, but improved on his example. They were professionals from very early on, and you would have to say they were good at it. They weren't Raffles, they weren't Professor Moriarty, they weren't Arnold Zeck, and God knows they weren't Willie Sutton or Al Capone. But they made a living at it and they didn't get caught, and isn't that enough for us to call them successful?

They always worked together, and more often than not they used other people as well. Over the years, they tended to team up with the same three men. I don't know that it would be precisely accurate to call the five of them a gang, but it wouldn't be off by much.

One, Louis Creamer, was a couple of years older than the Walkers— George, I should mention, was himself a year and a half older than his brother Alan. Louis looked like a big dumb galoot, and that's exactly what he was. He loved to eat and he loved to work out with weights in his garage, so he kept getting bigger. It's hard to see how he could have gotten any dumber, but he didn't get any smarter, either. He lived with his mother—nobody knew what happened to the father, if he was ever there in the first place—and when his mother died Louis married the girl he'd been keeping company with since he dropped out of school. He moved her into his mother's house and she cooked him the same huge meals his mother used to cook, and he was happy.

Early on, Louis got work day to day as a bouncer, but the day came when he hit a fellow too hard, and the guy died. A good lawyer probably could have gotten him off, but Louis had a bad one, and he wound up serving a year and a day for involuntary manslaughter. When he got out nobody was in a rush to hire him, and he fell in with the Walkers, who didn't have trouble finding a role for a guy who was big and strong and did what you told him to do.

Eddie O'Day was small and undernourished and as close as I've ever seen to a born thief. He got in trouble shoplifting as a child, and then he stopped getting into trouble, not because he stopped stealing but because he stopped getting caught. He grew up to be a man who would, as they say, steal a hot stove, and he'd have it sold before it cooled off. He was the same age as Alan Walker, and they'd dropped out of school together. Eddie lived alone, and was positively gifted when it came to picking up women. He was neither good-looking nor charming, but he was evidently seductive, and women kept taking him home. But they didn't keep him—his relationships never lasted, which was fine as far as he was concerned.

Mike Dunn was older than the others, and had actually qualified as a schoolteacher. He got unqualified in a hurry when he was caught in bed with one of his students. It was a long ways from pedophilia—he was only twenty-six himself at the time, and the girl was almost sixteen and almost as experienced sexually as he was—but that was the end of his teaching career. He drifted some, and the Walkers used him as a lookout in a drugstore break-in, and found out they liked working with him. He had a good mind, and he wound up doing a lot of the planning. When he wasn't working he was pretty much a loner, living in a rented house on the edge of town, and having affairs with unavailable women—generally the wives or daughters of other men.

The Walkers and their associates had a lot of different ways to make money, together or separately. George and Alan always had some money on the street, loans to people whose only collateral was fear. Louis Creamer did their collection work, and provided security at the card and dice games Eddie O'Day ran. George Walker owned a bar and grill, and sold more booze there than he bought from the wholesalers; he bought from bootleggers and hijacked the occasional truck to make up the difference.

We knew a lot of what they were doing, but knowing and making a case aren't necessarily the same thing. We arrested all of them at one time or another, for one thing or another, but we could never make anything stick. That's not all that unusual, you know. They say crime doesn't pay, but they're wrong. Of course it pays. If it didn't pay, the pros would do something else.

And the Walkers were pros. They weren't getting rich, but they were making what you could call a decent living, but for the fact that there was nothing decent about it. They always had food on the table and money under the mattress (if not in the bank), and they didn't have to work too hard or too often. That was what they'd had in mind when they chose a life of crime. So they stayed with it, and why not? It suited them fine. They weren't respectable, but neither was their father, or his father before him. The hell with being respectable. They were doing okay.

The years went by and they kept on doing what they were doing, and doing well at it. Jack Walker drank himself to death, and after the funeral George put his arm around his brother and said, "Well, the old bastard's in the ground. He wasn't much good, but he wasn't so bad, you know?"

"When I was a kid," Alan said, "I wanted to kill him."

"Oh, so did I," George said. "Many's the time I thought about it. But, you know, you grow older and you get over it."

And they were indeed growing older, settling into a reasonably comfortable middle age. George was thicker around the middle, while Alan's hair was showing a little gray. They both liked a drink, but it didn't have the hold on them it had had on their father and grandfather. It settled George down, fueled Alan, and didn't seem to do either of them any harm.

And this wouldn't be much of a story, except for the fact that one day they set out to steal some money, and succeeded beyond their wildest dreams.

It was a robbery, and the details have largely faded from memory, but I don't suppose they're terribly important. The tip came from an employee of the targeted firm, whose wife was the sister of a woman Mike Dunn was sleeping with; for a cut of the proceeds, he'd provide details of when to hit the place, along with the security codes and keys that would get them in.

Their expectations were considerable. Mike Dunn, who brought in the deal, thought they ought to walk off with a minimum of a hundred thousand dollars. Their tipster was in for a ten percent share, and they'd split the residue in five equal shares, as they always did on jobs of this nature.

"Even splits," George Walker had said early on. "You hear about different ways of doing it, something off the top for the guy who brings it in, so much extra for whoever bankrolls the operation. All that does is make it complicated, and gives everybody a reason to come up with a resentment. The minute you're getting a dollar more than me, I'm pissed off. And the funny thing is you're pissed off, too, because whatever you're getting isn't enough. Make the splits even and nobody's got cause to complain. You put out more than I do on the one job, well, it evens out later on, when I put out more'n you do. Meantime, every dollar comes in, each one of us gets twenty cents of it."

So they stood to bring in eighteen thousand dollars apiece for a few hours work, which, inflation notwithstanding, was a healthy cut above minimum wage, and better than anybody was paying in the fields and factories. Was it a fortune? No. Wealth beyond the dreams of avarice? Hardly that. But all five of the principals would agree that it was a good night's work.

The job was planned and rehearsed, the schedule fine-tuned. When push came to shove, the pushing and shoving went like clockwork. Everything happened just as it was supposed to, and our five masked heroes wound up in a room with five of the firm's employees, one of them the inside man, the brother-in-law of Mike Dunn's paramour. And it strikes me that we need a name for him, although we won't need it for long. But let's call him Alfie. No need for a last name. Just Alfie will do fine.

Like the others, Alfie was tied up tight, a piece of duct tape across his mouth. Mike Dunn had given him a wink when he tied him, and made sure his bonds weren't tight enough to hurt. He sat there and watched as the five men hauled sacks of money out of the vault.

It was Eddie O'Day who found the bearer bonds.

By then they already knew that it was going to be a much bigger payday than they'd anticipated. A hundred thousand? The cash looked as though it would come to at least three and maybe four or five times that. Half a million? A hundred thousand apiece?

The bearer bonds, all by themselves, totaled two million dollars. They were like cash, but better than cash because, relatively speaking, they didn't weigh anything or take up any space. Pieces of paper, two hundred of them, each worth ten thousand dollars. And they weren't registered to an owner, and were as anonymous as a crumpled dollar bill.

In every man's mind, the numbers changed. The night was going to be worth two and a half million dollars, or half a million apiece. Why, Alfie's share as an informant would come to a quarter of a million dollars all by itself, which was not bad compensation for letting yourself be tied up and gagged for a few hours.

Of course, there was another way of looking at it. Alfie was taking fifty thousand dollars from each of them. He was costing them, right off the top, almost three times as much money as they'd expected to net in the first place.

The little son of a bitch . . .

Alan Walker went over to Alfie and hunkered down next to him. "You did good," he said. "There's lots more money than anybody thought, plus all of these bonds."

Alfie struggled with his bonds, and his eyes rolled wildly. Alan asked him if something was the matter, and Mike Dunn came over and took the tape from Alfie's mouth."

"Them," Alfie said.

"Them?"

He rolled his eyes toward his fellow employees. "They'll think I'm involved," he said.

"Well, hell, Alfie," Eddie O'Day said, "you are involved, aren'tcha? You're in for what, ten percent?"

Alfie just stared.

"Listen," George Walker told him, "don't worry about those guys. What are they gonna say?"

"Their lips are sealed," his brother pointed out.

"But—"

George Walker nodded to Louis Creamer, who drew a pistol and shot one of the bound men in the back of the head. Mike Dunn and Eddie O'Day drew their guns, and more shots rang out. Within seconds the four presumably loyal employees were dead.

"Oh, Jesus," Alfie said.

"Had to be," George Walker told him. "They heard what my brother said to you, right? Besides, the money involved, there's gonna be way too much heat coming down. They didn't see anybody's face, but who knows what they might notice that the masks don't hide? And they heard voices. Better this way, Alfie."

"Ten percent," Eddie O'Day said. "You might walk away with a quarter of a million dollars, Alfie. What are you gonna do with all that dough?"

Alfie looked like a man who'd heard the good news and the bad news all at once. He was in line for a fortune, but would he get to spend a dime of it?

"Listen," he said, "you guys better beat me up."

"Beat you up?"

"I think so, and—"

"But you're our little buddy," Louis Creamer said. "Why would we want to do that?"

"If I'm the only one left," Alfie said, "they'll suspect me, won't they?"

"Suspect you?"

"Of being involved."

"Ah," George Walker said. "Never thought of that."

"But if you beat me up . . ."

"You figure it might throw them off? A couple of bruises on your face and they won't even think of questioning you?"

"Maybe you better wound me," Alfie said.

"Wound you, Alfie?"

"Like a flesh wound, you know? A non-fatal wound."

"Oh, hell," Alan Walker said. "We can do better than that." And he put his gun up against Alfie's forehead and blew his brains out.

"Had to be," George Walker announced, as they cleared the area of any possible traces of their presence. "No way on earth he would have stood up, the kind of heat they'd have put on him. The minute the total goes over a mill, far as I'm concerned, they're all dead, all five of them. The other four because of what they might have picked up, and Alfie because of what we damn well know he knows."

"He was in for a quarter of a mill," Eddie O'Day said. "You look at it one way, old Alfie was a rich man for a minute there."

"You think about it," Louis Creamer said, "what'd he ever do was worth a quarter of a mill?"

"He was taking fifty grand apiece from each of us," Alan Walker said. "If you want to look at it that way."

"It's as good a way as any to look at it," George Walker said.

"Beady little eyes," Eddie O'Day said. "Never liked the little bastard. And he'd have sung like a bird, minute they picked him up."

The Walkers had a storage locker that nobody knew about, and that was where they went to count the proceeds of the job. The cash, it turned out, ran to just over $650,000, and another count of the bearer bonds confirmed the figure of two million dollars. That made the total $2,650,000, or $530,000 a man after a five-way split.

"Alfie was richer than we thought," George Walker said. "For a minute there, anyway. Two hundred sixty-five grand."

"If we'd left him alive," his brother said, "the cops would have had our names within twenty-four hours."

"Twenty-four hours? He'da been singing the second they got the tape off his mouth."

Eddie O'Day said, "You got to wonder."

"Wonder what?"

"How much singing he already done."

They exchanged glances. To Mike Dunn, George Walker said, "This dame of yours. Alfie was married to her sister?"

"Right."

"I was a cop, I'd take a look at the families of those five guys. Dead or alive, I'd figure there might have been somebody on the inside, you know?"

"I see what you mean."

"They talk to Alfie's wife, who knows what he let slip?"

"Probably nothing."

"Probably nothing, but who knows? Maybe he thought he was keeping her in the dark, but she puts two and two together, you know?"

"Maybe he talked in his sleep," Louis Creamer suggested.

Mike Dunn thought about it, nodded. "I'll take care of it," he said.

Later that evening, the Walkers were in George's den, drinking scotch and smoking cigars. "You know what I'm thinking," George said.

"The wife's dead," Alan said, "and it draws the cops a picture. Five employees dead, plus the wife of one of them? Right away they know which one was working for us."

"So they know which direction to go."

"This woman Mike's been nailing. Sister of Alfie's wife."

"Right."

"They talk to her and what do they get?"

"Probably nothing, far as the job's concerned. Even if Alfie talked to his wife, it's a stretch to think the wife talked to her sister."

Alan nodded. "The sister doesn't know shit about the job," he said. "But there's one thing she knows."

"What's that?"

"She knows she's been sleeping with Mike. Of course that's something she most likely wants kept a secret, on account of she's a married lady."

"But when the cops turn her upside-down and shake her . . . ."

"Leads straight to Mike. And now that I think about it, will they even have to shake her hard? Because if she figures out that it was probably Mike that got her sister and her brother-in-law killed . . ."

George finished his drink, poured another. "Her name's Alice," he said.

"Alice Fuhrmann. Be easy enough, drop in on her, take her out. Where I sit, she looks like a big loose end."

"How's Mike gonna take it?"

"Maybe it'll look like an accident."

"He's no dummy. She has an accident, he'll have a pretty good idea who gave it to her."

"Well, that's another thing," George Walker said. "Take out Alfie's wife and her sister and there's nobody with a story to tell. But I can see the cops finding the connection between Mike and this Alice no matter what, because who knows who she told?"

"He's a good man, Mike."

"Damn good man."

"Kind of a loner, though."

"Looks out for himself."

The brothers glanced significantly at each other, and drank their whiskey.

The sixth death recorded in connection with the robbery was that of Alfie's wife. Mike Dunn went to her home, found her alone, and accepted her offer of a cup of coffee. She thought he was coming on to her, and had heard from her sister what a good lover he was, and the idea of having a quickie with her sister's boyfriend was not unappealing. She invited him upstairs, and he didn't know what to do. He knew he couldn't afford to leave physical evidence in her bed or on her body. And could he have sex with a woman and then kill her? The thought sickened him, and, not surprisingly, turned him on a little too. He went upstairs with her. She was wearing a robe, and as they ascended the staircase he ran a hand up under the robe and found she was wearing nothing under it. He was wildly excited, and desperate to avoid acting on his excitement, and when they reached the top of the stairs he took her in his arms. She waited for him to kiss her, and instead he got his hands on her neck and throttled her, his hands tightening convulsively around her throat until the light went out of her eyes. Then he pitched her body down the stairs, walked down them himself, stepped over her corpse and got out of the house.

He was shaking. He wanted to tell somebody, but he didn't know whom to tell. He got in his car and drove home, and there was George Walker with a duffle bag.

"I did it," Mike blurted out. "She thought I wanted to fuck her, and you want to hear something sick? I wanted to."

"But you took care of it?"

"She fell down the stairs," Mike said. "Broke her neck."

"Accidents happen," George said, and tapped the duffle bag. "Your share."

"I thought we weren't gonna divvy it for a while."

"That was the plan, yeah."

"Because they might come calling, and if anybody has a lot of money at hand . . ."

"Right."

"Besides, any of us starts spending, it draws attention. Not that I would, but I'd worry about Eddie."

"If he starts throwing money around . . ."

"Could draw attention."

"Right."

"Thing is," George explained, "we were thinking maybe you ought to get out of town for a while, Mike. Alfie's dead and his wife's dead, but who knows how far back the cops can trace things? This girlfriend of yours—"

"Jesus, don't remind me. I just killed her sister."

"Well, somebody can take care of that."

Mike Dunn's eyes widened, but he didn't say anything.

"If you're out of town for a while," George said, "maybe it's not a bad thing."

Not a bad thing at all, Mike thought. Not if somebody was going to take care of Alice Fuhrmann, because the next thing that might occur to them was taking care of Mike Dunn, and he didn't want to be around when that happened. He packed a bag, and George walked him to his car, and took a gun from his pocket and shot him behind the ear just as he was getting behind the wheel.

Within hours Mike Dunn was buried at the bottom of an old well at an abandoned farmhouse six miles north of the city, and his car was part of a fleet of stolen cars on their way to the coast, where they'd be loaded aboard a freighter for shipment overseas. By then Alan Walker had decoyed Alice Fuhrmann to a supermarket parking lot, where he killed her with a home-made garrote and stuffed her into the trunk of her car.

"Mike did the right thing," George told Eddie O'Day and Louis Creamer. "He took out Alfie's widow and his own girlfriend, but he figured it might still come back to him, so I gave him his share and he took off. Half a mill, he can stay gone for a good long time."

"More'n that," Eddie O'Day said. "Five hundred thirty, wasn't it?"

"Well, round numbers."

"Speaking of numbers," Eddie said, "when are we gonna cut up the pie? Because I could use some of mine."

"Soon," George told him.

Five-thirty each for Louis Creamer and Eddie O'Day, $795,000 apiece for the Walkers, George thought, because Louis and Eddie didn't know that Mike Dunn had not gone willingly (though he'd been willing enough to do so) and had not taken his share with him. (George had brought the duffle bag home with him, and stashed it behind the furnace.) So why should Eddie and Louis get a split of Mike's share?

For that matter, George thought, he hadn't yet told his brother what had become of Mike Dunn. He'd never intended to give Mike his share, but he'd filled the duffle bag at the storage facility in case he'd had to change his plans on the spot, and he'd held the money out afterward in case the four of them wound up going to the storage bin together to make the split. As far as Alan knew, Mike and his share had vanished, and why burden the lad with the whole story? Why should Alan have a friend's death on his conscience?

No, George's conscience could carry the weight. And, along with the guilt, shouldn't he have Mike's share for himself? Because he couldn't split it with Alan without telling him where it came from.

Which changed the numbers slightly: $530,000 apiece for Alan, Louis, and Eddie; $1,060,000 for George.

Of course we knew who'd pulled off the robbery. Alfie's wife had indeed suffered a broken neck in the fall, but the medical examination quickly revealed she'd been strangled first. Her sister had disappeared, and soon turned up in the trunk of her car, a loop of wire tightened around her neck. Someone was able to connect the sister to Mike Dunn, and we established that he and his clothes and his car had gone missing. Present or not, Mike Dunn automatically led to Creamer and O'Day and the Walkers—but we'd have been looking at them anyway. Just a matter of rounding up the usual suspects, really.

"Eddie called me," Alan said. "They were talking to him."

"And you, and me," George said. "And Louis. They can suspect all they want, long as they can't prove anything."

"He wants his cut."

"Eddie?"

Alan nodded. "I asked him was he planning on running, and he said no.

Just that he'll feel better when he's got his share. Mike got his cut, he said, and why's he different?"

"Mike's case was special."

"Just what I told him. He says he owes money he's got to pay, plus there's some things he wants to buy."

"The cops are talking to him, and what he wants to do is pay some debts and spend some money."

"That's about it."

"And if the answer's no? Then what?"

"He didn't say, but next thing I knew he was mentioning how the cops had been talking to him."

"Subtle bastard. You know, when the cops talk to him a few more times—"

"I don't know how he'll stand up. He's always been a stand-up guy before, but the stakes are a lot higher."

"And you can sort of sense him getting ready to spill it. He's working up a resentment about not getting paid. Other hand, if he does get paid . . ."

"He throws money around."

They fell silent. Finally George said, "We haven't even talked about Louis."

"No."

"Be convenient if the two of them killed each other, wouldn't it?"

"No more worries about who'll stand up. Down side, we'd have nobody to work with, either."

"Why work?" George grinned. "You and me'd be splitting two million, six-fifty."

"Less Mike's share," Alan pointed out.

"Right," George said.

They were planning it, working it out together, because it was not going to be easy to get the drop on Eddie, who was pretty shrewd and probably a little suspicious at this stage. And, while they were figuring it all out, Louis Creamer get in touch to tell them he'd just killed Eddie O'Day.

"He came by my house," Louis said, "and he was acting weird, you know? He said you guys were going to pull a fast one and rat us out to the cops, but how could you do that? And he had this scheme for taking you both out and getting the money, and him and me'd split it. And I could see where he was going. He wanted me for about as long as it would take to take you both down, and then it would be my turn to go. The son of a bitch."

"So what did you do?"

"I just punched him out," Louis said, "and then I took hold of him and broke his fucking neck. Now I got him lying in a heap in my living room, and I don't know what to do with him."

"We'll help," said George.

They went to Louis's house, and there was Eddie in a heap on the floor. "Look at this," George said, holding up a gun. "He was packing."

"Yeah, well, he was out cold before he could get it out of his pocket."

"You did good, Louis," George said, pressing the gun into Eddie's dead hand and carefully fitting his index finger around the trigger. "Real good," he said, and pointed the gun at Louis, and put three shots in his chest.

"Amazing," Alan said. "They really did kill each other. Well, you said it would be convenient."

"One of them would have cut a deal. In fact Eddie did try to cut a deal, with Louis."

"But Louis stood up."

"For how long?"

"That was nice, taking him out with Eddie's gun. They'll find nitrate particles in his hand and know he fired the shot. But how'd he get killed?"

"We're not the cops," George said. "Let them worry about it."

We didn't worry much. We looked at who was still standing, and we brought in the Walkers and grilled them separately. They had their stories ready and we couldn't shake them, and hadn't really expected to. They'd been through this countless times before, and they knew to keep their mouths shut, and eventually we sent them home.

A week later they were at George's house, in George's basement den, drinking George's scotch. "We maybe got trouble," Alan said. "The cops in San Diego picked up Mike Dunn."

"That's not good," George said, "but what's he gonna say? They'll throw the dame at him, Alfie's wife, and they got him figured for the sister, too. He'll just stay dummied up about everything if he knows what's good for him."

"Unless they offer him a deal."

"That could be a problem." George admitted.

Alan was looking at him carefully. George could almost hear what was going through Alan's mind, but before he could do anything about it Alan had a gun in his hand and it was pointed at George.

"Now put that away," George said. "What the hell's the matter with you?

Just put that away and sit down and drink your drink."

"You're good, Georgie. But I know you too well. I just told you they arrested Mike, and you're not the least bit worried."

"I just said it could be a problem."

"What you almost said," Alan told him, "was it was impossible, but you didn't, you were quick on the uptake. But you knew it was impossible because you knew all along Mike Dunn was where nobody could get at him. Where is he, Georgie?"

"Buried. Nobody's gonna find him."

"What I figured. And what happened to his share? You bury it along with him?"

"I tucked it away. I didn't want the others to know what happened, so Mike's share of the money had to disappear."

"The others are gone, Georgie. It's just you and me, and I don't see you rushing to split the money with your brother."

"Jesus," George said, "is that what this is about? And will you please put the gun down and drink your drink?"

"I'll keep the gun," Alan said, "and I think I'll wait on the drink. Now that Louis and Eddie are out of the picture, you were gonna split Mike's share with me, weren't you?"

"Absolutely."

"Why don't I believe you, Brother?"

"Because you're tied up in knots. Because they grilled you downtown, same as they grilled me, and they offered you a deal, same as they offered me a deal, and we're the Walkers, we're not gonna sell each other out, and if you'd relax and drink your fucking drink you'd know that. You want your share of Mike's money? Is that what you want?"

"That's exactly what I want."

"Fine," George said, and led him to the furnace room, where he hoisted the duffle bag. They returned to the den, with Alan holding a gun on his brother all the way. George set down the bag and worked the zipper, and the bag was full of money, all right. Alan's eyes widened at the sight of it.

"Half's yours," George said.

"I figure all of it's mine," Alan said. "You were gonna take it all, so I'm gonna take it all. Fair enough?"

"I don't know about fair," George said, "but you know what? I'm not going to argue. You take it, the whole thing, and we'll split what's in the storage locker. And drink your fucking drink before it evaporates."

"I'll take what's in the locker, too," Alan said, and squeezed the trigger, and kept squeezing until the gun was empty. "Jesus," he said, "I just killed my own brother. I guess I'll take that drink now, Georgie. You talked me into it."

And he picked up the glass, drained it, and pitched forward onto his face.

The room fell silent, but for the crackling of the fire and, after a long moment, a rumbling snore from the fireside.

"A fine story," said the doctor, "though not perhaps equally engrossing to everyone. The club's Oldest Member, it would seem, has managed to sleep through it."

They all glanced at the fireplace, and the chair beside it, where the little old man dozed in his oversized armchair.

"Poison, I presume," the doctor went on. "In the whiskey, and of course that was why George was so eager to have his brother take a drink."

"Strychnine, as I recall," said the policeman. "Something fast-acting, in any event."

"It's a splendid story," the priest agreed, "but one question arises. All the principals died, and I don't suppose any of them was considerate enough to write out a narrative before departing. So how are you able to recount it?"

"We reconstructed a good deal," the policeman said. "Mike Dunn's body did turn up, eventually, in the well at the old farmhouse. And of course the death scene in George Walker's den spoke for itself, complete with the duffle bag full of money. I put words in their mouths and filled in the blanks through inference and imagination, but we're not in a court of law, are we? I thought it would do for a story."

"I meant no criticism, Policeman. I just wondered."

"And I wonder," said the soldier, "just what the story implies, and what it says about greed. They were greedy, of course, all of them. It was greed that led them to commit the initial crime, and greed that got them killing each other off, until there was no one left to spend all that money."

"I suppose the point is whatever one thinks it to be," the policeman said. "They were greedy as all criminals are greedy, wanting what other men have and appropriating it by illegal means. But, you know, they weren't that greedy."

"They shared equally," the doctor remembered.

"And lived well, but well within their means. You could say they were businessmen whose business was illegal. They were profit-motivated, but is the desire for profit tantamount to greed?"

"But they became greedy," the doctor observed. "And the greed altered their behavior. I assume these men had killed before."

"Oh, yes."

"But not wantonly, and they had never before turned on each other."

"No."

"The root of all evil," the priest said, and the others looked at him. "Money," he explained. "There was too much of it. That's the point, isn't it, Policeman? There was too much money."

The policeman nodded. "That's what I always thought," he said. "They had been playing the game for years, but suddenly the stakes had been raised exponentially, and they were in over their heads. The moment the bearer bonds turned up, all the deaths that were to follow were carved in stone."

They nodded, and the policeman took up the pack of playing cards. "My deal, isn't it?" He shuffled the pack, shuffled it again.

"I wonder," the soldier said. "I wonder just what greed is."

"I would say it's like pornography," the doctor said. "There was a senator who said he couldn't define it, but he knew it when he saw it."

"If he got an erection, it was pornography?"

"Something like that. But don't we all know what greed is? And yet how easy is it to pin down?"

"It's wanting more than you need," the policeman suggested.

"Ah, but that hardly excludes anyone, does it? Anyone who aspires to more than life on a subsistence level wants more than he absolutely needs."

"Perhaps," the priest proposed, "it's wanting more than you think you deserve."

"Oh, I like that," the doctor said. "It's so wonderfully subjective. If I think I deserve—what was your phrase, Policeman? Something about dreaming of avarice?"

" 'Wealth beyond the dreams of avarice.' And it's not my phrase, I'm afraid, but Samuel Johnson's."

"A pity he's not here to enliven this conversation, but we'll have to make do without him. But if I think I deserve to have pots and pots of money, Priest, does that protect me from greed?"

The priest frowned, considering the matter. "I think it's where it leads," the policeman said. "If my desire for more moves me to sinful action, then the desire is greedy. If not, I simply want to better myself, and that's a normal and innocent human desire, and where would we be without it?"

"Somewhere in New Jersey," the doctor said. "Does anyone ever think himself to be greedy? You're greedy, but I just want to make a better life for my family. Isn't that how everyone sees it?"

"They always want it for the family," the policeman agreed. "A man embezzles a million dollars and he explains he was just doing it for his family. As if it's not greed if it's on someone else's behalf."

"I'm reminded of the farmer," said the priest, "who insisted he wasn't at all greedy. He just wanted the land that bordered his own."

The soldier snapped his fingers. "That's it," he said. "That's the essence of greed, that it can never be satisfied. You always want more." He shook his head. "Reminds me of a story," he said.

"Then put down the cards," the doctor said, "and let's hear it."


In my occupation (said the soldier) greed rarely plays a predominant role. Who becomes a soldier in order to make himself rich? Oh, there are areas of the world where a military career can indeed lead to wealth. One doesn't think of an eastern warlord, for example, slogging it out with an eye on his pension and a cottage in the Cotswolds or a houseboat in Fort Lauderdale. In the western democracies, though, the activating sin is more apt to be pride. One yearns for promotions, for status, perhaps in some instances for political power. And financial reward often accompanies these prizes, but it's not apt to be an end in itself.

Why do men choose a military career? For the security, I suppose. For self-respect, and the respect of one's fellows. For the satisfaction of being a part of something larger than oneself, and not a money-grubbing soulless corporation but an organization bent on advancing and defending the interests of an entire nation. For many reasons, but rarely out of greed.

Even so, opportunities for profit sometimes arise. And greedy men sometimes find themselves in uniform—especially in time of war, when the draft sweeps up men who would not otherwise choose to clothe themselves in khaki.

As often as not, such men make perfectly acceptable soldiers. There was a vogue some years ago for giving young criminals a choice—they could enlist in the armed forces or go to jail. This later went out of fashion, the

argument against it being that it would turn the service into a sort of peni-
tentiary without walls, filled with criminal types. But in my experience it
often worked rather well. Removed from his home environment, and
thrown into a world where greed had little opportunity to find satisfaction,
the young man was apt to do just fine. The change might or might not last
after his military obligation was over, of course.

But let's get down to cases. At the end of the second world war, Allied
soldiers in Europe suddenly found several opportunities for profit. They had
access to essential goods that were in short supply among the civilian population, and a black market sprang up instantly in cigarettes, chocolate, and
liquor, along with such non-essentials as food and clothing. Some soldiers
traded Hershey bars and packs of Camels for a fraulein's sexual favors;
others parlayed goods from the PX into a small fortune, buying and selling
and trading with dispatch.

There was nothing in Gary Carmody's background to suggest that he
would become an illicit entrepreneur at war's end. He grew up on a farm in
the Corn Belt and enlisted in the army shortly after Pearl Harbor. He was
assigned to the infantry and participated in the invasion of Italy, where he
picked up a Purple Heart and a shoulder wound at Salerno. Upon recovery
from his injury, he was shipped to England, where in due course he took
part in the Normandy invasion, landing at Utah Beach and helping to
push the Wehrmacht across France. He earned a second Purple Heart
during the German counterattack, along with a Bronze Star. He recuper-
ated at a field hospital—the machine-gun bullet broke a rib, but did no
major damage—and he was back in harness marching across the Rhine
around the time the Germans surrendered.

Neither the bullets he'd taken nor the revelations of the concentration
camps led Gary to a blanket condemnation of the entire German nation.
While he thought the Nazis ought to be rounded up and shot, and that
shooting was probably too good for the SS, he didn't see anything wrong
with the German women. They were at once forthright and feminine, and
their accents were a lot more charming than the Nazis in the war movies.
He had a couple of dates, and then he met a blue-eyed blonde named
Helga, and they hit it off. He brought her presents, of course—it was only
fitting, the Germans had nothing and what was the big deal in bringing
some chocolate and cigarettes? Back home you'd take flowers or candy, and
maybe go out to a restaurant, and nobody thought of it as prostitution.

He brought a pair of nylons one day, and she tried them on at once, and one thing led to another. Afterward they lay together in her narrow bed and she reached to stroke the stockings, which they hadn't bothered to remove. She said, "You can get more of these, liebchen?"

"Did they get a run in them already?"

"Gott, I hope not. No, I was thinking. We could make money together."

"With nylons?"

"And cigarettes and chocolate. And other things, if you can get them."

"What other things?"

"Anything. Soap, even."

And so he began trading, with Helga as his partner in and out of bed. She was the daughter of shopkeepers and turned out to be a natural at her new career, knowing instinctively what to buy and what to sell and how to set prices. He was just a farm boy, but he had a farm boy's shrewdness plus the quickness it had taken to survive combat as a foot soldier, and he learned the game in a hurry. As with any extralegal trade, there was always a danger that the person you were dealing with would pull a fast one—or a gun or a knife—and use force or guile to take everything. Gary knew how to make sure that didn't happen.

It was another American soldier who got Gary into the art business. The man was an officer, a captain, but the black market was a great leveler, and the two men had done business together. The captain had a fraulein of his own, and the two couples were drinking together one evening when the captain mentioned that he'd taken something in trade and didn't know what the hell he was going to do with it. "It's a painting," he said. "Ugly little thing. Hang on a minute, I'll show you."

He went upstairs and returned with a framed canvas nine inches by twelve inches, showing Salome with the head of John the Baptist. "I know it's from the Bible and all," the captain said, "but it's still fucking unpleasant, and if Salome was really that fat I can't see losing your head over her. This look like five hundred dollars to you, Gary?"

"Is that what you gave for it?"

"Yes and no. I was going back and forth with this droopy-eyed Kraut and we reached a point where we're five hundred dollars apart. And he whips out this thing of beauty. 'All right,' he said. 'I vill hate myself for doing zis, but you haff me over a bushel.' And he goes on to tell me how it's a genuine Von Schtupp or whatever the hell it is, and it's worth a fortune.

"The way he did it, I couldn't come back and say, look, Konrad, keep the picture and gimme a hundred dollars more. I do that and I'm slapping him in the face, and I don't want to rub him the wrong way because Konrad and I do a lot of business. And the fact of the matter is yes, we're five hundred bucks apart, but I could take the deal at his price and I'm still okay with it. So I said yes, it sure is a beautiful picture, which it's not, as anyone can plainly see, and I said I'm sure it was valuable, but what am I gonna do with it? Sell it in Paris, he says. Sell it in London, in New York. So I let him talk me into it, because I wanted the deal to go through but what I didn't want was for him to try palming off more of these beauties on me, because I saw the look in his eye, Gary, and I've got a feeling he's got a shitload of them just waiting for a sucker with a suitcase full of dollars to take them off his hands."

"What are you going to do with it?"

"Well, I don't guess I'll throw darts at it. I could take it home, but what's a better souvenir, a genuine Luger or an ugly picture? And which would you rather spend your old age looking at?"

Gary looked at the painting, and he looked at Helga. He saw something in her eyes, and he also saw something in the canvas. "It's not that ugly," he said. "What do you want for it?"

"You serious?"

"Serious enough to ask, anyway."

"Well, let's see. I've got five hundred in it, and—"

"You've got zero in it. You'd have done the deal for what he offered, without the painting."

"I said that, didn't I? Strategic error, corporal. I'll tell you what, give me a hundred dollars and it's yours."

"Let's split the difference," Gary said. "I'll give you fifty."

"What is it we're splitting? Oh, hell, I don't want to look at it anymore. Give me the fifty and you can hang it over your bed."

They didn't hang it over the bed. Instead Helga hid it under the mattress. "The Nazis looted everything," she told him. "Museums, private collections. Your friend is stupid. It's a beautiful painting, and we can make money on it. And if we can meet his friend Konrad—"

"There's more where this one came from," he finished. "But how do we sell them?"

"You can get to Switzerland, no?"

"Maybe," he said.

The painting, which he sold without ever learning the artist's name—he somehow knew it was not Von Schtupp—brought him Swiss francs worth twenty-eight hundred American dollars. The proceeds bought four paintings from the droopy-eyed Konrad. These were larger canvases, and Gary removed them from their frames and rolled them up and took them to Zurich, returning to Germany this time with almost seven thousand dollars.

And so it went. It wasn't a foolproof business, as he learned when his Zurich customer dismissed a painting as worthless kitsch. But it was a forgiving trade, and most transactions were quite profitable. If he was in doubt he could take goods on consignment, selling in Zurich or Geneva—or, once, in Madrid—and sharing the proceeds with the consignor. But you made more money if you owned what you were selling, and he liked owning it, liked the way it felt. And if there was more risk that way, well, he liked the risk, too.

All his time and energy went into the business. Art was all he bothered with now—there were enough other soldiers making deals in stockings and cigarettes—and he was preoccupied with it, with the buying and selling and, almost as an afterthought, with the paintings themselves.

Because it turned out he had a feel for it. He'd seen something in that first painting of Salome, even if he hadn't realized it at the time. He'd responded to the artistry. Before he enlisted, he'd never been to a museum, never seen a painting hanging in a private home, never looked at any art beyond the reproductions in his mother's J. C. Penney calendar.

He learned to look at the paintings, as he'd never looked at anything before. The more he liked a painting, the harder it was to part with it. He fell in love with a Goya, and held onto it until something else came along that he liked better. Then he sold the Goya—that was the one he took to Madrid, where he's heard about a crony of Franco's who wouldn't be put off by the work's dodgy provenance.

It was easier to part with Helga. They'd been good for each other, as lovers and as business partners, but the affair ran its course, and he didn't need or want a partner in his art dealings. He gave her a fair share of their capital and went on by himself.

Nothing lasts forever, not even military service. There came a time for Gary to board a troopship headed back to the States. He thought of staying in Europe—he had a career here, for as long as it could last—but in the end he realized it was time to go home.

But what to do with his money? He had run his original stake of cigarettes and nylons up to something like eighty thousand dollars. That was a lot of cash to carry, and it was cash he couldn't explain, so he had to carry it—he couldn't put it in a bank and write himself a check.

But what he could do, and in fact did, was buy a painting and bring that home with him. He chose a Vermeer, a luminous domestic interior, the most beautiful thing he'd ever seen in his life. It hadn't come to him in the usual way; instead, he'd found it in an art gallery in Paris and had been hard-pressed to get the snooty owner to cut the price by ten percent.

On the troopship, squinting at the painting in his footlocker by what little illumination his flashlight afforded, he decided he must have been out of his mind. He'd had all that cash, and now he was down to what, fifteen thousand dollars? That was a lot of money in 1946, it would buy him a house and get him started in a business, but it was a fifth of what he'd had.

Well, maybe he could run it up a little. It would be a week before the ship docked in New York, and there were plenty of men on board with money in their pockets and time on their hands. There were card games and crap games running twenty-four hours a day, and he'd always been pretty good at a poker table.

I suspect you can guess at the rest. Maybe he ran up against some card-sharps, or maybe the cards just weren't running his way. He never knew for sure, but what he did know was that he reached New York with nothing in his kick but the five hundred dollars of case money he'd tucked away before he started. Everything else was gone, invested in straights that ran into flushes, flushes that never came in, and bluffs some other guy called.

You'd think he'd be desolate, wouldn't you? He thought so himself, and was surprised to discover that he actually felt pretty good. If you looked at it one way, he left Germany with eighty thousand dollars and landed in New York with five hundred. But there was another way to see it, and that was that he had five hundred dollars more than he'd had when he left Iowa in the first place, and he'd been shot twice and lived to tell the tale, and he had a Bronze Star to keep his two Purple Hearts company, and he knew as much about women as anybody in Iowa, and more about art. The money he'd had, well, in a sense it had never been real in the first place, and, as for the paintings he'd trafficked in, well, they hadn't been real either. They'd all been stolen, and they had no provenance, and sooner or later they could very well be confiscated and restored to their rightful owners.

He figured he'd done just fine.

❧   ❧   ❧

"Soldier? Have you finished?"

The soldier looked up, blinked. "More or less," he said. "Why? Don't you like the story?"

"It's a fine story," the doctor said, "but isn't it unfinished? There's a sense of closure, in that our hero is back where he started. That's if he went back to his family's farm, which I don't believe you mentioned."

"Didn't I? Yes, he returned to the farm."

"And to the girl he left behind him?"

"I don't believe there was a girl he'd left behind," said the soldier, "and if there was, well, she'd been left too far behind to catch up with him."

"That must have been true of the farm as well," the priest offered.

The soldier nodded. "That proved to be the case," he said. "He had, as it were, seen Paree—and Madrid and Geneva and Zurich and Berlin, and no end of other places more stimulating than an Iowa corn field. He'd spent two days in New York, waiting for his train, and he'd spent much of it at the Metropolitan Museum of Art and in the galleries on upper Madison Avenue. He stayed in Iowa for as long as he could, and then he packed a bag and returned to New York."

"And?"

"He found a cheap flat, a fifth-floor walkup in Greenwich Village for twenty-two dollars a month. He made the rounds of the art galleries and auction houses until he found someone who was willing to hire him for forty dollars a week. And, gradually, he learned the business from the ground up. From the very beginning he saved his money—I don't know how he could have saved much when he earned forty dollars a week, but he managed. Half of it went into a permanent savings account. The other half went into a fund to purchase art.

"Years passed. Although there was often a woman in his life, he never married, never formed a long-term alliance. Nor did he move from his original apartment in the Village. The neighborhood became increasingly desirable, the surrounding rents went up accordingly, but his own rent, frozen by the miracle of rent control, was still under a hundred dollars a month twenty-five years later.

"His capital grew, as did his collection of prints and paintings. The time came when he was able to open a gallery of his own, stocking it with the works he'd amassed. Rather than represent living artists, he dealt in older works, and on more than one occasion he was offered work he recognized from his time in Germany, stolen paintings he'd brokered years ago. Since then they'd acquired provenance and could be openly bought and sold.

"He's in the business today. He could retire, he'll tell you, but then what would he do with himself? He walks with a cane, and on damp days he feels the pain of his second wound, the rib broken by the machine-gun bullet. It's funny, he says, that it never bothered him once it healed, and now it aches again, after all those years. You think you're done with a thing, he'll say philosophically, but perhaps no one is ever done with anything.

"He's respected, successful, and if I told you his name, which is certainly not Gary Carmody, you might very well recognize it. There were rumors over the years that he occasionally dealt in, well, not stolen goods exactly, but works of art with something shady about them, and I don't mean chiaroscuro. But nothing was ever substantiated, and there was never a scandal, and few people even remember what was once said of him."

"And that's the end of the story," the policeman said.

"Well, the man's still alive, and is any story ever entirely over while one lives? But yes, the story is over."

"And what does it all mean?" the priest wondered. "He was a rather ordinary young man, not particularly greedy, until circumstances created a great opportunity for greed to flourish. Greed led him into a marginally criminal existence, at which he seems to have thrived, and then his circumstances changed, and he tried to change with them. But greed led him to try his hand at poker—"

"Even as you and I," murmured the doctor.

"—and he lost everything. But what he retained, acquired through greed, was a love of art and a passion for dealing in it, and as soon as he could he returned to it, and worked and sacrificed to achieve legitimate success."

"Unless those rumors were true," the policeman said.

"It's a fine story," the doctor said, "and well told. But there's something I don't entirely understand."

"Oh?"

"The Vermeer, Soldier. He was working for nothing and living on less. My God, he must have been scraping by on bread and water, and it would have been day-old bread and tap water, too. Why couldn't he sell the Vermeer? That would have set him up in business and kept him living decently until the gallery started paying for itself."

"He fell in love with it," the policeman offered. "How could he sell it? I daresay he still owns it to this day."

"He does," the soldier said. "It hung briefly on the wall of his room in the farmhouse in Iowa, and for years it hung on a nail in that fifth-floor Village walkup. The day he opened his own gallery he hung it above his desk in the gallery office, and it's still there."

"A lucky penny," the doctor said. " 'Keep me and you'll never go broke.' And I'd say he's a long way from broke. I haven't priced any Vermeers lately, but I would think his would have to be worth an eight-figure price by now."

"You would think so," the soldier allowed.

"And he wouldn't part with it. Is that greed, clinging so tenaciously to that which, if he would but let it go, might allow him to reach his goals? Or is it some other sin?"

"Like what, Doctor?"

"Oh, pride, perhaps. He defines himself as a man who possesses a Vermeer. And so it hangs on his crumbling wall while he lives like a church mouse. No, make that like a ruined aristocrat, putting on a black tie every night for dinner, setting the table with Rosenthal china and Waterford crystal, and dining on stone soup. Made, you'll no doubt recall, by simmering a stone in water for half an hour, then adding salt."

"An old family recipe," the policeman said. "But would the painting be worth that much? An eight-figure price—that's quite a range, from ten to a hundred million dollars."

"Ninety-nine," the doctor said.

"I stand corrected. But if it increased in value from fifty thousand dollars to—oh, take the low figure, ten million. If it performed that well, how can you possibly argue that he should have sold it? He may have struggled, but it doesn't seem to have harmed him. Who can say he was wrong to keep it? He's a success now, he's been a success for some years—and he owns a Vermeer."

They fell silent, thinking about it. Then the priest cleared his throat, and all eyes turned toward him.

"I should think," he said, "that at least two of the figures are after the decimal point." He drew a breath, smiled gently. "I suspect Soldier has neglected to tell us everything. It's a forgery, isn't it? That priceless Vermeer."

The soldier nodded.

"By Van Meegeren, I would suppose, if it fooled our Mr. Carmody the first time around. That fellow's Vermeers, sold as the fakes that they are, have reached a point where they command decent prices in their own right. I don't suppose this one is worth quite what that young soldier gave for it half a century ago, but it's a long way from valueless."

"A fake," the policeman said. "How did you guess, Priest?"

"The clues were there, weren't they? Why else would his heart sink when he peered at the painting as it reposed in his footlocker? He saw then by flashlight what he hadn't seen in the gallery's more favorable lighting— that he'd squandered all his profits on a canvas that was never in the same room as Vermeer. No wonder he gambled, hoping to recoup his losses. And, given the state of mind he must have been in, no wonder he lost everything."

"An expert in New York confirmed what he already knew," the soldier said. "Could he have sold it anyway? Perhaps, even as the Parisian dealer, knowingly or unknowingly, had sold it to him. But he'd have taken a considerable loss, and would risk blackening his reputation before he even had one. Better, he always felt, to keep the painting, and to hang it where he would see it every day, and never forget the lesson it was there to teach him."

"And what was that lesson, Soldier?"

"That greed can lead to error, with devastating results. Because it was greed that led him to sink the better part of his capital into that worthless Vermeer. It was a bargain, and he should have been suspicious, but the opportunity to get it at that price led him astray. Greed made him want it to be a Vermeer, and so he believed it to be one, and paid the price for his greed."

"And hung it on his wall," the priest said.

"Yes."

"And moved it to his office when he opened his own gallery. So that he could look at it every day while conducting his business. But others would see it as well, wouldn't they? What did he tell them when they asked about it?"

"Only that it was not for sale."

"I don't suppose it harmed his reputation to have it known that this new kid on the block was sufficiently well-fixed to hang a Vermeer on his wall and not even entertain offers for it," the doctor mused. "I'm not so sure he didn't get his money's worth out of it after all."

❧   ❧   ❧

They fell silent again, and the policeman dealt the cards. The game was seven-card stud, but this time the betting was restrained and the pot small, won at length by the priest with two pair, nines and threes. "If we were playing Baseball," he said, raking in the chips, "with nines and threes wild, I'd have five aces."

"If we were playing tennis," said the doctor, who had held fours and deuces, "it would be your serve. So shut up and deal."

The priest gathered the cards, shuffled them. The soldier filled his pipe, scratched a match, held it to the bowl. "Oh, it's your pipe," the doctor said. "I thought the old man over there had treated us to a fart."

"He did," said the soldier. "That's one reason I lit the pipe."

"Two wrongs don't make a right," the doctor declared, and the priest offered the cards and the policeman cut them, and, from the fireside, the four men heard a sound that had become familiar to them over time.

"You see?" said the doctor. "He's done it again. Try to counteract his flatulence with your smoke, and he simply redoubles his efforts."

"He's an old man," the policeman said.

"So? Who among us is not?"

"He's a bit older than we are."

"And isn't he a pretty picture of what the future holds? One day we too can sleep twenty-three hours out of every twenty-four, and fill the happy hours with coughing and snuffling and snoring and, last but alas not least, great rumbling pungent farts. And what's left after that but the grave? Or is there more to come, Priest?"

"I used to wonder," the priest admitted.

"But you no longer doubt?"

"I no longer wonder, knowing that all will be made clear soon enough. But I'm still thinking of greed."

"Deal the cards, and we can do something about it."

"As I understand it," the priest went on, "crimes of greed, crimes with mercenary motives, fluctuate with economic conditions. When and where unemployment is high and need is great, the crime rate goes up. When times are good, it drops."

"That would stand to reason," the soldier said.

"On the other hand," said the priest, "the criminals in Policeman's story fell tragically under the influence of greed not when they lacked money, but when they were awash in it. When there was not so much to be divided, they shared fairly and equally. When the money flooded in, they killed to increase their portion of it."

"It seems paradoxical," the policeman agreed, "but that's just how it was."

"And your corporal-turned-art dealer, Soldier. How does he fit into the need-greed continuum?"

"Opportunity awakened his greed," the soldier said. "Perhaps it was there all along, just waiting until the chance came along to make money on the black market. We could say he was greediest when he bought the fake Vermeer, and again when he realized what he'd done and tried to recoup at the card table."

"A forlorn hope," said the doctor, "in a game like this one, where hours go by before someone deals the cards."

"His money gone," the soldier went on, "he applied himself like a character out of Horatio Alger, but was he any less avaricious for the fact that his actions were now ethical and lawful? He was as ambitious as ever, and there was a pot of gold looming at the end of his rainbow."

"So greed's a constant," said the priest, and took up the deck of cards once again.

"It is and it isn't," the doctor said. "Hell, put down the damned cards. You just reminded me of a story."

The priest placed the cards, undealt, upon the table. By the fireside, the old man sighed deeply in his sleep. And the priest and the soldier and the policeman sat up in their chairs, waiting for the doctor to begin.

Some years ago (said the doctor) I had as a patient a young man who wanted to be a writer. Upon completion of his education he moved to New York, where he took an apartment rather like your art dealer, Soldier, but lacking a faux-Vermeer on the wall. He placed his typewriter on a rickety card table and began banging out poems and short stories and no end of first chapters that failed to thrive and grow into novels. And he looked for a job, hoping for something that would help him on his way to literary success.

The position he secured was at a literary agency, owned and operated by a fellow I'll call Byron Fielding. That was not his name, but neither was the name he used, which he created precisely as I've created an alias for him, by putting together the surnames of two English writers. Fielding started out as a writer himself, sending stories to magazines while he was still in high school, and getting some of them published. Then World War Two came along, even as it did to Gary Carmody, and Byron Fielding was drafted and, upon completion of basic training, assigned to a non-combat clerical position. It was his literary skills that kept him out of the front lines—not his skill in stringing words together but his ability to type. Most men couldn't do it.

When he got out of the service, young Fielding wrote a few more stories, but he found the business discouraging. There were, he had come to realize, too many people who wanted to be writers. Sometimes it seemed as though everybody wanted to be a writer, including people who could barely read. And when they tried their hand at it, they almost always thought it was good.

Was such monumental self-delusion as easy in other areas of human endeavor? I think not. Every boy wants to be a professional baseball player, but an inability to hit a curveball generally disabuses a person of the fantasy. Untalented artists, trying to draw something, can look at it and see that it didn't come out as they intended. Singers squawk, hear themselves, and find something else to do. But writers write, and look at what they have written, and wonder what's keeping the Nobel Commission fellows from ringing them up.

You shake your heads at this, and call it folly. Byron Fielding called it opportunity, and opened his arms wide.

He set up shop as a literary agent; he would represent authors, placing their work with publishers, overseeing the details of their contracts, and taking ten percent of their earnings for his troubles. This was nothing new; there were quite a few people earning their livings in this fashion—though not a fraction of the number there are today. But how, one wondered, could Byron Fielding hope to establish himself as an agent? He had no contacts. He didn't know any writers—or publishers, or anyone else. What would persuade an established writer to do business with him?

In point of fact, Fielding had no particular interest in established writers, realizing that he had little to offer them. What he wanted was the wannabes, the hopeful hopeless scribblers looking for the one break that would transform a drawer full of form rejection slips into a life of wealth and fame.

He rented office space, called himself Byron Fielding, called his company the Byron Fielding Literary Agency, and ran ads in magazines catering to the same hopeful hopeless ones he was counting on to make him rich. "I sell fiction and non-fiction to America's top markets," he announced. "I'd like to sell them your material."

And he explained his terms. If you were a professional writer, with several sales to national publishers to your credit, he would represent you at the standard terms of 10 percent commission. If you were a beginner, he was forced to charge you a reading fee of $1 per thousand words, with a minimum of $5 and a maximum of $25 for book-length manuscripts. If your material was salable, he would rush it out to market on his usual terms. If it could be revised, he'd tell you how to fix it—and not charge you an extra dime for the advice. And if, sadly, it was unsalable, he'd tell you just what was wrong with it, and how to avoid such errors in the future.

The money rolled in.

And so did the stories, and they were terrible. Fielding stacked them, and when each had been in his office for two weeks, so that it would look as though he'd taken his time and given it a careful reading, he returned it with a letter explaining just what was wrong with it. Most of the time what was wrong was the writer's utter lack of talent, but he never said that. Instead he praised the style and found fault with the plot, which somehow was always flawed in ways that revision could not cure. Put this one away, he advised each author, and write another, and send that along as soon as it's finished. With, of course, another reading fee.

The business was profitable from the beginning, with writers sending in story after story, failing entirely to learn from experience. Fielding thought he'd milk it for as long as it lasted, but a strange thing happened. Skimming through the garbage, he found himself coming across a story now and then that wasn't too bad. "Congratulations!" he wrote the author. "I'm taking this right out to market." It was probably a mistake, he thought, but this way at least he got away with a shorter letter.

And some of the stories sold. And, out of the blue, a professional writer got in touch, wondering if Fielding would represent him on a straight commission basis. By the time my patient, young Gerald Metzner, went to work for him, Byron Fielding was an established agent with over ten years in the business and a string of professional clients whose work he sold to established book and magazine publishers throughout the world.

Fielding had half a dozen people working for him by then. One ran a writing school, with a post office box for an address and no visible connection with Byron Fielding or his agency. The lucky student worked his way through a ten-lesson correspondence course, and upon graduating received a certificate of completion and the suggestion that he might submit his work (with a reading fee) to guess who.

Another employee dealt with the professional clients, working up market lists for the material they submitted. Two others—Gerald Metzner was one of them—read the scripts that came in over the transom, the ones accompanied by reading fees. "I can see you are no stranger to your type-writer," he would write to some poor devil who couldn't write an intelligible laundry list. "Although this story has flaws that render it unsalable, I'll be eager to see your next effort. I feel confident that you're on your way."

The letter, needless to say, went out over Byron Fielding's signature. As far as the mopes were concerned, Fielding was reading every word himself, and writing every word of his replies. Another employee, also writing over Fielding's mean little scrawl, engaged in personal collaboration with the more desperate clients. For a hundred bucks, the great man himself would purportedly work with them step by step, from outline through first draft to final polish. They would be writing their stories hand in hand with Byron Fielding, and when it was finished to his satisfaction he would take it out to market.

The client (or victim, as you prefer) would mail in his money and his outline. The hireling, who had very likely never sold anything himself, and might in fact not ever have written anything, would suggest some arbitrary change. The client would send in the revised outline, and when it was approved he would furnish a first draft. Again the employee would suggest improvements, and again the poor bastard would do as instructed, where-upon he'd be told that the story, a solid professional effort, was on its way to market.

But it remained a sow's ear, however artfully embroidered, and Fielding wouldn't have dreamed of sullying what little reputation he had by showing such tripe to an editor. So the manuscript went into a drawer in the office, and there it remained, while the hapless scribbler was encouraged to get cracking on another story.

The fee business was ethically and morally offensive, and one wondered why Fielding didn't give it up once he could afford to. The personal collab-oration racket was worse; it was actionably fraudulent, and a client who learned what was going on could clearly have pressed criminal charges against his conniving collaborator. It's not terribly likely that Fielding could have gone to jail for it, but a determined prosecutor with the wind up could have given him some bad moments. And if there were a writer or two on the jury, he couldn't expect much in the way of mercy.

Fielding hung on to it because he didn't want to give up a dime. He didn't treat his professional clients a great deal better, for in a sense he had only one client, and that client was Byron Fielding. He acted, not in his clients' interests, but in his own. If they coincided, fine. If not, tough.

I could go on, but you get the idea. So did young Metzner, and he wasn't there for long. He worked for Fielding for a year and a half, then resigned to do his own writing. A lot of the agency's pro clients were writing soft-core paperback fiction, and Metzner tried one of this own. When it was done he sent it to Fielding, who sold it for him.

He did a few more, and was making more money than he'd made as an employee, and working his own hours. But it wasn't what he really wanted to write, and he tried a few other things and wound up out in California, writing for film and television. Fielding referred him to a Hollywood agent, who, out of gratitude and the hope of more business, split commissions on Metzner's sales with Byron Fielding. Thus Fielding made far more money over the years from Gerald Metzner's screenwriting than he had ever made from his prose, and all he had to do for it was cash the checks the Holly-wood agent sent him. That was, to his way of thinking, the ideal author-agent relationship, and he had warm feelings for Metzner—or what passed for warm feelings in such a man.

When Metzner had occasion to come to New York, he more often than not dropped in on his agent. He and Fielding would chat for fifteen min-utes, and then he could return to Hollywood and tell himself he hadn't entirely lost touch with the world of books and publishing. He had an agent, didn't he? His agent was always happy to see him, wasn't he? And who was to say he wouldn't someday try his hand at another novel?

Years passed, as they so often do. Business again called Gerald Metzner to New York, and he arranged to drop by Fielding's office on a free after-noon. As usual, he waited for a few minutes in the outer office, taking a look at the sea of minions banging away at typewriters. It seemed to him that there were more of them every time he visited, more men sitting at more desks, telling even more of the hopeful hopeless that they had talent in rare abundance, and surely the next story would make the grade, but, sad to say, this story, with its poorly constructed plot, was not the one to bring their dreams to fulfillment. What a story required, you see, was a strong and sympathetic lead character confronted by a problem, and . . .

Di dah di dah di dah.

He broke off his reverie when he was summoned to Fielding's private office. There the agent waited, looking younger than his years, health club–toned and sun lamp–tanned, a broad white-toothed smile on his face. The two men shook hands and took seats on opposite sides of the agent's immaculate desk.

They chatted a bit, about nothing in particular, and then Fielding fixed his eyes on Gerald. "You probably notice that there's something different about me," he said.

"Now that you mention it," Metzner said, "I did notice that." Years of pitching doubtful premises to studio heads and network execs had taught him to think on his feet—or, more accurately, on his behind. What, he wondered, was *different* about the man? Same military haircut, same horn-rimmed glasses. No beard, no mustache. What the hell was Fielding talking about?

"But I'll bet you can't quite put your finger on it."

Well, that was a help. Maybe this would be like soap opera dialogue—you could get through it without a script, just going with the flow.

"You know," he said, "that's it exactly. I sense it, but I can't quite put my finger on it."

"That's because it's abstract, Gerry."

"That would explain it."

"But no less real."

"No less real," he echoed.

Fielding smiled like a shark, but then how else would he smile? "I won't keep you in suspense," he said. "I'll tell you what it is. I've got peace of mind."

"Peace of mind," Metzner marveled.

"Yes, peace of mind." The agent leaned forward. "Gerry," he said, "ever since I opened up for business I've been the toughest, meanest, most miserable sonofabitch who ever lived. I've always wrung every nickel I could out of every deal I touched. I worked sixty, seventy hours a week, and I used the whip on the people who worked for me. And do you know why?"

Metzner shook his head.

"Because I thought I had to," Fielding said. "I really believed I'd be screwed otherwise. I'd run out of money, I'd be out on the street, my family would go hungry. So I couldn't let a penny get away from me. You know, until my lawyers absolutely insisted, I wouldn't even shut down the Personal Collaboration dodge. 'Byron, you're out of your mind,' they told me. 'That's consumer fraud, and you're doing it through the mails. It's a fucking federal offense and you could go to Leavenworth for it, and what the hell do you need it for? Shut it down!' And they were right, and I knew they were right, but they had to tell me a dozen times before I did what they wanted. Because we made good money out of the PC clients, and I thought I needed every cent of it."

"But now you have peace of mind," Metzner prompted.

"I do, Gerry, and you could see it right away, couldn't you? Even if you didn't know what it was you were seeing. Peace of mind, Gerry. It's a wonderful thing, maybe the single most wonderful thing in the world."

Time for the violins to come in, Metzner thought. "How did it happen, Byron?"

"A funny thing," Fielding said. "I sat down with my accountant about eight months ago, the way I always do once a year. To go over things, look at the big picture. And he told me I had more than enough money left to keep me in great shape for as long as I live. 'You could shut down tomorrow,' he said, 'and you could live like a king for another fifty years, and you won't run out of money. You've got all the money you could possibly need, and it's in solid risk-free inflation-resistant investments, and I just wish every client of mine was in such good shape."

"That's great," said Metzner, who wished he himself were in such good shape, or within a thousand miles thereof.

"And a feeling came over me," Fielding said, "and I didn't know what the feeling was, because I had never felt anything like it before. It was a relief, but it was a permanent kind of relief, the kind that means you can stay relieved. You're not just out of the woods for the time being. You're all of a sudden in a place where there are no woods. Free and clear—and I realized there was a name for the feeling I had, and it was peace of mind."

"I see."

"Do you, Gerry? I'll tell you, it changed my life. All that pressure, all that anxiety—gone!" He grinned, then straightened up in his chair. "Of course," he said, "on the surface, nothing's all that different. I still hustle every bit as hard as I ever did. I still squeeze every dime I can out of every deal I touch. I still go for the throat, I still hang on like a bulldog, I'm still the most miserable sonofabitch in the business."

"Oh?"

"But now it's not because I *have* to be like that," Fielding exulted. "It's because I *want* to. That's what I love, Gerry. It's who I am. But now, thank God, I've got peace of mind!"

❧    ❧    ❧

"What a curious story," said the priest. "I'm as hard-pressed to put my finger on the point of it as your young man was to recognize Fielding's peace of mind. Fielding seems to be saying that his greed had its roots in his insecurity. I suppose his origins were humble?"

"Lower middle class," the doctor said. "No money in the family, but they were a long way from impoverished. Still, insecurity, like the heart, has reasons that reason knows nothing of. If he's to be believed, Byron Fielding grew up believing he had to grab every dollar he could or he risked ruin, poverty, and death."

"Then he became wealthy," the priest said, "and, more to the point, came to *believe* he was wealthy and financially secure."

"Fuck-you money," the policeman said, and explained the phrase when the priest raised an eyebrow. "Enough money, Priest, so that the possessor can say 'fuck you' to anyone."

"An enviable state," the priest said. "Or is it? The man attained that state, and his greed, which no longer imprisoned him, still operated as before. It was his identity, part and parcel of his personality. He remained greedy and heartless, not out of compulsion but out of choice, out of a sense of self." He frowned. "Unless we're to take his final remarks *cum grano salis?*" To the puzzled policeman he said, "With a grain of salt, that is to say. You translated fuck-you money for me, so at least I can return the favor. A sort of quid pro quo, which in turn means . . ."

"That one I know, Priest."

"And Fielding was not stretching the truth when he said he was the same vicious bastard he'd always been," the doctor put in. "Peace of mind didn't seem to have mellowed him at all. Did I mention his brother?"

The men shook their heads.

"Fielding had a brother," the doctor said, "and, when it began to appear as though this scam of his might prove profitable, Fielding put his brother to work for him. He made his brother change his name, and picked Arnold Fielding for him, having in mind the poet Matthew Arnold. The brother, whom everyone called Arnie, functioned as a sort of office manager, and was also a sort of mythical beast invoked by Byron in time of need. If, for example, an author came in to cadge an advance, or ask for something else Byron Fielding didn't want to grant, the agent wouldn't simply turn him down. 'Let me ask Arnie,' he would say, and then he'd go into the other office and twiddle his thumbs for a moment, before returning to shake his head sadly at the client. 'Arnie says no,' he'd report. 'If it were up to me it'd be a different story, but Arnie says no.'

"But he hadn't actually consulted his brother?"

"No, of course not. Well, here's the point. Some years after Gerald Metzner learned about Byron Fielding's peace of mind, Arnie Fielding had a health scare and retired to Florida. He recovered, and in due course found Florida and retirement both bored him to distraction, and he came back to New York. He went to see his brother Byron and told him he had decided to go into business. And what would he do? Well, he said, there was only one business he knew, and that's the one he would pick. He intended to set up shop on his own as a literary agent.

" 'The best of luck to you,' Byron Fielding told him. 'What are you going to call yourself?'

" 'The Arnold Fielding Literary Agency,' Arnie said.

"Byron shook his head. 'Better not,' he said. 'You use the Fielding name and I'll take you to court. I'll sue you.'

" 'You'd sue me? Your own brother?'

" 'For every cent you've got,' Byron told him."

The soldier lit his pipe. "He'd sue his own brother," he said, "to prevent him from doing business under the name he had foisted upon him. The man may have achieved peace of mind, Doctor, but I don't think we have to worry that it mellowed him."

"Arnie never did open his own agency," the doctor said. "He died a year or so after that, though not of a broken heart, but from a recurrence of the illness that had sent him into retirement initially. And the old pirate himself, Byron Fielding, only survived him by a couple of years."

"And your young writer?"

"Not so young anymore," said the doctor. "He had a successful career as a screenwriter, until ageism lessened his market value, at which time he returned to novel-writing. But the well-paid Hollywood work had taken its toll, and the novels he wrote all failed."

They were considering that in companionable silence when a log burned through and fell in the fireplace. They turned at the sound, observed the shower of sparks, and heard in answer a powerful discharge of methane from the old man's bowels.

"God, the man can fart!" cried the doctor. "Light up your pipe, Soldier. What I wouldn't give for a cigar!"

"A cigar," said the priest, thoughtfully.

"Sometimes it's only a cigar," the doctor said, "as the good Dr. Freud once told us. But in this instance it would do double duty as an air freshener. Priest, are you going to deal those cards?"

"I was just about to," said the priest, "until you mentioned the cigar."

"What has a cigar, and a purely hypothetical cigar at that, to do with playing a long-delayed hand of poker?"

"Nothing," said the priest, "but it has something to do with greed. In a manner of speaking."

"I'm greedy because I'd rather inhale the aroma of good Havana leaf than the wind from that old codger's intestines?"

"No, no, no," said the priest. "It's a story, that's all. Your mention of a cigar put me in mind of a story."

"Tell it," the policeman urged.

"It's a poor story compared to those you all have told," the priest said. "But it has to do with greed."

"And cigars?"

"And cigars, yes. It definitely has to do with cigars."

"Put the cards down," the doctor said, "and tell the story."

There was a man I used to know (said the priest) whom I'll call Archibald O'Bannion, Archie to his intimates. He started off as a hod carrier on building sites, applied himself diligently learning his trade, and wound up with his own construction business. He was a hard worker and a good businessman, as it turned out, and he did well.

He was motivated by the desire for profit, and for the accoutrements of success, but I don't know that I would call him a greedy man. He was a hard bargainer and an intense competitor, certainly, and he liked to win. But greedy? He never struck me that way.

And he was charitable, more than generous in his contributions to the church and to other good causes. It is possible, to be sure, for a man to be at once greedy and generous, to grab with one hand while dispensing with the other. But Archie O'Bannion never struck me as a greedy man. He was a cigar smoker, and he never lit a cigar without offering them around, nor was there anything perfunctory about the offer. When he smoked a cigar, he genuinely wanted you to join him.

He treated himself well, as he could well afford to do. His home was large and imposing, his wardrobe extensive and well chosen, his table rich and varied. In all these areas, his expenditures were consistent with his income and status.

His one indulgence—he thought it an indulgence—was his cigars.

He smoked half a dozen a day, and they weren't William Penn or Hav-a-Tampa, either. They were the finest cigars he could buy. I liked a good cigar myself in those days, though I could rarely afford one, and when Archie would offer me one of his, well, I didn't often turn him down. He was a frequent visitor to the rectory, and I can recall no end of evenings when we sat in pleasantly idle conversation, puffing on cigars he'd provided.

Then the day came when a collection of cigars went on the auction block, and he bought them all.

A cigar smoker's humidor is not entirely unlike an oenophile's wine cellar, and sometimes there is even an aftermarket for its contents. Cigars don't command the prices of rare bottles of wine, and I don't know that they're collected in quite the same way, but when a cigar smoker dies, the contents of his humidor are worth something, especially since Castro came into power in Cuba. With the American embargo in force, Havana cigars were suddenly unobtainable. One could always have them smuggled in through some country that continued to trade with Cuba, but that was expensive and illegal, and, people said, the post-revolution cigars were just not the same. Many of the cigar makers had fled the island nation, and the leaf did not seem to be what it was, and, well, the result was that pre-Castro cigars became intensely desirable.

A cigar is a perishable thing, but properly stored and maintained there's no reason why it cannot last almost forever. In this particular instance, the original owner was a cigar aficionado who began laying in a supply of premium Havanas shortly after Castro took power. Perhaps he anticipated the embargo. Perhaps he feared a new regime would mean diminished quality. Whatever it was, he bought heavily, stored his purchases properly, and then, his treasures barely sampled, he was diagnosed with oral cancer. The lip, the mouth, the palate—I don't know the details, but his doctor told him in no uncertain terms that he had to give up his cigars.

Not everyone can. Sigmund Freud, whom Doctor quoted a few minutes ago, went on smoking while his mouth and jaw rotted around his cigar. But this chap's addiction was not so powerful as his instinct for self-preservation, and so he stopped smoking then and there.

But he held on to his cigars. His several humidors were attractive furnishings as well as being marvels of temperature and humidity control, and he liked the looks of them in his den. He broke the habit entirely, to the point where his eyes would pass over the humidors regularly without his ever registering a conscious thought of their contents, let alone a longing for them. You might think he'd have pressed cigars upon his friends, but he didn't, perhaps out of reluctance to have to stand idly by and breathe in the smoke of a cigar he could not enjoy directly. Or perhaps, as I somehow suspect, he was saving them for some future date when it would be safe for him to enjoy them as they were meant to be enjoyed.

Well, no matter. In any event, he did recover from his cancer, and some years later he died of something else. And since neither his widow nor his daughters smoked cigars, they wound up consigned for sale at auction, and Archie O'Bannion bought them all.

There were two thousand of them, and Archie paid just under sixty thousand dollars for the lot. That included the several humidors, which were by no means valueless, but when all was said and done he'd shelled out upwards of twenty-five dollars a cigar. If he consumed them at his usual rate, a day's smoking would cost him $150. He could afford that, but there was no denying it was an indulgence.

But what troubled him more than the cost was the fact that his stock was virtually irreplaceable. Every cigar he smoked was a cigar he could never smoke again. Two thousand cigars sounded like an extraordinary quantity, but if you smoked six a day starting the first of January, you'd light up the last one after Thanksgiving dinner. They wouldn't last the year.

"It's a damned puzzle," he told me. "What do I do? Smoke one a day? That way they'll last five years and change, but all the while five out of six of the cigars I smoke will be slightly disappointing. Maybe I should smoke 'em all up, one right after the other, and enjoy them while I can. Or maybe I should just let them sit there in their beautiful humidors, remaining moist and youthful while I dry up and age. Then when I drop dead it'll be Mary Katherine's turn to put them up for auction."

I said something banal about the conundrum of having one's cake and eating it, too.

"By God," he said. "That's it, isn't it? Have a cigar, Father."

But, I demurred, surely not one of his Havanas?

"You smoke it," he said. "You earned it, Father, and you can damn well smoke it and enjoy it."

And he picked up the phone and called his insurance agent.

Archie, I should mention, had come to regard the insurance industry as a necessary evil. He'd had trouble getting his insurers to pay claims he felt were entirely legitimate, and disliked the way they'd do anything they could to weasel out of their responsibility. So he had no compunctions about what he did now.

He insured his cigars, opting for the top-of-the-line policy, one which provided complete coverage, not even excluding losses resulting from flood, earthquake, or volcanic eruption. He declared their value at the price he had paid for them, paid the first year's premium in advance, and went on with his life.

A little less than a year later, he smoked the last of his premium Havanas. Whereupon he filed a claim against his insurance company, explaining that all two thousand of the cigars were lost in a series of small fires.

You will probably not be surprised that the insurance company refused to pay the claim, dismissing it as frivolous. The cigars, they were quick to inform him, had been consumed in the normal fashion, and said consumption was therefore not a recoverable loss.

Archie took them to court, where the judge agreed that his claim was frivolous, but ordered the company to pay it all the same. The policy, he pointed out, did not exclude fire, and in fact specifically included it as a hazard against which Archie's cigars were covered. Nor did it exclude as unacceptable risk the consumption of the cigars in the usual fashion.

"I won," he told me. "They warranted the cigars were insurable, they assumed the risk, and then of course they found something to whine about, the way they always do. But I stuck it to the bastards and I beat 'em in court. I thought they'd drag it out and appeal the judgment, and I was set to fight it all the way, but they caved in. Wrote me a check for the full amount of the policy, and now I can go looking for someone else with pre-Castro Havanas to sell, because I've developed a taste for them, let me tell you. And I've got you to thank, Father, for a remark you made about having your cake and eating it, too, because I smoked my cigars and I'll have 'em, too, just as soon as I find someone who's got 'em for sale. Of course this is a stunt you can only pull once, but once is enough, and I feel pretty good about it. The Havanas are all gone, but these Conquistadores from Honduras aren't bad, so what the hell, Father. Have a cigar!"

❦   ❦   ❦

"I don't know why you were so apologetic about your story, Priest," the soldier said. "I think it's a fine one. I'm a pipe smoker myself, and any dismay one might conceivably feel at watching one's tobacco go up in smoke is more than offset by the satisfaction of improving the pipe itself, as one does with each pipeful one smokes. But pipe tobacco, even very fine pipe tobacco, costs next to nothing compared to premium cigars. I can well understand the man's initial frustration, and ultimate satisfaction."

"An excellent story," the doctor agreed, "but then it would be hard for me not to delight in a story in which an insurance company is hoist on its own petard. The swine have institutionalized greed, and it's nice to see them get one in the eye."

"I wonder," said the policeman.

"I know what you're thinking," the doctor told him. "You're thinking that this fellow Archie committed lawful fraud. You're thinking it was his intention to make the insurance company subsidize his indulgence in costly Cuban tobacco. That's entirely correct, but as far as I'm concerned it's quite beside the point. Lawful fraud is an insurance company's stock in trade, and anyway what's sixty thousand dollars on their corporate balance sheet? I say more power to Archie, and long may he puff away."

"All well and good," the policeman said, "but that's not what I was thinking."

"It's not?"

"Not at all," he told the doctor, and turned to the priest. "There's more to the story, isn't there, Priest?"

The priest smiled. "I was wondering if anyone would think of it," he said. "I rather thought you might, Policeman."

"Think of what?" the soldier wanted to know.

"And what did they do?" the policeman asked. "Did they merely voice the threat? Or did they go all the way and have him arrested?"

"Arrested?" cried the doctor. "For what?"

"Arson," the policeman said. "Didn't he say the cigars were lost in a series of small fires? I suppose they could have charged him with two thousand counts of criminal arson."

"Arson? They were his cigars, weren't they?"

"As I understand it."

"And doesn't a man have the right to smoke his own cigars?"

"Not in a public place," said the policeman. "But yes, in the ordinary course of events, he would have been well within his rights to smoke them.

But he had so arranged matters that smoking one of those cigars amounted to intentional destruction of insured property."

"But that's an outrage," the doctor said.

"Is it, Doctor?" The soldier puffed on his pipe. "You liked the story when the insurance company was hoist on its own petard. Now Archie's hoisted even higher on a petard of his own making. Wouldn't you say that makes it a better story?"

"A splendid story," said the doctor, "but no less an outrage for it."

"In point of fact," the policeman said, "Archie could have been charged with arson even in the absence of a claim, the argument being that he forfeited the right to smoke the cigars the moment he insured them. Practically speaking, though, it was pressing the claim that triggered the criminal charge. Did he actually go to jail, Priest? Because that would seem a little excessive."

The priest shook his head. "Charges were dropped," he said, "when the parties reached agreement. Archie gave back the money, and both sides paid their own legal costs. And he got to tell the story on himself, and he was a good fellow, you know, and could see the humor in a situation. He said it was worth it, all things considered, and a real pre-Castro cigar was worth the money, even if you had to pay for it yourself."

The other three nodded at the wisdom of that, and once again the room fell silent. The priest took the deck of cards in hand, looked at the others in turn, and put the cards down undealt.

And then, from the fireside, the fifth man present broke the silence.


"Greed," said the old man, in a voice like the wind in dry grass. "What a subject for conversation!"

"We've awakened you," said the priest, "and for that let me apologize on everyone's behalf."

"It is I who should apologize," said the old man, "for dozing intermittently during such an illuminating and entertaining conversation. But at my age the line between sleep and wakefulness is a tenuous proposition at best. One is increasingly uncertain whether one is dreaming or awake, and past and present become hopelessly entangled. I close my eyes and lose myself in thought, and all at once I am a boy. I open them and I am an old man."

"Ah," said the doctor, and the others nodded in assent.

"And while I am apologizing," the old man said, "I should add a word of apology for my bowels. I seem to have an endless supply of wind, which in turn grows increasingly malodorous. Still, I'm not incontinent. One grows thankful in the course of time for so many things one took for granted, if indeed one ever considered them at all."

"One keeps thanking God," the priest said, "for increasingly smaller favors."

"Greed," said the old man. "What a greedy young man I was! And what a greedy man I stayed, throughout all the years of my life!"

"No more than anyone, I'm sure," the policeman said.

"I always wanted more," the old man remembered. "My parents were comfortably situated, and furnished me with a decent upbringing and a good education. They hoped I would go into a profession where I might be expected to do some good in the world. Medicine, for example."

" 'First, do no harm,' " the doctor murmured.

"But I went into business," said the old man, "because I wanted more money than I could expect to earn from medicine or law or any of the professions. And I stopped at nothing legal to succeed in all my enterprises. I was merciless to competitors, I drove my employees, I squeezed my suppliers, and every decision I made was calculated to maximize my profits."

"That," said the soldier, "seems to be how business is done. Struggling for the highest possible profits, men of business act ultimately for the greatest good of the population at large."

"You probably believe in the tooth fairy, too," the old man said, and cackled. "If I did any good for the rest of the world, it was inadvertent and immaterial. I was trying only to do good for myself, and to amass great wealth. And in that I succeeded. You might not guess it to look at me now, but I became very wealthy."

"And what happened to your riches?"

"What happened to them? Why, nothing happened to them. I won them and I kept them." The old man's bowels rumbled, but he didn't appear to notice. "I lived well," he said, "and I invested wisely and with good fortune. And I bought things."

"What did you buy?" the policeman wondered.

"Things," said the old man. "I bought paintings, and I don't think I was ever taken in by any false Vermeers, like the young man in your story. I bought fine furniture, and a palatial home to keep it in. I bought antique oriental carpets, I bought Roman glass, I bought pre-Columbian sculpture.

I bought rare coins, ancient and modern, and I collected postage stamps."

"And cigars?"

"I never cared for them," the old man said, "but if I had I would have bought the best, and I can well appreciate that builder's dilemma. Because I would have wanted to smoke them, but my desire to go on owning them would have been at least as strong."

They waited for him to go on; when he remained silent, the priest spoke up. "I suppose," he said, " that, as with so many desires, the passage of time lessened your desire for more."

"You think so?"

"Well, it would stand to reason that—"

"The vultures thought so," the old man said. "My nephews and nieces, thoughtfully telling me the advantages of making gifts during my lifetime rather than waiting for my estate to be subject to inheritance taxes. Museum curators, hoping I'd give them paintings now, or so arrange things that they'd be given over to them immediately upon my death. Auctioneers, assuring me of the considerable advantages of disposing of my stamps and coins and ancient artifacts while I still had breath in my body. That way, they said, I could have the satisfaction of seeing my collections properly sold, and the pleasure of getting the best possible terms for them.

"I told them I'd rather have the pleasure and satisfaction of continuing ownership. And do you know what they said? Why, they told me the same thing that everybody told me, everybody who was trying to get me to give up something that I treasured. You can guess what they said, can't you?"

It was the doctor who guessed. "You can't take it with you," he said.

"Exactly! Each of the fools said it as if he were repeating the wisdom of the ages. 'You can't take it with you.' And the worst of the lot, the mean little devils from organized charities, armored by the pretense that they were seeking not for themselves but for others, they would sometimes add yet another pearl of wisdom. There are no pockets in a shroud, they would assure me."

"I think that's a line in a song," the soldier said.

"Well, please don't sing it," said the old man. "Can't take it with you! No pockets in a shroud! And the worst of it is that they're quite right, aren't they? Wherever that last long journey leads, a man has to take it alone. He can't bring his French impressionists, his proof Liberty Seated quarters, his Belgian semi-postals. He can't even take along a checkbook. No matter what I have, no matter how greatly I cherish it, I can't take it with me."

"And you realized the truth in that," the priest said.

"Of course I did. I may be a doddering old man, but I'm not a fool."

"And the knowledge changed your life," the priest suggested.

"It did," the old man agreed. "Why do you think I'm here, baking by the fire, souring the air with the gas from within me? Why do you think I cling so resolutely, neither asleep nor awake, to this hollow husk of life?"

"Why?" the doctor asked, after waiting without success for the old man to answer his own question.

"Because," the old man said, "if I can't take it with me, the hell with it. I don't intend to go."

His eyes flashed in triumph, then closed abruptly as he slumped in his chair. The others glanced at one another, alarm showing in their eyes. "A wonderful exit line," the doctor said, "and a leading candidate for the next edition of *Famous Last Words,* but do you suppose the old boy took the opportunity to catch the bus to Elysium?"

"We should call someone," the soldier said. "But whom? A doctor? A policeman? A priest?"

There was a snore, shortly followed by a zestful fart. "Thank heavens," said the doctor, and the others sighed and nodded, and the priest picked up the deck and began to deal out the cards for the next hand.

# AUTHORS' BIOGRAPHIES

**F. Paul Wilson**'s novel *The Keep* was made into a successful movie of the same name, and also gave rise to several tangentially linked sequels, including *Reborn*, *The Tomb*, and *Nightworld*. His short fiction has appeared in *Night Visions IV*, *Predators*, *Weird Tales*, and *Analog*. He has also edited several anthologies, including *Freak Show* and *Diagnosis: Terminal*. He lives with his family in New Jersey.

**Doug Allyn** is an accomplished author whose short fiction regularly graces year's best collections. His work has appeared in *Once Upon a Crime*, *Cat Crimes Through Time* and *The Year's 25 Finest Crime and Mystery Stories*, volumes 3 and 4. His stories of Tallifer, the wandering minstrel, have appeared in *Ellery Queen's Mystery Magazine* and *Murder Most Scottish*. His story "The Dancing Bear," a Tallifer tale, won the Edgar award for short fiction for 1994. His other series character is veterinarian Dr. David Westbrook, whose exploits have been collected in the anthology *All Creatures Dark and Dangerous*. He lives with his wife in Montrose, Michigan.

**Gabrielle Kraft** is a former executive story editor and analyst at several major Hollywood studios. Her series protagonist, lawyer and deal maker Jerry Zalman, has appeared in four novels, most recently *Bloody Mary*. Her first novel in the Zalman series, *Bullshot*, was nominated for the Edgar award for best Mystery novel of 1987.

**Jack Ritchie** (1922–1983) was an author who excelled in short fiction. A master of the short, sharp detective, or suspense story, his work was reprinted in the Best Detective anthology series seventeen times and has appeared in virtually all of the hardcover Alfred Hitchcock collections. Adept at both humorous and serious fiction, his characters ranged from the vampire detective Cardula to a ten-year-old boy detective.

**Jeremiah Healy** is one of the private eye writers who helped change a moribund mystery field in the eighties. A former professor at the New England School of Law, his debut novel about private detective John Francis Cuddy, *Blunt Darts*, announced that here was a wise new kid on the block. Since then he has written more than a dozen novels featuring his melancholy PI, and his books and stories have done nothing but enhance his reputation as an important and sage writer whose work has taken the private eye form to an exciting new level. Winner of the Shamus award in 1986 for *The Staked Goat*, he is one of those writers who packs the poise and depth of a good mainstream novel into an even better genre novel. Recent books include *The Stalking of Sheilah Quinn*, and the latest Cuddy mystery *The Only Good Lawyer*.

The character of John Rambo became a part of world language with the release of the Sylvester Stallone movie *First Blood*. **David Morrell**, the English professor who wrote the novel upon which the film was based, has become a successful author the world over with more than ten international bestsellers, including *The League of Night and Fog* and *The Brotherhood of the Rose*. He is an accomplished writer in several fields, as his recent collection of horror and dark suspense stories, *Black Evening*, demonstrates. He also wrote a moving book about the death of his teenage son, *Fireflies*.

*Psycho* (book and film alike) is the dividing line separating old-style suspense fiction from new-style. After *Psycho*, all bets were off. Suspense fiction (as opposed to the straight mystery) could and did go anywhere. The man who started all this was an unassuming, friendly, and very witty writer named **Robert Bloch** (1917–1994), a talented professional whose other novels included such dark suspense masterpieces as *The Scarf*, *The Kidnapper*, and *The Night of the Ripper*. There are some who insist his short stories were even better than his novels. He published several volumes of his stories during his lifetime. You never quite knew what to expect from a Bloch story. He delighted in defying expectations, often by incorporating unexpected humor in his work. Even in the grim struggle of Norman Bates, Bloch managed to work in a laugh or two.

While The Nameless Detective series is very well-written, cleverly plotted, and steeped with fascinating characters, it is also, one senses, a kind of diary for its author. Stretching over several decades now, the series spotlights both San Francisco and an unnamed detective, and charts how both have changed over this period of time. *Shackles* (1988) and *Sentinels* (1996) are two of the series highlights. And author **Bill Pronzini** has proved he can write non-series novels, too, *Blue Lonesome* (1995) and *A Wasteland of Strangers* (1997) being among the most creative and moving novels of the 1990s—in or out of crime fiction. Nameless makes his most recent appearances in *Illusions* and *Crazybone*.

**Mat Coward** is a British writer of crime, sci-fi, horror, children's and humorous fiction, whose stories have been broadcast on BBC Radio, and published in numerous anthologies, magazines, and e-zines in the UK, US and Europe. According to Ian Rankin, "Mat Coward's stories resemble distilled novels." His first non-distilled novel—a whodunit called *Up and Down*—was published in the US in 2000. Short stories have recently appeared in *Ellery Queen's Mystery Magazine*, *The World's Finest Crime and Mystery Stories*, *Felonious Felines*, and *Murder Through the Ages*.

**John F. Suter** (1914–1996) wrote dozens of mystery stories for *Alfred Hitchcock's Mystery Magazine* and *Ellery Queen's Mystery Magazine* during his long career. His work reveals the sly workings of the human mind and how a crime can grow out of the most ordinary happenings. "Come Down from the Hills" is one of his finest stories.

The Canadian crime writers give out the Arthur Ellis award for excellence in suspense fiction. **Peter Robinson** has won the Ellis for short story ("innocence") and novel (*The Hanging Valley* and *Past Reason*). Most of his novels deal with the subtle changes in the life of one Chief Inspector Alan Banks, who presently works out of Yorkshire England's Swainsdale area. Robinson has often spoken of his fondness for Simenon, and this influence is especially marked in the clarity of his prose and the melancholy truths discovered during the investigations. Robinson is also a first-rate short story writer, and the piece chosen for inclusion in this volume hints at the long and successful career ahead of him.

**Dorothy Cannell** first introduced her unlikely pair of private detectives, Hyacinth and Primrose Tramwell, in the mystery novel *Down the Garden Path*. They subsequently made appearances in *The Widow's Club* and *Mum's the Word*. Her stories, whether they feature the two sisterly detectives or not, are often set in her native England, and "The High Cost of Living" is no exception. Her short story "The Family Jewels" won the Agatha for best short story in 1994. Her latest book is *Bridesmaids Revisited*. She lives in Illinois with her husband, Julian, and their two Cavalier King Charles spaniels, Bertie Woofster and Jeeves.

**Bill Crider** won the Anthony award for his first novel in the Sheriff Dan Rhodes series. His first novel in the Truman Smith series was nominated for a Shamus award, and a third series features college English professor Carl Burns. His short stories have appeared in numerous anthologies, including *Cat Crimes II* and *III*, *Celebrity Vampires*, *Once Upon a Crime*, and *Werewolves*. His recent work includes collaborating on a series of cozy mysteries with television personality Willard Scott. The first novel, *Death Under Blue Skies*, was published in 1997 and the second, *Murder in the Mist*, was released recently.

If versatility is a virtue then **Ed Gorman** is virtuous indeed. He has written steadily in three different genres—mystery, horror and westerns—for almost twenty years. He has also written a large number of short stories, with six of his collections of wry, poignant, unsettling fiction in print in the USA and UK. Kirkus said, "Gorman is one of the most original crime writers around," taking particular note of his Sam McCain-Judge Whitney series, which is set in small-town Iowa in the 1950s and winning rave reviews from coast to coast. It is no surprise that he captures the essence of life in the Midwest, since he lives in Cedar Rapids, Iowa. As for the wealth of detail he brings to every novel and story he writes, well, he's been there and back again, and the observations he shares about life, love, and loss make his books all the richer. His most recent novel is *Will You Still Love Me Tomorrow?*, the third Sam McCain book.

Female private eyes date back to at least the pulps. They were always "gals," saucy versions of guys, whose stories were told with a wink and a smirk. **Marcia Muller** reinvented the female private investigator, giving her pith, dignity, intelligence, and the kind of social sensitivity that had oddly been limited to the male PI's. All of her books about Sharon McCone, investigator for the All Souls Legal Cooperative in San Francisco, were sound and professional from the start. But Muller has proved to be one of those writers who constantly pushes herself to do more challenging work. *A Wild and*

*Lonely Place* (1994) and *The Broken Promise Land* (1996) signaled the start of longer and even more powerful McCone mysteries. And her audience was eager to accompany her on these journeys, turning Muller into a mystery genre brand name. Her most recent work is *Listen to the Silence*.

**Helen Neilsen**'s novels illustrate the underbelly of usually sunny California, although she is not hesitant to set her stories in other major metropolitan areas as well. Books such as *Gold Coast Nocturne*, *Stranger in the Dark*, and *Borrow the Night* reveal what is really going on in cities and towns across America. A former freelance commercial artist and draftsman, she turned to writing fiction in 1951. She lives in Laguna Beach, California.

**Gillian Roberts** is the pseudonym of Judith Greber, who writes an award-winning series featuring Amanda Pepper, a thirty-something high school English teacher at a Philadelphia prep school. She was introduced in the novel *Caught Dead in Philadelphia* in 1987. Greber is a native Philadelphian, a graduate of the University of Pennsylvania, and a former high school English teacher. Currently she lives and writes in the San Francisco Bay area.

**Susan Dunlap** is the author of seventeen novels, encompassing all three categories of mystery protagonists: private eye, police detective, and amateur sleuth. She has won the Anthony award and the Macavity for her short fiction. As she notes: "The unifying factor in all my books is a 'sense of place' because I think where people live has a strong influence on the way they think, live, react, and who and why they choose to kill." Ms. Dunlap's novels are state-of-the-art in style, theme, and thrills. A founding member of the writer's organization Sisters in Crime, she lives and works in California.

**Brendan DuBois** is the award-winning author of short stories and novels. His short fiction has appeared in *Playboy*, *Ellery Queen's Mystery Magazine*, *Alfred Hitchcock's Mystery Magazine*, *Mary Higgins Clark Mystery Magazine*, and numerous anthologies. He has received the Shamus award from the Private Eye Writers of America for one of his short stories, and has been nominated three times for an Edgar Allan Poe award by the Mystery Writers of America. He's also the author of the Lewis Cole mystery series—*Dead Sand*, *Black Tide*, and *Shattered Shell*. His most recent novel, *Resurrection*

*Day*, is a suspense thriller that looks at what might have happened had the Cuban Missile Crisis of 1962 erupted into a nuclear war between the United States and the Soviet Union. This book also recently received the Sidewise Award for best alternative history novel of 1999. He lives in New Hampshire with his wife, Mona.

**Lawrence Block**'s novels range from the urban noir of Matthew Scudder (*Hope to Die*) to the urbane effervescence of Bernie Rodenbarr (*The Burglar in the Rye*), while other characters include the globe-trotting insomniac Evan Tanner (*Tanner On Ice*) and the introspective assassin Keller (*Hit List*). A Grand Master of Mystery Writers of America, he has won the Edgar and Shamus awards four times each and the Japanese Maltese Falcon award twice, as well as the Nero Wolfe and the German Philip Marlowe awards. In France, he has been proclaimed a Grand Maitre du Roman Noir and has twice been awarded the Societe 813 trophy. He has been a guest of honor at Bouchercon and at book fairs and mystery festivals in France, Germany, Australia, Italy, New Zealand, and Spain, and, as if that were not enough, was publicly presented with the key to the city of Muncie, Indiana.

# PERMISSIONS AND COPYRIGHTS

"Come Down from the Hills" by John F. Suter. Copyright © 1987 by Davis Publications, Inc. First published in *Ellery Queen's Mystery Magazine*, April 1987. Reprinted by permission of the Executor for the author's Estate, John F. Suter Jr.

"The Wrong Hands" by Peter Robinson. Copyright © 1998 by Peter Robinson. First published in *Ellery Queen's Mystery Magazine*, April 1998. Reprinted by permission of the author.

"The High Cost of Living" by Dorothy Cannell. Copyright © 1990 by Dorothy Cannell. First published in *Sisters in Crime 3*. Reprinted by permission of the author and her agents, the Jane Rotrosen Agency.

"My Heart Cries for You" by Bill Crider. Copyright © 1988 by Bill Crider. First published in *14 Vicious Valentines*. Reprinted by permission of the author.

"Inside Job" by Ed Gorman. Copyright © 1988 by Ed Gorman. Reprinted by permission of the author.

"Deadly Fantasies" by Marcia Muller. Copyright © 1989 by the Pronzini-Muller Family Trust. First published in *Alfred Hitchcock's Mystery Magazine*, April 1989. Reprinted by permission of the author.

"Death Scene" by Helen Nielsen. Copyright © 1960 by the Toronto Star. Copyright renewed 1988 by Helen Neilsen. First published in *Ellery Queen's Mystery Magazine*, May 1963. Reprinted by permission of the author's agents, the Scott Meredith Literary Agency, LP.

"Goodbye, Sue Ellen" by Gillian Roberts. Copyright © 1992 by Judith Greber. First published in *Malice Domestic 2*. Reprinted by permission of the author.

"Death and Diamonds" by Sue Dunlap. Copyright © 1992 by Sue Dunlap. First published in *A Woman's Eye*. Reprinted by permission of the author.

"A Ticket Out" by Brendan DuBois. Copyright © 1987 by Davis Publications, Inc. First published in *Ellery Queen's Mystery Magazine*, January 1987. Reprinted by permission of the author.

"Speaking of Greed" by Lawrence Block. Copyright © 2001 by Lawrence Block.